THE EARTH
BETWEEN

G. B. CHASE

Third
Story
Window

ISBN 1-58169-046-0
For Worldwide Distribution
Printed in the U.S.A.

Third Story Window
An Imprint of Genesis Communications, Inc.
P.O. Box 91011 • Mobile, AL 36691
800-367-8203
Email: GenesisCom@aol.com

TABLE OF CONTENTS

DEDICATION

This volume is dedicated to the one
who is the earthly Light of my life…
the one person, besides the Lord's own dear presence,
who has been by my side no matter what has come our way…
my dear wife Mary Jo.
She has worked tirelessly as a co-laborer for over 30 years.
It is my hope that this story will re-affirm to her
the glorious hope that lies before us.

ACKNOWLEDGMENTS

I wish to give special mention and appreciation to my sister Judy, for her help introducing me to computerized word processing. No little chore.

And, as well, to a one time co-worker and now dear friend, Mark Sarver, whose help in technical matters has been beyond measure.

I offer to both my sincerest thanks.

In honor of a worthy heritage established by my grandfather and great-grandfather whose initials I share, I sign this volume
G.B. Chase III

CHAPTER 1
No Panic Allowed

The overpowering, explosive sound made Ruth freeze where she stood. It was not a bomb—it was more like an ear-shattering, vibrating scream that made her heart skip a few beats. It was even more unearthly due to the accompanying visual distortion of everything around her. It wasn't vertigo; yet everything material, even the atmosphere, seemed to melt into a writhing vortex around her. It was a mixture of warped form and space and color that made her wonder if she was hallucinating.

Strange, yet Ruth could almost swear it happened twice, the second time with everything occurring in reverse order, even though the time that passed was far too short for such a thing to happen. It lasted less than 30 seconds, yet seemed like a long time. She was distinctly aware of when it happened because she had just called her son Mike down for breakfast. She had not wanted him to be late for school again.

"Oh no!" she screamed, "Mikey! Mikey! Where are you? Are you all right?"

"Y-y-yeah, Mom. Are you okay?" Mike came crawling out from under the dining table where he had dove at the first loud blast.

Ruth grabbed her son in a quick embrace and both of them stood there panting as if they'd just run a race.

"I've never been so scared!" said Mike.

"I know," Ruth answered. "What in the world could it have possibly been?"

"I dunno, but it couldn't be anything nuclear because the light didn't keep building like Dad said it would." Mike was pretty quick at assessing a situation for a twelve-year-old.

"No! No!" she cried. "Hank! Oh no, not Hank! Mike, call your father at the lab. He went there early this morning—had a fresh idea he wanted to check out."

"Mom, y-you don't think some—"

"Mike, not now! Just call! Quickly!"

Dr. Cooper's lab had been built not far from their home, down inside of a half mile wide hill in the middle of the rolling countryside. The top

1

center of the hill had been cleverly excavated down to the surrounding ground level. The soil was pushed up the sides making the hill even higher and leaving a large crater in the center. This huge earthen berm concealed the lab complex from the sight of all the surrounding land, including his own house. The entire property was conveniently located about 10 miles away from all the surrounding communities.

Most of the area's population was unaware of the presence of such a facility. Only a small number of hand-picked people worked there in various buildings within the complex, and they were sworn to complete secrecy about the project. Each one only had knowledge of their own portion of the work, working various shifts and in different buildings. Dr. Henry Darin Cooper was the only one who understood what was being built.

"Mom—there's no answer. I can't reach Dad!"

They both ran out to the backyard and past the barn to look toward the hill. A large cloud of dust that looked almost like smoke was swirling around at the top of the hill. Their worst nightmare seemed to be coming true. Something had happened at the lab—Dr. Cooper could very well be in serious difficulty.

"Oh please, dear God," cried Ruth. "Don't let anything happen to Hank." She was near hysteria and sobbing.

"Mom, Mom!" yelled Mike. "Cut it out! That won't help Dad or anyone else out there."

"You're right, of course," Ruth gasped as she choked back the sobs. "Hurry, go get the first aid kit, and I'll find a couple of flashlights just in case the power's out."

"But Dad told us we were never to go near the place!"

"I'd say this is definitely an exception. I'm not just going to stand here and do nothing!"

"Yeah, Mom, me too. I don't see what could be so hush-hush and mysterious anyway. Let's go."

A small smile fell across Ruth's face. That boy was the joy of her life, and he was always braver than his years. Just last summer, he had climbed to the highest branches of an 80 foot oak tree to save a kitten that was stuck up in it for two days. The same summer he dove into a crowded pool to pull up a little three-year-old girl. He hadn't thought about calling the lifeguard; he just did what needed to be done.

Mike wasn't much larger than the average kid his age. He was clean-cut, as they used to say, and a good student, interested in many things. He particularly enjoyed anything having to do with technology. He got that from his father. His interest in spiritual things came from his mother. She saw to it that nothing kept her husband and son away from church activities. She believed that the best protection for her son was to teach him to know God and follow His precepts. Unfortunately, she hadn't had quite the same success in getting her husband interested in these things.

Just thinking about how they had waited more than five years to have children and the joy she had missed during that time made her wince a bit. Children really are a blessing, she had told Hank many times. It had seemed necessary to wait at the time because of Hank's studies and then his meteoric rise in scientific circles.

Besides a masters degree in electronics, that man of hers had earned four doctorates along the way—in physics, nuclear power, astronomy, and metallurgy. Ruth never could understand why he was suddenly so interested in metals. Jewelry always seemed to be one of the farthest things from his scientific mind. So, why all the interest in gold?

Ruth suddenly shook herself out of her reveries as she heard Mike yelling. "Hey, Mom, are you going to drive to the lab or what?"

"You're right. Let's go!"

She put the car in gear and sped down the long driveway to the doctor's private short cut to the lab complex.

Ruth was the type of woman who thoroughly enjoyed the role of wife and mother. She was strong of heart where loyalty was concerned, yet had a very tender and compassionate spirit. Although average in looks and build, she had hazel eyes that seemed to look deep into the one caught in her gaze.

Just as they were almost to the top of the berm, Ruth ground the car to a halt.

"Now listen real close to me," she told Mike. "The first thing we will do is just look over the whole scene. We need to be sure that nothing is going on that will endanger us."

"Hey! I don't care," retorted Mike.

"You better, young man. You can't help anyone or anything if you get in trouble yourself." Ruth's adrenaline was working, and she was up to the challenge, come what may. After all, Hank needed her clearest thinking and steady nerves right now. And she couldn't bear having anything happen to Mike.

"Now, are we clear? Do you understand?"

"Uh huh, I got it; I'll be careful."

"Okay then. Lets get up there and see what Dad's big mystery is, and if there's anything we can do to help. Keep a sharp eye out for your him."

CHAPTER 2
An Alien Ship?

When Ruth and Mike looked over the upper rim of the hill, they saw rubble piled high in the middle of the complex. Most of the buildings around the perimeter, however, were not damaged greatly, having only a few broken windows apparently caused by flying debris. The corner of one roof closer to the center of the complex was torn off, but at least there was no sign of a general fire or any charred remains, as would be expected in a typical explosion. The trees and other vegetation around the buildings looked untouched, making them both relieved to think that radiation was probably not a factor.

In the middle of the complex, what had been the largest building was reduced to shreds of metal and crumbles of concrete. At what looked like "ground zero" was the strangest machine, or craft of some sort, that either of them had ever seen.

"Hey, is that some alien ship, Mom? Naw! What do you think it really is? Is this what Dad's been working on? It looks like it's still moving some. Mom...Mom! Is it really gold or is it colored glass?"

The machine was still throbbing and shuddering a little, as if trying to shut down. It didn't really look like a saucer—more like a nut bowl with a raised center that curved in and up to a point. It was thick and heavy at the bottom center of the bowl form and very narrow and thin at the rim.

Ruth finally gathered her thoughts. "I've never even imagined anything like this. I knew it was classified. Your dad would not talk about it at all. How in the world could he make something like this, and how could he afford it?"

She stood silent for a moment remembering his interest in gold. "It does almost look like gold, doesn't it?"

The outer shell seemed nearly transparent, but Ruth could make out the lines of interconnecting layers and other parts that locked together almost like scales. Mike thought it looked almost like the 3-D computer drawings that could be rotated every which way and yet still be transparent.

"It seems safe enough for now," Ruth said. "Let's get down there and see if we can find your father or anyone else."

They followed the road that spiralled down around the inside of the crater. At the bottom, the gate which gave access to the complex was closed. There was no one at the guardhouse to open the gate, and they saw no switches or levers that would open it.

"Well, if he could afford to build that thing out here, he can afford to fix a gate," said Ruth. "Buckle up and hold on, Mikey; we're going in the hard way." Backing the car up about 50 yards, she aimed it at the center of the double gate, and floorboarded the accelerator. *Wow! I'm really doing this! I always wondered what it would feel like.*

From Mike came a long "M-M-Mo— — —m!!!"

Before they had time to think, they had crashed through. Riding a little taller in her seat, ever faithful Ruth had done the job.

They headed straight for the center of the complex and "that thing" sitting there. Ruth stopped the car about 50 feet from the edge of what had been a considerable building. *Or was it a hangar,* she wondered. From the ruins, it was evident that the roof was meant to be retracted out of the way. It was like an enclosed launching pad she had seen in a movie years ago.

Up close, the craft was a lot larger than they had originally thought it was. They could see interlocking plates under the surface. It didn't look like it had joints and seams, though, just parts laying in various positions. It was much like something alive, with one tissue blending into the next, so you really didn't see very deeply inside.

The area surrounding the machine was a mess. What looked like entire banks of computers and control stations were demolished. There were just a few machines left that still had a power source of some sort and were spitting and sputtering.

Ruth and Mike picked their way through the rubble to get around to the far side where there was a ladder going up the side of the craft. Still no sign of life was evident. Mike was becoming more and more excited and curious, but Ruth was becoming worried.

"Please, dear Lord, let Hank be safe," she whispered. She was too overcome by all she saw to be able to pray anything else.

"Mom? Is it possible that Dad didn't build this thing, and maybe it really is alien?"

Even a 12-year-old kid's imagination was being strained. *After all, Dad is just Dad. How could he have built something like this?* By now, Mike had arrived at the ladder. He hesitated, looked back toward his mother and saw that her attention was elsewhere. He started up just a couple of steps and froze at the sound of a husky, panicky voice crying out, "No! No, Mike, don't go into the ship! Get down quickly! Get away from there!"

Mike and Ruth both turned suddenly to see where the voice was coming from. About 20 feet away, they saw Dr. Cooper hunkered down under a large piece of the fallen roof. His eyes were glazed with panic. He looked too weak to stand, or maybe he was too frightened. There was blood around his ears and his nose. Ruth had been a nurse for 10 years, but from where she was standing, she couldn't tell if it was from a surface injury or if it had come from an internal head injury.

Ruth rushed over to him and began sobbing, "Hank, oh darling, I was afraid I'd lost you." Mike jumped off the ladder and ran over to his dad, throwing his arms around him. But Hank pushed him back as if he were afraid of something or someone.

Mike knew his father had recognized him. *Why is he pushing me away now? Is he mad 'cause we're not supposed to be here?*

After making sure that his bleeding was from purely superficial wounds, Ruth began trying to make sense out of the situation. "Hank—just what's happened here and what is this thing?" she demanded. "Are we safe, or should we all get out?"

Right away they could see that they weren't going to get very far asking questions. Dr. Cooper seemed almost incoherent. The only thing Hank seemed to be able to tell them was that no one else was in the compound; or at least, they shouldn't be.

Ruth knew she had to quickly decide on a plan of action. "Stay here with your father," she told Mike. "I'm going to the car to phone for some help. We've got to get a doctor for your father." Needing some moral support, she added, "I better call our pastor, too," and she was gone. Mike kept on edging closer to his dad until the older man let him put an arm around his shoulders. They just sat there, saying nothing.

When Ruth ran to the car, she was glad that Hank had seen to it that they had the satellite linked cell phone. She had a hard time getting through. Doc's line was busy, and when she tried the pastor, she got the answering machines both at the parsonage and the church. She left a message for Pastor Steve to call her A.S.A.P. and turned her attention to contacting Sheriff Morgan.

"Hello, Sheriff Morgan?" Ruth was almost yelling.

"Speaking," answered the sheriff.

"Oh, thank God I could reach you. I've been ..."

"Please calm down. Tell me who you are, where you are, and what's the emergency."

"This is Ruth Ann Cooper. You know my husband, I believe—Dr. Henry Cooper?"

"Sure do. Go on," the sheriff encouraged her.

"Well, he's got real trouble out here at the lab. Oh…maybe I better ask you something first. Do you know anything about his work out here?"

"Very little," the sheriff answered.

She hesitated, "We were never allowed out here, and Hank can't speak for himself right now. I don't know if the government is involved in his project, or for that matter if I should ask you about your clearance concerning it."

"Oh, I've got you. Some time ago, I was given directions to the lab's location, a sealed list of personnel, and a provisional top clearance. I guess that means my clearance would be on a "Need to Know" basis—to be used only in case of emergency."

"Great," answered Ruth. "This is that time. Something has happened out here at his lab complex. There's no danger to the surrounding population as near as I can tell. I do need this from you right now: I need help reaching Dr. Payne right away. I'll let him decide if we need the paramedics. The fewer people who see what's happened here the better. I need you to station your men at all the roadways that lead anywhere near the complex so that no one will enter the grounds—no one, that is, but Dr. Payne and yourself. Oh, and I'm trying to get ahold of our pastor—Steve Lichtmann. Please have them let him through also."

"Can do, no problem. Just give me your cell number so we can reach you in the meantime. Say, is that a secure line?"

"No, it isn't, Sheriff; so we'll need to be careful. For now, I can tell you that Hank is alive. I don't think he's in any imminent physical danger from what I can tell."

CHAPTER 3

Gathering the Troops

Sheriff Morgan was able to connect Ruth with Dr. Payne within a few minutes. Doc's wife had been chatting with a cousin in the next state when the sheriff broke in and told her that her husband was needed for an emergency at the Cooper's. In a few minutes, Doc was on the line. "Now, Ruth, pull yourself together. What's happened?"

Ruth sketchily filled him in, hoping he wouldn't ask too many questions.

"Everything's going to be all right. Whatever has happened, your husband's a tough bird. You know that. I'll come right away and bring some extra things I might need."

"Doc, you're right about Hank. But could you do one thing for me on your way out? Could you stop by Pastor Steve Lichtmann's and see if he's there? I would really appreciate it if you could bring him with you."

Promising to stop by Steve's, Doc hung up. Ruth's phone immediately rang. It was Steve. "I just got in the house and played your message. What's wrong, Ruth?"

Again Ruth shared a few details and told him that Doc Payne would be stopping by shortly and asked if he would ride out to their place with the Doc. Agreeing to come, Steve shared a few verses with Ruth and prayed with her for strength before he went outside to wait for Dr. Cooper. As soon as Doc drove into the pastor's driveway, Steve hopped in the car, and they sped off to the Cooper's place.

The two men were certainly a study in contrasts and yet similar in their approach to life. Doc was a practical man of science dealing with facts and diagnoses, while Steve dealt with people's souls. They were a good team and worked well together in emergencies. Many times Doc would ask that Steve be summoned at critical times to add a spiritual dimension when it was needed.

On their way out to the site, they encountered the sheriff who motioned for them to pull over. He made sure that both the doctor and the pastor knew they would be exposed to classified information, and that they would be bound by complete confidentiality.

Sheriff Harold Lawrence Morgan had been needing a reason to show off with some of his expertise since the small county seat of Willow Springs was usually quite calm. The sheriff was about six feet tall and fancied himself a bit of a cowboy. He always walked tall with a long stride. He had a full head of reddish brown hair that covered his ears when he wore his tan Stetson.

The sheriff told them, "I'll escort you to the access road and block it behind you. When we get to that point, you just keep going and I'll follow after I secure the area with my deputies."

With the Sheriff's siren's blaring, it took only a few minutes for them to reach the turnoff. Steve and Doc hardly had time to gather their thoughts. Their minds were racing with unanswered questions. Before they knew it, the sheriff was turning on to the access road and over to the side. He waved them on through and parked across the road. He was already on the radio, calling someone.

Both men had never been down this road before and thought it looked strange. At the entrance, there was a widened area so cars could turn around once they had read the warning sign. A heavy, short chain link fence came up to the edge of the road from each side, and ended at a gate that had been flung open by the earlier blast. To the side there was a simple warning sign, a bit too small to be seen from the highway. It read:

WARNING - PRIVATE PROPERTY
RESTRICTED AREA
Security Provided by U.S. Government
Unauthorized Persons Will Be Shot As Trespassers
Level 5 or Over Government Clearance ONLY

Doc spoke up. "Looks like a good time to start praying, Pastor. I don't know what we've gotten into here." He looked over at Steve and found him already bowed in prayer.

After a bit, Doc added, "Well, whatever you asked for Pastor, it just got my amen." They both laughed.

Doc and Mrs. Payne were longtime members of the church he had pastored for about 10 years. Dr. Cooper, Ruth, and Mike were also members, and they were all good friends. Doc had even occasionally taught a Sunday School class.

Steve was of slight build and blond, but balding, with bright blue eyes that seemed to have an eagerness about them. He was an avid lover of history, especially archaeology. He had received his masters in pastoral studies and had minored in antiquities. Not quite six feet tall, he had a ready smile and was a warm presence to those in his flock.

Dr. John Quincy Payne, on the other hand, carried himself in a practiced mode. He had a heart bigger than his own sizable carriage but enjoyed approaching many things as a bit of a curmudgeon. His bushy, gleaming white head of hair helped support that image. His wit was dry but almost aggressive at times.

"I'm a little concerned about what we might find, Pastor. I hope the dear Lord hasn't cut him off at the pass. I'm not too sure where Hank stands with the Lord."

"Just hang in there, Doc," answered Steve. "We'll know soon enough. I'm sure the Lord will be faithful to answer our prayers."

After swinging the gate wider, they drove on down the access road. As they rounded the top of the berm, they caught a full view of the complex. Doc hit the brakes. "What the blue blazes is that, Pastor? Did we just drive into the twilight zone? Have you ever seen anything like it?" Doc finally took a breath.

Steve answered, "I don't know; I hope not; and No, definitely not—in that order, Doc."

Both were dumbfounded, and Doc cautiously started driving on down into the crater. When they got to the bottom, they looked at each other in surprise as they drove through the security gate that Ruth had mowed down with her car. As they rounded the corner of the guardhouse, they saw Mike waving his arms wildly to get their attention.

Slamming the car to a halt, Doc ran over to Hank's side and started examining him. He checked his eyes and vital signs and started asking simple questions. "What's your name? How old are you? What day is this?"

At first, Hank was still rather incoherent, or what he was saying in panicky fashion was beyond their understanding. Finally, with the help of a sedative Doc gave him, he calmed down enough to realize who he was talking to. Hank took a deep breath and tried to gather his thoughts. He had to let out his big secret, and then possibly these friends might be able to help him figure out what went wrong.

Dr. Henry Darin Cooper was normally clean shaven, unless he felt on occasion that he wanted the professorial look. Then he might sport a goatee for a couple of months, just for its effect. At a well-built 6 feet, he had a ready humor and deep warm brown eyes.

This particular morning, though, he was entirely different. Not only were his clothes a mess, but he had also managed to grow a complete beard since morning. He no longer looked well nourished, but more as though he had been on a protracted fast. The term Doc used in his initial examination was *emaciated,* which created quite a concern with everyone.

They had been too happy to find him in one piece to notice much more at first.

Hank settled down and answered Doc's questions, convincing everyone that he was of sound mind.

"I have to tell you right off that you've been pulled into the middle of a highly classified project. You have to swear to keep whatever you see or hear in complete secrecy until such time as it becomes apparent that secrecy either couldn't or shouldn't be maintained. And if the story has to be told to outsiders, I will be the one to tell it."

About that time, the sheriff walked up to the group standing in the center of the hangar. No one had noticed that he had driven in to the complex. He was so shaken by what he was seeing that he hadn't made a sound while approaching the group. He acted like he expected something to leap from the shadows.

"Is everyone all right?" he asked.

"Yes, we're fine," they chimed in unison.

"I have to ask," said Sheriff Harold Morgan, pointing to the craft, "What *is* this thing, and where did it come from?"

"First things first," responded Dr. Cooper. "Sheriff, you do have "Need to Know" clearance; and clearance or not, the rest of everyone here has the same need to know. I need to have your vow of secrecy just as I have theirs, and I'll fill you in as best I can."

"You've got it, Dr. Cooper—you know you can count on me. My men have the whole area secure. I know for sure they could never guess anything like this was down here. And we'll leave it that way!"

"Just call me Hank, Sheriff. It'll make it easier."

"Of course, Hank; my pleasure."

"I guess that leaves the ball in my court now," said Dr. Cooper. His eyes started misting up, and he swallowed several times. His emotions were obviously right on the surface. "What do you think, Doc?" Hank asked Dr. Payne. He was hoping Doc would tell him to wait a while.

"Well," said Doc, "you seem pretty lucid right now. Your blood pressure is doing fine. I think the sooner you get off your chest what in the world has scared you nearly to death, the better. My instincts say, ask Pastor Steve to pray a blessing of protection on whatever is happening, and then get on with it."

"Oh, good gravy, Doc," Hank started to object. Then he stopped in deep thought. *There's my blooming pride popping up again. Like I must always be in control for myself. S'pose that's why I tend to hold the church and the idea of the Almighty at arms length. I always rather "bought it," but with reservations. After all, I am a scientist. Doc, on the other hand, is so devout, he wouldn't even treat a patient without a prayer. I should just shut up and...*

"Dear Father," Steve had already begun. "You are looking down right now on a bunch of people who are startled by very strange happenings. We don't know for certain why we are here, what has happened, or what to expect next. Our friend Hank seems to the rest of us to be right at the center of it all, and it's obviously frightening him quite a bit. We weren't sure if he would even survive, for a little while; and that has us frightened. I know, Lord, that You control all things. So, we put ourselves, our minds, and our futures in Your hands. We know You will make all things work eventually for our good and according to Your will. Keep us by Your strong and faithful hand. In the name of your Son, Jesus, we ask this. Amen."

Five other voices echoed in unison, " Amen."

After hesitating a minute, Dr. Hank Cooper finally spoke. "This is going to take a while, so find some way to get comfortable and we'll start."

Sheriff Morgan interrupted, "Hey, wait a minute. I need to know how many other people could be in all this rubble, Hank. I haven't seen any movement in the whole complex."

"It's all right, Sheriff, there shouldn't be anyone within miles of this place. I gave everyone two weeks of vacation and told them to get lost until I called them back."

"Okay, then. Go on."

"Let's begin with a question," started Dr. Cooper as they all made themselves as comfortable as possible on fallen pieces of the roof. "It's not a test or anything. Give me your guess. Now that you've been next to that gizmo over there for about an hour or more, answer me this: What is it? Come on, what do you think?"

Harold Morgan spoke up first. "I've always considered everyone talking about flying saucers to be kooks, nuttier than fruitcakes. This doesn't mean they're right, does it?"

"Thank you for your insight, Sheriff," answered Hank. "Who else has an idea?"

Doc sputtered a bit, then said, "Well, it is round, and I've never seen material that looks like that. Maybe those kooks *are* on to something."

Steve broke in almost cutting Doc off in mid-sentence. "Yeah, that material looks like metal, gold even, but it's too transparent or is that an illusion?"

"Do you mean it doesn't remind you of anything?" queried Hank.

"It looks alien to me," said Ruth.

Steve started to say something but was forcefully interrupted by Mike.

"No, no. It doesn't look like any spacecraft I've ever seen from anyone's imagination either in movies or books or anywhere. It seems almost backwards to anything you'd expect to fly. But, maybe that doesn't matter all that much. Anyway, there's a ladder, but where do you get in? You stopped me from finding out, Dad."

"Why did you mention anyone's imagination, son?" asked Hank.

"Well, 'cause I play a lot of video games, and read sci-fi stories. And it's all imagination. Isn't it?" Mike really wanted an answer this time.

"Yes, Mike, imagination for sure. Fiction or made up stories, most likely. But, sometimes truth is stranger than fiction. Imagination starts everything, whether it deals with truth or not."

Turning to the others, he continued, "Most of the people who have worked in this complex were the best at what they did. This was because their imagination, concerning their interests in their own special fields, was more developed than that of their contemporaries. Even then, they were so focused on what they were accomplishing that I believe none of them ever imagined what the end product would be. They just wanted to push their particular technology to the limits and beyond. They were also glad that someone would hire them and support them in their efforts.

"That's why it was easy to maintain secrecy and security. Each unit that worked here did so when none of the other units were around. Controlled access thereby controlled interchange of information between units. The head of each unit reported to and conferred with me only. I was the only person who knew what all the pieces were, let alone how or why they fit together."

Doc spoke up. "I think you must be feeling a lot better, the way you're going on. It all sounds neat, but you haven't told us a thing yet. Are you stalling? Are you still scared to face what nearly killed you? In short— what is that thing?"

"Touché, Doc," Hank answered. "Maybe I was, but I did think the guessing game would be interesting. Well, let's start this way. We usually think of UFO's—saucers, starships, or just plain rockets—in terms of travel through space. That's natural because we can see spatial relationships visually. A fellow with an imagination by the name of H. G. Wells tried to think in terms of time travel."

"Time travel—like Time Cop?" asked Mike excitedly.

"Well, yes and no," answered Hank. "That's kind of the way H.G. Wells thought about it, though. But there's the rub. A sled or car mysteriously moving back and forth in time is so simplistic; it's just silly. Too many problems. The worst one is speed.

"Our whole concept of time is measured according to how we break up

13

the length of days, hours, minutes, and seconds. The fastest and most constant speed we measure is the speed of light. And, since light carries what we can see visually with it, we suppose we must travel much faster than the speed of light to catch up to it.

"Even if we went 10 times the speed of light, we would have to be gone two years approximately to reach a time, say, eight to ten years into the past and return to the same moment we left. So, to go 1000 years into the past to 'see' what happened would still take 100 or more years. If that were possible, and the traveler returned to the same time he left, everyone he left would seem the same age, but he would be more than 200 years old.

"You see the whole concept becomes silly if we approach it that way—like a dog chasing its tail. Because all the time needed to re-live time would only really waste away your physical body. Also, the speed of sound is only 600 or 700 miles per hour in our atmosphere. It is far too slow to accompany the pictures carried by light. And, since space doesn't contain that same atmosphere, sound would not go beyond earth anyway. All such a process would accomplish would be to chase image and illusion, rather than substance. It really isn't time travel. Thus the conclusion: chasing light rays to see what was, is a practice in futility."

Her patience starting to wear thin after having the fright of her life, Ruth looked down at her husband patronizingly, "Well, are you saying, Dr. Cooper, that this isn't a time machine either?"

"Yes and no," answered her husband, in a similar tone. This showed both of them that Hank's nerves were a little more under control. They played this game at home, often, as a tension breaker. They had a basic dislike of what they called the "hoity-toity" arrogance of academia in general. Any servile attitude of those with lesser academic accomplishment made them very ill at ease.

Sheriff Harold Morgan didn't catch on quite so fast. "Hold on there," he broke in. "Let's not go at each other yet. We still don't know what we're up against." His residual panic was still showing.

"It's all right, Harold," counseled Pastor Steve. "They were just playing a bit. Right, guys?"

"Yes, that's right," said Ruth. "But it's still a question, and I don't understand the answer."

"Okay, then," responded Dr. Cooper. "Here it is right out front. It's an IDEA."

"A what?" four voices chimed in unison.

"That's an acronym," said Dr. Cooper, "standing for Inter-Dimensional Entry Activator."

CHAPTER 4
The Sixth Dimension

Hank had their attention now. All four mouths were hanging open. He went on to explain, "It's hopefully a way to travel to different times and space *without* passing time. Then your speed can get you anywhere, spatially, that you wish to be, again without spending a lot of time. I think of it as an apt extension or expansion of a small piece of Einstein's Theory of Relativity. Did you ever hear of his theory of a warped universe called the 'Mobia Circle'?"

Three heads were twisting, nodding no. But Mike spoke up. "Do you mean that strip of paper trick, Dad?"

"Yes, son," answered Hank, "but far more than that. Run over that way, Mike. You should find what's left of a few desks. There should be some paper around that area and maybe some tape. We'll make an example of what started all of this."

That was all Mike needed. He was off in a flash and seemed to be back almost as fast. This was great! He was finally able to do something to help. He came back with an armful of computer paper.

"Yeah, that's just exactly what we need," said Hank and took the paper and a roll of tape from Mike. "I hadn't thought of it yet, but this paper is perfect. It's already perforated to separate into narrow strips. Now watch this," he urged as he picked up one long strip.

"If you take this and just make a ring out of it you have a circle. That has always been a symbol of an unending anything—from eternity in time, or infinity, etc. But, it's all in the wrist folks; watch close...

"If you take this other strip, twist it 180°, and hook up the ends, you then have an infinity that is twice as long as the other infinity. But, there's more." He made an (x) as the beginning point on the strip of paper, and started to draw a line down the middle of the strip to the other end. When he had made a complete circle, he was only half way there. The starting point was still on the opposite side of the strip.

"Now, pay attention," quipped Hank in his playful tone and a small snort. "We are now at the 'farthest point' from where we started; yet, just the thickness of the paper from where we started."

"Wow!" said Sheriff Morgan in a half-hushed tone. "Who could possibly think that up?"

"Einstein did," answered Dr. Cooper, "but there's much, much more to be considered. Einstein's genius was not just in mathematics. He could quietly sit and follow through with his mind, and see what he was seeing through formulas. Most of us need a 'known' ending target before we can even try to do something similar. We need to know what we are trying to visualize, before we begin a mental picture. The problem is that if we visualize a completely useless thing, we spend a lifetime going up dark alleys and down dead ends that get us nowhere. We think we know something only to find we know nothing. So we test, test, and test again. At least we learn what not to try again, if we were paying attention. Einstein just explained what he already saw with formulas, and that led him directly to new knowledge.

"He did get many others of lesser capacity thinking and testing his new ideas. Now watch. I mentioned dimensions as well as time. Look what happens when we put several strips of paper together in the same way."

Hank turned five or six strips into a multiple helix, all running together. Everyone looked on, stunned by the imagination stirring within themselves. They just looked at each other and back at the mass of twisted paper.

"Dad! You showed me the first circle before, but you never showed me this. How many dimensions are there?"

"We all live with four dimensions every day. One dimension is just that matter we can perceive exists. Two dimensions is like seeing a picture we can interpret because of light and shadow. But it is also like having only one eye. With two eyes we can see three dimensionally—height, width, and depth. So in art, a painting is two dimensional and—"

"A statue is three. All right!" Mike interrupted.

"Exactly right," said Hank. "Now the fourth dimension is seeing through things like glass, etc. The fifth dimension we see in a form almost like the fourth. Remember the stained glass windows at church?"

"Uh-huh, sure," answered Doc. "It's selective in what gets through the glass. I s'pose that's why you seem to look out the window in church all the time."

"Ya got me, humph! Well, right again, Doc. You see, light has mass and material just like everything else. Yet it is able to pass through transparent or translucent things of different mass and weight without harming the material. So, the colored glass only lets through its particular color of the spectrum. The rest is reflected away. Electronic pulses also travel

16

through many materials the same way; thus, we have radio and TV, etc. Sometimes a simple frequency change makes sound possible or blocks it altogether."

"It may be simple to you, Dr. Cooper," said Sheriff Morgan, "but I'm getting lost already."

"We're just about finished, Sheriff, but we need to see at least dimension number six. This is where a person would walk though a wall, and not harm himself or the wall."

"Ooh, neat-o!" cried Mike.

Hank continued: "Even though some may argue with the way I catalog the differences between the fourth dimension and the sixth, this is the way I have chosen to think about it. You see, we're able to sense with our own bodies so little of what is really out there that it becomes hard for us to grasp how things are made.

"If the light spectrum in total length were about 1000 miles, we would be able to see, with the naked eye, only the center two or three inches of it. The same is true of sound and also of the so-called hard to soft things we can feel—the things we use for tools and building things, for shelter, food, comfort, etc.

"We now can sense and measure other things near the fringes of that same dimension with instruments we build for that purpose. So we have some of these things, within our ability to control, that pass right through us, and we through them every day of our lives.

"These are such things as radio and TV frequencies, microwaves, etc. All of these are just light waves of different lengths and at millions of different frequencies. So, to some degree we already have a little control of the sixth dimension. How many more there are doesn't even matter right now, but that is enough for you to grasp the next point."

Doc interrupted. "I'm still where I was some time ago—all this has my head swimming. The question that concerns me right now is—are you alright or should I call the medics? You sound okay, your vitals are good, but you are still a torn-up mess from whatever happened here. I want to be sure my patient doesn't need anything."

"I understand, Doc. I feel fine now because I'm sharing old stuff with you. When I get to the nitty-gritty, I don't know how I'll be. There are some things I really don't want to remember. But, I also don't want too many people knowing what is involved here, or even have them see enough to make wild guesses. I sure don't want word to get out that there was a problem."

"Are you worried about panic?" asked the sheriff.

"Yes and no. What I don't want is for my backers to get wind of it and panic for their own reasons."

"Here's an idea. Let me call one of my deputies to get us some pizza and drinks, or something. It'll give them something to do and keep them from fearing the worst has happened."

"Okay, Sheriff, but don't bring them in here. We don't want to them to see all of this."

"You got it, Hank," Harold said as he grabbed his radio. "Sheriff to Gate Watch, come back."

"Yeah, Sheriff, this is Johnny. I read you clear; what's up?"

"I can't get into that right now, but everything's all right here. We just need some lunch. I think we'll be here for awhile. Leave the others there to block access and…Wait, you're at the main access from the highway, aren't you?"

"Yeah, right out front."

"Good. Go get us three large pizzas and about a dozen large drinks, and bring them to the blockade. I'll come down there and get them in about 45 minutes. Get yourself and the others whatever you need, as well. All you guys at the other points can send one man to get you lunch, too. Morgan out."

"Roger that," answered Johnny.

Dr. Payne spoke up, "Well, that much is settled, Hank. I'll reserve medical judgment a little longer. Let's all go sit over under those trees while we wait for the food. Let's see if we can find your 'nitty-gritty.' Did you say there was a next point?"

Everyone laughed for a time as they arranged themselves on the grass. The group closeness had built enough to start having inside jokes.

"Yes," said Hank, "and that next point brings things into a sharper focus." He continued, "I just want us now to think in terms of solid, or semi-solid material. The same material, anything or everything, of which we are part. The things we say have dimension and substance. Rock, chairs, cars, our own bodies, these trees, etc. You get the picture. We say our bodies are fairly soft, mostly water. Thus, diamonds are very hard, and lead and uranium very heavy. Are you with me?

"Okay now, think of what we call the cosmos—space, asteroids, stars, planets, galaxies, etc.—all very huge and far apart…at least, most of the time."

Everyone chuckled.

"What most people don't realize is that for their comparative size, there's about the same percentage of space between the atoms of a single cell in a piece of wood, as there is between the stars of a galaxy…as much space between the atoms in a molecule as in a solar system…as much space between most planets and their moons as there is between the electrons, protons, quarks, etc., in a single atom. The forces of mass, matter, gravity, and electrical charges is what holds all of these together.

"This means that from our vantage point in the spectrum of things, we are close to the center. In one direction, the cosmos is massive. It is equally unimaginably minuscule in the opposite direction. We probably have only just begun to realize how little we have comprehended in either direction.

"It would not be stretching things too far, and I'm sure Doc Payne can confirm this biologically, to say that each living creature, or even each rock, is almost a universe in itself—itself being the huge side of the equation.

"You know, the smaller things become, the longer time would seem to be. And, conversely, the larger they are, the more meaningless time is. I imagine that truism may break down somewhere, though. It's just a passing thought. But, just think how short a time can produce millions of deadly bacteria or viruses!

"What I have been trying to do here, though, is find a way to move into the ultra-microscopic world—to take something of considerable mass and force it to collapse in upon itself much the way a dying star might condense to a size so small that its density would form a black hole. But I don't want anything that dense, or it would swallow everything with no escape."

Ruth turned ashen white and cried, "You mean you've been trying all this time to commit suicide for the sake of some knowledge?"

After Steve and Doc managed to calm her down, Mike spoke up.

"I don't think that's what Dad was thinking. Remember he was talking earlier about time travel. You did intend to come back, didn't you, Dad?"

"Yes, of course," said Dr. Cooper. "I wasn't even sure enough about my calculations yet to consider manned flight. I hoped to send the IDEA by itself first. After all, who knows how or where to navigate? You can't just..." he broke down. The fear was returning and starting to spread to everyone else again.

Doc knew how to lighten the scene. He yelled, "There he is!"

Everyone looked up suddenly, and the sheriff asked, "Who?"

Doc answered, "The Nitty-Gritty that we were going to get down to, of course."

The whole group was so much on an emotional edge that even with such an inane joke, laughter got started, and it became a roar.

Pastor Steve spoke seriously after a bit and asked, "Hank, is that what happened—did you ride that thing?"

CHAPTER 5
Thanks to Hans Reicher

After a long, silent pause, when everyone stared at Hank while he kept looking at the IDEA, the others began to get anxious again. They kept trying to get him to focus on Pastor Steve's question.

"Well, I guess...no...oh, I can't be sure," Dr. Cooper finally responded. "I was inside adjusting a program, and I remember noticing the dissembler activating. So I started to get out quick. Nothing like that should happen without my command. The next thing I know for sure I was outside, and the whole place was falling in all around me.

"I began seeing all kinds of visions, memories, or whatever. I finally came to realize that Mike was sitting next to me, trying to hold me close. I kept hoping it had just been a wild dream."

Doc spoke again, "I think we're finally getting close to the point. Hank, what did you mean about a dissembler—what is that?"

"Well," started Hank, "that's going to be a shocker. You remember when I talked about forcing something to collapse into itself? That's another way to say shrink; but, that word is inadequate."

"Yeah...yes...oh sure..." everybody stated, responding all at once.

"I'll have to start talking about the material in the machine for you to grasp it."

"Hey," Doc broke in. "Let's break for awhile and look at the damage around here while the sheriff gets that pizza for us, okay?"

Ruth and her son went poking around the ruins while Doc was doing another check on Dr. Cooper. "Hey Mom, what do you think about Dad? Is he gonna be all right?"

"I think so, Mike. Just be careful and not get him too excited right now."

After the sheriff came back with the pizza and everyone had their fill, Dr. Cooper picked up where he left off.

"It was Einstein again, talking about the 'Mobia circle' that suggested that modern astronomers, who are mostly atheists, may not have the whole story. They already were measuring an expanding universe. He blew their minds with a couple of thoughts. Number one, if the universe was truly expanding, there had to be a beginning. Would that be 'creation'?

"Number two was this: Since light has substance, and all we can see and measure is light that started our direction billions of years ago, as the astronomers say, we can't be sure what the universe is like right now. The material substance of that light is subject to the laws of gravity, momentum, direction, etc. That means everything we see probably moved along a continuum of dimension to reach our telescopes.

"Hence, to Einstein this was probably a single plane, if you will, of yet undetermined depth or thickness. Compared to infinite nothingness, however, it would probably be relatively thin. The crust of the earth, our atmosphere, or the like is like a substantial ribbon or perhaps like a wood shaving. His mobia circle gives it much time to expand, in fact at least twice as much, but still eventually brings it back.

"Skeptics of biblical prophesies—the prophesies that speak of the stars falling from the skies—say an expanding universe makes that impossible. Yet, Einstein's theory raised the question. What if he were correct, and what if that ribbon didn't have the strength to keep both sides of the ribbon apart completely? Asteroid showers could devastate the earth as it is. Imagine what a filmy cloud of debris at the edge of a galaxy could cause in the way of destruction.

"Einstein's big question was, 'How can you be so sure? What if I am right? Are we nearly as bright and knowledgeable as we think we are?' He died before we heard a clear answer from any conclusion he may have made. The question that he did express was what if a way could be found to puncture that ribbon and come out on the other side?

"Since his death, black holes have been postulated—small dense crushes of stellar material with gravity so intense that even light cannot escape. Some have theorized that these holes that swallow galaxies would become so dense that ultra-critical mass would cause a new big bang on the other side and start things all over again. It's a wild idea and impossible to test—so it's quite useless.

"All of this was enough to get me thinking. All material that we are aware of, and comfortable with in our dimension of space, has plenty of room for compression. The question is how to compress it, and what materials to try.

"Now hang on to your hats," Dr. Cooper continued. "There is only one material from which my vessel is constructed. That material is gold—pure, specially processed and formed gold."

Everyone looked suddenly at the machine and back at Dr. Cooper. It was as if they all wanted to yell something, but their mouths just hung open. Myriads of questions flooded each mind, but they didn't know which ones to ask.

Ruth finally stuttered her way through one question. "H...Hank, is this why you were studying m...me...metallurgy?" Then she started almost yelling. "How could you...you...we...well, we just can't afford that. And, how could you make it look like glass?"

"Yeah, and where did you find so much of it?" Sheriff Morgan wanted to know. "Did you rob Fort Knox? I didn't know that much gold existed."

"Whoa, hold on folks," responded Hank. "Those are good questions, but not the ones I expected. I'll answer them though. Ruth— Yes that is why I studied metals, that and more. Also, you're right, we never could afford this; but I didn't pay for it, or any of this complex. It is mine, but it was funded by a massive grant that also paid the salaries of everyone involved. As to its looking like glass, that's the next part of the story, and I'm not responsible for that effect. That was just the way it happened. Someone else knew how to do it."

"Now Harold," Dr. Cooper turned to the sheriff. "No, I didn't rob anyone. Also, there's not nearly as much there as it looks like."

"Steve," continued Hank, "don't you have a question or two? I thought you would."

"Well, maybe," Steve responded. "Have you been reading Ezekiel and Revelation?"

"Right on target, Steve," answered Dr. Cooper, "except the answer is: No, not lately. I knew that was what you would think of, though, because as this project progressed, the same thoughts you just had passed by me as well. I believe I can tell you, though, that they have nothing to do with it."

"Are you really so sure?" responded Steve. "Ahem, to quote a famous man I heard of recently."

"Touché to you, too," answered Hank. "But, if we take time discussing the differences there, we'll never get on with this. I'm still shaky on how much weight I give that stuff anyway."

"I'm sorry to hear that, Hank," said Doc Payne, "but please continue. You sure have my attention."

"Okay then," said Hank, "back to the subject at hand. We already covered how much space there really is in all things material. The reason these things seem to be so solid is because, in my theory, we are in their same dimension. Yet borderline parts of our dimension, and whatever is next door does pass through us and other solids all the time. Examples—radio waves, microwaves, Xrays, and many lesser known and sometimes dangerous substances.

"What I wanted to do was to take something that was solid and, keeping it that way, cause it to pass on through other things in my material dimension.

"A friend of mine, Hans Reicher, seemed to have stumbled on a way of expanding metals in their atomic structure while still maintaining their identity and structural integrity. In short, he could refine metals to such a purity that the atoms would still hang together even though their volume was 1000 or even 2000 times as great. There wasn't more metal; it just displaced that much more space."

"Was Hans from Circleville?" asked Ruth.

"Yes," answered Hank. "He was the first person I hired for this project 12 years ago. He was the only other person, besides myself, to have any idea what IDEA is about. It scared him half to death, but he couldn't resist the challenge."

Ruth remembered attending Hans' funeral a year ago. She secretly wondered if the fright hadn't finished off his bad heart.

"Wait a minute, Dad," said Mike. "Didn't you say you wanted to make things smaller? What's this expansion stuff about?"

Dr. Cooper looked at Mike with raised eyebrows and a deep peering look into his eyes. Then he turned to Ruth and said, "Honey, this little genius you've given me is scaring me. If he keeps this up, he'll be telling me where I went wrong."

"Ah, Dad, cut it out."

"Just kidding, son, I think," said Hank. "But you hit on the real question coming up next. If a man wants to ride in a time machine, it has to be big enough to get into and hold the power source and all the controls, so it has to get big first."

"What?" said Doc. "You also just said something about un-manned flights, or trips, well you know what I mean…."

"You, too, eh Doc?" At least Hank could tell they were listening. He continued: "I said unmanned flights first; but if the thing came back like it should, getting in and seeing for yourself is the next step."

"Oh, I hope you don't mean that," cried Ruth. This got everyone talking at once. Finally Sheriff Morgan whistled sharply, cutting off all the talk.

"Just listen to us," he said. "You could almost think we believed we knew what we were talking about. This is really getting good. Let the man fill us in enough and possibly we might."

"Thank you, Sheriff," said Dr. Cooper. "I really appreciate your devoted attention to my work."

Everyone had a good laugh.

Dr. Cooper continued, "The reason for expansion, other than the one already given, is to allow the utmost compression from the starting point. My calculations indicated that there was enough compression space available, even in an element as dense and heavy as gold, to become at least 1000 times smaller spatially, and still maintain its identity and integrity. What Hans was able to do was to increase the space in the opposite direction by 1500 times. That meant the effect I wished to achieve, by my best calculated guesses, was quite possibly doable. The compression I hoped to achieve was then multiplied by the factor of 1500. I felt that would hit my projected window.

"The goal was to make IDEA so dense that it came close to the projected 'Gravity Equivalent' that others expected from a collapsed star. However, since IDEA isn't even a good microscopic size compared to a star before its collapse, the result shouldn't create any real havoc to our own dimension. The thing I wanted was to be able to puncture that dimensional ribbon we just talked about and see if Einstein was right. If I could see what is next door, I might be able to learn how to transverse time."

"Hey, Hank, you've got me worried," interjected Steve. "If this thing is to collapse in on itself to a factor of several thousand times, how do you expect to ride in it?"

"I'll get to that in a bit," answered Hank. "But something just hit me when you asked that. Don't get all excited because I'm probably wrong, but I suddenly got a disturbing feeling that maybe I already did ride in it."

"Hank!" cried Ruth.

"Easy, Hon," urged Hank, "I said I'm not sure. Anyway, at this point it is after the fact, whatever that fact is. I *think* I'm all right, so don't fret."

"Yeah, and don't you be too sure either," quipped Doc Payne.

"Let me explain just a little more about the material structure—just the barest essentials and no real detail," continued Dr. Cooper.

"Look close inside and you can see many overlapping plates, almost like scales. They're very thick on one end compared to the other," he said.

Everyone said they could see what he was talking about so he went on. "The joints are both flexible and solid, but without hinges or any other connection. They are joined with an atom to atom bond, much like the cells of your body are bonded to each other. I mean that the joints are so molded together as one that it is almost like the basic structure of living tissue.

"If it's bent, crumpled, or otherwise changed under pressure, it will, when released, eventually retake its original shape. The bulk of each plate is at the lower and most central location, in relation to its place in the total machine. It's also important that there's no other material or ingredient in the entire machine. It's expanded gold only.

"Gold was chosen not only for its density properties, but also because it is less likely than some other choices to reach a critical mass and explode. I would never expect it to do so. And electronics is needed for control, and gold is a most excellent conductor. The trick was making the whole ship to be, for all practical purposes, one big memory and calculation chip with an absence of insulating material.

"It must also comprise the power source within itself, and everything must be compressible without there being damage to any function. I won't go into how this is accomplished."

"Compression is achieved by centrifugal force," continued Dr. Cooper. "The..."

"Hey, wait a minute, I know something about this," interrupted Dr. Payne. "I use centrifuges all the time. Centrifugal force throws things out, not in!"

"Uh-huh, go on," challenged Hank.

"Go on? That's it," retorted Doc.

"Basically you're right, of course," said Hank. "That's the reason for the strange shape of this craft. As it starts spinning, it's actually very aerodynamic and uses the atmosphere to fly. It can be flown laterally; but for a time machine, lateral flight capability isn't important or even used initially. The craft gains enough altitude so nothing but the air is jeopardized, while all the time the speed of rotation is increasing. At a critical juncture, the central power source starts an added outward pressure. The ship would probably seem to balloon for just a moment if were not for the upward velocity compensating visually. It gives the craft the illusion of sitting still because its growth in size and its speed away from the viewer would cancel each other out.

"As the internal pressure builds, the mass of the overlapping plates start a lever process that makes the outer and upper plates turn inward, blending together in the center. This is due to the greater mass still pushing outward. But the forcing or by now pulling of the outer edges in toward the center increases rotation much as a skater performs a long spin. The control mass wants out but can't get there.

"Suddenly the mass collapsing into the center builds the rate of rotation exponentially. The craft changes shape from the crazy bowl you see here to something more like a rugby ball, then to a seed, and poof! You wouldn't be able to see it any more until, and *if*, it returned using roughly the reverse process. But not too roughly—it would need to be quite precise."

Ruth was stunned, but quickly spoke up. "Hank, I hadn't told you what Mikey and I went through this morning. The thing that made us come up here. Would what you just told us account for the feeling that what we saw, heard, and felt seemed to happen twice, but the second time in reverse? It left us not sure which way it really happened."

"Yes, very likely," answered Hank. "Do you mean to say there was an effect as far away as the house?"

"Yes, that's what I'm saying, and it was quite frightening."

"Sure was!" added Mike.

"Oh boy," said Hank. "I was sure the crater created by the berm would deflect any possible ripples. I wasn't even sure there would be such an effect anyway."

Doc Payne spoke up. "How much *more* were you unsure of Dr. Cooper?" His tone of voice revealed a little irritation. He wasn't too sure he really liked what he had just learned.

"I'm afraid, Doc," Hank answered, "there are many things of which I am unsure. Isn't that why we explore the unknown?"

"All right, Hank, I'll buy that for now. Please, tell us how a person can ride something that is being crushed to a 'massive nothingness' and still survive." Doc was getting edgy.

"You'll have to hang on for a real ride now," answered Dr. Cooper. "The next thing could curl your hair unless you've seen a recent sci-fi movie that had something similar in it. We're talking about the dissembler. That is, if I'm not just boring you to death. If so, I could stop going on and on, and turn my attention to cleaning up around here."

"Whoa there! Not so fast," retorted Doc Payne. "I think you're trying not to face what's happened here. I, for one, don't want to be left hanging at this point."

"That's right, Dr. Cooper," said the sheriff. "You already agreed we have a need to know, so don't start stalling now. So far, we don't know much. Get on with it. Right, guys?"

Everyone agreed. This was no place to stop anything.

CHAPTER 6
The Dissembler

"Well, let's see," began Hank. "You've all seen these magic shows where illusionists seem to make something or someone disappear in one place and reappear in another. I'm sure you all realize that it's an illusion, a sham, show biz trickery.

"However, for quite a few years, electronic science has been attempting what could be called teletransportation of various objects. They haven't been very successful in a version of this called levitation, which requires overcoming gravity.

"What has been done is the disassembly of, for example, a key into its electrical component parts. Those molecular pieces are then put into the receiver and then into a transmitter—something like microwave messages—and transmission of them to another receiver some distance away. This receiver sends them to another type of transmitter that reassembles these parts back into a key. The key has then moved from point A to point B. As astounding as that is, the transmission of even complex inanimate objects, with different parts, became reasonably routine."

"How in this world are we supposed to believe that?" Steve said. "This really does sound like sci-fi stuff. Don't you think so, Sheriff?"

"Huh? Yeah, I guess it does," answered Harold, "except ..."

"Except what?" asked Doc abruptly.

"Well," said the sheriff, "with what he was telling us before this, with us eating it up, maybe we should hear the rest of it, I guess."

"I told you we could stop if..." Dr. Cooper was interrupted by Mike.

"No Dad, keep going, this is just getting good."

Everyone reluctantly nodded in agreement, so Hank continued.

"Well, the hard thing was accomplished quite a few years later. At first only the highest government and military officials even knew the attempts were being made. One lab finally managed to teleport a simple single cell organism and not kill it. Gradually higher and more complex living things such as plant life were successfully teleported.

"The real difficulty came with small mammals or warm-blooded creatures. Even when it became possible to teleport them, it could only be done very rapidly and in a closed system. That meant it had to have a permanent receiver locked into the system at least within the same building.

"Higher orders of living animals and yes, even humans, were eventually teleported as well. All of this was accomplished by others, before I ever conceived of 'The IDEA'. There were real problems all along. They never got beyond the closed system, and there were often disastrous results."

Steve spoke up again. "I don't like being a killjoy, or horrified moralist, Dr. Cooper, but this is too much like playing God for my tastes. I had no idea you were mixed up in this kind of thing."

"I know, Steve," answered Hank. "But I just explained that I wasn't. If the populace knew some of the things our governments have been involved in, there would have been a revolution. Some of our officials would have been strung up next to monsters like Mussolini and Hitler. But what was done was done, and the knowledge passed on.

"You've seen science fiction use these same techniques. It's common movie fare now for starship personnel to be transported electronically through space to computer chosen sites that don't even worry with a receiver. That's fantasy—thus it's fun. But, you see, our thought patterns are already making these massive leaps of faith. In this case, faith has been placed in something as flimsy as scientific imagination with no real evidence to base it on. As often happens, someone managed to turn it into reality, to some degree. Men of science often get trapped for years with flimsy fantasies and don't know how to extricate themselves. So, they get even more inventive in their imaginings. One classic case, with no real evidence working for it, is that scenario called evolution. More and more scientists are waking up on that issue, though. But there will always be diehards."

Ruth spoke up. "As much as this whole thing is scaring me, I think there may be a sermon in there somewhere, Pastor. Do you suppose?"

"Maybe, Ruth," Steve replied, a little mollified.

"The bottom line, Pastor," said Hank, "is that I managed to make use of this knowledge and give it a few twists of my own. I was able to physically test, in a beginning way, the thing I hoped to achieve. By using the same materials used to build the IDEA, I was able to make a small compartment large enough to contain a mouse. This container was equipped with similar electronic teleporting instruments as found in the IDEA.

"The dissembler was activated, and the mouse disappeared as expected. It was theoretically expected to be assimilated into the circuitry of the compartment. After 30 seconds, the procedure was reversed. As expected, the mouse was reassembled on the pad. He was agitated but seemingly in good condition. I had succeeded in step one."

"Wow!" shouted Mike, "was he alive?"

"Yes, son, alive and seemingly well."

Doc and Sheriff Morgan shook their heads in disbelief. Ruth just sat on the box she had found, obviously stunned. This was all getting way beyond their credibility.

"I know I'm throwing too much your way and too fast," Dr. Cooper said very apologetically. "But there's more. Try to stay with me.

"Step two was a repeat of step one, but with an addition. After the mouse was put into the electronic circuitry, the container was placed in a heavy press. It was pressed one way, then another, until the whole thing was not any larger than a grain of sand or a small gold nugget. I had no way as yet to reverse the compression, except to depend on that material's own tendency to return to its original shape and size. Only the natural atomic level forces could operate.

"In this case, it took a little more than 48 hours for the container to achieve its original measurements and appearance. Initial voltage checks seemed to show that the circuitry had not been damaged. But, what about the mouse?

"I reversed the teleport procedure, and he appeared right on cue. This time, although he was not in such good condition, he was still alive. I was able to nurse him back to health. Step two was enough of a success that I proceeded with the rest of the project."

Doc Payne jumped to his feet shouting, "Are you out of your mind, Dr. Cooper? Did you really plan to zap yourself into electrons so you could ride that contraption?"

"Someday...maybe...but only if the IDEA could make some trips by itself first."

"How would you know what it did on its own?" retorted Doc.

"Oh, the IDEA is equipped with its own sensory instruments as well. It carries a complete log of what it sees or hears. I would be able to learn a little from that about where and when it went. I hoped to get a little advance knowledge for navigational purposes, before I would risk a ride. In the meantime, I would just set up programs by guesswork, but accurately enough to reverse them exactly. This would cause the IDEA to return to the same time and location from which it left—an electronic or atomic 'homing pigeon' of sorts."

By this time Ruth's nerves began to give her fits. She began hyperventilating enough for them all to become concerned. Doc sent Mike to get some towels and water from one of the restrooms left standing. Hank was really concerned about his wife and decided to wait until she was okay before he went on.

During the break, Hank had time to think to himself a bit. It was amazing how telling a story interfered with internal thought. He started comparing his condition earlier this morning to the condition of his mouse after step two. He began to throw around the idea in his head that maybe he really had been on a long trip.

Ruth was able to finally settle down. As everyone began to relax and gather their wits again, Steve brought them back to their main idea. "Tell me, Hank," he said, "isn't it a real possibility, that if all you told us is true, you might have actually taken your first ride accidentally? You were in terrible shape physically, mentally, and emotionally when we first saw you today."

Doc chimed right in with, "I think the answer has to be yes— come on, Hank, open up and face it."

This was the part he didn't want to face. *How could I admit such a thing, and have no way to prove it? I'd be a laughingstock of everyone in the sciences, let alone my backers.* Hank brought himself up short. *There goes my stupid pride again—wanting to control my image first. But there are possibly terrible implications wrapped up in all these happenings...things that could affect all of mankind, not just me.*

"Like I said before, guys," answered Hank, "I'm not really sure. All I really know is that something terrifying took place. If only I could remember..."

"You can, Dad," said Mike. "You said the IDEA was equipped with a log or the stuff to collect the info. Isn't that right? Isn't that what you said?"

"You're right, son. Except, I hadn't gone far enough to program all of that 'stuff,' as you call it, so I don't think it was possible yet. It couldn't be."

Sheriff Morgan cut in. "Hank, didn't you have other security equipment, or launch observation stations, capable of observing what happened? That could be a start."

"Another good thought, Sheriff. Why don't you and Doc come with me. We'll see if we can find those tapes and discs and a way to play them. I think we have some power available, the way some of this 'stuff' was sputtering awhile ago."

Everyone laughed, glad to relieve the tension.

"Anyway," Hank continued, "I can get a generator from maintenance if we need it. Boy, this place could sure use workers in that department right now."

As the three men left to look for evidence, Ruth pulled a picture from her wallet. They just had a family shot taken last week. She called Mike and Steve over to take a look. She thought she saw a great difference in how old Hank looked then, and the way he looked now. Had he really aged 10 or more years? Did the new gray temples and sagging chin come from today's trauma?

The three of them just sat quietly, waiting for the men to return. They had decided that Hank still had too much on his plate to sort his possible aging out right now. There was a bit of denial on their part as well. Ruth was so edgy about Hank's close call she didn't like the subject much. They would wait and see how Hank moved into the topic on his own. For now they would just wait.

CHAPTER 7
Rolling the Log

Before long, the men returned in an upbeat mood. They had indeed found three tapes of that morning in the cameras. Hurriedly, they set up a tape player and monitor from one of the computer stations and put in one of the tapes.

The first part of the tape showed an exterior shot of the hangar and continually panned in a somewhat circular motion—up, right, down, left, and across the middle left to right. Suddenly without warning, the hangar seemed to just blow apart.

Right out of the center of the rupture came the IDEA. It was spinning rapidly and rising steadily. It climbed suddenly and looked like it was swelling, but the top edges were curling in like the crashing crest of a wave. It seemed to move away so fast as to be unbelievable. The next minute it was a mere shining ball about the size of a basketball, but not quite spherical. "The rugby football," yelled Mike. Before the others could comment on his idea, it was barely visible, and quickly it was gone. Then flash—there was the IDEA sitting back on the pad still pulsating and spinning.

A moment later a ring around the peaked center section began to glow almost white. The top tipped abruptly to one side, opening the central hatch. Suddenly a man scrambled out into the bowl, clawing his way over the narrow lip. A ladder suddenly appeared where he was, and he scrambled down it so quickly that he almost slid down the rungs, rather than take them individually. He was obviously panicked and was screaming something, but there was no sound track on this tape.

Everyone was yelling at once. "Hank, that was you. You did ride that thing!" The tape had gone dead by that time, probably due to an interruption of its power supply.

Hank was visibly shaken. Those pictures stirred up the memories that were getting lost in all the talking. It was all he could do to control his feelings of panic and not start babbling again.

There was no more guesswork about the fact that Dr. Henry Cooper had indeed gone somewhere in the IDEA and had managed to return alive. But...now there were even more questions.

The sheriff spoke first. "I saw the ship leave, just the way you expected, Dr. Cooper. How did it return? The next thing I knew it was just there."

"Well...ah...ah... I don't know why it looked that way," answered Hank. "Unless...ah...maybe we were just distracted, like in a magic show, and our attention was in the wrong place."

"Play it again," said Mike, "Maybe we'll see what happened."

"I have a better idea," said Dr. Cooper. "Put in the tape from the east side tower, instead of replaying the west tape. Maybe a different angle will show a different picture, and we can see around the different obstacles."

The sheriff put in the east view tape, and it began playing similar panning motions. Everyone was bracing for the blow out of the hangar when Hank yelled, "Look!"

He pointed to the corner of the screen. There was a bright pinpoint of light racing by that became a large ball. Then it turned into a spinning bowl, just uncurling at the rim. Suddenly the hangar blew apart, and just as suddenly, the IDEA was back sitting on the pad and slowing down.

Sure enough, right on cue the hatch opened. They could see a panicky Dr. Cooper once again clawing his way out of the still quivering bowl. Then the screen went blank, due to the same power loss.

Dr. Cooper ran to another part of the hangar and came back with another player and monitor. They put the west tape in one and the east tape in the other. They synchronized the hour and minute symbols on both tapes at 7:06:00 AM. Then Dr. Cooper patched in a third monitor that would play both pictures overlaid on the one screen. "On my mark, Sheriff, 3,2,1, mark." Both men pushed the switch.

It was soon very clear, that in a 30 second period of time, the trip out and the trip back had both taken place. On the first tape the hangar walls hid what was happening inside until the blow out occurred, so it had originally seemed the trip back was starting before the trip out.

Dr. Cooper was almost giddy with joy for a bit. He had just seen proof that, whatever else happened, his program had been so very perfect that there couldn't have been more than two seconds difference in his time of departure and his return. The IDEA was able, even in an accident, to come back and land on its still clean pad before the debris from the roof could settle down on it.

For all practical purposes, Dr. Cooper was only in the machine's circuitry for about two to five seconds at the most. Indeed, after he found shelter, the debris was still falling around him.

So why am I feeling so bad? I ache, and have a general feeling of weakness and malaise. I just feel old and worn out.

Doc noticed his feeble actions and began his checks on Hank's vital signs etc. all over again. After seeing all of this, Ruth was trembling all over. She didn't know whether to laugh or cry, so she just stared at the pastor, hoping for some help.

The only one really getting a kick out of it all was Mike. His mind was racing with all kinds of thoughts and possibilities. In fact, his ideas seemed to be racing each other for attention. He couldn't really latch on to any single one. His mind was just too, too busy. He finally caught one and thought, *My Dad did all that?*

Ruth wondered if she should bring up how different Hank really did look. She looked again at Steve. With a questioning twist of her cheek and a raised eyebrow, she held up the recent family photo. Steve understood immediately, stared back for a couple of seconds, and shook his head. Ruth nodded agreement and they waited for a better moment to broach the subject.

SluRRR - P ! SchSSS !

Everyone jumped with a start, then started laughing at each other and their case of nerves.

Ruth roared, "Mikey, I only had one nerve left, and you just shattered it with your opening that can!"

"Oh, Mo-o-o-o m, I didn't mean it!! That first soda was just so good, I wanted another one."

This turned into a very timely release of tension that everyone appreciated. They sat quietly for a bit, breathed deeply a few times, and assured themselves that everyone was still in stable and sane condition.

Dr. Cooper finally broke the silence and said, "We'd better get on with this because my telling stories is not buying any time, if you'll pardon the pun.

"I guess you've realized that what happened was accidental—at least I think it was. If a launch was planned, the roof would have been retracted and out of the way. Also, all manner of guidance, control, and observation devices would have been in place and operational. You don't pull off something like this without planning, measurement, documentation, and redundant verification. Yet this happened with almost none of these things even nearby, let alone operational. However, because of the tapes, we were able to get some verification of what happened. And, we have a massive mess I might add. I can just hear NASA asking if this is my 'clean' room." That brought another round of laughter.

Hank continued, "I still don't remember doing enough programming and plotting calculations to even make the occurrence happen in the first place. That's why I'm so surprised that I was actually trapped in the IDEA

34

with no control. Yet there are amazing and horrifying pictures coming to the surface of my mind. I know something happened."

"What kind of memories, Hank?" asked Steve.

"I guess the best overall word I know is 'apocalyptic' type pictures from beauty to disasters, both natural and manmade. There's a feeling of familiarity to them. If I really did breach the time barrier, they might seem familiar because they were history I had learned earlier. I just can't be sure. I've always been a skeptic about people claiming to have visions. Anyway, I don't even know if I could have seen anything. Not for sure. And of course I have no way of knowing what my mouse felt, saw, heard, or anything else. It doesn't seem realistic to believe anything could happen to a creature turned temporarily to atoms. The bottom line is—I just don't know!"

Hank held his head in his hands for a bit. He seemed to sob lightly for just a moment. Then he shook his head and said, "I just can't let this thing drop me here and leave me that way. We're going to find out something. But, how?"

"Dad?"

"Yeah, what is it, Mikey?"

"Didn't you say none of these things were ready to work yet?"

"Yes, I did."

"Then why did they?"

"I don't know, son. What are you getting at?" Hank seemed a little irritated.

"Well, what I mean, I think, is that all these things couldn't work yet, but they did….Isn't it possible…I mean…what if the log of the IDEA worked when it really wasn't ready either?"

Steve jumped up, "Out of the mouths of babes! Listen, Hank, the Lord made it clear, for those who would listen, that the faith of a child was the key to most things."

"Man, there's a sermon here, Ruth."

"All us grown ups, including scientists," Steve continued, "are so sure of what we think we know, that we shut up our minds about the things we think 'can't' be. So we ignore them. Yet the boy could see the obvious. If it happened in part of the machine, it should at least be possible, if not probable, that another part of the machine might malfunction, and actually work as well. Now there's an oxymoron for you, or a paradox."

"Whoa! Take a breath, Pastor," said Doc. "Let us know if you're excited or what!" Laughter all around again.

"Sure 'nuff, Hank," said Sheriff Morgan. "The kid may be on to something. How would we find out?"

Dr. Cooper looked at everyone quizzically. "Do you all think it's possible?" he asked.

Everyone nodded.

"Sheriff, how brave are you? I'm going to need some help. It would mean going inside the central control or the equivalent of the bridge on a ship."

"Hey, can we all see inside, Dad?" begged Mike.

"I'll have to consider that very carefully, son. Let Harold and me check it out first, then a very slim maybe. We'll see."

"C'mon, Sheriff, let's put a couple of us nuts in this nut bowl and see if I can get the log unit out. Go on up the ladder, that's not the part that bites," added Hank.

"Okay, coach, I'm goin' in," Harold yelled back.

Dr. Cooper spoke more soberly once they were inside the rim. "Always step in the darker toned areas, Sheriff, there's more support there. And stay over next to the rim until I get the hatch open."

Hank put his hand out, palm down, on a very bright spot, about chest high. "Welcome, Dr. Cooper," said a voice very much like Ruth's. About knee high, a bright ring glowed all the way around, and the hatch gently opened.

CHAPTER 8
Takeoff!

Ruth gasped loud enough for Hank to hear her. He turned and winked at Ruth with a smile. He hoped that would keep her calm. He then turned back toward the center of the ship, looked all of it over carefully, and gingerly stepped over the low wall of the hull and went on in. It was rather like stepping into a small boat. After a moment he called, "Sheriff, come on in but step lightly."

What Sheriff Morgan saw when he stepped inside was astounding. Different areas of the walls all around were pulsating with activity. It was like being inside a great computer, but this one almost looked and felt alive.

Hank spoke up right away and said, "Listen carefully—do not speak. Just nod or motion your responses to me. Much of what you see here can be voice activated, and I don't want any sudden accidents. I know what words must not be said unless I want a certain response. And, Harold, don't touch anything that is blinking, and nothing at all in this area." He pointed to a spot that was dead center on the bridge. He continued, "That's the infamous dissembler."

Harold Morgan put his right hand to his face and made a zipper type motion across his lips. He closed his eyes and crossed himself, and then made a similar motion in front of Hank.

Dr. Cooper smiled and quipped, "It can't hurt."

After checking a few control areas around the bridge, Dr. Cooper was satisfied that the IDEA was as secure as he knew how to make it. He called to the other four and told them to come on up to take a short look.

When Mike scrambled up the ladder, his father stopped him at the rim. "Go slow, son. Step softly and only on the darker areas inside the bowl rim." He said it loudly enough for all to hear. "Now, stop. There isn't enough room for everyone, so just look from where you're standing."

Hank took a few minutes to explain things no one understood completely. "If all had gone as planned, then the circle in the center was where the pilot would have stood. He would have pre-programmed his coordinates and the exact reversal of those same steps, moved into the central

37

target zone, and given a verbal command. The hatch would close over the top of the bridge. That would activate the dissembler that would envelope him in a bright ray of particle beams. This would break the whole person down into electronic particles, recording their exact order. In an instant, the pilot would be contained as an electronic recording, of sorts, and held in the memory chips of the IDEA. If it worked properly, a man would be alive inside a machine—not really disembodied—but it would seem so to our dimension. Now his new 'body'—the IDEA—could function according to its own capabilities, without harming its passenger.

"At this point, the seam of the hatch would be sealed at the atomic level. This is about the same as being welded, except it becomes actually seamless—truly one continuous piece of material. With that accomplished, the IDEA begins to spin, and the rest is what you saw on the surveillance tapes."

Ruth just stood staring with her hand across her mouth. Mike started to speak, but was silenced by Hank giving him the hush sign. After another moment looking around, Hank dismissed everyone but the sheriff, and they climbed to the bottom. Now, he hoped that the two of them could go about retrieving the log without causing another accident.

After about 10 minutes, the sheriff came out to the rim and held up a small disc, a little larger than an old L.P. record. The disc or wheel was really several separate discs in a neat stacking compartment. They were very much like the older laser discs that had been used in some large frame computers.

Behind him came Dr. Cooper, who had very carefully closed and re-sealed the central cone hatch. He placed both hands in a different place than he used to open the hatch and softly spoke a security code that no one could hear. To the uninitiated eye, there was just no access to the inside of the ship. He nodded to the sheriff and they both climbed down.

When they were on the ground, he gave the ladder a friendly slap, and it just shriveled up almost like water balling up on wax. Then it seemed to melt right into the wall of the rim and disappear, leaving no visible seams.

Without question, everyone else was utterly astounded. They had seen computer generated special effects in clever sci-fi movies. But, they had watched the 'real' thing happen here.

"I did mention, didn't I," asked Dr. Cooper, "that truth can seem stranger than fiction?"

"You got that right," answered Steve. "Is that the log you have there?"

"That's it," replied Hank, "I just hope Mike is right and we find something on there. I would hate to think the memories that are surfacing are only hallucinations, even though it might be better for everyone if they are!"

"Are they really that bad?" asked the sheriff.

"Terrifying," answered Hank. Dr. Henry Cooper wasn't a squeamish sort of man, but he knew what fear was—this trip had given him a large dose. He wasn't a bit ashamed to admit it.

After they found the various pieces of equipment he needed, he assembled a playback array that could decode the log and show whatever was on it. He believed he had enough room to record several years of earth time experience.

He was expecting and hoping for dimensional time travel. Yet, he couldn't be sure if what he saw on the exterior surveillance tape indicated that, or just a going and coming back from who knows where. If it was just another version of space travel, he would have failed, no matter how great the rest of the achievement was. The fact that the timing of the going and coming were almost at the same instant gave him hope for success.

"Are we ready to find out?" asked Hank.

Everyone nodded, especially Mike. He was having the time of his life, as some of his friends would say: "to die for."

"Okay then." With that, Hank pushed the button.

The beginning of the log actually showed Dr. Cooper on the bridge, pushing or touching a bright spot here, a dark one there. He was occasionally speaking instructions to the computer, and sometimes receiving a verbal response back. The ship's voice was the same as Ruth's. She blushed a little the first few times she heard it. In one way he had kept an image of her with him in everything he had done. That gave her quite a warm glow.

Right away, though, Hank stopped the tape. "I feel I must acknowledge right now," he said. "What we just saw should not be possible. The log is only supposed to operate on an actual mission. Early tests of the log were done long ago in another building before the bridge was finished in its construction. This thing should not have even been on. According to that panel, it wasn't." With that he pointed to an outlined area on the wall in the still frame that was showing.

"I have to hand it to you, Mikey," he said. "You can really keep your mind on the core of the matter. You're the one who saw the possibility of the log having worked, too."

Mike grinned, stood, and took a deep bow. While everyone else chuckled a bit, Hank gave his son an affectionate jab on the arm.

"Well let's see the rest of this thing," said Hank, as he restarted the log.

Almost immediately, everyone's eyes grew wide. The cone shaped top that was the hatch had begun to move. They saw that as soon as Hank had become aware of its movement, he turned suddenly and ran toward the point where he should exit. He tried to get there before the hatch closed completely. As he passed the control panel, he tried to flip the abort switch in order to stop the hatch from closing but had missed it.

The log showed that he stepped back to hit the switch again, but it was too late. He had stepped onto the dissembler target. There was a shrill pulsing sound, a column of greenish pulsing light, and in an instant Dr. Cooper was gone. A laser beam came from the center of the cone and locked onto the joint between the hatch and the hull. It made a full circle around the bridge along the joint seam. The circle glowed for two or three minutes and just disappeared. The hull was now one solid unit.

Immediately the control panel showed a golden glow, and various parts of it started blinking and pulsating.

Captivated by what the log was showing, Dr. Cooper broke the awe-filled silence and said, "It looks like I became part of the control center."

Ruth started uttering rhythmic gaspings as if she were stifling sobs. Hank put his arm around her and said, "It's okay, Hon, I'm back; I'm here. It's a shocker, but I'm okay. Please take a deep breath and relax." Ruth pushed herself into his arms and tried her best to do as he asked.

There began a loud humming, and then a sudden sound almost like a car wreck. The picture jerked and danced around a bit, then smoothed back out.

"What happened, Dad?"

Hank answered quickly, "That must have been when the IDEA smashed through the roof. If this had been planned, the roof would have been out of the way, completely retracted. I'm just surprised that the IDEA itself wasn't destroyed."

Doc spoke up again. "I wonder, could the IDEA be spinning fast enough to create a vortex powerful enough to rip the building apart?"

"Hey, Doc, good thinking. I don't know if that could be it or not, but it sounds like something worth checking out."

The sheriff said, "Hey look, that's the same image we saw on the first exterior tape."

He was right. The IDEA was able to receive data from the observation cameras, as well as its own. It was watching itself fly away. This was indeed unique.

Suddenly the image changed. It seemed that a stream of particles was coming straight at the camera but bouncing off of it like raindrops or snowflakes bouncing off a windshield in a heavy storm. The surrounding space seemed to range from almost black to blindingly bright light and became like a huge twisting tunnel. It reminded Steve of the descriptions some people reported after near death experiences.

Doc thought about similar things he had heard. He always considered that they were simply oxygen loss illusions, but that couldn't be the problem with the IDEA.

CHAPTER 9
6,000 – 8,000 years?

As suddenly as the light tunnel began, it ended. The pictures returned and there was water in all directions, as if the IDEA was flying over an ocean. Rugged looking land appeared, and a moment later there was a small thump. The IDEA had landed on a flat-topped ridge in a mountainous area.

On another ridge, across a deep valley, was a large number of animals. Some were grazing while others were picking their way down the valley toward an even larger group. The vegetation seemed young and tender as in early spring.

The log switched to the inside of the craft where suddenly the green light column returned, and Dr. Cooper appeared on the target. The laser opened the hatch, and he climbed up to take a look outside over the rim. There were more animals than he had ever seen in the largest of preserves or zoos. He looked up the side of the mountain, checking from side to side as if panning a camera. The log was doing the same thing using a pre-planned program to search out any area, primarily for security and reconnaissance purposes.

Near the top of the mountain in a deeply shadowed crevasse, he saw a long tall building similar to a barn, but with the ends neither flat nor gabled. They were rounded toward the center on the walls, with a heavy column running vertical at the center of each end. There were a couple of large holes on the side, similar to some doors of big barns. The doors seemed to be hinged at the bottom so that they opened by laying down, much like a truck's tailgate. Hank couldn't see the bottom or base of the building due to large boulders close in front of it. Yet it was obviously several stories tall.

There was another opening near the top and close to one end. From a distance, it appeared to be an open window. There were birds, large and small, flying in and out of one of the openings. A small way down the slope at another level spot was a structure much like a flat-topped pile of stone. Smoke was rising from either on top of it or directly behind it, Hank couldn't really be sure which.

He was just beginning to climb over the rim to try for a better look, when a shrill alarm sounded from inside the IDEA. Startled, he went back inside to see what was wrong. While he was studying the far wall where the alarm came from, the hatch closed. Sensing what was happening this time, Hank stepped into the center of the target. The green column of light pulsed, and he was gone again. The familiar hum began and the light tunnel effect reappeared. This time it seemed shorter, and the pictures again appeared. Soon there was another thump followed by deathly silence.

The IDEA was on a wide plain. There was an extremely tall structure—similar to a skyscraper—about a quarter of a mile distant, which rose in a graceful spiral.

The dissembler placed Dr. Cooper back on the target, and the hatch opened once again. Hank could be heard mumbling to himself, "I didn't program this! What can be going on?" He looked out over the rim and began the same panning observation in all directions, as did the cameras in the ship.

Looking at the screen, Dr. Cooper's memories came back more clearly to him. He had realized that this portion of the protocol he had programmed was working properly, and so had purposefully followed it himself. He was sure he should not try to interact with anything, at least until he knew what he was doing and where he was. His location in time or space was a mystery at this point. (So was even the fact that he *was* here, wherever that was.) If he ever ended up in a position to hear anyone speak, he would likely not understand their language.

That thought brought his attention back. Around the tower-like structure was a fairly large city with no walls. All the other structures were rather small in comparison and similarly made of brick or stone as was the tower. The city seemed to be built in five or six distinct clusters or districts. Even those had smaller areas.

At the top of the tower stood a regal looking man. He held a very large bow in his hand. He seemed to be yelling something to the city below. He turned every which way, and occasionally pointed into the sky with the bow. A large quiver of arrows hung on his back. A few people were struggling with large stones. It looked as if they were trying to get them to the top.

Most of the people seemed to be leaving the city. It was as if each district was evacuating away from the tower in the center, except for one. There was very animated speech and yelling, and some seemed almost violent at times.

When speech was exchanged between different districts of people, it eventually ended with the waving of their arms, as if they were saying goodbye in disgust. The scene was not a happy one. The figure on top of the tower became increasingly agitated. He took an arrow and shot it skyward; it was not to be seen again. The man started walking angrily down the spiral path with his head down.

After some time had passed, the alarm sounded again. Hank looked inside very quizzically, then he shrugged and stepped onto the target. He asked, "Is this the idea?" The hatch shut, and the green light pulsed, and Hank Cooper disappeared from the screen once more.

At this point Dr. Cooper reached over and turned the player off. He said, "I don't understand this at all. I know I hadn't planned this program. The alarm was supposed to indicate the danger of a breakdown. Yet, here it looks like the IDEA has a mind of its own and was just telling me to obey and get aboard. Are you guys sure this isn't a wild dream?"

Doc spoke up, "It's wild all right, Hank; but I'm wide awake and watching your show, too."

Steve excitedly asked, "Don't any of you understand what we just saw?"

Mike spoke. "I think I do. After the first time the IDEA went through the light tunnel, it looked like what I would think was Noah's ark after the flood. The animals were still hanging around for a while."

Doc Payne added, "And…wasn't that an altar of sorts with smoke rising from it?"

Steve agreed immediately, and started to go on, but was interrupted by Dr. Cooper. "That's impossible," he said, "there wouldn't be enough time to go—what—8000 years in the past!"

Doc jumped up. "Don't be so cocksure, Hank. You just told us you hoped to poke through the fabric of space and time. Maybe you did and had no idea how far you went or exactly where. Right?"

"Oh, my… I guess you might be right," answered Hank.

"THIS is so-o-o neat!" exclaimed Mike. "Isn't it, Mom?"

"Uh-huh…" moaned Ruth. She was awestruck.

Hank spoke again. "But, why and how could the IDEA be giving the orders, so to speak?"

"I'm not sure yet, though I'm beginning to wonder," said Steve.

"Wonder what, Pastor?" asked Doc.

"I'm not ready to commit on that yet," answered Steve. "But, I could almost swear the second stop was the tower of Babel and a very defeated Nimrod."

"Two events out of the Bible?" asked Hank.

"Well they were reported in many other traditions as well," answered Steve.

"Please!" urged Sheriff Morgan, "Turn that thing back on. Let's see if that idea holds up."

Everyone nodded in agreement, and Dr. Cooper restarted the playback of the log.

CHAPTER 10
The Beginnings of Fear

At once the monitor was ablaze with the twisting stream of the light tunnel. This was also a short ride, and with a thump the ship had quickly landed. Everything happened right on schedule as before, and they saw Hank stepping out toward the rim. Again he was in a mountainous area.

Dr. Cooper interrupted and said, "I think we can stop questioning whether I rode the IDEA, or if it works."

There was muttered and chuckled agreement, but Hank continued. "I'm just confused about this whole sequence if it keeps up. How long did I really do this? We've jumped a lot of years."

Ruth gasped and pointed at the monitor. It showed what Hank and the IDEA were observing this time. There was a fire built to one side of what looked like another altar. On the altar was a neat crisscross laid stack of small branches. Laying on the branches was a young man, possibly in his upper teens, wearing only a loin cloth. Standing over him was a very old man—tall and muscular, but quite old.

As the old man stepped forward and bowed his head, he reached inside his tunic and withdrew a large knife. He then raised it as if to slay the boy, when suddenly a whirlwind became as if it were a fire that took nearly human form.

This form stopped the old man's hand and pointed to a nearby bramble. There was a young ram caught by the horns. The old man untied the boy, then slaughtered and burned the ram. He stood there weeping while holding the lad in his arms.

Just as the old man lifted his arms and his eyes to the skies, the IDEA set off the alarm. Hank hurried to the target, and the sequence began once more.

Steve could hardly contain himself this time. He blurted, "I'm ready to commit to what I believe happened right now. You're right, Hank, this has nothing to do with your program. Your IDEA was made to work, but not by you. I believe that God Himself, or His angels, have caused this to be recorded...purposely recorded to confound all who think they are so wise—those who would denigrate His Word and pretend it isn't true.

"How better to reach those who worship the 'science' of the creature, rather than even acknowledge the Creator Himself? He is showing once more, thousands of years after the fact, which things in all of history are really important, from His point of view. His grace is attempting to open a few more blinded eyes, and unstop the deaf ears. His Word and His plan are really all that matters."

"Wow, Pastor," said Doc, "I think you've got it nailed this time."

Everyone slowly nodded in agreement.

Ruth said, "I think I know why I called for Doc AND you, Pastor. You needed to be here after all."

Hank spoke in a subdued manner. "I think you're on to something, Pastor. Even I recognized the story of Abraham, being ready to offer Isaac on Mount Moriah."

No sooner had he said this than the next landing thump was heard, and the next scene unfolded. As he went to the rim and the hatch opened, it was obvious the ship was sitting on a small point of land, like a coastal cliff. On one side was a sea and on the other was a huge crowd of people. Men, women, young, old, and even babies were there. Mixed in was every conceivable domestic animal, as well as fowl. There were carts, wagons, litters, and every manner of carrying vehicle filled with bundles and bags, and poles from which hung different kinds of food.

Quite a distance from the IDEA, stood a man. His arms were lifted high, and in his right hand was a long stick—longer than he was tall. All at once he brought his hands down rapidly, and all was still for a moment.

Suddenly the water level just below Hank started dropping, and a mountain of spray shot straight up into the air. It was massive, as if a tidal wave had hit a mountain. Some of the mist from this huge mountain of water hit Hank in the face, and he began mopping it off with the handkerchief he always kept in his pocket.

Then came a wild backwash of water, with waves colliding from all directions. It looked like the city swimming pool with 100 kids taking turns doing belly flops., but this was gigantic in comparison. The camera switched to the debris. There were bows, arrows, spears, helmets and odd bits of clothing, mostly sandals, floating on the water. The whole crowd started shouting excitedly.

Suddenly the alarm went off again. Once again Hank stepped onto the target pad and disappeared into the circuitry.

In the hangar, all was silent. Everyone knew what they had just seen—the destruction of Pharaoh's army during the exodus of the Hebrews from Egypt.

Dr. Cooper spoke again. "It was about here that I really became afraid," he said. "I knew that I only meant for the IDEA to go once to one point, and then return by the same route but in reverse. Multiple stops had been impossible for me to plan because I really didn't know how to find any particular time or place, yet. I was afraid I was lost in time and would never return."

Ruth started quietly crying, but this time it didn't last long. The others realized that she was "on the edge" emotionally. Just the suggestion of Hank being possibly lost in time with no way back was almost enough to push her over. Actually Doc was surprised to see her stay so strong.

The next trip was over almost as fast as it started. The landing sequence, now familiar, grabbed everyone's attention as pictures returned to the monitor.

Again the craft was in hilly country, not on top of a mountain, but more like in the foothills. On another wide dome of land stood a sizable city. The high stone walls of the city looked quite formidable. They were tall and thick enough to have occasional windows, indicating to Hank that some people had their homes or businesses inside the wall itself.

There were gates into the city facing at least four directions, and possibly more. There seemed to be a gate in the center of any long straight line of wall. What was strange to Hank was the fact that all the gates were closed. They were built of massive beams a foot or more wide, and probably as thick. It would probably take several men to move them in any direction.

Without a sound, there came from around a corner many armed men of war, followed by seven priests in linen robes walking side by side in a single rank. They were carrying large 'shofars' or ram's horn trumpets. Behind them were four men holding each end of two long poles. Slung between the poles was a large chest. There were two winged forms on either end of the top of the chest. They were bowing toward the center. All of it was golden.

Mike let out a loud whisper. "The Ark of the Covenant! We just studied about that in Sunday School."

"I think you're right, Mike," Steve agreed.

On the monitor, the parade continued. It grew wider as it grew longer. The whole nation of Israel was marching around this city. That meant it had to be Jericho, they all concluded. Among the marchers were many more men of war, mingled with the people.

Doc spoke up, "You better watch close now!"

Shortly after Doc said that, the parade stopped. Trumpets started blowing, and all of the people started shouting, making a terrible racket. The earth began to quiver, and in a mighty cloud of dust the walls all over the city, especially in front of the parade, crumbled into a meaningless heap.

As the men of war charged into the city with their swords, bows, and spears, the six people in the hangar sat stunned. Were they really viewing the actual fall of Jericho? Just then Steve pointed to a small section of wall that was still standing.

"Look over there," said Steve, as he pointed to a strip of red cloth hanging from an upper window. "That was the signal of Rahab, who later would be a great, great, great, grandmother of King David. She was saved because she had helped Joshua's spies."

Doc spoke up. "Pastor, I heard some years ago that there was no evidence of this kind of destruction at Jericho."

"That's old info," answered Steve. "In just the last five to ten years, archaeologists have found it. It was buried deeper than they thought before. That was because the city was rebuilt on top of itself several more times than they knew."

"The Hebrews' victory sure was awesome," piped Mike.

As the city began burning, with heavy smoke rising in billows, the alarm sounded. Hank had to get back on the target once again. The next light tunnel trip seemed a little longer this time.

When Hank looked over the rim to survey the area, the scene was quite a bit different. He seemed to be on a flat rooftop overlooking a rather quaint city that looked more like a village, except for one building—it was a rather impressive mansion of several wings built of heavy beams of cedar. Much of it was stained in either red or blue. It also had decorative stones inlaid in the wood at well-chosen points to accent the rich decor. Some of the pillars were overlaid with gold in intricate patterns. It was obviously the home of a very wealthy person.

South of the town, a fair-sized parade of joyful people were coming toward the palace amid much music and singing. They looked like they were indeed quite happy. The scene focused on some men who were carrying a large chest on two poles.

A young man was singing and dancing wildly just ahead of the trunk. As he saw people gazing on the sight, he motioned for them to join in with the crowd. The rather odd part of this picture was the fact that the man who was leading the dancers was just barely dressed. Everyone else had on a full compliment of clothes, yet this fellow was wearing a linen ephod, wrapped around and through his legs, girding his loins—he was in his underwear!

He carried a timbrel and played as he sang and danced. And there were many other musical instruments being carried in the procession. This was a major street party and looked like a time of jubilee.

As the procession passed the palace, a dark-haired young woman stuck her head out of an upper window. She was obviously unhappy with what she saw and slammed the window shut as she left. It didn't seem to matter. The procession went up one street and then down another, winding its way through the whole town.

Again the alarm inside the IDEA sounded. Hank, quite obedient now, stepped back inside, ready for the next ride. This time the light tunnel lasted for the longest time since the first trip, second in length only to the initial take off.

This gave all of them time for reflection on what they were seeing...time to gather their thoughts...time to study each other.

Doc remembered why he was there. He rechecked Hank's vital signs and examined his eyes. He then turned his attention to Ruth. He knew she had been hanging on an emotional edge since she arrived.

Mike was obviously fine, and Steve was musing. He was intrigued by what he had seen and was privately wondering if he might possibly be able to anticipate any of the next scenes. He was sure he was right about the trip being orchestrated by God. The question was how far would all this go. Steve took a long deep breath and decided to see if the others saw what was happening as he did.

CHAPTER 11
Enemies

Steve asked, "Dr. Cooper, as amazing as all this is, do you see a definite pattern here?"

"Well," said Hank, "It's like reading a Bible story book, with many of the stories missing."

"Is that all?" asked Steve.

"Yes, except for the fact that it seemed to almost go to the farthest point back in time, and is, so far, working its way back toward the present."

"That's what I'm getting at," said Steve, "but I think there's more."

"How so?"

"Look at it this way," urged Steve. "You went to the only time that we know of when the whole earth was destroyed. After that, the Bible says that God told Noah the world would never again be destroyed by water. God helped Noah save his own family and pairs of other land animals and birds; all else was doomed.

"The rest of your trip, thus far, has picked out very important times according to God's redemption plan—types and shadows of what was to come, moments when God showed His power, and moments He received praise."

"I'm not sure I follow you," said Hank.

"It's almost as if God is showing these things for a second time, now to all of you. You see, all through the Scriptures, one pattern is constant. If something was urgently important for man to pay attention to, God said it twice, sometimes several times. These things confirm, by use of your scientific knowledge, that what was written is true."

"Are you saying that God is using me as a prophet? I can tell you, I'm no prophet! In fact I've never been sure about much of this Bible prophecy, or even if the stories were credible."

Doc joined in. "Maybe it's time for Dr. Henry D. Cooper to open his own eyes and mind. What do you think, Hank? But...prophet—no...neo-archaeologist—maybe."

"Right now, I'm scared," said Hank. "I'm remembering some of the rest of the trip."

Mike said, "Dad, remember the verse I was learning a couple years ago?"

"What verse is that, son?"

"The fear of the Lord is the beginning of wisdom."

Steve suggested, "Let's see where this leads. We should figure it out soon enough."

About that time the light tunnel on the screen faded, and Hank and the IDEA had landed again.

This time the ship was sitting on an open plain. There was lush vegetation and to one side a forested area. A little distance away on a dome-like rise sat a beautiful city. The hill was more like a mound almost totally covered by this tall city. It seemed like the hill was much taller inside the walls. The walls, even from several miles away, seemed massive. A large river was flowing nearby, and looked as though it flowed directly into the city.

At the horizon in the opposite direction, Hank could see very rugged stony mountains. As he was surveying the land and watching various animals, a new sight caught his eye. Every once in awhile, groups of cattle or deer would act startled and move in nervous patterns. They never went far but just moved quickly one way and then another.

Finally, Hank could see the cause. There was a sizable man crouched down among the animals. He was crawling around eating grass and roots. Occasionally he would jump and grab berries or leaves from low hanging tree limbs. If a deer was eating tree leaves that would look good to him, up he would jump and get some for himself. Then he might go after the grass the cattle was grazing on. If a badger was digging for grubs, he was there for his take.

As Hank watched, he noticed this man's clothing was very dirty and torn to rags. There were shreds left of an outer garment made from fairly heavy material. Even with all the filth, he could see beautiful colors in the garment. There was crimson red, deep blue, and purple. Once in awhile, Hank saw the glint of gold in a few places on the garment.

Suddenly the man stopped foraging for food, stood tall and lifted his fists toward the sky. He waved his arms violently and screamed unintelligible rantings. When he exhausted himself, he would crouch low and shake, sometimes in a rocking motion. Once rested, he would begin all over again. His clothes suggested royalty, but his demeanor said "raving lunatic."

Hank jerked up with a start. The alarm was calling him again. Steve began to talk, so Hank turned off the log.

"I'm pretty sure now," Steve said, "You returned to Babylon after the southern kingdom of Judah was taken captive. We just watched the great king Nebuchadnezzar. God reduced him to foraging in the fields to humble Nebuchadnezzar and bring him to repentance. The king had claimed all glory for himself and did not continue to acknowledge the God of the Hebrews as the one true God. His pride had taken hold of him, and God hates pride. It really is the original sin, beginning with Satan. It took many years for Nebuchadnezzar to come to his senses, but it happened."

"What are you getting at?" asked Hank.

"All of Scripture refers to Babylon as the base, if you will, of earthly evil—its center of operations. From Nimrod and his tower to the reign of Nebuchadnezzar, it was the bloodiest of the bloody. The Chaldeans gained their would-be knowledge through sorcery, conjuring, a warped version of the zodiac that we now call astrology, witchcraft, spiritism, and even satanism. Most of the surrounding countries in the Middle East had spin-off occult religions that came from this source. They worshiped idols whose rituals involved all manner of perversions of anything sacred or sexual, even involving human sacrifices. Most of the sacrifices were children." Steve hesitated.

"Go on," urged Hank. He was getting anxious now.

"The IDEA could have stopped any number of places. That would have just given us historic lessons and insight. However, what happened is that only those things important to God's message became the depots at which you stopped. By coming back to Babylon, you finished one cycle.

"God's men—Noah, Abraham, Moses, and Joshua—built things to the point of establishing Israel. Then David was Israel at its best and greatest. Then we went back to Babylon, the enemy of a disgraced and fallen Israel. Yet, even the great Nebuchadnezzar bows to his maker. He established the first of four great empires that Daniel had foretold."

"What are those four great empires?" asked Hank.

"I can answer that," quipped Doc. "The first was Babylon, the second one was the Medes and Persians, the third one was Greece under Alexander the Great, and the fourth one was Rome. I taught a Sunday School lesson on this. The prophecy about these empires is found in the book of Daniel, chapters 2 and 8, I think."

"That's right, Doc," said Steve. "So, I'm thinking this could be a prophetic trip after all. You may not be a prophet, but you could be the reminder and verifier to a 'science' addicted generation. Maybe we can see some of this coming up if we continue. If we're not on the right track, we'll find out soon enough."

With that, Hank reached over and restarted the log.

This scene was set high in the mountains almost to the tree line.

Below were beautiful forests as far as the eye could see. Above were many rocks and further up on some of the higher peaks was snow and icy glaciers.

There was a trampled down ridgeline that showed signs of being used as a path. As the picture continued to scan, it stopped for awhile at what looked like a pass through the mountains. The other way, the path seemed to grow to a purposeful roadway. It was a quiet and beautiful scene.

Without warning there was a startling blast of sound that echoed back and forth between the peaks. It was followed by a chorus of similar wailing blasts. It was hard to tell if it was a loud horn or a frantic scream.

Mike hollered, "Dad! That sounds just like what we heard at the zoo last summer! Wasn't that an elephant?"

"More like elephants, big plural!" answered Dr. Cooper.

"You've got that right," chimed in the sheriff. "Look up there!" He was pointing to the top corner of the monitor. Through the narrow pass, near the snow line, came three large bull elephants. They were large enough to have massive tusks. Every few minutes one of them would raise his trunk as high as he could and trumpet to those behind. Sometimes many of the others would answer in like fashion.

By this time it was apparent that there were hundreds of elephants. They weren't all of the massive size of the lead three, but elephants are still large compared to other animals. In this case, they were the main beasts of burden for a huge army.

There were men on horseback, as well, carrying long spears and swords who seemed to comprise a fighting cavalry. The elephants, though, were carrying or pulling enormous loads of supplies and war machinery. These loads were so massive that no other beast could have possibly gotten them over mountains. This was truly a world class, world-sized supply regiment.

Walking among, in front, and behind the elephants was an enormous army. They were a strange sight to behold. Every man among them looked rough hewn and unshaven enough to frighten any foe. Many wore heavy long vests of shaggy sheep or goat skins, slung with belts and straps that held all sorts of hand weapons. Most of the soldiers wore some sort of hard helmet, but they were of all different kinds of metal, each uniquely shaped, and very different in comparative sizes. Each man had added his own choice of different decorations, to make his helmet as awesome and fearsome looking as possible.

A great percentage of this horde also carried long weapons of varied types: some were spears with jagged prongs for points; others could broadly be described as battle axes; still others would qualify as lances.

Sheriff Morgan blurted out, "Those dudes should have the elephants carrying all that metal. I sure wouldn't want to walk across the street lugging all that, let alone climb mountains on the way to a fight."

That drew a little chuckle of agreement, but everyone was mesmerized by the sight of this huge army that seemed to go on and on. These were obviously trained men under military control. The end finally was just in sight as the front of the line was disappearing near the far horizon at a bend in the pass. Through this whole time, the constant chilling sound of trumpeting elephants drowned out all else.

As the alarm beeper sounded again, it was obvious that everyone present knew and understood what they had just witnessed. Even Mike had heard the story in school. This was the Goth hordes, led by Hannibal, moving against Rome. The IDEA had been sitting on the southern slope of the Alps, just to the north of the Adriatic Sea.

Steve threw in a quick update on what they were watching. "There it is—the evidence that the fourth great power of Daniel was becoming a force to be reckoned with. It had to be considered at least a potential super power, and a threat to Greek-Syrian control, for an army of this size to try such a bold move. History tells us that it didn't destroy Rome. It just made them mad enough to get ready for their turn to take over the world, in what was called 'Pax Romana'—the Roman peace."

When the IDEA landed again and Hank looked over the rim, he pulled back for a bit. Where was the ground? He edged up for another look and realized the IDEA was somehow balanced on the corner parapet of a city wall. It dropped below him to only a steep ledge that fell away sharply to a deeper ravine. As Hank moved to the other side, he could see the city. It was recognizable in short order. This was almost an exact picture of drawings and models he had seen in his youthful studies of ancient history.

That knowledge plus the fact of what scenes he had observed so far meant that this was Jerusalem, the holy city of the Hebrews. As he looked further to his right, he had a good view of the temple hill and the temple itself, courtyard and all. He could see smoke coming from the altar. Yet, something seemed strange. There were statues in the courtyard. They looked more like something Hank expected to see in the Greek temples like the Parthenon, or even the idols of Syria and Asia Minor. The temple guards wore armament that looked more Syrian than Hebrew to him.

There was a commotion in the streets about a quarter of a mile away. An armed contingent was leading a procession of some sort. There were two large men dressed in brightly colored robes carrying something on a pole between them. A small group followed singing and dancing and carrying small bells. It was strange indeed.

Following this group and lining the streets were other distinctly dressed men and boys. Their basic clothing was light brown to gray in color. The outer garment was like a long tunic of similar color with various types of blue edging at least on the hem, but sometimes at the front edge and around the neck. A couple of men even had blue edging around the arm holes. The men were mostly bearded, and both men and boys wore fairly long, curly hair. This group was obviously antagonistic toward those in the procession. They shouted epithets and occasionally pelted them with stones.

As the procession rounded a corner in this winding street, another noise became noticeable—the squealing sound of frightened and irritated swine. As the two brightly robed men came into view, they turned directly toward the temple. Between them, hanging by its feet from this long pole, was a young pig. Screaming his displeasure, he twisted against the bindings, trying his utmost to break loose.

As they came closer to the temple, the bystanders increased their stone throwing confrontation to just short of a riot. It stopped only when the guards pushed them back and thwarted their efforts.

The procession danced its way into the temple and directly into the inner court, and to the area before the altar. Even the altar was a bit strange. It was as if another layer or shelf was sitting atop the bottom altar, which had horns on each of the four corners and was a bit broader at the base where the troughs were.

The two large men grabbed the writhing, young pig by the feet, slipped the pole from the rings of the bindings, and heaved him upon the altar. As these men forcefully held it upon the altar, the squealing increased in volume. Another man dressed in flowing robes raised a large knife above eye level with both hands. He bowed in the direction of one of the statues and then turned back to the struggling pig. The knife came down suddenly, the squeal reached its highest peak, and then there was silence. A small drum began an exotic beat and was accentuated by the bells which began an orgy of obscene and vulgar dancing.

Suddenly Hank's attention was grabbed by the alarm. He obediently stepped on the target, and the IDEA was on its way again.

After this short trip, Steve spoke up once more. "I was wrong awhile ago. 'This' is the point of the complete cycle. We have seen the point when Rome became a significant world power, to start the last of the four great empires. And this was the abomination of desolation that was prompted by the Syrian who imagined himself the new Zeus. That was Antiochus Epiphanes, the name implying the return of the Greek god of Olympus, Zeus.

"This desecration is the beginning of the end of this cycle. It is considered by prophetic scholars to be the type of the Anti-Christ, old 666, who at the end of the world will personally do something similar. This will happen for similar reasons. But, this time he will claim that 'he is god'."

As everyone was nodding that they understood, Ruth began to protest that the vulgarities they just observed were not a fit thing for her son to see. She wanted to protect him.

After a while, Mike was able to convince everyone, including Ruth, that he understood right from wrong and good from evil. They were a little shocked when he told them about some of the things his classmates showed around the school.

This trip was over, and they all took a deep breath wondering what was next.

CHAPTER 12
The Gates of Hell Shall Not Prevail

The next scene that came up on the monitor was like a one act play, depicting a Christmas postcard. It didn't last long and was very different from the other more active scenes. It looked like it was some hours before the dawn. A very different looking star, or at least a shining object resembling a star, had been moving across the sky. Yet compared with the east to west movement of all the usual stars, this one was different. From where Hank stood in the rim of the IDEA, this star was moving from north-northwest to south-southeast. It was moving slowly, and was lower in the sky as well. To the eye of a 20th century man, it looked rather like a beacon from a slow moving, nearly hovering aircraft.

Hank was again at the edge of a small village. It seemed vaguely familiar, almost like the village he had seen several stops back where the half dressed man was dancing and singing.

Along the road, from the northwest came a sizable caravan. There were several camels, quite a few horses, and many people. Three handsomely attired men were in the lead—two on horseback and one riding a camel.

They stopped at the edge of town and pointed to the star and several buildings. They started up again and nearly passed that side of the village. There didn't seem to be any interest for them in the village. Suddenly they stopped, looked back over their shoulders and pointed again. After coming to some agreement, they turned around and rode to a small house right on the edge of town.

One of the leaders dismounted and knocked on the door. A moment later the door opened, and a tall middle-aged man appeared holding a candle. There was a short conversation, and the man went back inside. The one who knocked on the door came back to the others, and a flurry of activity began. He kept pointing to various areas right in front of the house, as if arranging a certain order or protocol.

More candles could be seen moving around inside the house. The man of the house returned with a small bench and two small tables. He set the chair in the center and went back inside. He returned with candle stands for each table and went back to the house. After several minutes, a very young woman appeared in the doorway holding an infant son. The boy seemed about a year old and stood by the chair while the young woman seated herself. She reached over and lifted the child to her lap and held him close. The man, obviously her husband, stood behind her and held her shoulders gently.

He then nodded to the caravan, and the three leaders approached the little family. Although the three men were dressed regally, they moved cautiously and seemed almost servile in their demeanor. They each spoke just a little and then fell to the ground nearly prostrate, as was the oriental custom before a king. The child looked into the face of his mother for a moment, and then back to the men before him. She looked at the child's face, and then took the corner of her scarf and patted his cheek just below his eye.

The three men motioned to the others further back, and they all bowed low, joining in the honor of the moment. The three raised up to their knees and clapped twice, loudly. Three other persons of lesser rank came forward and handed each a handsome chest of moderate size. One by one, the three visitors stepped forward and presented their gift. Again they spoke, but with few words. Each in turn left their gift and walked away backwards, bowing as they silently returned to the caravan. They waved and bowed as they left, continuing to the southeast.

Hank started looking around, searching the sky for the beacon-like star. It was gone as well. He looked back at the house. The bench, tables, and candles were gone, and the house was dark again. Without warning, a shimmering light appeared a short distance away. It was a swirling blur of light, very similar to the entity he had seen stopping Abraham. It went directly to the small house and right through the wall. Light could be seen inside the house. Soon there was a quick burst of light, like a flashbulb, and then all was dark.

In an instant, candlelight shown from inside. The first light of dawn was appearing at the horizon's edge. The door opened and the man rushed out. He went behind the house and emerged a few minutes later leading a donkey. The young woman came out with the child and two heavy bags. Her husband tied the bags together, wrapped the bindings with a blanket, and hung them on the back of the donkey. He then laid the child on a blanket, lifted his wife onto the beast, and handed her the child and a blanket to wrap around both of them. He started leading the donkey away toward the south.

Mike spoke immediately and asked, "What's going on? That wasn't a stable, and there were no shepherds."

"That's correct, Mike," answered Steve. "The Wise Men really didn't arrive in time for Jesus' birth. They came nearly a year later. We just tend to show everyone together in our celebrations because it's easier to do.

"The three kings had to go to Jerusalem and ask King Herod where the new King, the Messiah, was supposed to be born. Herod didn't like that at all and wanted to kill the baby. That's why an angel told the Wise Men to return home a different way. Then the angel warned Joseph of the same thing and told him to take the child to Egypt. Three years later, the king died and Joseph moved back home, this time back to Nazareth where Jesus would grow up. All of these things fulfilled specific prophetic details about the promised Messiah."

"Okay," said Mike, "I feel better now."

There it was again. The alarm alerted Hank, and he was on his way. But, this time there was hardly any time in the light tunnel. In fact, the next three scenes came so rapidly, they might have seemed to be one. The only thing that indicated otherwise was the alarm sounding; and each time it did, Hank returning to the dissembler target.

When Hank looked over the rim, he came up with a start. The IDEA was right up against a huge stone wall. He could reach out and touch it. He hesitated, at first, not really sure he should. Finally he could resist no longer. The stone was cold and clammy. He pulled his hand back quickly and looked up. There were no windows, but it towered above him. Hank concluded it was the wall of a city. It was night again, but the first glimmer of dawn was showing over the hill nearby. All was silent.

A fowl odor hung in the air from the smoke of a smoldering fire. It was coming from a deep ravine, a little way from the city wall. Hank walked carefully around the rim to get a wider view. On a tall cliff at the other side of the ravine he saw the silhouette of three crosses. His hand went to his mouth as he gasped. A more startling sight was just a bit farther. There were several terraces cut into the escarpment. Along these ledges were large stones pressed tight against the wall formed by the face of the cliff.

Sitting on one massive stone was the form of a man, but he was shining like the sun. The whole area was filled with the brightness of daylight. Another similar figure was moving swiftly away around the hill. Several soldiers in Roman style battle gear were lying on their backs. They looked like bodies stretched out on the field of battle. Gradually they began to stir. They slid along the ground with arms raised in a defensive position. Eventually some got to their feet while others were still crawling away from the blinding light. They all headed as quickly as they could into the ravine where there was an opening in the wall. They seemed determined to go in the opposite direction of that taken by the second figure shown on the monitor.

Again the alarm, and Hank ran to position. Zap and zap. The tunnel wasn't even noticeable. The IDEA was somewhere inside the city on a flat rooftop. This time it was daylight, and crowds of people were in the street and market area below. It seemed to be a festival day, yet there was confusion. People were arguing and pointing toward the windows of a room across the way. No one was looking in the direction of the IDEA and Hank. Even though he was extremely close this time, no one seemed aware of Hank's presence. The room they were pointing to was a large one on an upper floor.

The sounds coming from there at first seemed to be a jumble. Yet the people inside seemed to be speaking in unison, but with different sounds. They were obviously very excited.

Arguments in various languages were going on in the street. On and on it went, and Hank wished he was also a linguist so he could understand what was being said. Suddenly a burly man in rough attire stepped onto the porch in front of the room. He raised his hands high, and the crowds became silent.

The alarm went off, and the routine continued again. The time in the light tunnel seemed like a blink of an eye. The IDEA was stopped on a small rise in a relatively barren area. Just below was an oasis that provided a bit of shade and some water. A well-traveled road was running through it. Almost to the horizon were a wooded area and the walls of a large city.

Coming from the south was a small caravan. As it came closer, one could see that a large part of this group were soldiers of some sort. They didn't seem to be Roman. In the lead with three of the soldiers was a well-dressed young man. He was obviously the one in charge and was signaling directions, as if he hoped to rest there awhile.

He no more than turned his attention forward again, when he was stopped in his tracks by something like a bolt of lightning that knocked him to the ground. Yet, the blinding light continued. It was similar in form to some of the lights they had seen before. Every time a sound like thunder would come from the light, the ground seemed to tremble a bit. The young man was terribly frightened and remained on his knees with his face pressed to the ground, covering his head with his hands. He started to reach one hand toward the light, and suddenly it was gone.

All of the people accompanying the young man remained frozen in shock for several minutes. When he finally did cry to them for help, they found that he was blind. By now Hank was almost able to anticipate the incessant alarm, so he went to his mark and was gone.

This time Steve reached over to the button and turned off the log. "I don't know about you folks," he said, "but I'm exhausted. Anyway, this seems like a good place to compare notes.

"Is there anyone here," he continued, "who doesn't know what we've seen here? We've seen the three Magi visit the infant Jesus, His flight to Egypt, and His resurrection from the dead. This was followed by the gift of the Holy Spirit at Pentecost, and then the conversion of Saul of Tarsus." Everyone nodded in agreement.

"How much more is on the log, Hank?"

"I really don't know, Pastor," answered Dr. Cooper. "I only know this isn't what terrified me. At this point, if you watched my actions it looks like I was getting used to the procedures, even if the machine was giving all the orders instead of me."

"I think that's quite an interesting comment," said Doc. "It really does seem like you were a stowaway or a captive in your own creation."

"If you ask me," said Sheriff Morgan, "it's spooky."

"I believe there's a purposeful message here, Hank," said Steve.

"How's that, Pastor?" said Hank.

"Do you believe in God, Hank?"

"Sure."

"And His Son, the Messiah?"

"Yes, I guess so, why?"

"Why do you believe, Hank?"

"After all we've see here today, how could I not?" retorted Dr. Cooper.

"But haven't you always resisted committing yourself to Him, taking Him as your own Savior?" asked Steve.

"What's your point, Steve?" asked Hank.

"Just this," answered the pastor. "James 2:19 says: 'If you say you believe there is one God you do well: The devils also believe and tremble.' He means by this that mental knowledge is not enough. To believe in Christ means to trust Him completely with everything you are. You trust His work, not just acknowledge His existence.

"I believe He is trying to draw you to Himself by means of a craft He *let* you build, and ride in, and He kept you safe. How many of these trips do you think that mouse of yours could survive? And, how many have we already seen you take, right before our eyes?"

"You know, Pastor, I think you're right," Hank responded. "All my life, I've really been an idiot run by pride. I was sure all of this was my own invention. But I could never have imagined, for at least another 50 years, how to navigate a trip like this in a straight line time-wise. And never could I have picked precise times and locations—I don't know if I ever would have gotten that far. You're right, Steve, and I do believe that Jesus is exactly who He claims to be—my God and Savior. I am His for whatever it is He wants of me."

"Wow, I've been waiting a long time to hear that," said Doc rejoicing. Ruth began to softly weep and enveloped Hank in a warm embrace. "That means so much to me, Hank," she whispered.

Beep-beep. "Sheriff, this is Gate Watch. How much longer do you need us?"

"I read you, Gate Watch," answered the sheriff, "I'll get back to you on that."

Everyone looked around and realized that most of the day had passed by now. It was really getting late.

"What shall I tell them, Hank? You still don't want too much known about this, do you?"

"You got that right," answered Dr. Cooper.

Hank didn't want to leave the machine uncovered in case any word had leaked out. His big concern was how his backers might respond if they got any hint of what had happened. It had been awhile since he had checked in with a progress report to them. These people knew only just enough to keep them interested, but that fact would probably cause them to be quite curious. He had promised them technical breakthroughs for future travel in the areas of materials, miniaturization, new fuel sources, and propulsion.

The group threw some ideas around about how to handle their situation and decided they should all spend the night at the complex. They would find some way to camouflage the ship, and try not to make it obvious that anything had happened.

The sheriff called his men and told them to meet him at the edge of town. Then he went to his car and sped up out of the complex and headed for town.

Hank led Doc, Steve, and Mike to an untouched building a short ways from the hangar. There were so many boxes of supplies there that it almost had the feeling of a survivalist camp. They grabbed six cots, six bedrolls, some lanterns, pillows, and several long coils of nylon rope. Once they had those back in the hangar, they went back for more supplies. On the last trip, Hank finally found what they needed to cover up the ship—two large trunks full of what looked like big sheets of fishing net.

Hank also took a couple of machetes and two small camping hatchets. He said, "Okay guys, we'll act like we're in the Boy Scouts now. Let's each work in a different area. Cut down small branches and bushes to put back here in a big pile. But be sure not to cut everything from one small space. Scatter it out so it won't be obvious from the rim or the air."

"Ruth, you know how to set up cots, right?" When Ruth nodded, Hank pointed to a row of rooms at one side of the hangar. "If those rooms are in as good shape as they seem to be from here, you can pick one or two that you like and set up the cots in there. That way if it rains, we'll have shelter." With that, each person set out to complete their assigned task.

When the sheriff got to the edge of Willow Springs, all the deputies were waiting. He pulled them into a roadside park and gathered them around.

"Okay troops, here's the deal. We have a security situation out there that is so classified, I can't share it with you. Just believe me, it is important for us to stay on alert. That's why I called some of you back on your day off. I don't know how long this will last, or when we will be relieved.

"So, we have to play this totally 'black out' quiet, but we must be careful enough not to raise anyone's curiosity, or disrupt our own lives too much. Willow Springs, and everyone passing by, must be sure that life is just 'moseying by' as usual.

"You fellows that have been off a day, get with the night crew just coming on. We won't set up the roadblock anymore, because we don't want to draw attention to the area. But, for tonight, I want this shift to keep an eye on the access road without letting themselves be seen. So far we've been fortunate to not raise any interest."

"Sheriff," interrupted Johnny Thompson, "I'm not too sure that's totally correct. One black Lincoln, I believe, stopped out on the highway this afternoon. It just sat there, watching us. When I got in my car and approached them, they sped away toward town."

Sheriff Morgan's second in command, Lt. John R. Thompson, was a "man's man." More than six-and-a-half feet tall, he had the shoulders of an ox. It was no wonder he was such a great half-back in his Willow Springs high school days. His wavy blond hair matched with bright blue eyes added to his impressive appearance. Although he was even tempered, he took his job seriously and was known to be one not to be messed with. Johnny, as everyone called him, was definitely the sheriff's most effective weapon.

"Okay, thanks, Johnny. If any of you spot such a vehicle in town, don't approach it or even act like you notice. But alert the rest of us. We'll just watch to see what those people are up to.

"That brings up something else. Any time you talk to each other about any facet of this situation, or those people, do this. Just say the code phrase "Calling Animal Control" and everyone will switch to our secure channel to do any talking. No one will pay any attention to someone trying to get ahold of a dogcatcher. For everything else, use channel 10 as normal.

"While you're watching the secure area from a distance, if you see any vehicle—any vehicle on land or air—approaching the hill, call it in immediately. Especially call me, because I'm going back out there to spend the night after I get some food to take with me. Johnny, I want you to set the schedules for the squads tonight, then you can go home. At 8:00 AM, I want you to meet me at the front blockade point with breakfast for six. All of you keep your beepers and radios on call all night, just in case. Otherwise it's been a long day. Get some rest. Dismissed."

Before Harold Morgan picked up the food for supper, he went personally to Doc's house and let Mrs. Payne know that Doc would be staying at the complex. He made sure she understood that it was quite official and classified, and that she should just be happy he was back when the time came. He assured her that Doc was overseeing health matters, primarily, but she should not even ask what he had seen or heard.

Then the sheriff went to Steve's home. He went through the same general story with Mrs. Lichtmann. She said she understood, and that she would be praying that all would be well.

Sheriff Morgan went home, changed clothes, and got new batteries and a charger for his phone and radio. He left the same message with his wife and told her she could call Johnny for anything she might need. He drove to the grocery, made a stop at the local hamburger establishment, and headed back to the lab complex.

CHAPTER 13
That Isn't Nice At All!

When Sheriff Morgan got back to the complex, it was obvious everyone had been making good use of their time. He could hardly believe how different everything looked. Machinery that had been laying in piles of rubble was standing upright now. Small clutter was cleared, and the IDEA was totally covered up with net and brush—at least enough to break up the golden glow.

The monitor and players they had been watching were already placed in one of the undamaged rooms. The cots were set up around the walls, and a table and chairs were in the center of the room. The monitor was set with its back to the door and the large window. How that window had survived all the flying debris was a mystery all in itself.

Hank called out. "Hey, Sheriff, it's nice you could get back when most of the work's done."

Harold quipped, "Sure is. Well, since you don't need me, I'll just take all this food back."

A roar went up from everyone—they were definitely ready for some food. Hank told them that if it became necessary there was a large supply of freeze dried foods stored in the complex which they could use. All they needed was water, and they had plenty of that since the water lines were still working fine. They had already found the restrooms were okay, so things were pretty good for now.

Ruth mentioned how torn up Hank's clothes seemed, and that she could stand a change of clothes. The sheriff hollered "Surprise! I thought of that already, too." He had brought a change of clothes for everyone. He had gotten Doc's and Steve's from their wives. He thought there was a chance that Ruth and Mike might have been in such a hurry this morning when they left that the house would still be open. When he got there on his way back from town, he found he was right. He went in, found everyone's closets, and just grabbed some things and put them in a suitcase from the master bedroom. Then he left a couple of lights on in the middle of the house to show a glow in other parts of the house. He closed blinds and drapes so no one could see in and locked the place up.

Hank asked Harold to help him and the other men lift some large beams and lean them onto the rim of the IDEA. They also put a couple other ones crosswise on them to break up the circular look. Hank and the sheriff rode to the top of the rim to look down on the hangar. It still looked like something had damaged the building, a tornado, maybe, but the IDEA wasn't visible from overhead.

As they ate, Sheriff Morgan told them all about Johnny's report on the large black sedan. He noticed a wince in Hank's facial expression.

"Do you have some inkling on who that might be, Hank," he asked?

"Well, maybe. I don't really know. When you're writing grants and dealing with the government, you're never quite sure who is behind anything. I've met some pretty eccentric characters and some overly stiff security types. People who take themselves too seriously just naturally make me nervous. To tell the truth, they get under my skin, and it irks me to death.

"The problem is in the fact that these strange sorts always are the ones with the deep money wells. They all seem to be part of the federal military complex in some way. It's impossible to wade through all the alphabet soup of acronyms for their organizations. So when I found one with international ties to our main allies, as well as our own government, I became interested. They were immediately attentive to my work. Their name intimated that this group was interested in new ideas and applications. Their demeanor was that of very self-assured intelligencia to the point of secretive snobbery. Since I certainly was interested in security, I overlooked the weirder sides of their attitude."

"What is this great organization's name?" asked Doc.

"The acronym is NICE. That stands for National Illuminate Coordination Extension. Their work, as they explain it, is to find worthwhile research and development efforts that will effectively keep them on the cutting edge of truly new knowledge. They say they wish to shed the light of fresh new knowledge upon all those capable of parlaying what they gain from each other into even greater advancements. NICE then becomes not only the funder, but also the clearing house and trading post of whatever is learned. They also promise autonomy. In fact, I have had little contact with them that wasn't involved in my need for more money. I spent millions just preparing the crater to hold the complex. Millions more on buildings and equipment, until we were able to raise a little of our own funds through some unconnected research. But since they supplied the money and have yet to see a return, I know they would get the jitters real fast, once they found that something went wrong."

"I must say," responded Steve, "I'm already getting the jitters since I heard their name. It's a vast confederacy of many secret societies or lodges that have one thing in common—they believe themselves to be the only true minds, or the 'enlightened few.' Their members are bound to each other by oaths of secrecy to the point of death. They support each other as the movers and shakers while pretending no common allegiance. The pretense is that these organizations are separate from each other.

"Once the members move up several levels or degrees, they learn more of the truth, but it's too late. They are trapped by the increased secrecy and the fact that they have been sucked into more serious things. Their fear of disclosure is overcome by the greater power they are given. They will spout anything to look good to the populace, whether religion, charity, morals, etc. But, they will be ready to *do anything* in secret in order to keep their power secure."

"Pastor," said Ruth, "you're frightening me now. What have you gotten into, Hank?"

"I guess I don't know," answered Dr. Cooper. "I've always been too busy to be a joiner. I just presumed that everyone who said the right things probably meant them."

"I'm afraid I have worse news," responded Steve. "These various groups, if not the confederacy itself, are international. They are largely European and go back sometimes hundreds of years. They were spread worldwide by the imperialism and colonizations of the 17th, 18th, and 19th centuries. In fact, some of that lasted well into the 20th century. They had at least enough members to put them into the inner circles from which political leaders are chosen. That happens mainly because they can get the backing. Occasionally an outsider breaks through due to his own ambition or "cause celeb," but he soon finds he's owned by the insiders as well."

Doc spoke up. "Pastor, you sound like we the people have nothing to do with it all."

"Well, Doc," answered Steve, "there are some people out trying to warn others, especially Christians and Jews, of just that fact. They say the UN is about ready to spring the trap of world government on all nations. The power supposedly behind all this is a whole list of groups like the Illuminate, Tri-lateralists, environmentalists, etc. Others, though, shrug all these people off as paranoids, seeing conspiracy around every corner. Rather like the sheriff, here, thinking UFOs were just for nutcases.

"There's more," continued Steve. "Some people, who watch Bible prophecy closely believe that these groups and their control of something like the UN could easily be the framework from which the Anti-Christ could quickly take over."

"You mean old 666?" asked Doc.

"Yes," answered Steve.

"You're right, Hon," Hank said to Ruth. "The question definitely is: what have I gotten myself into?"

"Is this going to mean trouble, Dad?" asked Mike.

"I don't know, son. I hope not. I really do question whether I should report the success of my work, though. If all this is true, I wouldn't want this technology to fall into the wrong hands."

Everyone sat in silence, trying to absorb and sort through the things just said. The fear was almost palpable.

"Dear Lord," Steve began to pray, "I know the others here are feeling the same thing I am right now. We feel impending trouble. We know that we can put no trust in the goodwill of the people who have been financially involved in this project. But, Lord, we do know that we can trust You. You're ever faithful and true, never changing. We thank You that through what we have seen, Hank has finally turned loose of controlling things himself. He has given himself to You and whatever is Your will for him. He has said so to us and thus claimed Your salvation. Now, Lord, keep Your mighty hand over us. Walk before us and guide us. We trust our safety and our future to You. Give us Your peace now, Lord, that we might rest well. In Jesus' name we ask this. Amen."

Five other voices joined, "Amen!"

"It's late," said Doc, "and we've been through a lot. Especially you, Hank. You need rest desperately. Let's all go to bed."

"You're right, Doc," said the sheriff. "I'll set my watch alarm and come check on everyone about 2:00 - 3:00 AM, just to be sure all is well."

Everyone agreed, said their goodnights, and went to their cots for the night. Tomorrow promised to be a very full day.

CHAPTER 14
Judgment in the House of the Lord

Everyone but Dr. Cooper woke up about 7:30 AM. When Ruth saw that Hank was still sleeping soundly, she gave him a gentle nudge. Hank came up off the cot yelling and flaying his arms. After a few seconds, he realized where he was, and that he was having a bad dream. After he settled back down, Doc came over to examine him once more. Getting a thumbs up from the doctor, Hank went to the restroom and slapped his face with cold water.

Breakfast was already smelling good. After they ate, everyone agreed that Sheriff Morgan and his men were proving they could handle the situation like a well-oiled machine. So far, everything was going well.

Hank got the day rolling quickly. "I think we should continue what we started. At least we don't have to bother with a lot of preliminary details. We can just pick up where we left off." Since everyone agreed, Hank turned on the power again and started the log.

The time shown in the light tunnel had by now become so routine that they barely noticed it and, for the most part, it was now quite short.

In today's first sequence, the IDEA had stopped on another precarious perch. It was the same corner of the city wall it had stopped on when the swine was carried into the temple. As Hank surveyed the area from the rim, he could see a large army camped in siege around the city. There were thousands of what he thought were probably Roman troops. Whenever any of them moved near the wall they moved in solid units marching in close order.

Officers were barking orders to units of various sizes. They seemed to be stationing their men at strategic points around the city walls. Catapults were being drawn back to firing position.

Atop the walls were similar units of defensive troops. It was obvious that they were ill-equipped by comparison. The men also did not seem to carry themselves as men who felt strong and alert. Their demeanor was that of an exhausted, cornered animal—tired yet anxious, on edge, and a bit jumpy. There was a definite look of confusion and dissatisfaction on their faces.

Down in the streets, the city doors and window shutters were closed tight. There was only an occasional movement as very few people were out and about. Bodies were scattered in the street with most looking as though they had died of starvation or some disease. Some were quite thin with bloated bellies. The smell of death was everywhere.

On a nearby hill to the other side was the same grand building Hank had seen before. One glance told him that this was the temple of Jehovah, and so the city was obviously Jerusalem again. The courtyard was empty, and there was no activity near the altar either.

In front of the gates to the temple stood great numbers of men in white linen robes. Some held shofars and other various musical instruments and made lackluster attempts at playing them. In front of them stood armed men with swords, bows, and spears. At each gate there were probably 50 of these guards standing rather forlornly. A sense of impending doom was in the air.

Outside the walls, deep toned drums began beating a pattern that most certainly gave specific directions. Occasionally, this was answered by blaring trumpets or bugles and drums. The sound moved like a wave around the city till it was back at its beginning point. Then a steady cadence was beaten on the drums as they made their way around the city. The cadence built in volume and tempo until…silence. Everything stopped on the same beat. Such a sudden silence was deafening in its own way. One could feel the terror of confusion. What was coming next? And, how soon?

Without audible signals, at least any that could be heard at the city walls, the catapults all fired in unison. The dramatic clash of cymbals at their appointed time during a symphony could not have been more precise. Besides the huge stones that they hurled well over the walls and into the city, some catapults tossed large skins full of oil. Others nearby pitched burning bales of straw and brush in the same direction. When the skins hit a building or the ground, they burst like balloons spilling the oil over everything, and the flaming bales ignited the oil almost instantly. There were no explosions as would be heard with modern bombs. The resultant fires, however, were almost as devastating, for they quickly turned into a firestorm, drawing in the air like a blast furnace.

The instant all these missiles were airborne, the entire army let loose a scream that sent chills through the defenders. As they did so, they scaled the walls with hooks, ropes, and ladders. Dual teams of charging horses—one on each side—pulled huge tree trunks on wheels toward each gate. The tow ropes were long enough so that, as the teams approached the gate, they could peel off to the right or to the left without unhooking the log.

This acted like a sling shot hurling a mighty battering ram into the gate. On only two of the gates did they need to turn back and hit the gate again.

The defenses on the wall fell quickly before the huge onslaught. The defenders became swiftly frozen in fear and easy fodder for their enemies' swords and spears.

When the other troops reached the temple, the story was much the same—a sudden massacre and all fell silent. Everything and everyone was covered with blood. It was even flowing readily down the streets.

What followed was a systematic search throughout the city. Everyone who could be found—men, women, and children—were herded into the largest open area in the city, right in front of the temple. Hank winced, thinking about his own son, as he watched all the young men old enough to fight be systematically killed in front of the entire assembly. The old men and women, and the younger women and children, including males about 12 years old and younger, were separated into much smaller groups of 200-300.

Before too much time had passed, several of these groups were being held next to one of the gates of the city. It looked from the IDEA as if each gate had about the same number of groups stationed near it. A small contingent of soldiers swept the city once more. Anyone else found this time, no matter what age or gender, was instantly killed. As the troops passed through the city, they set any remaining buildings on fire. There was a huge pillar of black smoke still rising up from the center of the city.

The soldiers then proceeded to the temple grounds and were met by others with horse drawn carts loaded with all manner of tools of destruction.

Suddenly the drumbeats began again. It was now nearly evening. The wails of mourning and loss were a constant sound from the captives. One by one, each group was marched through a nearby gate by a centurion and his troops. They continued to march in whatever direction they began, until they were all out of sight.

Back at the temple mount, a systematic destruction of the magnificent building had begun. First the valuable furnishings and golden treasures and vessels of worship were plundered and packed into the same carts that had brought the tools of demolition. Several hundred men were working stone by stone, removing any signs of the building ever having been there. Anything made of wood, that was not a fine piece of furniture, was thrown into a huge pile to be burned. The work would obviously take some time, but the city had fallen.

Steve hit the button again.

"Hey," hollered Hank, "if you keep that up we'll never finish, Pastor!"

Everyone joined in teasing Steve, just for fun. They felt the need for some release after the carnage they just witnessed.

"Do any of you remember the phrase that shows up in the Old Testament?" Steve asked. "'Judgment begins at the house of the Lord.' Remember? That is what comes to my mind right here. The very city and temple that was destroyed before because of God's great and powerful judgment is the same city and rebuilt temple judged once again.

"We saw the chosen people dispersed in all directions from a fallen Jerusalem. This was, except for the military, identical to the dispersal of all humanity from a defeated Babylon its first time around.

"The next time when Babylon attacks God's chosen people, it prevails for a short time and is then defeated itself. History tells us that the same thing happened to Rome. Prophecy tells us it will happen to both Babylon and Rome once more at the end of the world as we know it."

"You're getting a lot out if this, aren't you, Pastor?" quipped Hank as he chuckled to himself.

Pastor Steve grinned his biggest grin and shrugged as Hank flipped the switch to the log back on.

The light tunnel was a little longer this time. Just long enough for a few more teasing remarks about Pastor Steve's "fast finger of fate." Then new pictures began to flicker across the monitor.

CHAPTER 15
Exit Fourth Empire – Enter Four Horsemen

This time the pictures seemed more confused. It was as if the IDEA had not really settled in one spot. It just moved from one location and situation to another. If any sequence was dream-like, this one was it. Dr. Cooper mentioned several times that this type of imagery was involved in his nightmares as he awakened. Also quite noticeable was the absence of any picture of Hank himself. The group finally concluded that for a considerable time, Hank was "one with the IDEA," contained in the circuitry and sensing all of these scenes in exactly the same fashion as the machine itself.

They also decided that this group of pictures spanned several hundred years. It began with different scenes of knights on horseback clad in heavy armor. One group was riding in long winding columns, each with a contingent of foot soldiers and other supplies. Many carried banners with large crosses emblazoned on them, similar to many of the paintings of the crusades.

Doc picked up on this and told the others: "The crusades were caused through the attempt of Constantine to revive the already fallen Roman Empire into what he would call the 'Holy Roman Empire.' Constantine had adopted Christianity and thought his edict, which declared all of the Roman Empire to be Christian, was enough to make it so. Many others believed this to be the case so they set out to 'liberate' the Holy Land. They wished to drive out the Saracens or who we now generally call Moslems."

Mixed in with the crusaders were scenes of hundreds of thousands of raggedly dressed people dying of starvation or some sort of plague. There were a couple of earthquakes and one volcanic explosion, then more knights and more plagues. It became almost a whiplashing sequence from pageantry to poverty, and woven throughout was desolation. It was beginning to look as if all mankind had lost its civilized nature. All grandeur was gone. Everything was bleak and dreary.

Suddenly there was a short burst of the light tunnel and then another plop. The IDEA landed once again. As the camera panned the scene, Hank realized he was in a large city. The buildings around him seemed well

74

kept. Just down the street was a large Gothic cathedral. As he looked around at the people, their style of dress, and their large wheeled carts, he felt like something was familiar.

The others watching the monitor noticed the same thing. Then Doc spoke up. "That has almost the same style about it as a painting by Rembrandt." They all agreed and realized that they were now observing more modern history.

As the picture continued, a dark cloaked figure came around the corner of the cathedral with a long roll of parchment in his hand. He looked in all directions and saw no one. He unrolled the paper, took off his shoe and, using the heel as a hammer, nailed the paper to the door.

Curious passers-by started going to look at this paper. Those who could read it aloud to the others, until a sizable crowd had gathered in front of the cathedral. After some time had passed, the doors opened and a priest demanded to know what was going on.

When he was shown the paper on the door, he began to read. Suddenly he tore the paper from the nail and started waving his arms at the crowd. He was obviously angry and trying to run the people off. He turned and stormed back inside the cathedral, paper in hand.

Steve knew that story well. It was Martin Luther's 99 theses nailed on the door of the Wittenberg cathedral. A schism had definitely begun within the Church that was destined to start a new kind of dispersal. First a dispersal of God's Word, then an even wider one of His people.

The next landing was startling indeed to Hank. As he looked over the rim of the IDEA, he was sure he had seen this place before. He was on the shore of a rocky coastline. The general shape and lay of the land looked both familiar, yet strangely different. In the slight cove of the bay sat a tall masted wooden ship. It was still a fair distance from the shore and was firmly anchored in the rather calm water. Though there were moderate swells, there weren't any crashing waves.

The sounds of singing and prayer could be heard wafting across the water. It didn't take much imagination to know that these were hymns of praise and that those present aboard this ship had an attitude of thankfulness.

Shortly after the singing stopped, people started appearing on deck. A tall middle-aged man, dressed in some military fashion, seemed to be directing the activity. The men wore wide-brimmed hats and dark suits, and the women had large white linen collars on their black or brown dresses. The children's clothing was made from mainly tan or gray rough hewn material.

Small boats began to be lowered over the side of the ship, and one by one, people climbed down a rope ladder to the boats. There were quite a few rough moments for them as a swell would suddenly cause the rowboat to temporarily splash away from the ship. When the rowboat reached the shore, the passengers disembarked on an outcropping of rock that made nearly a perfect, natural dock. Of course, a few of the boys preferred wading ashore, but everyone else used the rock.

Hank didn't have to guess why he thought he knew this place. He just hadn't been here 300 years ago. It was obviously what later would be known as Plymouth, Massachusetts. Just as the alarm began calling Hank inside, a new swell and a broadside wind caused the ship to turn in the water. On the broad beamed stern was painted the ship's name, MAYFLOWER. As soon as Hank ducked inside, the hatch closed and the light tunnel began.

When the hatch opened this time, a blast of north wind and the glare of the sun off an endless expanse of snow left no doubt to Hank that wherever he was, it was definitely winter. Again the IDEA was on a fairly high piece of ground, but there were taller mountains on both sides. He had actually landed in a large valley next to a river that bisected part of it.

Not far away, two huge armies were facing each other with infantry, cavalry, and artillery. The army to the northeast was extremely larger in infantry while the other army in the southwest was heavy in artillery with many cannons of all sizes.

Even though the cannons from the west kept up a steady barrage, the infantry and even the cavalry seemed spent. They were not dressed nearly well enough for this freezing weather. At first glance, this western army seemed to have the advantage in weaponry, but their lack of effective action quickly became evident to Hank.

As the ship's cameras zoomed in, Hank realized that the eastern cavalry wore the heavy outer wear and the distinctive hats of the Cossacks of Russian legends, while the western troops wore the garb of 19th century France—indeed the French flag was visible. They also held to the old rank and file formation designed for a standard duel type of warfare.

With a bloodthirsty scream, the cossack cavalry charged. About two thirds of the way, they were met by the opposing cavalry. As the fight between horsemen continued, the Russian infantry followed the horses. As they came across the weapons of fallen comrades, they picked them up to use as spares.

It was no contest. The western cavalry, or what was left of it, began withdrawing, and the two infantries were soon engaged in hand-to-hand combat. Large portions of the French forces began to bolt and run. Their commander ordered retreat and fled for his own life.

As the alarm sounded, Mike blurted out, "I know that story, too. In fact, our band plays music about it—the 1812 Overture."

"You got that right, boy," said Doc. "We hear it every 4th of July, too, for some reason."

"The defeat of tyranny," said Ruth. "Napoleon has just been defeated by the Russians. Or rather, he was defeated by a bad Russian winter. If this was not the final battle, at least it was a decisive one. Napoleon lost his war of 1812, and his own hopes for a new 'Holy Roman Empire.'"

IDEA was suddenly opening to a new place. The fields were green, mostly pasture land. It would have been a beautiful pastoral vision, but for three things—broken fences, scarred trees with torn and broken limbs, and heavy ruts filled with ashes making the meadows' thick sod look as if it had been host to disaster.

There was a huge crowd gathered in both Sunday finery as well as workers' everyday clothing. Everyone seemed somber and grim as if in mourning, which was readily explained when they saw the large area behind the people covered with grave markers.

Between the graves and the assembled crowd was a small platform with a roof, draped with black crepe and banners of red, white, and blue. A couple of carriages arrived at the scene, and a small group of men, dressed in black, walked up to the platform. The man leading them was much taller than his companions. The tall black top hat accentuated his stature. To those watching the tape, there was no mistaking his identity—it was President Abraham Lincoln. He was about to deliver one of the world's most profound messages that the world had ever heard in support of liberty, heroism, and righteous responsibility.

As the crowd hushed and gave their attention, Abe began, "Four score and seven years ago, our fathers…"

"Beep-beep"—the alarm had a mind of its own. Hank could be heard protesting as he stepped inside, "I really would like to hear the real thing all the way through." But, the hatch closed, and he was off again, like it or not.

Once again, the pictures on the monitor were flashing by, just like the ones that had shown the Dark Ages. These pictures were more than dark— they were grim. The first was of a city built on a hilly area between the sea and a huge bay or harbor. This was a sizable neck of land like a peninsula because of a deep rift that cut it off from the rest of the coast, allowing the ocean to flow into the bay. There were two or three islands in the bay itself. Except for the fact that there were few tall buildings as compared to say New York City, this was indeed a large metropolis. All of the housing seemed to be row houses, all tied together.

Ruth said, "I believe that's San Francisco."

Just then everything began moving. They could see buildings bending and waving like straw in a wind. The water in the bay built up massive waves that pushed several blocks onto the land. Buildings began to break and crumble into a heap. Fires started almost simultaneously as gas lines ruptured and sparked to life from crushing debris.

"This has to be 1906," cried Doc. "Good grief, I heard it was terrible, but I never imagined it was like this...."

By now you could hardly see the city because the smoke mingled with the light fog from the bay. There was just a horrible orange glow, and an occasional brighter flame.

A flash of light and the scene suddenly changed. Each time the IDEA would hover for awhile, it was either in the midst of horrendous warfare, or the devastation left behind by such a war. There was one major aggressor whose troops were recognizable by heavy steel helmets with ornately sculpted spikes right on top. The opposing forces were much smaller, and kept changing attire and appearance as a different nation was involved. The last defensive or counter-offensive forces were obviously an allied group of nations. They wore olive drab woolen uniforms, and their typical head protections were steel helmets shaped like shallow bowlers with wide brims.

The battlefields were covered with deep trenches, some of which were connected for miles. "World War I," Ruth and Doc said in unison. Doc shook his head. "That was supposed to be the war to end all wars. The mass destruction weapons of poisonous gas were the most horrible thing the world had ever seen. Also this was the first time that airplanes were used in combat. Hand-dropped bombs and mortar type shells were devastating to their victims." The IDEA played back some of these things. Then for a moment, it went blank.

The next views were of the worst of poverty and hardship. There were but small differences in how deadly was the devastation. They saw people standing in soup lines blocks long.

Doc said, "All over the world starting in Europe, probably due in part to the war's aftermath, then spreading to Asia and Africa, it was the same picture. People were unable to work, because the economies of the whole globe seemed to collapse. In the first stages during the 1920s, people in other parts of the world were starving, while in the U.S.A. and Canada, they were having a merry old time. Then suddenly, at the end of the decade, business as usual didn't exist anymore. The stock market had crashed, and some of the wealthiest men jumped out of skyscraper windows, paychecks ceased for many, and life as usual stopped.

"For the next 10 years, men stood in long lines to get some meager morsel in the cities. In the rural areas, people were able to grow some of their own sustenance. Drought and famine fell upon the earth, even where crops were normally the greatest. Dust blew from the south and southwest in large enough amounts to cover buildings in the otherwise fertile plains. Starvation increased.

"In Ireland, the potatoes were ruined year after year. In the U.S.S.R., the winters were so devastating, hundreds of thousands couldn't survive. As if this wasn't bad enough, a new regime under Joseph Stalin was slaughtering anyone who was a Jew or dared name the name of Christ. He was sure he could wipe out religion, especially any claiming connection to Jehovah. Jews were killed where they stood and/or their homes and villages ransacked and destroyed. Christians were herded onto cattle cars and shipped to Siberia. Before they arrived, many were taken from the trains in the middle of the frozen wasteland, stripped of their clothes, and driven off into the snow to freeze to death. Asia and Africa had droughts beyond belief, followed by floods that destroyed everything in the way."

These were deadly times, and the IDEA recorded samples of it.

"How about stopping here for a minute, Hank?" asked Steve.

Hank reached over and stopped the playback. "What's up, Pastor?" asked Hank.

"I am becoming so sure that we are in for more than a history lesson that I want to ask a favor—it may be asking a lot."

"Well, aren't we getting mysterious today," chimed in Doc Payne, a little irritated that his history lesson had been interrupted. "You can find a lot of ways to stop the show. Are you hungry, already?"

"No, Doc," answered Steve. "I hope you're jesting. I really don't want to be an irritant here, but I believe we're headed right past our time and into the future before long."

"Whoa, Pastor," said Hank. "That just isn't possible. The future doesn't exist yet."

"Why, Dad," said Mike, "if you went to the past, and maybe actually met someone there, you would have come from his future."

"Oh-wee, Ruth!" hollered Hank. "I told you this kid was going to show me up!"

"I'm serious, Dad," said Mike.

"I know, son. Trouble is you're probably right."

"I know he is," said Steve. "Everything we have seen so far has been reported or prophesied in the Scriptures. Those prophets were shown the future. It was one they couldn't understand, but they saw it."

"Well, now," said Hank, "I don't remember anything about Martin Luther, the Pilgrims, WWI, or the depression in the Scriptures."

"Oh, really," responded Doc Payne. "We already noticed the pattern on the log that seemed to pick on things relating to the plan of God, shown in the Scriptures. Anything that was helpful in that plan fits that part. As for WWI, and the depression, I think they might be part of the 'Four Horsemen'."

"The four horsemen?" asked Hank.

"Yes," answered Steve. "The Four Horsemen of the Apocalypse, or of Revelations. They're talked about in Revelation 6—a 'White Horse' going forth conquering and to conquer; a 'Red Horse' given power to take peace from the earth; a 'Black Horse' symbolizing shortages of food or famine; and a 'Pale Horse' bearing the name hell and death, given the power to kill a fourth of the earth's inhabitants.

"Many prophecy scholars believed this began with WWI, when nation rose against nation and continued to the present. They conclude that the Four Horsemen have been riding through the 20th century. They feel that it signified the seals being opened to make ready the final days on earth as we know it."

"Then what's your favor, Pastor?" asked Hank.

"I have a friend, Dr. Charles Carver, who is a scholar of prophecy whom I know personally. I trust him and his insight, and I trust his ability to honor confidentiality," said Steve. "Could you, would you agree to call him in on this? If the log does go into depicting future things, I believe he would be like a living encyclopedia. If there is a prophecy connection, he will spot it."

"Oh, boy! That would make seven people in on it all. I don't know…"

Ruth spoke up. "Hon, if this whole thing does turn out that way, you'll have to let a lot of people know anyway. And seven sounds like one of those perfect numbers to me."

"How would you get him here?" asked Hank.

"I have his card in my wallet. If you will let me use your cell phone, I'm sure I can reach him. He's only about 200 miles away, if he's home."

"I think we better work out some security protocol, so we know how to handle this," said Hank.

"Here's an idea, Hank," offered the Sheriff. "Have your friend get here ASAP and go to Miller's Grocery. Then, Pastor, you and I can be there shopping for a few items that are fresher than Hank's survival food, here. Have Charles look for me in my uniform and, of course, he'll recognize you. He can ask us for some directions since he's from out of town. And since his truck is 'broken down,' we could offer to drive him somewhere. It should all seem very normal and innocent if there is anyone watching. Then, Hank, if you like, once we're in the car, we can blindfold Dr. Carver until we arrive inside the crater, and he will not know where he is. We could even fill him in on some of it during the drive and save a little time that way."

"My! You thought that up pretty quick for a hick town sheriff," quipped Doc.

"Doc's right; it sounds workable. Here's the phone. Do it," said Hank.

CHAPTER 16
Call a Specialist

Steve reached Dr. Carver on the second ring. He agreed to come right away since Steve thought it so important. It was determined that with packing a few things for a possible stay over, he could be in Willow Springs in three hours.

With that arranged, Sheriff Morgan called on his radio to Fred Farnsworth, the proprietor of the local truck stop and garage known as Fred's Fill-up and Fast Food. He told Fred to switch to the sheriff's secure band, and with that accomplished, they proceeded to make arrangements for Dr. Carver's old truck, when he arrived, to be parked in the garage waiting area, as if it needed work. Dr. Carver said, "Anyone looking at it would believe it."

With those details taken care of, everyone agreed to continue their exploration of the log. Hank pushed the play button once more.

It was readily apparent that the IDEA still was not landing. It just hovered and recorded scene after scene—most of them nightmarish.

A huge army moved all over Europe. Massive tank brigades and now aircraft were armed with heavy guns and bombs. Men were marching with stiff arms saluting.

Mike was the first to shout, "Hitler!"

"Yes," said Ruth. "This is Hitler's bid to rule the world. Even his Romanesque marching symbols showed that he, too, desired a revived Roman Empire. There's the V2 rockets landing in London as they did in other parts of England. The poor English never knew when or where they would hit. Oh no, look! There's a cattle car train filled with prisoners. The poor people inside are probably Jews headed for the death camps."

Cities and villages were devastated. People were starving and dying from exposure to the elements. The contrast between the dead, dying, and displaced populace, against that of stomping and arrogantly prancing troops was ludicrous. The firepower of the German tanks, cannons, and bombs seemed overwhelming.

Suddenly the light tunnel returned, and when it stopped, the IDEA was sitting atop an extremely high rock escarpment. Hank showed up again and looked over the rim. To one side he could see nothing but ocean. The other direction showed he was on the high point of a large island. A sizable city was near the other end, and in the ocean directly out from the city was a whole fleet of navy vessels. In fact, almost hidden from him, around the corner of the island was a large port. Nearly all of the ships looked like navy. Most close in to port were destroyers or battleships with massive cannons. One or two of the largest ones were anchored a bit farther out.

Just over the horizon the sun was sending its first glow, an orange edge breaking over the waves. Gradually a persistent hum turned into a loud buzz. It was as if a huge swarm of bees wanted to make the IDEA into its next hive. As Hank looked back over his shoulder to find out where the hum was coming from, it changed to a deafening roar. Several hundred small fighter-bomber planes came screaming up over the huge mountainous rock where the IDEA was sitting. They had obviously been flying near sea level so as to come from behind this high point of the island. Some were white and others silvery grey, but all had the symbol of the sun painted on them. Everyone knew that their target was Pearl Harbor.

One moment the port looked almost asleep; the next moment there was pure chaos. Planes were diving in to drop bombs and returning to strafe the area with machine gun fire. They soon were moving in all directions, much like a swarm of bees when on attack. Ships were trying to both shoot back and escape to the open sea. Very few made it. Most were sunk where they sat. If they didn't sink, they were at least badly burned. Most of the city looked burned to some degree.

The picture suddenly changed. A woman and a tall man wearing a general's uniform were shown hanging in the middle of the city. They were hanging upside down by their feet. Their bodies were riddled with bullet holes. They had been slaughtered like a couple of pigs.

Doc remembered seeing that picture before. "That was Mussolini and his mistress after rebel forces caught them. One third of the Axis powers, as they called themselves, had fallen."

He had no more spoken those words when cliffs and beaches all of a sudden came into view. An armada was opening up its landing doors near the beaches, and waves of men were wading ashore. The carnage of the battle was beyond description. Death was everywhere, yet through it all, some troops actually were scaling the cliffs. Others were dropping by the hundreds on parachutes behind enemy lines. Many were killed by gunfire before they reached the ground; others were snagged in trees and shot where they hung. But others got through and destroyed the heavy concrete bunkers that held the largest armament.

The next view showed the skies over several cities. It was as if the IDEA was at an extremely high altitude, looking down on several hundred American B17 and B24 bombers, as well as many smaller British bombers that flew in tight formations. Each group nearly blotted out the sun on the ground and blocked the IDEA from seeing large parts of the ground.

The first group made a bombing run and lost a lot of planes. Then the second group would drop their bombs followed by the third and fourth. After their run, each alternate group would peel off in opposite directions, turn around and fly back in for a second run. So four groups followed each other going north on their first run. But, on their second runs, they came from the east, then west, and then east and west again. Finishing their task, they regrouped as best they could and flew toward the horizon. The destruction they left behind was absolute and nearly unbelievable. Yet the worst damage was the swarms of incendiary bombs that had turned whole cities into firestorms. Death, once again, was everywhere.

Two or three camps, shown quickly, revealed bony, starved bodies huddled behind wire fences and furnaces full of bones. There were huge deep pits filled with piles of dead bodies, most of them emaciated. There were several black jackets laying outside with an applique of the Star of David.

Beep-beep, Hank returned again to the target. Zap, flash,and pictures. When the pictures returned, it looked, once again, like the war they had just been watching. The ship moved quickly from one sample scene to another. There were flashes of ships being bombed by kamikaze suicide planes; a massive battle between huge fleets; ships blowing apart; other ships, torpedoed, losing fuel into the sea, with the fuel catching fire and sailors swimming in a sea of flaming fuel. Long marches of prisoners tortured or beheaded for not keeping up; quaint island villages plundered and women raped. Then came horrible scenes of hand-to-hand fighting. Death again was everywhere.

Suddenly the scene changed. The monitor showed cities on a coast—port cities of some import. A similar picture happened twice in rapid succession. A lone bomber flying very high and fast approaching the city, dropped a large barrel looking object. The plane immediately veered 90° to the side, accelerating and climbing as fast as possible. The barrel fell a considerable distance till a parachute opened and slowed its fall. While still in the air, the bomb exploded with a flash of blinding light, several times brighter than the sun. A circle moved out along the ground at unimaginable speed, crushing everything in its path for three or four miles. In the center was a fireball that made it seem as if the sun had landed on earth. In only seconds, a mushroom shaped cloud of smoke, dust, and debris climbed four or five miles high and spread out about 15 miles wide.

The circle that blew out now came crashing back in as the fireball pulled air back to the center. The air and the fuel of debris created a firestorm that combined them all in the center, and the fireball continued to climb its way right up through the mushroom cloud.

Almost immediately the IDEA moved to another area and kept moving. This time it was hovering over what looked to everyone like the Great Wall of China. Then they saw the large red stars on everything and they had no doubt that one of the armies was that of Mao Tse Tung. There were horrendous battles between two forces. From village to village, and then to the cities, the communist forces were victorious. Finally the other army was forced to flee to a nearby island. The monitor then showed the genocide that followed. It looked like everyone above a certain age was slaughtered, which left only the young. Scenes of people being martyred filled the screen.

A quick flash of the light tunnel and the IDEA was moving quickly from Moscow with its recognizable spires to nearby cities where they saw nearly identical pictures of millions of people being tortured and mur-dered. Then there were tanks rolling into country after country. Darkness and terror was everywhere, and death ruled the day.

Another quick flash and the IDEA was showing jet fighters, MIGs and sabre jets, flying over what seemed to be continuous mountains.

This changed quickly to several different scenes showing almost iden-tical action. U.S. soldiers were holding their positions on a ridge, while ac-tual waves of soldiers, dressed in quilted uniforms, charged the front line position. It was like the tide coming in when the moon is at its closest. The first wave of soldiers were mostly cut down by automatic or machine gun-fire. As soon as one group of soldiers came into view they were mowed down. The few who made it were met by overwhelming numbers in hand-to-hand battle.

The next wave came in similar fashion, climbing over the piled up bodies of the wave preceding them. It seemed each wave had half again more men than the one just before. The screams of blood lust would change to screams of agony and then fall silent, only to be followed by an-other wave of them. As ammunition grew short in supply, fewer guns fired. By about the fifth wave, some of the soldiers would skirt the ends of the piled up bodies and approach the other line from the flanks. The battle would end in a hand-to-hand combat with bayonets, knives, and rifles.

In each case the advancing troops were annihilated, with almost no prisoners taken. The casualties among the opposing troops looked to be anywhere from 10% to 30% depending on how well each contingent was supplied with ammunition. Within the next few days, the whole thing would start again. Tens of thousands, then hundreds of thousands died in a matter of a few days or weeks on the mountains.

"Korea," said Hank sadly. "My uncle was wounded there. So many men died there, and it was a long time before it was even called a war."

CHAPTER 17
Runaway Horses

Another quick flash of the light tunnel and thump, the IDEA landed again. This time Hank felt almost at home. The IDEA was on another precarious perch. When Hank looked over the edge this time, he sharply sucked in his breath. At first it seemed as though there was no bottom. As he looked around, he was able to relax when he realized he was atop a skyscraper quite near the Empire State Building. Some distance the other way was the Statue of Liberty. But the scene the IDEA zoomed in on was directly ahead—the United Nations complex. It looked impressive with its circle of flags from all member nations. The picture zoomed in to a close-up of the centerpiece sculpture interpreting the scriptures from Isaiah 2:14 and Micah 4:3, "They shall beat their swords into plowshares, and their spears into pruning hooks."

But a strange thing happened. While remaining focused on the "swords to plowshares" sculpture, the monitor would suddenly block the picture with a frame of gray and blood red stripes. It would then come back to the still picture of the sculpture. Each time the stripes would be in a different direction or angle across the screen. This happened six times. Then beep-beep the alarm said it was time to resume the journey.

Once again it was a "fly over" with no landing. In the first scene, the IDEA was directly above a wall built to divide a city in two. Next to it was a heavy fence of barbed wire, and a wide open area of about 100 feet lay between the wall and a second heavy fence. This fence was topped with dual coils of razor wire. Along the inner or east fence, every 1000 feet was a tall guard tower with armed military guards.

As they watched the monitor, they saw a disturbance in the open area—bursts of gunfire erupted at four people attempting to run across the area—and a man, a woman, and two small children lay dead. The picture blinked white and then returned in a different position over the wall. A large explosion was seen and then the mangled body of a young man who had stepped on a mine. Again white light and a new picture showed a man sliding on a cable from a rooftop on the right side to the top of the wall on the left side. Shots rang out and he fell. But this time he fell on the left side of the wall and was helped up by soldiers. He was wounded but alive. Flash again, and another scene showed three young people being dragged from a cave-in of a tunnel they tried to dig. They were promptly shoved to their knees and shot in the back of the head.

Suddenly the light tunnel came back for a few seconds. It was evident that the term "fly over" still applied. The IDEA was in orbit and could move to any point it wanted to show. At first it was over the western North American continent. There was a sudden flash of blinding light about 40 miles east of a large river in what would be in the middle of the desert. A very compact column of a cloud moved rapidly skyward and then expanded in all directions. The IDEA moved suddenly west across the Pacific and far north, and in rapid succession the same scene happened twice.

It was like riding the end of a teacher's pointer, as he pointed to one place after another. Back to the U.S. desert, and several more detonations. It took no guess work to notice the IDEA was paying attention to the development of nuclear power, particularly its weapons. Three or four locations would take turns with their tests. Each one seemed bigger that the ones before.

Again the IDEA moved, this time west and north, and flew over the ocean to a place covered with snow and ice. In rapid succession bombs were being detonated like popcorn. The slight break between scenes were mere blinks of light before the new picture appeared. All the IDEA needed to do most of the time was to stay well north over the Pacific to see the fireworks show being put on to the left and right of the water. Each country plainly knew what the other was doing.

"This must have been during the 'cold war' which to me was like WWIII being played out through the scientists," said Doc. "It was the war of research to outdo one another—a war of mutual intimidation. It was not a war without casualties either." The IDEA showed pictures of animals, wild and domestic, getting very sick and dying. The human population seemed to thin out rapidly in parts of the country.

"These death scenes were near and downwind from favored test ranges," Doc continued. "Radioactive fallout was exacting a heavy toll. Many of the plains states in the U.S. were covered with fallout as were Siberia and Alaska."

Suddenly the IDEA moved to the South Pacific and hovered near the water. The flash and fireball created this time was 1000 times bigger and brighter than the first detonations had been. This time the lovely atoll that had grown from the ocean floor to make a circular island just disappeared completely. The resulting tidal wave swamped naval vessels watching from miles away. Several similar blasts occurred in the same general area of small islands.

In a flash, the IDEA was over land again as a massive earthquake nearly wiped out towns at the southern end of a group of mountains.

Soon the IDEA moved on, and its vantage point was high above the desert floor where eruptions began occurring. These eruptions looked almost as if the earth had a hiccup, except they were always circular. A whole large area would lift just a bit, stir up some dust, and then lay back down. It would end up almost as flat as when it began.

"Underground tests?" Steve asked. Hank nodded.

North over the vast frozen wastleland, they saw more massive explosions. These kept moving further north and east. They saw two large earthquakes occur in the Aleutian Island chain and another one in mainland Alaska. They watched horrified as a resultant tidal wave gathered strength and height, moving south and west to Japan and Hawaii. Mauna Loa began erupting violently on the island of Hawaii, and earthquakes began shaking up the land.

The screen zipped quickly to the other side of the world where more earthquakes were occuring.

"Look at the monsoon rains in Bangladesh—they killed thousands of people, I remember, and the resultant warfare that was triggered between India and Pakistan killed even more," said Chuck.

Another zap and the IDEA moved ahead once again, showing them a new volcano push its way up through the middle of a maize field and begin building a new mountain.

"That's Mexico. I had an old friend who was there at the time," Ruth said.

Many of the scenes were still vivid in most of their memories.

Then the monitor started showing ships leaving ports in Cuba, loaded with huge missiles, and heading northward in the Atlantic.

"That was the end of the Cuban Missile crisis. Boy, I thought I might be drafted for that one if it developed into a war," said Doc.

They watched rockets being launched. "That's Sputnik. That rocket sure changed the course of science," said Hank. "Gave us the impetus to get cracking as far as outer space went. And that next one is probably John Glenn going around the world for the first time."

"Wow!" Mike's face was a study in awestruck wonder. "I can't believe I'm seeing the real thing."

Everything quieted down for a very short scene showing soldiers before what everyone knew was the Wailing Wall in Jerusalem. A general with a patch over one eye was holding their flag aloft, his arms raised in a V for victory.

"That's Moishe Dayan celebrating Israel's bid for independence," said Steve. "That was a day of real significance for the Jews!"

Then a myriad of rockets and missiles of all shapes and sizes were launched. One scene showed views that all but Mike recognized from news shots—the mad scramble of U.S. personnel, and some Vietnamese allies, scrambling to get aboard helicopters atop the U.S. Embassy. This was the ignoble departure of U.S. forces from South Vietnam.

The IDEA moved again back over the western U.S. Suddenly the whole southern half of Mount St. Helens blew apart in a blast that dwarfed hydrogen bombs. A short flash of light, and a huge volcano on the other side of the world sent ashes thousands of miles away.

The IDEA flashed the light tunnel long enough to hover over an area they had seen twice before. Steve said, "That's the Tigris and Euphrates rivers area again. You can see the Persian Gulf in the south. To the north are the mountains around Mount Ararat. To the west a more arid yet fertile area we know today as Iraq. This is a return to Babylon.

"To the south you can see the cities of Kuwait," continued Steve. "I remember from all the pictures on CNN of Desert Storm." Tanks and military trucks were everywhere. All through the desert floor were armaments of every description. Tanks were buried in sand bunkers, ready to pounce like trapdoor spiders. There was an armada of carriers and a battleship in the gulf with another armada in the Mediterranean. The skies to the north were full of military planes. Suddenly the night sky was filled with the fires of jet and rocket engines. Also lighting the sky were the tracer bullets from the defensive fire of the Iraqi forces, and from exploding bombs. It seemed to never let up. Then Beep and flash and the IDEA moved again.

The light tunnel flashed for only a moment and another battle was in progress. At first, all fighting parties were blacks. Guerilla warfare type battles occurred between groups that looked more like gangs rather than armies. They saw huge warehouses loaded with food supplies, which contrasted against the thousands of people they saw starving. Suddenly a few tanks arrived, then a dead white soldier in a U.S. uniform is shown being dragged through the streets. "That's Somalia," Mike informed the questioning adults. "We read about that in our current events class."

IDEA moved again to view more warfare between Europeans. Mass graves. Long lines of refugees. Starving men behind wire fences, mountains, snow, while soldiers stood around with rifles and light blue helmets. All recognized the conflict in Bosnia. There were flashes of similar pictures—plane crashes, bombings of military barracks and office buildings—all things they had just recently seen on the news.

Again a move to the south Pacific and volcanic eruptions with ash going around the world. Sudden climate changes and one strange scene—the picture of a newspaper headline about a Bolivian earthquake that didn't do that much damage on the surface, but was a record breaking 400 feet deep.

"Whoa! Enough already!" shouted Doc. "I think after all that we need a break. Anyway, it's like reading today's newspaper right now."

Everyone present agreed. Anyway, it was about time for the sheriff and Steve to go meet Dr. Carver. Before they left, though, the sheriff spoke up.

"About that headline that was pictured—I think I even got some official notice about that. Federal authorities wanted law officers ready for possible emergency measures if strange things began to happen. It seems some seismologists were concerned about the magnitude of that Bolivian quake. Since its center was so deep, they were afraid it might cause the continental plates to begin to shift. That sounds rather extreme to me, but what do I know? I just thought that would make your day."

Dr. Cooper made another observation. "What got me this time was how the IDEA bounced around to show specific things, and this time not in a straight line. It was as if a point were being made, and not just chronologically."

"So you did recognize that point," said Steve.

"It seemed to me it was tied to that strange sequence with the U.N.," said Ruth.

"Yeah," added Mike, "What about those weird lines?"

"Well," said Steve, "I believe it is implying something found in prophetic scripture. The phrase about beating of swords into plowshares, etc., is being misused by the U.N. That reference in the Bible text speaks of the world after the Lord returns and is running the show. In fact, it could be a reference to heaven itself. It never implies that man will cause it to happen with his own devises and institutions. He is always too corrupt to make it possible. The U.N. plaque was but wishful thinking on the part of an artist and the politicians who take advantage of peoples' longings.

"Beyond that, I believe everything we saw, after those stripes, only confirmed what the stripes meant. Those who pay much attention to Bible numbers consider 'six' to be the number of man. Those stripes covered the monitor six times. That brings one prophetic scripture to my mind from Jeremiah 6:14: "They have healed also the hurt of the daughter of my people slightly, saying 'Peace, Peace, when there is no peace.'"

"Precisely, Pastor," said Doc. "That is the picture of our generation."

"And beyond that," said Steve, "it seems that the IDEA is not just o
serving and recording; it is talking back with additions of its own."

Hank said, "Hey, you guys better get to town if you expect to meet Dr.
Carver."

CHAPTER 18
The Carver Cavalry

As Sheriff Morgan and Pastor Steve were approaching Willow Springs, they were flagged over by Lt. Johnny Thompson.

"I'm sure glad to see you here, Sheriff," said Johnny. "We caught sight of that Lincoln again this morning, right after I met you with breakfast. They saw me driving back into town coming from the direction of the Coopers. I met Bo by the Chevy dealer and had him check on them in his private car. He watched them drive a ways past the access road and park awhile. Then they came back past it real slow before returning to town.

"I picked them up across town and followed a little distance back until I saw them turn toward the airport. I came back to the office and phoned Barry at the tower. He said they had pulled up close to the fence by the tarmac and just sat there for a couple of hours."

"Did you get a look at the people in the car?"

"Not real good, Sheriff, but they looked 'Hollywood Federal,' if you get my drift—dark suits and large dark shades."

"That's spooky," said Steve.

"You got the picture," quipped Johnny.

"Why spend so much time at the airport?" asked the sheriff. "Do you suppose they're expecting some sort of surveillance backup?"

"Something like that is my guess," answered Johnny.

The sheriff picked up his radio. "Calling Animal Control," he said. Then he switched to the secure channel, "Each one respond if you are on line." One by one the others came on and reported their positions. All except Bo.

Sheriff Morgan had two units start a search for him. Their orders were to stay on the secure channel and just listen as they searched. If they found him, they were to call in.

Just as the sheriff and the pastor were about to leave, a call came in. "Sheriff, this is Rick. Bill and I found Bo. He's not in uniform, and he's been badly beaten. We found his car about a block from where we found him. It was pulled over funny, like he was forced off the road. Either he was beaten there and managed to get this far before he passed out, or he tried to run and was caught here—I don't know which. As soon as we get off, I'll call the ambulance."

"No, don't do that!" hollered the sheriff. "Take him to the back of the hospital yourself. I'll call ahead and make arrangements for some staff to meet you there."

"Roger that," answered Rick. "Out."

There was a pay phone a few steps away. Harold Morgan ran to it and called his friend, Leon Schmidt, the hospital administrator. After a brief explanation about security, he left the rest in Leon's hands.

When he got back, Steve asked, "How are we going to hide this?"

The sheriff drew himself up tall and said, "Vee are a tiny village, Ja? But vee half our vaysss!"

They all laughed and climbed into the cars.

"Johnny," said Harold, "You stay on top of this. I'll go back to the work channel. If anything pertaining to this develops, just 'beep' me back to the secure channel."

"You've got it," said Johnny, and they parted company.

They had been in the market only a moment when Steve saw Dr. Carver walk in. Steve and the sheriff positioned themselves where Dr. Carver had to run into them. After a short pause, Dr. Carver stepped closer.

"Pardon me, please," he said. "The local constabulary should be able to direct me."

"Why sure, Mister," said the sheriff in his best John Wayne voice, "How kin I help ya?"

Dr. Carver looked at Steve with one raised eyebrow and a quizzical grin. He turned back to the sheriff and answered in the same vein, "Well, ahy jus' got in from Drahy Guulch and..."

Steve stuck out his hand to greet an old friend while still pretending not to know him. "That'll teach you to goof off when a stranger asks for directions," he said to the sheriff and nodded, adding, "Yup."

After fooling around with their roles a little more, they left with the sheriff saying he would take him to Fred's garage. Harold called ahead and Fred Farnsworth was waiting for them when they reached the truck stop. He waved them around back to the garage waiting area where they parked Dr. Carver's truck. They raised the hood, stuck their heads under it, and remarked a bit about the weather. Fred stepped back and shook his head yes, real hard. "I sure hope this charade throws off any one who's watching," Doc said.

"I'm glad my old truck finally came in handy," said Dr. Carver as the men shook hands, and Dr. Carver walked around front where Sheriff Morgan was filling his tank.

For the benefit of anyone who was watching, Dr. Carver said,

"Thanks, Sheriff. I'd really appreciate a ride. Looks like my truck is going to need a piece of work." He climbed in the back of the squad car and they took off.

"Calling Animal Control," it was Johnny's voice. Once on the secure channel, Johnny reported. "Say, Boss, Bo is going to be all right after a couple of his ribs mend. He said he started following that black Lincoln again. Trouble was they 'made him' this time. They forced him over, pulled him out of the car, and asked him what he wanted. He thought it best to act belligerent and dumb. So he threw them a bunch of city street, tough guy lingo and told them he would follow whomever he wanted to follow. When they asked if he thought they were someone to rob or otherwise mess with, he said, 'What if I do?'

"Right away, one guy took a punch at him. But Bo swung back and decked the guy, breaking his glasses. Then he ran, but they caught him and beat the tar out of him. There were four of them in all. They said something about heavy official business, and if he valued his life or freedom, he would butt into someone else's business. They said, 'You better make yourself scarce.' Then they beat and kicked him more until he passed out."

Bo was a smaller, but well built, and spunky sort of guy—one you might expect to be a Marine. He enjoyed his job thoroughly, and if need be, would gladly take on someone the size of Johnny. He never said much, unless he was sure something needed saying. Yet he had the ability to mimic the would-be tough guys. That got him in trouble this time. Most of the population considered him a real gentleman.

"Where are they now?" asked the sheriff.

"They're back at the airport."

"At least the Coopers place is over on the other side of town. We'll get on back now. Do you think they know we've spotted them?"

"I don't think so, Sheriff. They were near the lab once when they drove off from in front of the blockade and then when Bo was tracking them," said Johnny.

"Okay, let's hope we can keep it that way. See you later, out."

The sheriff pulled off to the side of the road and told Dr. Carver that for his own protection they needed to blindfold him. He didn't object, so they gave him the type of eye mask some people use in order to get to sleep. He put it on and then began asking a bunch of questions. "What had Johnny been talking about? What was so mysterious and classified that they needed these kinds of security methods? How did he get mixed up in this?"

Steve answered most of his questions after reminding Chuck, as his friend preferred to be called, about their phone conversation that had brought him to Willow Springs. Steve tried to give him a quick thumbnail sketch about the IDEA, its hoped-for purpose, and the astounding results they had seen in these two days in the compound. Chuck was incredulous over what he was hearing, but finally came to the key question.

"Do you mean, Steve, that you really believe this thing-a-ma-jig is going to show us the future? I've heard of reading bones and tea leaves, but this is just—"

Steve broke in. "Slow down, Chuck, you know I wouldn't call you on a lark. You have to understand that we have already seen scenes from 'The Flood' to the present day. The ancient pictures, from Noah until the fall of Rome, mostly showed scriptural stories that pertained to God's dealings with His people and the salvation plan. Are you with me?"

When Chuck nodded that he understood, Steve continued. "Anything since then showed points in history that we could recognize, most of which pertained to botched attempts to revive the 'Holy Roman Empire,' or the fulfillment of biblical prophesies of the four horsemen. Others continued the themes of dispersal of God's people and/or His Word. With all that, it is already showing things so current that we remember reading them in the paper not long ago."

"So, since it showed things that could be tied to prophecy, you believe it will now show the future?" asked Chuck.

"Something like that," replied Sheriff Morgan.

"And somebody rode the IDEA already?"

"Yep, sure did, Pilgrim." It was John Wayne's voice again.

Ignoring the jesting sheriff, Steve said, "We just felt we needed someone with more scholarship in prophecy than all of us, in order to keep us straight if that really happened. And you're the one I know and trust."

"How much is left on the log?" asked Chuck.

"We don't know till we watch it," answered the sheriff.

Just then they were getting to the top of the berm, and Harold stopped the car. He grabbed a pair of field glasses and panned the countryside as far as he could see.

"Well, I don't see anything out of the ordinary. Maybe we aren't being watched that well yet," he said. "I'll come back after dark and try with my night-vision infrared gear."

They started down into the crater, and when they neared the bottom, the sheriff told Dr. Carver he could remove the blindfold. Chuck remained silent, drinking in everything he saw with a look of astonishment on his face. He couldn't imagine where anything like this could possibly be located. He thought sure he knew this part of the country well. Yet, this was obviously not some underground facility.

Once they reached the hangar, Pastor Steve immediately launched into the introductions. Then Hank got Dr. Carver's commitment of complete confidentiality. Chuck confronted Hank with the need to tell the story as widely as possible if this did turn out as prophetic as Steve thought. Hank agreed, but made it clear that when that time came, he, himself, would release the information first. Chuck had no problem with that, thinking it a reasonable course of action.

Hank then took Chuck over to the IDEA. His utter amazement was immediately evident after Hank touched the side and quickly and as quietly as possible stated the code. The familiar small line near the top of the rim glowed and Ruth's voice was heard saying "Welcome, Dr. Cooper, please come aboard." Suddenly the side of the ship seemed almost to melt, and the stairway treads appeared in almost liquid fashion. Once they were steady, Hank started up and said, "Follow me, Chuck. Let's do this quickly."

Chuck stepped up to the ladder gingerly at first, but then when he felt its solid rungs, he quickly climbed on up. Dr. Cooper opened the hatch and stepped inside enough to give Chuck a quick tour. Then, as they left, Hank repeated the same closure routine he had used before. Chuck's mouth dropped open when Hank placed his hand on the proper spot, spoke the code softly, and gave the ladder a little swat. As the ladder flowed back into the IDEA, Chuck stood there shaking his head.

He was still trying to absorb what Hank told him about riding that thing when Ruth hollered, "Soup's on!"

"Coming, Hon," Hank responded. Then turning back to Chuck he said, "I set up a separate monitor to save us some time. It will be repetitious to the others, but I'll bet they'll enjoy watching your response, as they remember theirs. I'll play the outdoor surveillance tapes from the security monitors for you. Possibly we'll have time to show the first few minutes from the log. We'll try to finish all of this while we eat lunch."

Chuck responded, "I got some general rundown from Steve as we drove from town so I probably don't need to see much to catch up with the rest of you. Then will we jump to the approximate present day where you stopped viewing?"

"Yes, I think that's best. The sheriff made it sound like we may be attracting too much notice. So time is of the essence right now."

The whole group sat down to eat, and Steve prayed over the meal. Hank switched on the tapes for Dr. Carver to watch as they ate so that he could join them after lunch with a little experience of how the IDEA worked.

CHAPTER 19
Revelation Satellites

When lunch was over, and all discussion about Chuck's reaction had subsided, Hank took control once more to get started. He was concerned about Harold's report on Bo's run-in with the strange visitors. He felt that if it really had something to do with him and the complex, he should have been contacted in normal fashion. If he was the subject of their curiosity, yet they hung around without direct contact, then their presence in town felt sinister, as if they were stalking him. Steve's concerns about the funding organization were getting to him.

He had Steve fill Chuck in with what he thought was important about the last three or four scenes, then Hank restarted the log.

The log was still in a similar mode of darting around, back and forth with very little time warp involved. Light tunnel periods were short, and they acted almost like a glitch in transmission or tracking. They were still unique, though, so they couldn't be confused with static snow.

At first the IDEA seemed to be in orbit again, moving in next to a satellite that was quite bulky with huge long panels of solar voltaic cells. From a direct frontal angle, the panels looked like wings. There were many other antennae and aerials and some parabolic dishes. Dr. Cooper identified it as one of the communication satellites in geo-synchronous orbit.

Then, 'blip' and the IDEA was looking down on a large stadium—something like looking at it from a blimp. There was a large stage set on one end of the field. Behind the stage, a large group in the seats were dressed alike. It looked like a large choir, with men sitting separate from the women. Eight or 10 people were on the stage along with musicians and their instruments. One speaker was front and center, motioning to the crowd. As they watched, people started leaving the stadium seats and going onto the field. Some were even running. As the field filled up, all stood with bowed heads. Some had uplifted hands. Then 'blip' and on they went to the next scene.

Another satellite appeared, similar to the first, yet somehow it was different. It was definitely over another part of the earth. Then "blip." This was a different stadium. The people were different, but all else was very similar. These scenes went back and forth from stadium to satellite and back to another stadium a total of 10 different times.

Some places and situations were recognizable to those watching— U.S., South America, Africa, India, and Russia. There were several each in America and South America, and one even had a big PK drawn out on the field of the stadium. There was a definite message here, and Dr. Carver got right into the swing of it. Hank saw it coming and stopped the log.

Chuck rose to his feet, obviously excited. He said: "You are really right, Steve, this is very specific in its prophetic picture." Then he opened his Bible and read from Revelation 14:6,7:

> *and I saw another angel flying in the midst of heaven, having the everlasting gospel to preach unto them that dwell on the earth, and to every nation, kindred, and tongue, and people, saying with a loud voice, Fear God, and give glory to Him, for the hour of his judgement is come: and worship Him that made heaven, and earth, and the sea, and the fountains of waters.*

"There are many scholars who believe these communication satellites are what John saw in Revelation," said Chuck. "There are many of them in order to be able to reach the whole earth, but they are a single system. The word we translate as *angel* is mainly used for the word *messenger*. In Scripture that's what angels are, God's messengers. Angels are sometimes winged, and most of these satellites have that appearance."

Hank broke in, "Wait, Chuck, those satellites carry all sorts of messages, and not just from mass evangelism rallies."

"Absolutely right, Hank," answered Chuck, "But just as there was a lot of other history besides the scenes your IDEA looked at, God is only interested in His message. Also, within that same message, it is getting out on those satellites in other forms as well. There are local church services, Bible teachings, missions outreach, and on and on. You're being shown what can quickly make a clear point. It is also apparent that the earth and humanity will have no excuses.

"There's are few inhabited spots on earth that have not heard the Gospel in some form. The Bible has been translated into thousands of languages and dialects. But the satellite system has beamed TV and radio, adding to that shortwave radio, so that the whole planet is covered. This has just been within the last 50 years at most. That's about 50/12,000ths of recorded history or 1/240th of just recorded history.

"You've already covered the Four Horsemen, signs in the sun, moon, and stars found in Luke 21:25. Also, Joel 2:30 reads, 'I will shew wonders in the heavens and in the earth.' And now, the angel proclaiming the Gospel to the whole earth. I would say you're already deeply into final days prophecy at this point."

"Would you listen to you, Chuck," chided Steve. "For an old skeptic, you act like you're having fun."

"Yeah, you caught me," laughed Chuck.

"That must mean it's time for more fun, presuming there is any more," said Hank as he hit the play button.

The next scenes were both disturbing and dull. The IDEA moved from one church door and parking lot to another. Most, but not all, were large imposing buildings with grandiose architecture. But there were very few people going through the doors. Then the IDEA would show up at lakes, parks, golf courses, swimming pools, and various nightclubs, casinos, etc. All were full.

Then it would go back to similar church properties and zoom in on bumper stickers with shallow "feel-good" messages, similar to "I'm all right, you're all right," "If it feels good do it," "I'm for women's choice and I vote," "Down with capital punishment," and "It's OK, that's MY truth."

Next it was looking over a city area, watching two gangs of young people kill each other. Just around the corner, a police squad car was parked next to a Cadillac, with an officer accepting an envelope full of money.

Next were scenes in air terminals and bus stations. One group with shaved heads and rusty orange robes were dancing around with bells and tambourines and passing out literature. Another group with literature was selling flowers.

Other scenes showed people going into houses with signs advertising psychics, spiritists, and channelers.

The IDEA went back to the same dead-looking churches and showed church signs with sermon topics such as "Self image, your strength," and "Thou shalt love Mother Earth."

Then there was a sudden change to large groups of people meeting together with posters and banners reading, "Just Believe"; "Say it, see it, and make it so"; "Self esteem made easy"; and "We are all gods."

Suddenly the monitor went blank for several minutes, and everyone thought that they might have seen the end of the log. Just as Hank reached for the "off" button, the light tunnel returned. Hank soon realized that the pause was only to let the machine switch to a new disc. He was sure more conversation was bubbling up, so he stopped it anyway.

Ruth spoke up first and said, "Correct me if I'm wrong, but I got the distinct feeling, with that mixed up sequence, that judgment is about to take place in the house of the Lord. Do you remember, Pastor, that you said that yesterday about the temple?"

"I think you're right on target," answered Steve.

"It sure made the point about some people thinking other things were more important," observed the sheriff.

"It's that and more," said Chuck. "It's a separating process already started. The wheat from the tares, sheep from the goats, followers of the Lord and pretenders. In Matthew 7:21-23, Christ says:

> *Not everyone who says to me Lord, Lord shall enter into the kingdom of Heaven, but he that doeth the will of my father which is in Heaven. Many will say to me in that day, Lord, Lord, have we not prophesied in thy name? and in thy name cast out devils? and in thy name done wonderful works? And then I will profess unto them, I never knew you: Depart from me, ye that work iniquity.*

"Not everyone that attaches themselves to a church congregation really means business. They may not be trusting Christ's work, on their behalf, for salvation, or for the basis of communion with Him. Many are too proud of what they think is their own righteousness to admit they really need a Saviour. They believe they're good enough to earn their own way, by some subjective sliding scale. The trouble is, they feel smug and secure because they're comparing themselves with the bottom of the scale.

"As the final days get closer, the rift between the real and the unreal will be increasingly evident. The obvious split has already caused many to leave from some of the oldest parts of the church that many call liberal or compromised. Their seminaries took part in the worst of the 'higher critical' denial of the Scriptures. They've been quick to denigrate Scripture, because of their exalted opinion of their own scientific interest and understanding. As time has gone by, their 'science' has more and more proven their opinions wrong, and actually supports Scripture. Yet, they refuse to be honest and accept that fact. They may call themselves Christian or Jew, but they have switched to a different god of their own creation. They worship their pride and 'non-knowledge' concerning science, and in the process have become totally unscientific. When they willingly lie about what they've found to be true, they fulfill the scripture in Romans 1:21,22:

> *Because that, when they knew God, they glorified Him Not as God, neither were thankful, but became vain in their imagina-*

tions, and their foolish heart was darkened, professing themselves
to be wise, they became fools.

"This arrogance is their idol, made in the image of themselves. This creates the low morals problem that destroys any society that embraces it. When the righteous cease teaching righteousness, most people fall for all the ploys pushing false freedom. Then new generations have no foundation, and man's own natural bent toward evil desires takes over. Before long, all freedom is lost."

Steve broke in, "I can't agree with you more, Chuck. You've all heard it said, 'If you believe in nothing, you're likely to fall for anything.' This is also very true of some very fervent believers who become easily led by charismatic speakers who claim new revelations going beyond and even counter to Scripture. They are mentally lazy enough that when they hear some things they want to hear, things that sound good on the surface, they eagerly jump on board, without taking time and effort to rightly divide the word of truth. They test the spirit of the message against what they *like* to hear, rather than against what the scripture has already stated."

"That's right, Steve. And that's why another part, probably a second one-third, will be in danger of following false teachers and prophets. They are especially susceptible to those claiming to see visions and performing signs and wonders.

"In Matthew 24:24, Jesus Christ said:

For there shall arise false Christs, and false prophets, and shall show great signs and wonders, in so much that, if it were possible, they shall deceive the very elect.

"And in 2 Corinthians 11:13-15, we read:
For such are false apostles, deceitful workers, transforming them-selves into the apostles of Christ. And no marvel, for Satan him-self is transformed into an angel of light. Therefore it is no great thing if his ministers also be transformed as the ministers of right-eousness, whose end shall be according to their works.

"These folks also end up worshiping the same idol—themselves—with their imagined self-righteousness."

"Okay, I have a question," broke in Hank.

"Yes, of course," answered Dr. Carver. "I tend to get started and rattle on and on."

"No! No, that's no problem. I'm learning things the last two days that I hadn't known before, but I am curious about one thing. Being somewhat learned in the sciences, I have a mathematical mind. I noticed that you made a point about one-third of the church and implied that it was the same as another third. That rings a bell with me, but I don't know why or what note the bell is playing. Will you fill me in?" asked Hank.

"Oh, yes, that's a good point, and it does have significance. I believe you picked up on that because God definitely expresses His mind often in mathematical terms such as number patterns. Scripture uses them in specific contexts.

"Now there's a lot of discussion and disagreement among scholars as to how much attention and significance is to be given to numbers. I won't try to cover most of that now. As with any point of view, men are prone to be extremists—pro and con.

"But try this—what do you think of when you see a string of threes or a string of sixes especially if there is a decimal?"

"That's easy," said Hank. "I think of one-third or two-thirds of whatever is involved."

"Exactly," responded Chuck, "and God uses the same principle in Scripture. Three is equated broadly with God's perfection and righteousness. Six is broadly equated with Satan and his evil imperfection and unrighteousness, as is also true about sinful humanity."

"Oh—and that's the reason the anti-Christ's number is 666?" asked Hank.

"Yes," answered Chuck. "And more. I'll refer you to a story, that even if you've read or heard it, you may not have given it much attention. It is found in 2 Samuel 8:2. King David's men had just won a battle against Moab. And, when the Moabites, still alive, surrendered, David had them lie face down in three long lines. He then touched the man at the end of one line with his sword. He said, 'These shall live.' His soldiers then killed everyone in the other two lines. The Moabites that were given life then went with David as captives and served Israel for the rest of their lives.

"If you'll notice, each man chose which line he would be in. Then the king had mercy on the one-third he chose. This is considered by many scholars to be one of the moments in David's life when His actions were a prophetic type or picture of what Christ would do, or the picture of the salvation of a remnant of humanity, who once were slaves to Satan but now belong to Christ.

"Two other scriptures somewhat clarify this picture. One of them is when the prophet Jonah, a rather disobedient type himself, let his pride and self-righteous attitude show. This was because Nineva had repented and God, in his sovereignty, spared the city and did not destroy it as He originally had said He would. Jonah pouted and threw a real snit. 'You mourn for a gourd plant you did not grow, should I not spare that great city with 120,000 persons?'

"Also, in Exodus 33:19, God told Moses: '...and I will be gracious to whom I will be gracious, and will shew mercy on whom I will have mercy.' He thereby stated His sovereignty in final judgment.

"Then Christ told his followers: 'Narrow is the way, and straight the gate that leads to eternal life, and few there be that find it. And, likewise, broad is the way that leads to destruction and everlasting torment, and many shall walk in that way.'

"He further said, 'My sheep hear my voice and they follow me, I am the good shepherd.' Again he said: 'I am the gate,' meaning the gate to the sheepfold. 'If any man comes into the fold any other way he is a thief and a robber.' And finally Christ said: 'I am the way, the truth, and the life, no one comes to the father except by me.'

"That last statement is the stumbling block for the vast majority of people because they are prideful and sinful men and women. It doesn't sound on the surface to be broadminded and tolerant enough, even though the complete message is 'Whosoever will, may come.' The gate, as narrow as it may seem, is wide open to any who want to enter. It is open enough for all to enter if they will, but most will be upset that they can't use a different door if they wish.

"All of this makes a picture of a great host of people who are obedient to God, yet in actual percentages only a small part of humanity is saved. Now what we saw on the monitor showed the same pattern even within the corporate structure of the Church: about two-thirds of it being those who either add to or detract from the true Gospel message of 'Christ and him crucified' and intermingled in the true Church, 'The Israel of God,' spoken of by Paul, who walks straight down that path and through that gate and does not look right or left. They keep their eyes, ears, and heart attuned directly on their Lord.

"Ruth was right," Chuck concluded. "The process is already started. Judgment is beginning in the house of the Lord."

CHAPTER 20
Heads Up!

As Hank reached over to restart the log, the sheriff's radio came back on with the familiar pager noise. Then a voice said "Calling Animal Control" in low bass tones. On the secure channel, Johnny's voice came back, "Sheriff, do you read me?"

"Yes, Johnny, go ahead," answered Harold Morgan.

"That's affirmative, Sheriff. This is Johnny. I just heard from Rick and Bill. They were hanging around the airport, trying not to be seen by those guys in the Lincoln, when a helicopter landed at the far end of the field. They switched to the channel used by the tower and heard the controller demanding that the chopper identify itself, but no one responded. The Lincoln was driven down to where the helicopter was parked, and two men got out and approached it. Two men from the chopper met them. And get this—they were wearing black suits and had big bubble helmets on like some of the bikers use. They acted really weird, Sheriff. Instead of a regular handshake, they bowed to each other. Can you beat that?

"The meeting didn't last long, and the helmeted guys got back in the chopper. Oh—by the way, Rick and Bill made a big deal—I'm not sure why—about the fact that the chopper was a dull black color. About the time the controller got on the channel to tell the chopper it didn't have clearance to be on the field, it just up and flew away from the field and over the next little hill along Bush road.

"Rick said the other strange thing was that they didn't remember hearing much sound when the chopper first approached and landed. But, when it left, it made an awful roar like you usually get from military choppers. I can't prove it yet, Boss, but my hunch is that these guys are up to no good. I don't know what to expect next, or how to watch for it."

"Rick, Bill, and Johnny," said the sheriff, "I want you to stay right where you are. Better yet—Rick and Bill, station yourselves close to the tower. Keep this radio on the secure channel, but keep a backup on the tower channel. If that chopper comes back, it will mean they're totally arrogant and sure of what they can do—regs or no regs. If that happens, lock in with your radar gun and clock 'em."

"You want me to give those guys a ticket?"

"Thanks a lot, Bill. No…I'm just playing a hunch of my own."

"Johnny," said the sheriff, "I want you to drive back across town and get into position to see anyone approaching us here at the complex from the highway—especially those guys in the Lincoln. If they do come near here, let me know pronto. The rest of you go to the nearest road out of town and watch for anyone you think could possibly be in league with these guys—even motorcycles—especially if the riders are all in black with full bubble helmets. They would most likely be riding all-terrain styled bikes. Now stay on this secure band; I have a feeling we're in for some surprises. Morgan out."

Doc spoke up right away and said, "Sheriff, do you really think maybe these guys know we had some trouble here?"

"I have to cover that possibility, Doc. I'm concerned about all the black colored sedans, clothing, choppers, and uniforms. That's consistent with many reports of problems I've been getting the last few weeks from all over the country. There are also reports that these Black Forces are a covert arm of the UN, and that they operate with the permission of our own government. In fact, some of the stories and denials from the Feds are reminiscent of UFO stories and the subsequent charges of coverup. It's like they're practicing to see how much they can get by with. Congressmen and senators aren't much help either. They're told it's a matter of national security, and they back off investigating them. Put that together with what you fellows were saying about the Illuminate, and I really get nervous."

"Did you…did you say Illuminate?" asked Dr. Carver.

"Yeah," answered the sheriff. "Hank said they had something to do with finances on this project, and Steve gave us quite a scary lecture about secret societies, including that group."

"Steve is quite right if he made them seem scary. You combine these groups with the UN and some of its treaties, and given the right turmoil around the world, you could have world domination overnight. In fact, it wouldn't be beyond these guys' modus-operandi to create the turmoil on purpose, so they could have a 'legitimate' reason to grab control. And the Black Forces may be the easy tool. Didn't Johnny say the men at the airfield greeted each other with bows?"

"That's correct," answered the sheriff.

"Does that mean they're oriental?" asked Mike.

"Right on, young man," answered Dr. Carver. "If they're operating for the UN, then it would make sense to use foreign troops wherever they're needed. Orientals could be operating here, while our boys are shipped off somewhere else. That way they won't hesitate to use force on innocent civilians. If they ever wish to overtake our relatively Christian country, it would make sense to use troops from atheistic, oriental, or Moslem countries. The individual soldiers would likely feel righteous in taking harsh action."

Doc went over to Ruth. She was beginning to show signs of stress and on-coming panic. She was sobbing almost in a whisper, "What have you gotten us into? What could happen to Mikey?"

No one answered her. She really wasn't wanting an answer right then anyway, but she was worried for her son. Hank just stood next to her with his arm around her. Steve motioned to Dr. Carver, and they all joined hands as Chuck began to pray.

"Our Father, who is ever faithful, we thank You that You always hear us, and that You always answer. You have told us to trust in You with all our hearts and not lean on our own understanding. And You have promised, Father, to give Your angels charge over us to lead us in all our ways, and to protect us from the evil one. We are trusting You for that right now. Our welfare and future are in Your hands. Provide whatever we may need. This we ask in the name of Jesus and for His sake. Amen."

After everyone murmured an amen, Hank decided that it was time to get on with things. "Well, Sheriff," said Hank, "is there anything else we need to do right now?"

"Not that I know of."

"Okay then, let's get on with this and see what else is on that log."

Everyone settled themselves around the monitor once again. This time, the light tunnel segment was over almost instantly. To everyone's surprise, the next scene was at night with the city lights dazzling. A huge crowd was in the street below. At the end of the street, high atop a tall building, was the Waterford crystal ball. At the bottom, in blue lights was the number 1999.

Mikey yelled, "Hey, that's New Year's Eve in New York!"

"For sure, young man," joined in Doc. "You're looking at Times Square. At least we know the date for once. Do you realize, folks, that this is the first time that we're in the future? Can you beat that!"

Everyone gasped in awe, hardly able to fathom it. It was one thing to view what was in the past, but quite another to see what had not happened yet.

"The real future!" cried Mike. "This is better than Star Wars 'cause we know it's gonna happen for sure!"

Then the crowd in the street started counting down. Excitement was in the air. Two million people were packed like sardines in the streets. Very few generations get to say goodbye to one millennium and hello to a new one. As the countdown continued, the ball dropped slowly as it had for many years. This had truly become not only a New York tradition, but a national one as well.

When the ball reached the bottom, right on the zero count, the numbers 1999 that had been dimming slightly suddenly went off. With a blaze of light, new numbers twice their size flashed 2000. The crowd went wild with cheers and laughter. A mass band composed of members from all across the five burroughs of the city broke into an amazing sequence of fanfare that eventually worked its way to the traditional song, 'Auld Lang Syne.'

Suddenly the IDEA's alarm beeped and the light tunnel flashed onto the monitor for just a moment.

"Guess not much will happen that night since we moved on so quick," said Mike.

"We must have fixed all the Y2K bugs that were important," said Hank.

Then the monitor brought the next pictures up. "Hey, wait a minute. Are we right back in Times Square?" asked Mike.

The IDEA had stopped at nearly the same place it had been just before. Crowds were singing, fireworks were going off, and office lights and billboards all over the city were flashing their lights furiously.

"At this angle I can't make out exactly what year it is on the sign," said the sheriff. "Since we traveled a little in the light tunnel that means the year is more than 2000, but how much more we don't know."

The street was full of celebrating dancers. Parties abounded in skyscraper penthouses and on many rooftops. Planes and helicopters were mingling with each other in the air above the city, and at times, between the taller buildings. This was a special moment every year, and everyone looked determined to enjoy it to the fullest.

Then the lights blinked for a moment, and suddenly everything was dark. This darkness seemed even blacker due to the sudden contrast from the bright lights that had just been flashing everywhere. People's eyes needed time to adjust. It was even darker because of the cloud cover and made even worse because the skyscrapers created a canyon so deep that the sky was hardly visible anyway. Patches of black sky at the most could be seen directly overhead. Everything else was blocked by dark, forbidding buildings.

In the midst of the sudden darkness, one small plane and one helicopter lost their bearings and smashed into the walls of tall glass buildings about a block from each other. The falling debris and fireballs of burning fuel landed on the crowds below. Panic was instantaneous. People were trampled upon in everyone's frenzy to escape.

In horror, the seven of them watched the sight of New York City falling apart right on their monitor.

"What's going on? I know this sort of thing was supposed to happen with Y2K. I think you were right, Mike, nothing must have happened then since the IDEA bounced us here right away," said Hank as he pushed the pause button. "I know lots of people who are mad at the government for spending so much money the last few years over something that may not happen. They don't realize how important it is to spend all that money and what they can avoid because of it."

"Avoid is the key word, my friend," said Dr. Carter. "I read that a number of those programmers are writing some code for the computers that will put off any such problems for 20-30 years. They've been so swamped with work that they have had to do a 'quick fix.'"

"You're right," said Steve. "I read about that, too. Looks to me like, here in the future, either no one wanted to spend any more money after nothing happened in the year 2000 or else the programmer's fix didn't hold very well."

Hank pushed the pause button to continue the scenes. Streets jammed up quickly due to numerous auto accidents occurring with the sudden absence of working traffic lights. Some of the drivers caught in this horrible midnight melee started losing their tempers. Within range of the IDEA's viewers, three people were mortally wounded in "road rage" type arguments. The new year was starting with a bang.

"Boy, this is no friendly blackout like it was years ago," Hank said. "I remember I had a friend who lived on the east coast when the electric grid went out back then, and he said they had a ball. He met more people in that one night than he had in the previous six months since he'd moved there. Met his wife that night, too."

"No, Hank, it's not the same world it was back then, unfortunately," Steve said. "The whole mood of the country seems to have changed."

In a little while, tens of thousands of people slowly started pouring into the street. They had walked down flights and flights of stairs from skyscraper restaurants and high-rise parties to find their way out of the downtown area. Since there was no power, the elevators failed to work; and in the darkness, it took a long time for people to stumble down stairways from 40, 60, 80 or 100 floors up.

It took a similar amount of time for emergency personnel to be able to get anywhere near Times Square, unless they were already stationed there. Huge lines of people, four or five abreast were trying to get to the subways, but the trains weren't running either.

Ruth spoke up and said, "I wonder how many people are stranded on the trains." Everyone in the room groaned at the thought of all those people stranded below ground in the dark.

Suddenly, the scene changed as the IDEA began hovering over various parts of the city. The scenes seemed to almost sputter onto the screen, interrupted with short bits of the light tunnel. Doc even questioned whether they were all in the city or just nearby in time and/or space. Crowds of angry and opportunistic people with no moral compunction began smashing into stores and grabbing as much as they could carry. Others were forcefully robbing people where they stood. Every once in a while, the IDEA would spot a fire. People were looting store after store. In the pawn shops, people were stealing guns and knives, arming themselves as they pleased.

"Dad, do you think that's what's really going to happen?" Mike asked.

"Son, we really don't know. Maybe this is just a warning we're supposed to share with others. If the utility companies and other businesses work hard enough, maybe they'll prevent this."

Dr. Carver spoke up and said: "Well, it may not be the fulfillment of biblical prophesy yet, but many people warned us that these things could happen. They're telling us to work now to prevent these problems. They've predicted power outages, financial collapse, failure of our defenses, etc., if we don't deal with it. The trouble is that since nothing much happened before, and it seems so far off right now that they will have to change a 'quick fix' into a permanent fix, people are just ignoring the warnings."

"Even though this isn't yet reflective of any specific prophesies, it may be the triggering force that will make some of them possible," said Steve. "I wonder, too, how much time has elapsed here between short bursts of the light tunnel. Could it be that it all didn't happen exactly at midnight?"

Doc broke in, "I read in a science magazine that a lot of people think it won't all happen at once. Some people say the problems will surface gradually. People are definitely warning of government interference. The IDEA hasn't shown us anything yet from the rest of the world. It will be interesting to see what is going on there."

Hank had hit the pause button when Chuck started talking, so he reached over and released it.

Similar scenes continued. All mass transit seemed at a standstill. When the IDEA flew down the coast, it was obvious that the power grid had failed.

"Even if some power plants were ready with their computers, the ones who were not ready probably overloaded the grid and the capacity of those that were still working," said the sheriff.

The IDEA followed the time zones all the way west and showed much

110

the same chaos. Planes landing at airports across the country crashed in the sudden blackouts. Trains collided because their switching signals were out of commission.

"What a way to begin a new year," Mike said. "I sure hope things won't really be like that, whatever year it is."

CHAPTER 21
What a Way to Start a Year

After taking a somewhat longer journey through the light tunnel, the scenes began again in Washington, D.C. They weren't sure if it was days, weeks, or even months later. The sun was shining and the IDEA was passing over the the mall between the Capitol and the White House. The area was as beautiful as always, except for one thing: Crowds of agitated people were milling around. Some held signs of protest, but most were walking aimlessly around.

Toward the downtown area, crowds lined up in front of banks, many people screaming and yelling in a fruitless attempt to gain access through the locked doors. Angry people were picketing in front of the Treasury Department and the Social Security headquarters. Protest signs, rock throwing, and screaming seemed to be the order of the day.

"Mom, what do you think this is?" Mike asked.

Ruth shook her head in distress. Then the viewers of the IDEA zoomed in on newspaper headlines. They read: "Computers Crash— Worldwide Economic Disaster."

"Oh, no. Those poor people!" Ruth sighed.

The scene shifted first to grocery stores. People were gathering in long lines outside waiting for new stock to arrive. Then it moved again to show even longer lines of either very new or very much older autos waiting for gas.

"They don't have any computer chips in the old cars. Hey Chuck, I think your old truck may have a bright future!" Steve joked, trying to relieve the tension building up because of the one thought on everyone's mind—*this may be our future, too!*

Chuck broke in on the picture: "The Black Horse is still riding. The pale one isn't far behind!"

Then the picture on the monitor did another strange sequence. It was as if the IDEA was in orbit again. It seemed to be interested in the continental U.S.A., zooming in on one familiar city after another. From L.A. to Chicago, to San Francisco, to New York, to Miami, to Kansas City, to Dallas, to Seattle, it covered them all, eventually leading back to Washington DC.

Angry crowds in front of banks or stores, usually grocery stores, were becoming more unruly. Then in at least one place, and sometimes more, they began to riot. Local police were unable to control the situation. National Guard troops would come as reinforcements, and finally a contingent of the Army, Marines, or Navy would be sent in. As martial law was becoming established, a new contingent of military would take over control. Local police would stay on "reduced control" status. All "normal" military would then leave to be available elsewhere. The big guns and armaments were all in the hands of this new group who had tanks, troop carriers, and helicopters of their own.

"Everything's black!" Mike pointed out. The color of their uniforms and equipment was all black and the military salute of this group was a clenched fist.

Freedom looked like it was rapidly disappearing in America. The Black Forces were very quickly taking control. With the Capitol under martial law, it was a hazardous time indeed.

The IDEA quickly went to Europe showing them similar scenes from six large cities there. The shock to the viewers increased when the IDEA went back to New York and landed back in front of the UN complex. The color black was everywhere, including the UN flag.

Suddenly there was a flash, and the light tunnel began again. Quickly, Hank stopped the log. They all looked like they were bursting to make some comments.

Dr. Carver was the first to speak. "I don't expect this to show up on the log, but we could easily be some of the first victims of the Black Forces we just watched. If not, there must be something remarkable in store for us."

"You think those guys at the airport are part of this Black Force bunch then?" asked Sheriff Morgan.

"Yes and no. The structure of the organization may not have gelled that much yet."

"Say, Chuck," queried Hank, "why do you refer to us as victims? It seems to me that what we watched was a group just bringing order out of chaos. What are they supposed to do when so many are rioting?"

"Don't be so naive, Hank. That's exactly what the thinking was in Germany when Hitler and the Nazis took over. Only later did it become clear that much of the disorder was purposely started by Hitler's Brown Shirts, only so that his other forces would have to step in with martial law to restore order. That made them look like the heroes of the moment. Only when Hitler was in office and had complete control did Germany and the rest of the world learn anything about his true agenda.

"There are many who make it their business to check into secret societies and find out what their involvement is with public institutions. Almost all of these researchers agree that something is going on covertly connected to the UN. These same people I.D. the Black Forces as the UN's enforcement tool. Up until now, every contact the Black Forces has had with the public has been in remote areas and usually involved actions so weird and occultish as to make anyone who dared report it look like a complete idiot. This allowed them time to polish their procedures. They've been in this country openly, on a limited level, for several years. Their actions, as well as their plans, though, are very secretive."

"Once control is solidified, then, restoration of order won't be their goal. Is that what you're saying?" asked Hank, finally catching on to Chuck's explanation.

"Now you got it," answered Chuck. "The last pictures we saw may be implying that the line between freedom and tyranny may have been crossed by that time. If that's the case, anyone who seems to be an impediment to complete control will have to be victimized. They'll have to move quickly to silence or remove any people they perceive to be a possible threat. Any contrary viewpoints cannot be allowed."

"We better get as much knowledge about all of this as possible," said Hank. He reached over again and restarted the log. As the light tunnel resumed, everyone could feel the collective anticipation combined with dread.

Thump, the IDEA had landed again. It was sitting on a small high spot again. As Hank appeared near the rim, the first thing he noticed was a sizable body of water. All the land around it was quite desolate. The few plants and scrub trees growing near the water looked quite scraggly. A few bushes that were in the water had a strange appearance. As the picture zoomed in for a close-up, it became clear what happened. The water had risen, gradually drowning all of the plants' roots and killing the bushes. The branches still sticking out of the water were covered with heavy crystal forms.

Hank personally knew of only three places where this was likely: First the great Salt Lake in Utah, second the Salton Sea in California, and third the Dead Sea in Israel. As he moved around the rim, the question of his location was answered—there was an encampment flying the Star of David on another high spot in the terrain. This tented complex had a small radar unit, some missiles loaded on trucks, an armored troop carrier, one tank, and a mobile communications center. The troops seemed relaxed but occasionally used their equipment, including binoculars, to scan the horizon in all directions.

A bit farther down the valley floor was a large drilling rig. A single glance told Hank that this was an oil drilling rig. The signs seemed to imply, as did the military presence on the hill, that this was a joint venture between a private company and the government of Israel.

This didn't seem to be a wildcat venture. A good sized pipeline was already nearing completion. There were three huge above ground tanks in place. Expectations were obviously high. They must have believed they were atop a major field. As the viewers paid more attention to the pipeline, they saw two more branches, spaced just right to be joined to two more wells with instant connections. Indeed, the well that was being drilled was already connected to a cap-off valve.

As Hank and the IDEA were still watching, the drilling crew began running away from the rig, and the operator was attempting to pull the power head away. Suddenly, as if fired from a gun, the links of the drive rod that powered the drill, came flying out of the top of the casing. The first ones came out slowly, compared to the ones 30 seconds later. Finally they were firing out the full height of the rig and came crashing down in a tangled pile. Soon there was salty water spraying out with the rods. Suddenly, the last rod blew out with the drill still attached. What followed was a mighty fountain of salt water 80-100 feet high. Eventually it began looking like muddy water. Soon it was obvious that oil was mixed in the water. In only a few minutes, the fountain was all black—a real gusher was born.

When the flow had stabilized and proven itself, a few men rushed up to the cap and closed it off. They then opened the valve to the pipeline and started to fill one of the three tanks. As the celebration began, the IDEA called Hank back to the target. Time to go.

It was a short trip back to New York and the UN. As the IDEA sat on its now familiar spot, the very striking thing everyone noticed was that even though martial law was no longer evident, the Black Forces seemed now to be clearly the UN's main security organization. They were on the streets accomplishing traffic control and were posted at all the main doors running I.D. checks. They also seemed acquainted with any official delegates on sight. It seemed that they must have been functioning in that capacity for quite a while.

A speaker's stand was being set up just outside the doors to the Assembly Hall. There were enough microphones to satisfy all the major TV channels. Crews were jockeying for position when the U.S. and the Israeli ambassadors approached the stand. They were obviously quite upset but were struggling to maintain a dignified front. The U.S. delegate spoke concerning his great sadness and utter dismay that the UN General Assembly had voted a complete condemnation of Israel. He told his listeners that it was forced by mostly the Arab nations and their allies, through economic extortion. The Arabs threatened to cut off all oil supplies to member nations unless they agreed to Israel's denunciation. He shared his belief that the OPEC cartel was at the center of it all. The OPEC nations tried to say that Israel was stealing their oil. Israel denied their accusation saying that they only had a few wells near the Dead Sea, hundreds of miles away from most of the complaining countries.

The ambassador explained, "What some geologists have surmised is that the Mideast oil field is composed of only one single large pool of oil. Iran, Iraq, Kuwait, Saudi Arabia, Yemen, Abu Dabi, etc.—all of which are above sea level—have oil fields which seem to be somewhat separate pools. These countries had to drill quite deep to reach them. However, all these fields were like multiple necks on a bottle. The bottle itself is much broader and deeper than anyone had imagined.

"When Israel saw oil seeping through the ground southwest of the Dead Sea, of course it began drilling. It had hit from below sea level the much lower side of the bottle, if you will. They didn't need to spend money pumping. Gravity did all the work. Where gas pressure had caused a few gushers in the upper 'neck like' pools initially, that had now dissipated. But on the low end, gas pressure wasn't needed. In fact, the pool at the low end seems to be much deeper still."

The Israeli ambassador was quite defiant toward the vote of the UN Assembly. The UN had wanted to sanction Israel as if they really were stealing oil from the other countries. He thanked the U.S. for vetoing such an action. The Russian ambassador pushed his way to the speaker stand and stated his condemnation of the U.S. veto. He was afraid Israel would drop the price of oil too far, which would be devastating to the profits of the Russian oil. He warned both countries not to be too sure of themselves.

Before he could finish, the ambassador from Iraq pushed him aside to make his own point. "Our brothers of Islam now know the truth. Iraq has been picked on and overrun by the U.S. and its allies in the west. They have caused us trouble and starved our people. Now they want to help Israel steal our oil. We will not allow this any longer."

The arguments among the ambassadors were becoming more and more heated and looked like they might lead to physical blows. The officers of the Black Forces moved in quickly. They separated the delegates and sent the press away. The confrontation was over for now.

The alarm sounded, and Hank was seen going to the target. As the green particle beam appeared, and Hank disappeared, Chuck shook his head and exclaimed, "Whoa, I'll never ever get used to seeing that!"

"I could program the IDEA to stay put," said Hank, "and you could try it for yourself, Chuck."

"No way! I'll wait till the Lord does it."

"Fine, whatever you say. I want to know, though," said Hank, "if anyone else noticed what happened with the IDEA's log clock. What I am talking about is how we have been watching things for short periods of time. Yet anyone who knew these events would know it should take many hours or days longer to view them. An example being that oil well. We watched for only minutes, but I noticed that the clock said the gusher blew wide open for 48 hours before they closed the cap valve."

While everyone was excitedly discussing this phenomenon, they were interrupted by the sheriff's radio.

CHAPTER 22
Be Prepared

"Calling Animal Control." It was Johnny's voice. The sheriff switched to the secure channel.

"I read you, Johnny, go ahead," said Sheriff Morgan.

"Okay, back at you, Boss. I'll get off and let Rick fill you in, come on, Rick."

"Yeah, Boss, I think we got an answer to your hunch. We were just down the street that leads to the airport entrance, you know, watching the Lincoln right in front of the control tower. We were sitting there with our windows down. The car was not running. We couldn't hear or see anything out of the ordinary. The only thing that was running was the radar gun, just in case a speeder came by.

"All of a sudden, we heard the loudest roar from a helicopter, and that black chopper from before buzzed the tower with such a racket it broke one of the big tower windows. I grabbed the radar gun and tried to clock it. It didn't show up in the slightest. I know I was behind it, but I had it in my sights for 10-15 seconds. It went straight and then turned right. They certainly weren't going faster than sound. This gun has a range of three miles. It was like it was a ghost."

"Okay, Rick, you did fine. Now we know that the chopper is probably built out of that stealth type material. It just absorbed your signal, or reflected it away from you. It sounds like they can be quiet or noisy at will."

"Rick, did you say they turned right as they were leaving?"

"Affirmative, Sheriff."

"They may be coming this direction after all," said Harold. "All units not in place already, go to your previous stations and stay out of sight. In case you see anything like these guys in black in the chopper, cars, bikes, or whatever, have your larger armament ready. We may need to intercept them. Just remember, we don't know how well they're equipped. If you need to, load up on ammo from headquarters. We will do our best from here. Any questions? — No? — Okay, out."

As soon as he was finished talking with his men, the sheriff turned to Dr. Cooper. "Hank, what kind of defenses do you have around here...anything?"

"Do you mean guns and the like?"

"That might help, but other things, too—barriers for the roadway, mines, traps, more cover for the IDEA. You get the picture."

"We do have a small arsenal of automatic weapons and loads of ammo. As far as the IDEA is concerned, the only thing I could do to hide it better would be to get in it and fly it off. Problem is, I wouldn't know how or when to bring it back."

"You can forget that, Mister." It was Ruth, putting her foot down.

"I know, Hon, but you don't have to worry. I don't know how to do it anyway."

"We just need to keep them from flying overhead and outside the compound," spoke the sheriff. "Hank, do you have aerial flares?"

"Yes, I sure do, and four guns to fire them."

"Let's collect what we can. I can teach everyone how to use them. Then we can station ourselves up on the rim. With the Lord's help, we can manage to defend the place, I think. A lot depends on how much they throw at us."

Doc spoke up. "I can be helpful with any wounded. I don't like the idea of shooting at anyone to take their life."

"I understand," said the sheriff. "I'm sure Steve and Chuck might feel the same way. Right? —I thought so. Well, I have my deputies as a small flanking force. In the compound, I believe Hank and I can handle the rest. Ruth, you just keep Mike down and out of the way, unless we need a nurse's help, okay? —Fine. Now Pastor Steve and Dr. Carver, you can find a lot of ways to help, but as far as I'm concerned you can concentrate on prayer."

Everyone nodded, but everyone was afraid of what was about to transpire.

The sheriff still insisted that everyone, including Mike, learn how to operate the weapons, if only for self-defense if things became really ugly. He didn't think anything would get that bad, but he just wanted to be prepared.

"I really believe these guys are just testing things, a reconnaissance of sorts," he said. "They may have been watching more than you ever knew and might have some idea what happened here. But they probably don't understand what they observed."

Hank cut in. "That may be an explanation, but it's not a good reason to act in such a sereptitious manner. If these guys are some competitor trying to steal secrets, that's one thing, and we can defend against it. However, if this is connected with my backers, it's plain crazy. They know how to reach me openly. If this is them, they are proving they're not trustworthy. My question is *why*? What is so urgent that they might storm the complex?"

"I think I may have a clue about that," said Chuck Carver. "What if someone else did have some information about your real purpose and project? And what if they leaked that information by accident or for profit? The next question, then, is your last one. What is so urgent? Well now, we've already talked about secret societies and the Illuminate as one of them. From what we can tell, they seek only power and any wealth that accompanies such power. We're also sure they have extensively infiltrated the UN bureaucracy and the administrations of nations. Coupled with present day technology, this makes world domination within reach. This could easily be the tool used by old 666 to fulfill the prophesies of revelation."

"If this *is* all connected, then we also know that the power behind the Antichrist, whomever he is, really is Satan himself. By understanding Satan's original sin and the nature of God, we may find the clue…"

"What clue?" asked Hank, a bit edgy, wanting to get on with securing the weapons but anxious to know what Chuck was talking about.

"Why, time, of course," answered Chuck, "and the knowledge of the future. Just think about it. We know that God, the creator of all we know about, and the creator of a mighty angel Lucifer, has characteristics that apply only to Him. One of these is what we call *omnipotence*—the greatest power that exists. The second, which increases the first immeasurably, is what we call *omniscience* or all knowledge—the ability to know the beginning and the end. In other words, God knows the future and is thus able to cause things to fulfill His final objective or will. He has never been surprised by anything, even Lucifer's rebellion. He doesn't find himself saying, 'Oops.' A third part of His nature is that God cannot change. He operates in total integrity and goodness; we call it holiness.

"Satan's big problem was pride—'The Original Sin.' By the way, pride is the basis for *all* sin, even now. Satan was so arrogant that he tried to overthrow God. He lost that battle, but the war is continuing. Scriptural prophesies tell the end result, but the ingredients that bring it to pass remain the mystery lost in the future. Satan is arrogant and vengeful enough to believe he can still win. He would do anything to get control of something possibly capable of giving him such knowledge."

"Well, the way you've put it," said Hank, "we may be caught between God and Satan. In that crossfire, we're probably doomed."

"No way!" said Doc. "If we are caught between, God knows all about it already. We just trust Him to take care of the details. In the meantime, we just stand firm. Right, Pastor?"

"Absolutely," answered Steve. "We all live our entire lives caught between God and Satan."

"Hank," called Sheriff Morgan, "we better get up on the rim and see if anything's going on. I've loaded guns, binoculars, ammo, flare guns and radios in the car. Let's go." They left the sheriff's extra radio with the others and headed for the top of the berm. They stationed themselves to view the area between the complex and Willow Springs.

Sheriff Morgan took out his night vision equipment and turned the controls as low as possible. "This wasn't meant for daytime, but I hope I can pick up on any hot spots out there. Any engine will create extra heat. I guess I'll find out if this works," he said.

"It should be possible," answered Hank. "It will depend on the quality of your contrast controls."

"Calling Animal Control." It was Johnny again. "Sheriff, that black Lincoln is on the move again. They've been talking on their phone a long time. Now they've gone in the direction of the highway turn off. If they're coming your way, they'll be there in about five minutes. "

"Sheriff, Rick here. We just saw three black cycles drive out of a semi, over at the truck stop. They left town going in the opposite direction. It's my guess they intend to circle around on one of the farm roads and come up behind you."

"Any other reports?"

"Yes, sir, Frank here. There's a black suburban in town now. It has started out south on Maple street. If it's coming your way, it would be about in the center of the other two vehicles. This could be the flank approach. The car can't get all the way, but it might carry several troops who could continue on foot."

"Has any one seen the chopper again?" asked Sheriff Morgan.

"Not since it buzzed the airport and turned toward your direction," answered Johnny.

"Okay, all we can do is wait and see what happens, troops. Just stay on this channel, and everyone get in your riot gear, all of it. I don't want to lose any of you. Wait until you hear anything from us that indicates contact of any sort. Spread yourselves out in teams of four or more. Johnny, if you place your men behind where you think the Black Forces are approaching, that will be good basic cover. Then if you have enough for an over-terrain team between those points, it will be even better."

"Roger that," said Johnny. "Phil and Mark got back from vacation yesterday, so we have 20 pairs of legs here. I could send the in-between, over-terrain guys in early so they can get in place about a half mile from the complex. We have four rough terrain bikes. Those eight men could ride double, if that sounds all right to you."

"Good thinking, Johnny. Just make it clear that we do everything as silently as possible unless the fighting does break out. One other thing—if any of you have the targets in view, don't say anything to rock the boat. But if you see any of them act like they are on to us and have figured out our secure channel, then get on the horn quick and yell, 'Silent Running.' Then we'll maintain radio silence. Everyone got that?"

"Roger, " "Yes," "You bet," a chorus of voices responded.

"Okay then, Johnny, you handle that end. Morgan out."

The sheriff then called down to the five in the hangar. "Switch to this secure channel and you'll be able to hear anything that happens." He grabbed his binoculars and looked toward the highway and the main entrance to the access road with its turn-around area.

"Hank, there isn't just one black Lincoln now; there's two of them."

Hank told the sheriff that the Suburban had already reached the end of its road. It was not a four-by-four so it had not attempted any overland travel. He counted eight men with automatic rifles walking toward the berm. They had about a two mile hike ahead of them.

Harold Morgan switched to his infrared gear. He looked back at the Lincolns. If it worked, he could pick up the extra heat of the engines. As he looked very closely, he could see some movement from what had to be their personnel. Next he looked at the Suburban. They either had left it idling, or there was a driver still behind the wheel.

As he panned a little closer to the berm, he could make out a very slight movement coming his way. It was eerie, almost as if the vegetation was not quite visible where this shadow passed. The nearest thing he could relate it to was heat waves rising from the pavement, if you could get just the right angle from the sun. That had to be the eight man team from the Suburban. He then checked for any movement from his own cycle teams in between the Lincolns and the Suburban, and whatever else was out there. He did eventually pick up on the first group nearest the highway, and finally just trusted the others to be in position as well.

Hank had seen the sheriff's other men coming up behind the Black Forces. Everything seemed to be going as planned. Then the sheriff spoke excitedly, "I've got it, I'm sure of it. Hank, see that long row of barns just to the northwest?"

As Hank trained his binoculars in that direction, the sheriff continued, "There's a massive wave of heat coming from behind those barns. It has to be a jet engine of some sort, and I'm sure that chopper is jet driven. It certainly can't be from livestock, unless of course old Schmitty is raisin' a herd of dragons."

Hank chuckled a little, then quipped, "Will you consider settling for a dragonfly?"

Sheriff Morgan responded, "R-iiiiiight!"

Just then Hank interrupted him. "Hey, it looks like Schmitty and his wife are being hassled by those dudes in black! They're pushing them into their house at gunpoint. I sure hope no one gets hurt."

Steve came on line. "Easy, Hank, this is the time for trusting in the Lord. I know the Schmidts will be. Just stay alert, and stand firm. It sounds like it's just beginning."

"I second that," said Chuck. "Stand!"

Just then the two Lincolns passed the gate and started up the road to the berm. When they got to bottom of the hill, the first car kept going, but the second stayed. What made Sheriff Morgan uneasy was the fact that for a few minutes the first car was out of sight, since the roadway went all around the complex. It didn't reach the top until it had come full circle.

The sheriff had Hank move down the road about 100 feet so they would not be able to see over the rim yet. He stayed on top and watched the opposite side with his binoculars just in case anyone would try to come up that side, using the car as a decoy. He also alerted Doc to be watching the far walls of the complex, so he could sound the alarm if anyone did show up. Hank stationed himself right in the middle of the road, with his automatic at the ready, and waited.

CHAPTER 23
Barbarians at the Gate

"Okay, I can see them, Sheriff," called Hank. "I think I could use a little help now."

"On my way, Hank."

The sheriff joined Hank just as the Lincoln pulled up to within 25 feet of where they stood. One man got out of the front passenger door while three men exited the back seat. They all looked like bad news. The fellow in front was somewhat smaller and older and made it plain that he was in charge as he approached Hank and Harold accompanied by one of the other men.

"Since you're not in uniform," said the older man, "I'm guessing you might be Dr. Henry Cooper. Is that right?"

"You are correct," answered Hank. "Please state your business here. You see this is a classified area. Unauthorized visitors are not allowed."

"Oh, believe me, Doctor, we are definitely authorized," responded the elderly man.

"You haven't even introduced yourself or shown any ID yet," said Hank. "What is your name, and whom do you represent?"

"My name is not important, Doctor."

Hank and the sheriff pointed their guns right in the faces of the two men. The two men waiting by the Lincoln pulled their weapons as well. The elderly man held his hand up and motioned his men to lower their weapons. Then he spoke again. "If you insist, you can call me Ivan. I come from a unit high in the government."

"I'm sorry," said Hank, "but I don't believe you. This has been a government project. They could contact me at any time with proper protocols. You guys have been skulking around here for days. If you have any connection at all, you're not acting according to procedure. In my book that makes you a renegade group. Now what do you have to say to that?"

"Oh, aren't we wound tight!" sneered Ivan. "I assure you we are connected. I was told you were to be…wait, what is this hick sheriff's security clearance?"

"Watch it, scum ball," retorted Harold as he pushed the gun into Ivan's face.

"He has total need to know," answered Hank. "In my book, he has twice the clearance you do. I still don't know who you are, so why don't you pack up your dogs and clear out."

"Boy, first he's uptight, and now he's testy." Ivan was obviously getting to the boiling point. He continued, "As I was saying...I was told you were to be considered 'nice.' Get my drift?"

"No. Explain yourself," answered Hank.

"Come on, Doctor. You're a smart guy; spell it—N-I-C-E," said Ivan. "You do have some recollection of your benefactor organization, don't you?"

"Of course I do, but why does that have anything to do with you? I still don't know you."

"I've been sent to observe your progress, inspect your facilities, and report back to them," said Ivan.

"I still don't believe you," said Hank, "and I'm getting tired of telling you so. If you were on the level, you could have followed protocol and come in at any time. But when you sneak around town, call in all kinds of backup for who knows what, and then don't want to show proper credentials, I have only one conclusion: You are a renegade. You're sticking your nose in where it doesn't belong. And you better call off your other Lincoln, the Suburban with the eight guys, your three bikes, and that poor excuse for a chopper, and get out of here."

Ivan was instantly over the edge with anger. "You are defying the wrong person. You have no idea what you are in for, because the one who sent me will not stand for failure. That's why I will not go back and offer that to him. How do you know about my people?"

"Okay, now we're getting somewhere," said Sheriff Morgan. "We know about your scum because we are not the hicks, as you put it, that you thought we were. Now you answer this: Who is the person who sent you here?"

"He's the same one," said Ivan, "who has been signing those millions of dollars worth of checks—the money man who made this all possible."

"Made what possible?" asked Hank.

"Your whole project, including your salary."

"Then what is his name?" prodded Hank.

"You got the checks, you tell me," chided Ivan.

"Cut that out!" yelled Hank. He was about to lose it. "I'm trying to find out if *you* know anything besides how to act like a total jerk. Besides, the handwriting is so terrible, who can read it. The bank always honored it. It seemed to be A.P.L...something."

"That's his signature all right," said Ivan. "It's one of the aliases he uses for security. You see, powerful men need to be cautious at all times. That's the signature of A. Paul Lyons, one of the world's richest men, and one whom no one knows. Now can we get on with business?"

"No...I'm afraid I still don't know who you are, nor do I trust you. You go back to town, and I'll check around. If you check out, I'll find you."

"Sorry, Chump," said Ivan, "it just doesn't work that way. If you want to do it the hard way, then here goes." With that he raised his hand in the air, and dropped it hard and fast. The two men by the car shot into the air just over the heads of Hank and Harold. Ivan and his bodyguard ran to the car and got in. The second Lincoln started moving slowly up the road.

A few shots were heard from down below in the brush. Then the sound of the chopper could be heard closing in. As it got closer to the berm, Sheriff Morgan gave a flare gun to Hank and two extra flares, then he picked one up for himself. He said, "Keep an eye on those cars, but for now let's light this place up. When the chopper gets closer, you fire a flare to its left, I'll put one to its right. That should help our guys get a bead on it. It's getting a little dark already. Maybe the night vision stuff will help."

Just then the black chopper came around the edge of some trees and started laying down a strafing pattern near Hank and the sheriff. Some of the deputies had already flushed out the eight troops on their flank. Gunfire could be heard easily.

Harold hollered, "On three: one...two...three!" Two flares flew toward the chopper as planned. Hank asked, "What would happen if we got one inside the chopper?"

"Don't try it; you'd have to be too close. They would cut you down. Leave that to Johnny and the boys."

Suddenly the whole scene changed.

The two flares starting acting very strange. They began growing, and soon they were like fiery spinning pillars. Hank and Harold looked at each other astounded at what they were seeing. With mouths agape, in huge grins, they turned back to watch what would happen next.

One of the pillars of fire looked as if it reached out and grabbed the helicopter's tail, rotor and all. The other one grabbed the main rotor, and the engine stopped cold. Instead of letting it fall to the ground, the two pillars started spinning the chopper like a weather vane. They would drop it suddenly, and then shoot it up a couple thousand feet. It was like a dance of derision. All the while, the men on board were screaming in terror.

Then suddenly the pillars carried the chopper over the compound as if to show it to the people inside, and then shot it straight up and completely disappeared.

Without any warning, the three bikes came part way up the berm, chased by the two lights. Three flashes like lightning bolts came from the light pillars and hit the riders at the same time. Three empty bikes went crashing downhill. The riders were nowhere to be seen.

Then the lights moved toward the two Lincolns, which were now racing back down the access road in full retreat. When the one in the lead didn't move fast enough, the men in Ivan's car started shooting it. A shell hit the fuel tank, and the car became a fireball. One of the pillars of light then pushed Ivan's car into the fireball, and it exploded.

In unison, the two pillars moved side by side to the valley in the direction of the Suburban. On the way, they crossed the point where the eight Black Forces troops were crouched, their weapons for the moment forgotten as they were watching what was happening to the other members of their team. As the pillars passed over the Black Forces position, screams of terror and pain could be heard for a moment. Then everything was silent. The pillars continued toward the Suburban until they hovered over it and its horn began blasting steadily. Their task completed, they returned to where they first encountered the chopper and began to shrink in size. The two men watched them become, once again, two burning flares attached to their parachutes, drifting toward the ground.

"Hallelujah!" Dr. Cooper and Sheriff Morgan shouted victoriously as they held on to each other for support while their emotions overflowed. Ruth drove down the hill bringing everyone together to jubilantly celebrate. The radio was popping with everyone talking at once.

Sheriff Morgan regained his composure and realized the need for some order. He grasped his radio and let loose a shrill note from his 'authentic' police whistle. Everyone fell silent.

The sheriff spoke. "Wow, I haven't used that thing in years. That was fun! Okay, troops, it looks like we didn't have as much to do with this whole thing as we thought we would. For that, I'm quite thankful. However, I want to commend all of you for doing exactly as you were ordered. You did it all quite well. For now though, which group is closest to the Suburban?"

"Sheriff, this is Rick. Bill and I came in behind them, and Frank and Phil joined us from their bike position."

"Okay, Rick," said Sheriff Morgan. "Frank, get on your bike and get that guy off the horn. The rest of you go to Rick's position and help drag the bodies to the Suburban. Stay on this channel, and I'll get back to you. Morgan out."

The sheriff turned to Hank and asked, "How do you propose to keep your secret from my men now, Dr. Cooper? They have to be curious about what just happened, and they put their lives on the line. Wait a minute; hold that thought, Hank."

"Morgan to Johnny...Morgan to Johnny...Do you read me?"

"Yes, Sheriff, what's up?"

"Did you take a casualty report? Is everyone all right?

"Yes sir, to both, Sheriff. We were just wondering what kind of miracle we have witnessed here. It certainly isn't our everyday mode of operation."

"I'll get back to you on that. Just keep everyone at the Suburban for now. Morgan out."

"Well, Hank, the question has returned. What do we do now?"

"Hank, listen close," said Ruth. "Your better half, as you always say, has something important to say now."

Hank grinned and motioned for her to continue.

"Who do you think this needs to be kept from right now? Your benefactor obviously knows there is something here that he wants, and he is now your enemy. I hope your savings and budgetary needs are taken care of for awhile. You certainly will not get any more from this Mr. Lyons. The sheriff's men have as much need to know now as anyone. Maybe some of them need to consider the Lord and the Gospel as well. If they care as much about right and wrong as their profession implies, they should be trustworthy. So, if you can still find a good reason to keep them in the dark, you will be well beyond genius."

"Whoo-eee!" yelled Doc Payne. "Isn't marriage great? Only a wife can cut to the long and short of it like that."

"Ruth, you're right," said Hank. "We have to let them in on it. In fact, it may make control of the situation that much easier. They don't have to tell their families. Go ahead, Sheriff, bring them in. We also have a large refrigerated room where we can keep eight or nine bodies. Doc might be able to tell exactly what happened to them."

"Morgan to Johnny, come back."

"This is Johnny. Go ahead, Sheriff."

"As soon as you have those bodies and anything they had with them loaded up, bring them all to the lab complex. Use the highway and front gate approach. Just be sure you don't leave anything out there in the brush. Bring that Suburban with you, too. I'll meet you all out front. Make sure everyone comes in and, Johnny; no calls back home just yet.

"—Oh, yes, we saw trouble at the Schmidt's farm. I believe that's where the chopper was hiding. Send four men over there to check on them. Be careful, just in case they left one of their goons behind. If the Schmidts are okay, bring them here as well. All explanations will be given here, and no one, repeat, no one else is to know anything. Out."

CHAPTER 24
A Warm Glow

The seven of them on the hill looked at each other, and their emotions began to break loose. One giant wave of relief, awe, tears, and laughter let down and felt like it all rolled into one huge foamy breaker. They gathered themselves into the two cars and surfed that feeling all the way down the crater and into the hangar.

Sheriff Morgan called dispatch to confirm they had been listening and make sure that they would not leak any information. He was relieved to hear that reporters at the local paper had not heard anything so far. He told Herb, at dispatch, to call Lieutenant Johnson of the State Troopers to find two or three men to watch over Willow Springs for the night. The lieutenant was an old friend on whom he knew he could rely.

The Sheriff, Hank, and the other men grabbed a few lengths of chain and drove out of the complex to the two burned out Lincolns. The smell of gas and overly cooked meat was heavy in the air. It was all most of them could do to control their stomachs right now. It wouldn't have been so bad, but for the knowledge of seven or eight human bodies charred to near nothingness. They needed to get the road open so the others could get by. They needed help moving the cars, so they just waited till the posse arrived.

Within minutes, they saw the caravan coming up the road. The cycles were in front and the Suburban right behind. The sheriff had the Suburban come up close to the first car. He tried to tell the guys on the cycles that it would be best if they didn't look too close. Two of them didn't listen and were shortly in the brush losing their composure and everything in their stomachs.

Once the Suburban was firmly chained to the shell of the burned out Lincoln, and as much equipment as possible was thrown in the back for traction, they were able to drag it down the road and over the embankment. They repeated the process on the second Lincoln and the road was clear. All that was left was a huge spot in the road where all the asphalt was burned away, but the road was still passable.

"Okay everyone, listen up," Hank said. "Follow us on into the compound. We'll go by one particular building first in order to put those bodies in the freezer. Then we'll go to the main building where all of this started. Hold your questions till then. There will be far more for you to learn than you can imagine. Let's go."

They were almost to the bottom of the crater when Rick called from the Schmidt's farm house. He said, "We found them tied and gagged, but they're okay. By the way, Schmitty said their accent sounded oriental. He wasn't sure what their plans were if they ever returned. He called his son, so he and the grandson will come take care of livestock and secure things. It must have sounded pretty mysterious to his son, but Schmitty is sure his son would never pry into his reasons for needing help."

"Okay, Rick," said the sheriff. "You bring the Schmidts and all four deputies and come to the compound. I'll meet you and show you the way in. Morgan out."

Karl and Hilga Schmidt still maintained a successful family farm in the old traditional eclectic style. They grew a moderate amount of several different grains and raised a broad range of livestock from animals to fowl. It was the type of farm that's disappearing all too quickly from the American scene. The old homestead was started by Karl's grandparents after they immigrated from Germany. His son and grandson still helped work the whole place. It was well run and supported the two families in comfortable style. It was a self-sufficient type of operation, growing their own feed and seed to support family, livestock, and start next year's crop with some left over to sell. As Hilga was careful to say, "They were blessed beyond measure."

Karl, now 70 years "young," was the robust and rotund image of the all-American farmer, with a full head of black hair that showed no sign of graying. He still outworked almost anyone around and was strong enough to wrestle the livestock into submission. He and Hilga were constantly doing for others and sharing the love of the Lord wherever they went.

Hilga seemed to share in the same strength that Karl was known for. However, she was quite petite. "Little but wiry," she liked to say. Her long silvery hair was usually pulled back in a ponytail that kept it out of her way. She was nearly always smiling and on the edge of some joyous outburst. Her green eyes sparkled and, at times, could look right through you. However, if she was quite serious or put out over some offense, her response was consistently full of compassion. Karl and Hilga were highly prized by the community of Willow Springs.

In the compound, after all the chores and unloading was finished and everyone had collected in the hangar, they all sat around and waited for the rest of those who had been summoned to arrive. Hank had made it clear that he had no time to go through explanations more than once, so "hurry up and wait" was the order of the day, as it was in the Army. Sheriff Morgan called back to the dispatcher so he could let the deputies' wives know that their husbands would be home late. Hank took a couple of the deputies to get the new exterior surveillance tapes. Then the sheriff went to meet Rick and the rest and bring them in.

Once everyone was present, Hank first made clear the need for confidentiality. Introductions were made all around; and then in quick and simple terms, Hank explained what the IDEA was all about. Then he told how he had accidentally taken the ride that tore up the hangar. Next he played the first surveillance tapes and the first three or four trips on the log—the same series he had used to orient Dr. Carver.

Once he had finished with that and answered their questions, he filled the newcomers in on the fact that the log was already moving into the future and the problem that lay ahead. Some of the deputies were not believers and objected at first to the obvious scriptural content of what he shared. Then Steve asked them a question that got them all thinking: "Can you explain what you saw happen out there this evening?"

They really weren't sure what they had seen. It seemed like a nightmare to them, and all this new information wasn't helping much. That's when Hank asked them to relate, as best they could, what they *thought* they saw. He then pointed out that they all agreed on what they observed. He put on the surveillance tapes that had just been taken from the cameras.

All of the cameras showed the same thing from different angles. They showed the two pillars of spinning fire carrying the black chopper over the compound with their dance of sorts, and then shoot straight up, with the chopper disappearing in an instant. This was all that was visible from inside the crater, but exactly what everyone, except the Schmidts, had seen. That was established as fact. Now it was time to consider what all the recent events really meant.

Hank began to tell them how the Illuminate or NICE had funded his work, and that he had not realized the evil nature of the group until two days ago. That nature had been confirmed today with Ivan's sinister introduction. At this point, Hank had a nagging question. "Who is this A. Paul Lyons?"

"What's that name again?" asked Dr. Carver.

"Ivan said it was A. Paul Lyons," answered Hank.

"I've got an idea about the answer to your question," said Chuck, "but only time or more of the log can tell us if I'm accurate."

"Go ahead," urged Hank, "tell all of us what you're thinking."

"We've already covered certain things common to today's secret societies, although many of you weren't in on this. Most of these societies that also secretly work together have infiltrated the UN and most national administrations. The Black Forces that we had dealings with today are part of this organization. This critical fact was confirmed by Ivan and his thugs.

"Many believe the presence of these societies, coupled with present and future advances in technology, will make world domination possible. The book of Revelation prophesies say this will come to pass with a man called the Antichrist in control. He is called Antichrist because even though he is Satan's evil pawn, he will claim to be the Messiah. He will claim to be God. He and all who follow him will eventually be identified by the number 666. We've been referring to him by that number because we don't know his name yet.

"Satan does everything as a statement of defiance and mockery. Most secret societies play these same games. Initiates think it is only 'coded fun' and eagerly get involved. Only later do they learn exactly what they have joined. And, in many cases, possibly most cases, Satan has long since gained control at the upper levels of their hierarchy. Ivan, today, gave us this name—A. Paul Lyons—as the man who is the head of NICE, which stands for 'National Illuminate Co-ordination Extension.' This fellow A. Paul Lyons has made it to the inner circle.

"His name, as given to us, sounds like this type of mocking play on words. A. is just an initial, Paul as spelled in Greek or English is a homonym that is really spelled pol, with a soft o, and the last name is just missing the grammar mark of an apostrophe between N and S. The true spelling then is A pol lyon's, or when it is shoved together 'Apollyon's' becomes a statement of possession stating 'He belongs to Apollyon.' Apollyon is the Greek name for Satan or Lucifer.

"The Antichrist—'old 666' as we have been calling him—will, according to Daniel's vision, revive the worldwide Roman Empire for one last time. It is possible we have learned one of his names. Ivan made it clear that this is the alias he uses for the Illuminate. Other names may be due to surface."

"So then," queried Hank, "you think we're headed for the Big Cosmic Showdown?"

"Certainly," answered Chuck. "We've always been headed that way. It's possible it is upon us now, and we may have been involved in one of the early skirmishes."

Steve spoke up and said, "And now that brings us to what we witnessed today. For sure there was a small fire fight between the sheriff's deputies and those guys from the Suburban. No one really got hit, isn't that right?"

Everyone nodded assent.

"Well then, is there anyone who saw the battle this evening and has seen the tapes, who does not realize what happened here?"

Mike raised his hand as if in school.

"Yes, Mike, go ahead," said Steve.

"I just think we are way past guessing games. Any idiot knows that just like God fought the battles many times for Israel, His angels took over the whole thing today. All we had to do was stand and watch."

With that, most of the group, led by Hilga Schmidt, stood and cheered, clapped their hands, and boisterously lifted remarks of thanksgiving to the Lord. Bill and Frank stood toward the back of the group with a few of the other deputies, mouths agape and an uncomfortable expression on their faces. They never had seen anything quite like it. They had gone to a church service only a couple of times in their lives. This was something they didn't understand.

Yet, regardless of the strangeness they felt, there was a desire to know more. They knew what they had seen and heard, but it was a little hard to process it. Ruth noticed their discomfort and went over to talk to them. After they opened up and expressed their dismay, she told them that the ones who were rejoicing knew without doubt that they had been protected from evil men because of their trust in Jesus. She told them that if they would like to know Christ in this intimate way, all they needed to do was say so. Then she went back next to Mike as things were beginning to calm down.

Hank thought it best if everyone left for the night at a similar stopping point. The Schmidts, in particular, had known nothing of these recent events. The deputies were just beginning to understand what all the ruckus of the past few days was about. The only one still out of the loop was the only casualty, Bo. He would be in the hospital another day or so. And since they did not know when any other Black Forces might return, it was time to turn the log on again.

To get them all up to speed first, Hank explained what happened on the last journey—the UN row and the Israeli oil field problem. Then he hit the play button.

CHAPTER 25
Brazen Babylon's Boner

The light tunnel was short again. When the IDEA released pictures this time, it was at a very high altitude over the Middle East. As it panned toward earth in a full circle, it was midway between the Mediterranean Sea and the tip of the Persian Gulf. Hank and Chuck both thought it was around the eastern border of Syria, close to both Jordan and Lebanon. That would make it north of the Golan Heights.

It was clear right away to them that there was military movement in Iraq. Yet there did not seem to be any response from all the opposing forces in the area. There were no NATO planes flying out of Turkey, and no American planes taking off from the Saudi Arabian bases. The embargoes were still in place, as far as anyone viewing could know, but then this was several years into the future, so who could know anything for sure. There were large carrier support fleets in the Persian Gulf and Arabian Sea. There was another in the Mediterranean, west of Syria. Nothing, though, showed any response from any of the fleets.

Soon Iraq fired six missiles in rapid succession. The first three went in different directions and landed right next to three different aircraft carriers—one in the Mediterranean and the others in the Persian Gulf and Arabian Sea. They each released a canister that contained yellow and green smoke just before impact. The sheriff surmised that what they released were mustard and chlorine gases. While the crews in these fleets were choking or running for cover and gas gear, the IDEA showed that the next two canisters landed on air bases used by NATO forces. The sixth missile headed for Jerusalem and scattered several cannisters across the city. The winds from the west and south started blowing the poisonous cloud across the southern part of Jordan and across the desert of Saudi Arabia.

Still there seemed to be no real response from any country. The log seemed to be stuck except for an occasional 360° pan of the whole viewing area. Most places hit by the gas attacks were in chaos. This time the IDEA didn't sound an alarm or show a blip of the light tunnel or anything. It just sat there panning again every few minutes. This gave the 30 people in the hangar a chance to discuss what they were seeing. They tried to guess where and when the next shoe would fall. The gas clouds were causing trouble all the way eastward. Cities in the Persian Gulf and in Saudi Arabia eastward were due for a second wave of gas, though somewhat dissipated.

Hank went to his controls again to fast forward until they saw a difference. He said, "I don't know what the hold up is, but I'm sure the IDEA is waiting for an important change of events. I know I was there, but I have no concept of how much time has gone by."

"Hold it," yelled Sheriff Morgan. Hank stopped the log. "Now," said the sheriff, "reverse just a few seconds." Hank complied. "Can this set-up stop on a freeze frame?"

"It sure can," answered Hank. "Just say when."

The replay started for less than a minute. "Stop," yelled Harold. Then he pointed down in the lower right hand corner. "Is it my imagination or is that a formation of aircraft? They're coming over the beach from out at sea and flying low."

"Look over here," said Hank. "It's another group just taking off, but they're going out to sea."

"They're all part of the same group, just in two waves," said Doc Payne. "I'll bet that's the air base outside of Tel Aviv. The Israelis are out for revenge. Instant retaliation has always been their policy."

"You're exactly right," said Hank. "They're taking off into the winds and in the opposite direction they intend to go. Look at the clock. This is six hours after the initial attack on Jerusalem. Iraq's big mistake was not hitting Tel Aviv."

Now that they knew what to watch, they saw the first group come inland just a few miles, flying at treetop level, turn north across Lebanon and Syria and turn east, straight for Baghdad. The second group continued deep inland across Jordan and part of Saudi Arabia, then they turned north, heading straight for southern Iraq.

In both groups, as the formation of six bombers approached Iraq's border, the first three stayed low and went straight in. While they were striking the targeted radar and communication centers, the other three climbed to the stratosphere in a spiral that kept them outside Iraq.

After several large explosions and columns of smoke, the first three, still flying low, came out and headed for home. As they were going out, the last three were flying in at top speed and very high. All six of these last planes went to specific targets. The prime target was, of course, Baghdad. Hank speculated that the others were probably suspected nuclear, chemical, or biological weapons depots. Each of the planes crossed their target and turned sharply in a climbing, looping maneuver. Taking various routes in all directions, they left Iraq behind.

Suddenly in nearly simultaneous order, like popcorn popping, six blinding flashes of monstrous proportions were seen. Immediately, six huge mushroom clouds soared to the top of the atmosphere. After a considerable time as the stems and bases of the mushrooms lifted away from the earth, another horror became apparent. Besides the normal smoke of burning ruins and debris outside the huge circles of nothingness left behind, very near ground zero were different colored clouds coming from the depths beneath the craters. They weren't just hanging in the air. They were spewing out of the ground as if more were being generated every second. Monstrous geysers of gasses or biological agents were being thrown up into the atmosphere. For a considerable time, everything within the circles looked as hot as magma. The rising heat pulled in air from surrounding areas fueling even more fires and carried much of the venting gasses to the upper atmosphere. Everything below these clouds turned as dark as night as the sunlight was blotted out. By watching this horrid shadow move eastward on the prevailing winds, everyone knew that it was the shadow of death. Radioactive fallout, poisonous gasses, and the most terrible diseases were now airborne. The cloud continued to spread, and in its path lay Iran, Afghanistan, Pakistan, India, Indonesia, and all parts east. The air pollution wasn't as bad as Mount Penetubo's eruption, but it was thousands of times more deadly. Babylon had definitely fallen.

Suddenly the light tunnel started again. Hank hit the pause button and said, "Chuck?" He was looking at Dr. Carver. There was no doubt that it was time for him to tie this together.

Chuck Carver responded right away. "Babylon is fallen! This is the theme that repeats itself in Revelation 14-18. These five chapters seem to tell a similar story from different aspects or viewpoints. Chapters 16-18 cover the seven last plagues. What causes some debate among scholars is the fact that the real ancient city of Babylon no longer exists. Yet Saddam Hussein, who considers himself the reincarnation of Nebuchadnezzar, has been trying to rebuild it. This only confirms that the 'evil spirit' of Babylon is still a reality.

"Another aspect is that chapter 18 makes it clear that when Babylon has finally fallen, nothing but the vilest of animals will ever live there again. Since that hasn't happened yet in our own time, something like we just watched will need to occur close to the end of things.

"One troubling aspect is that chapter 17 speaks of a mystery Babylon, mother of harlots and abominations of the earth. Some scholars believe this implies a false church, for various reasons. Another aspect of this mystery Babylon is that it is the center of world commerce. Some, but not all, scholars think this is a reference to the United States. That's a troubling prospect indeed. Yet when we see the moral decay, considerable greed, the dependence on drugs, then we must wonder if there really are two Babylons. It would not be uncommon for such dual pictures or meanings to be found in scriptural prophesy. Also common would be God using one evil country to bring judgment to another, in order to fulfill His plan and will.

"In another place or two, similar prophetic statements and judgments are attributed to the 'daughter of Babylon.' Any of the great nations we have mentioned, as well as the U.S., could be the subject of those passages."

Ruth started objecting. "I don't like the sound of that at all. It sounds like the righteous that do exist in this country, and have spread the Gospel around the world, really count for nothing!"

Steve answered, "That's not what Chuck was alluding to, Ruth."

"That's okay, Steve," said Chuck. "Much of what is being mentioned has to do with timing, number one; and, number two, general ruling principles as regards a total nation. In other words, Billy Graham has been cited as saying something to this effect in the late sixties: 'If God does not judge America severely, He will owe an apology to Sodom and Gomorrah.' In short, our nation has changed from a Christian nation, God-fearing and morally righteous, to a pagan nation hardly knowing who God is. Even many of the churches deny or ignore God and His will. Many more who call themselves ministers teach falsities concerning God—they teach a different Gospel. The rest of God's people have lost the effectiveness of their witness because they have had a difficult time staying clear of apostasy. All they have managed to do is stand firm. A few small communities have missed much of this degradation, but the country as a whole is in serious trouble. They have believed the lie. Indeed, they increasingly care nothing about truth as long as their finances are reasonably good. Even so, whenever God caused judgment to fall on Israel, He always protected and saved His remnant. We can trust Him for that now.

"Now timing may be the major factor," continued Chuck. "If we have come to the end of God's timing, and His will says 'Close the books,' then everything will be separated from His own people. Then the end will come. In the meantime, we may witness some things we would rather not see. In any case, the Lord and His angels will provide for us."

"Pardon me for interrupting," said Rick, "but I'm curious about something. When Iraq was obviously up to no good, can you figure out why all these super powers, especially the U.S., did nothing?"

"I can answer that, I think," said Hank. "The computer crashes we saw earlier may have affected our surveillance and communication satellites. Of course, the IDEA was able to observe and record, but the satellites possibly could not. Even if they could, they may not have been able to communicate it. I imagine that any of the damage in the satellites would take quite a long time to repair, with a lot of shuttle trips needed. And I think that the super powers wouldn't want to admit to having a lot of trouble fixing everything."

"And that," said Chuck, "could lay the perfect scenario for Babylon to be destroyed, with finality, by Israel. But that puzzles me, because Jeremiah says that Babylon would be totally destroyed by a nation from the north. That may be our opening to expect another Babylon to be identified by such a destruction."

"Well, now what?" asked Mike.

"That's probably found on the log, son." With that, Hank started the log again.

When the IDEA settled this time, it was just outside a heavily fenced, high security military compound. There was a very large bunker-styled building nearby. It was very strange because it had a large covered entrance and door reminiscent of a fine hotel or palace, but the rest of the building looked like a fortress.

As Hank watched from the rim of the IDEA, a regiment of infantry came to the front of the bunker. By their uniforms and flag, it was obvious he was in Iran. This bunker was very likely a command center. If it was built like most command centers, it very likely was many stories deep, and who could tell how large. Shortly a whole parade of VIPs arrived in one limo after another. The camera zoomed in on the flags at the front of each car.

"Hey, most of those are OPEC nations. I had that on my geography test last month," said Mike. "And there's also the former Soviet countries, too."

Saudi Arabia, Yemen, Oman, Kuwait, Jordan, Syria, Pakistan, Afghanistan, Libya, Algeria, also Russia, Ukraine, Georgia, Kazakhstan, and Uzbekistan were all represented here.

All of these delegates entered the lavish doors and were not seen for many hours according to the log clock. The IDEA seemingly knew what to expect, so it didn't bother to record "dead" time. Just before the delegates came back out, the area was filled with news crews and their cameras. A large crowd arrived and started chanting something that sounded vaguely familiar. Chuck understood the language of the area, so he interpreted for the rest. "They're saying, 'Death to America, and its pet pig Israel. They can never steal our oil again.'"

138

When the delegates stepped out of the doors and into their respective limos, the crowd grew louder. Then they set fire to the flags of the U.S. and Israel. This was followed by gunfire that lasted for five or 10 minutes. By that time, the limousines had sped off and the show was over.

"The controversy over the Israeli tap into the Middle East oil field looks like it's continuing," Hank speculated. "Probably as the pressure was released below sea level, the wells of the other countries began drying up at the higher altitudes. They probably know that it will just get worse and cost them millions or even billions of dollars to sink deeper casings to reach the lowering pool. I'm sure they've got some plan to counter this."

The alarm sounded, and Hank was seen and then not seen again. The familiar light tunnel returned and then suddenly stopped.

CHAPTER 26
The Pale Horse Gallops

The IDEA was in a low orbit position over the western hemisphere, the same one used by a couple of the communication satellite systems. As it moved from one satellite to another, it was apparent that most were non-functioning or shut down.

The IDEA moved to a spot over the Caribbean, fairly near the coast of Colombia, and again it just sat there.

Doc Payne spoke up and asked, "Do you suppose we just got our answer as to why there was no retaliatory response in the Mideast? Could the IDEA be showing us that there was no response because broken communications left many countries with no knowledge of those occurrences? And is this still a carry-over from the old computer crashing problem we saw when we first entered the future?"

"I'll bet you're right," answered Hank. "Although I hope you're not. The U.S. could be a sitting duck if that's the case."

Just then IDEA zoomed in on several dark shadows in the aqua waters of the Caribbean. One was almost directly below and slightly out to sea, nestled not more than 100 miles northeast of the Panama Canal. Another was just 40 miles south of Jamaica. The third was just barely visible in the gulf of California, between Mexico proper and the Baja. At first glance, one would think they were large whales, but at the Baja a large pod of whales was swimming nearby, many times smaller than the three shadows.

It finally became apparent that these were large submarines when they began surfacing. Almost as if it were choreographed, each sub, in sequence, opened two hatches near one end.

Hank yelled, "Hey, they're preparing to fire!"

Right on cue, as if Hank had ordered it, each sub fired one rocket. It seemed to be almost too steep a trajectory, though, if it was a bombing attack. Then a few minutes later, each sub took their turn and fired another rocket. They fired it at a much steeper angle, and everyone wondered why.

Then with almost the same popcorn effect as had been seen over Iraq, six huge nuclear blasts took place. The light was blinding, yet there were no huge mushroom clouds of debris.

"These blasts are taking place just at the upper edges of the atmosphere. Their purpose is not surface destruction, but an electromagnetic shockwave that will overload and destroy anything electronic in its path—a homemade solar flare of sorts," said Hank. "I think the reason for two launches, at different angles, is to let the three rockets in the first launch travel several hundred miles farther, yet detonate at nearly the same time and altitude as the ones in the second." He stopped the tapes so he could explain better what just had happened.

"From the Jamaican launch, two east coast areas seems to be affected. The one that hit Washington, DC, and Annapolis, Maryland, and its naval yards reached almost all the way up to New York City. The southern one covered southern Florida including Cape Kennedy, as well as several Naval, Air Force, and Coast Guard facilities.

"The Colombian area launches put a big footprint over Houston, Galveston, Corpus Christi, Dallas, and other military facilities in the area. And to the north, air bases having to do with SAC, whether current or reported closed, and army bases in the plains seem to be affected.

"The Baja launch covered most of the coastal area near Seattle, Washington, and points south in parts of Oregon. The southern target was what I recognize as Vandenberg Air Force base, and it looks like the devastation reached nearly to San Francisco to the north and the L.A. harbor to the south. This means that all power, communications, batteries to run emergency units, all aircraft, and many autos can no longer function. Anything unsheltered from this electromagnetic radiation was instantly burned up. In quite a few instances, this started fires that nobody could respond to because of the lack of electric power."

There seemed to be a pause as far as the IDEA was concerned. During that pause, Hank spoke somberly this time. "Those electro-pulse detonations have paralyzed the machinery that protects the nation. We're not just sitting ducks. We're more like blind fish in a bowl. We can be seen, but we can't see out. This may be preparation for a real attack."

No sooner had Hank finished than different problems arose. From several places within the pulse bomb footprints came massive columns of greenish gray smoke. The cameras on the IDEA zoomed in for close-ups. They were nuclear power plants that were in melt-down. With the loss of electricity, there was no way to stop them—no way to pump cooling water and no way to pull the rods. It was already too hot for manual effort. With the prevailing wind coming from the west, the dosage of radiation over the next week for anyone to the east grew exponentially. It was doubtful that anyone in the Federal Government could survive long enough to function at all, unless they were forewarned and had gotten out of the country. Even Air Force One couldn't fly if caught in any of the rockets' pulse patterns.

There were many smaller fires around the country from coast to coast that could have been started by falling aircraft or other transportation mishaps, caught by the pulse beam. There was no real way to tell about those smaller cases. Who could know how many small planes fell into the sea on either coast?

While the group in the hangar contemplated all they were seeing, Sheriff Morgan jumped up and pointed to the top of the monitor. "Is that what I think it looks like?" he asked excitedly.

"Oh, no," cried Doc, "the people don't even see them!" As the observers watched, they saw over the north pole about five missiles just beginning to glow as they entered the atmosphere. To the west, number one blew apart into three separate warheads. One dropped early on the southern coast of Alaska; another one hit close to the Space Needle in Seattle, Washington, and the third dropped in Salt Lake City. Missile number two also divided into three more—going to Chicago, Kansas City, and Denver. Missile number three split in only two parts—Detroit and St. Louis. Missile number four split three ways to Toronto, Canada, Akron, Ohio, and Pittsburgh. Missile number five hit Boston, New York City, Newark, and Philadelphia.

"No, no," hollered Hank. "Look at those subs!"

From the sub near Jamaica came separate missiles to Washington, DC, Atlanta, Georgia, and Niceville, Florida, near the Eglin Air Force Base. From near Colombia came missiles that streamed to New Orleans, Houston, and Dallas. From the Baja were missiles flying to San Diego, Phoenix, and Albuquerque.

No more missiles were seen, yet large mushroom clouds appeared in San Francisco, Fort Bragg, Los Angeles, and Long Beach—all in California.

By the time all this had occurred, the group of 30 people were in shock. The knowledge that this was supposed to be the future of their country had many of them in tears. On the monitor screen, the clouds were spreading like a heavy shroud of doom over the entire continent. They knew this would blow its way around the globe with its terrible blanket of death. Did they even want to see what else lay ahead?

Suddenly the IDEA moved to the south Pacific. The cameras zoomed in on a huge asteroid moving rapidly toward earth. There was no advance warning possible since most communication centers tied to space efforts were having the same computer problems as everyone else. Soon flames were trailing it from friction when it entered the atmosphere. It suddenly exploded and threw monstrous chunks many miles in all directions, although there was still a mountain-size chunk left when it smashed into the ocean.

The impact was immeasurable. Besides the waves created, the impact with the solid sea bed created a shattering earthquake that certainly would help other quakes move the tectonic plates. Almost instantly, Mount Penetubo in the Philippines exploded once again, several times more violently than a few years before. Within the hour, Mounts Kilehuea and Mauna Loa also blew apart violently, taking most of their island with them. Large portions of Sidney and Melbourne, Australia, were almost instantly flattened. Many of the islands in the entire area crumbled at their base and sank into the sea. The term "tidal wave" cannot begin to describe the monster wave sent out from ground zero. It was thousands of feet high—possibly even a mile; it was hard to tell from the monitor. At its southern side, Antarctica stood in the way and eventually sent a large backwash into the void. The rest began washing across the frozen land headed for the Atlantic side. Moving in all other directions, with equal force, the islands were destroyed, and the edges of all continents were in for flooding horrors that were unbelievable. Suddenly the IDEA turned off this transmission.

A few minutes later, there was a very small blip of the light tunnel, and the IDEA had relocated. It was still in a high orbital position. Now, however, it was above the Mediterranean Sea, probably 100 miles west of Lebanon and Israel. It was in perfect position to view all of the area we call the fertile crescent. To the north could be seen Turkey, to the south was Egypt. To the east could be seen everything from Afghanistan and Iran to Saudi Arabia and its small neighbors. To the southeast they could see Israel and the desert.

Coming over the mountains of Afghanistan and north of Turkey were large Russian troop planes. They dropped thousands of paratroopers and their equipment in Afghanistan, Iran, and Saudi Arabia. The ones coming over the Crimean and Turkey went all the way to Libya and Sudan and also dropped a similar force. While these advance troops set up their headquarters, and readied for their push, huge columns of thousands of tanks, that were already waiting on the borders, rumbled across the desert. They all stopped when they had to take time to construct a temporary bridge across the Tigris and Euphrates rivers.

While that was going on, Egypt massed its forces on three borders— Israel, Sudan, and Libya. It was obvious they had been left out of these plans, and now they were surrounded. "I bet they still don't trust Israel, treaty or no treaty," Steve said.

The first battle was in Libya and Sudan. Hank began a running commentary on all of the battles. "Looks like the Russian troops are surprising them." In a few minutes, Hank commented on the swiftly moving log: "I guess they go by the motto, 'If you can't beat 'em, join 'em.' Now they're joining the Russians to overrun Egypt joined by Moslem radicals who are fighting Egypt from within and Palestinians from the East. They probably feel like they're punishing Egypt for having a peace treaty with Israel."

Egypt fell rapidly with terrible devastation wreaked on their country. The radical forces were so completely ravenous they killed everyone in sight. Every building of every village was burned to rubble. Animals were killed and most left to rot in the sun. Sanitation techniques were notoriously bad to begin with, but now they just helped to spread disease. Cairo all but disappeared. Ships in the locks of the Suez Canal were stopped and used for bridges to the Sinai. Biological toxins were sprayed in the soil and farmable land covered with salt dropped out of airplanes. All of Egypt that wasn't just sand looked thoroughly poisoned.

When this was over, the joint forces began moving on Israel. As Israeli planes began to defend to the south, Russia and her northern allies began attacking from the northeast. Just as they had moved through Syria and Jordan with permission, they began shelling Jerusalem.

When this began, Palestinians in Israel began rioting. The forces coming from the south began shelling Tel Aviv, but all of Israel's planes were now airborne and ready to counterattack.

They bombed the main artillery and field rocket units, both north and south, concentrating mostly on mobile radar centers. They were only able to make one pass when suddenly the weather made flying impossible, and they were forced to return to base. Rockets from the south tried to hit the airfield, but each one was destroyed by lightening.

It seemed the entire Middle East was under a single massive storm. Hurricanes usually form over water and dissipate when land interferes with their source of moisture, but today exactly the opposite was occurring.

One other anomaly was noticed right away by the group watching the monitor.

Mike jumped and pointed to several places on the screen. "Look, there they are again," he said.

"The angels are back," said a chorus almost in unison.

Around the edges of this massive storm, columns of light or fire were spinning. It was almost like they were holding up the storm. Since only one side of the storm was visible underneath, it was not possible to tell how many there really were. No matter. They were a frightening sight all by themselves. Before much time at all had passed, lightening began striking like automatic rifle fire. There had to be millions of strikes all told, in just a few minutes time. Occasionally one could see explosions as ammo stockpiles, trucks, etc., would blow up. At times the lightening was so intense at to make one believe the storm was really a fire.

144

As quickly as it had begun, it was suddenly over and quiet. The immense storm just lifted and disappeared. The IDEA zoomed in on many specific areas where troops had been located. Dead bodies were everywhere, and most of them wore Russian uniforms. In many cases, they were charred beyond recognition. One strange thing was noticeable—most of the weapons from guns to tanks were not terribly damaged. They were wrecked but not burned up as one might expect. It was as if each soldier had encountered his own private lightening bolt. Also many civilians in Syria, Jordan, and Palestinian areas in Israel were also dead. Buildings, though, were reasonably untouched. A few were damaged early on in the artillery and rocket attack. Nothing, though, seemed like it had been set afire by lightening. There also had been massive 100-pound hailstones, crushing anything and everyone they hit. They were still lying on the ground melting, helping to wash the land.

It was obviously time to check in with Chuck, so Hank hit the pause button.

"Why is it you think the U.S. is to be hit?" asked Hank.

"Like I said before, some scholars have gone so far as to call the U.S. the new Babylon. That is because the name Babylon is attached to several different things. One is the physical place where the ancient kingdoms were found. Another refers to the false religions, cults, and occultic activity for which Babylon and the Chaldeans in general were known. For instance, the story of man's salvation drawn in the stars in the original zodiac that is referred to in the book of Job, was degraded into what is now called astrology. This was done by the Chaldeans, and God makes it clear that He hates this. It took His truth and changed it to a lie. This is what Satan constantly gets men to do. The third way Babylon is used is to label the world system of economics that leads men to love riches and debauchery, rather than God.

"Some scholars look for a second Babylon because several prophetic statements use the phrase, 'Babylon is fallen, is fallen.' This could refer to more than one, but also could mean it was a very great fall. Some also think it strange that a nation like the U.S. is not even mentioned specifically in Revelations. That, though, can be answered several different ways—the major one being that the U.S. is not a single people, it is a mixture of people from the whole world. It also never sought worldwide domination. But the fact it is such a mixture of peoples could also be why we saw such drastic judgment meted out. It is like a warning of worldwide woes to come.

"In a more political sense, though, it may not mean anything more than this: Russia knew it could not pull this off unless it paralyzed the U.S.

first. As it turned out, God didn't need the help of the U.S., and Russia still couldn't pull it off.

"Speaking prophetically, though, everything we have observed was pictured in Ezekiel 39:1-22. The first few verses refer to Gog, and in the later verses Magog. These are identifiable as Russia and her eastern Europe allies. In these verses God tells His enemies, Gog and Magog, that He will draw them to Himself in Israel so He can utterly destroy them on the mountains of Israel or Judah. One version translates it, 'I have a hook in your jaw, and you will come to do battle.' These are also stated as peoples from the far or 'extreme north.' The capital most directly north, and extremely so, from Jerusalem is Moscow. One passage elsewhere refers to the prince of Rosh as being Gog. However, a few discount this as only being the same word that means prince. I just don't think Ezekiel, in context, meant to say 'Prince of Prince.'

"This prophesy also talks of the utter destruction, by burning, of Gog, and of 'those who dwell carelessly in the Isles.' Another translation uses the words 'surrounded by their waters.' This denotes a false sense of security. This could easily refer to the U.S. and Canada, for that matter. It certainly couldn't mean ancient Babylon, in my view, even though the context implies a mention of Babylon's fall as well.

"Verse nine then states that the weapons left behind by Gog and his allies will provide Israel fuel for seven years. We know now that many of the weapons we build out of steel are, in Russia, built out of 'lignite,' an extremely fire hardened wood that grows in the forests of Russia and Siberia. Under extreme heat, it will burn even hotter than coke made from coal. Also, noticing the seven years statement, could it be that this will mark the beginnings of the seven years of Jacob's trouble? I don't know, it just seems possible.

"Again, verses 11-16 say it will take seven months just to bury the dead, and cleanse the land. This may refer to an earlier verse that says that only a 'sixth' of Gog would remain. The body count in Israel and in Russia will be overwhelming. Yet, the 'cleansing' may be the issue, to be ready for a holy day, possibly Passover.

"The key or trigger that made all of this possible, though, could very well be the computer problem. That made the sneak attack possible."

When Hank turned the log back on, they saw confirmation of what Chuck had just said. They found that the sequence of events was not yet over. There was more that pertained to this incident.

The IDEA had repositioned itself high above the north Atlantic and the North Sea. Just to the south of its location was a string of submarines. They were lined up like a pearl necklace, running just 50 or 60 feet from the surface. All hatches to missile bays opened together. As if carefully synchronized, all the ships started firing at once. The subs that were on the southern part of the string fired on targets along the western parts of Russia, Ukraine, Belarus, and the Crimean and Black Sea ports. Those strung across the north, toward Greenland and Iceland, were sending missiles over the north pole and arctic regions to various bases, cities, spaceports, power centers, and a huge central storage and pumping center for the Russian oil and gas pipeline. The first stage missiles that were fired numbered in the dozens. The IDEA was high enough to view them as they split into three, four, six, or more separate warheads. If every one arrived at their targets functional, the devastation was going to be immense. In a matter of minutes, it seemed like one whole side of the globe lay under one horrible cloud of radiation.

The IDEA moved a bit south and turned its viewers toward North America. In several cities along the eastern part of the U.S., there were more mushroom clouds, even though no missiles were detected. There were no more naval fleets or submarine packs to be seen. Hank and the rest surmised that these few bombs may have been carried in by terrorists. They remembered that 100 or more suitcase bombs had been lost track of in Russia, or so they claimed. Also missing were larger ones called barrel bombs. All of these were easily transported by individuals. Hank hit the stop button again, as Dr. Carver spoke up.

"I believe the rest of the verses in Ezekiel 39 have just been fulfilled. We may not know for sure which scenario is the real reason that the U.S. is to be devastated so terribly. But, whichever reason is the right one, it still fits the total picture. I feel like the most likely reason is that because the U.S., which started out purposefully built on God's Word, has now slipped so far away from God and His will for men. America was a shelter for righteousness and covered the world with God's Word. But, now we are guilty of the slaughter of the innocent, for our convenience. I'm speaking of abortion. God has said in many ways that people who spill innocent blood are to be cursed. Even in many churches we seem to ignore this, and then also go against God when we protect killers from the consequence of their actions. We turn truth into a lie, and care not what truth is. Our society even idolizes those who mock and resist righteousness. We even ask such people to be our leaders, as long as our greed is satisfied.

"It's just so hard to watch it happen. Maybe it's not too late to reach a few more people and help them be ready for what lies ahead. How about you three or four fellows who seemed to be such skeptics? Don't you think it's time to reconsider? Have you not seen the power of the Lord through everything that's happened here?

"That horrendous destruction you've witnessed is the wrath of a holy God, and is reserved for His enemies. However, He is a God of love that doesn't want this to happen to anyone. His love went so far that He gave his own life to pay for the justice that His Holiness must demand. He paid the price for you. Won't you just receive it, and love Him in return? For then there is no need to fear, but you will have the ability to live and love God, as well as be loved by Him."

"That's right," said Mike. "I learned two verses of scripture that say just that. 'The fear of the Lord is the beginning of wisdom,' and 'Perfect love casts out fear.'"

And for a moment, all was quiet.

Frank and Bill spoke up and referred to the moment when Ruth explained why the others were so happily praising the Lord.

"We couldn't understand what she was talking about at the time, but we've seen enough now to make it clear," Frank said, and Bill nodded in agreement. Both of them prayed with Dr. Carver, a prayer of repentance for what they now saw as their sin. There was a considerable time of rejoicing and praise.

Dr. Cooper said that it seemed like no matter what else happened to the IDEA, this made it truly worth it. Chuck then said, "This same kind of joy, the scriptures say, is going on in heaven, over each sinner who turns to the Lord. In the book of Zepheniah it says: 'I will rejoice over my people with joy and with singing.'"

After a small break, it was time to start again.

CHAPTER 27
Take a Deep Breath

As the log started again, the IDEA set down near an old salvage yard, somewhere in the U.S. The location was obvious to them because of the large number of American brand autos and equipment lying around. Dressed in jeans and winter jackets with football teams logos emblazoned on the back, people were milling around. It looked as if they were seeking shelter inside the old wrecks.

Even though the time of day on the monitor read 12:00 P.M., the sky was dark as if it were twilight. The monitor also said it was late August, yet there was snow, or what seemed to be snow, everywhere. This was what scientists had warned about repeatedly—a nuclear winter. The fallout particles that still remained aloft in the upper atmosphere were holding out the sunlight. Light and warmth was actually being reflected back into space. The ground was growing colder day by day.

There was a short blip of the light tunnel and the IDEA settled again, somewhere in Russia. An old bronze statuary that was typical of the U.S.S.R. was lying in disarray. People here were in at least as bad condition as those in the U.S. Considering their basic welfare before the holocaust, the Russian and Asian peoples were probably closer to starvation than the Americans. Yet, Americans had become so accustomed to ease that their skills of survival were not quite as developed.

The last winters had been hard due to power losses. Now winter was starting in August, and everywhere there was desolation and despair. There was no real hope for great changes soon. Many were without communication with the rest of the world. The more violent population often just took what they wanted from the others. The strong were overcoming the weak.

"Could we stop again, please?" asked Chuck.

Hank shut down the log and said, "Of course, Chuck."

"I must apologize to all of you," said Chuck. He saw the puzzled expressions on their faces, so he continued quickly. "Oh no, not that I've done anything, but you supposedly were depending on me to tie anything we saw to prophecy, if it did indeed fit."

When everyone nodded, he continued, "Watching all this warfare, especially in Israel, was so overwhelming I forgot about other things, like that asteroid. It hurt so much to see America burn and the forces of evil try to destroy Israel, all I could think of was the passage in Ezekiel 39. But, in Revelation 8 it was prophesied that the asteroid in the sea would destroy one third of the ships, and one third of all life in the sea. Or, that a third part of the sea would turn to blood.

"This chapter also describes a star falling on a third of the waters, and it would make those waters and rivers bitter and poisonous, killing many who drank the water. That star would be called Wormwood. I'm sure you remember the melt-down problems of Chernobyl. What you may not know is that the English translation of that name is 'Wormwood.' We know that radiation-poisoned water is bitter, and if people drink much of it they will die. I believe John saw nuclear war and only knew to describe it as a star falling from heaven. Warheads look like meteorites or shooting stars. A single star isn't likely to land on a third of the waters and rivers, but a nuclear holocaust is, at least when you include the fallout.

"So, the asteroid in the south Pacific and the nuclear exchange implies Revelation 8. And the invasion of Israel and the nuclear disaster in North America sounds like Ezekiel 39. So, we see why some people get so confused with prophesy. There is overlap, and different prophets were shown sometimes the same things, but from a different point of view. I'm sure we haven't heard the last of that 'Mountain Cast Into the Sea.' It's possible, in my mind, that much of the damage done by a chain reaction of earthquakes, caused by that asteroid, was covered up by nuclear explosions. The seismologists wouldn't be able to separate them in very convincing fashion. If the continents were caused to shift, look out."

"Have we covered it for now, then, Chuck?" asked Hank.

"I suppose so, Hank."

Dr. Cooper started the log again.

Sure enough, the IDEA gave a tiny blip of the light tunnel and stopped over the mid-Pacific Ocean. The tidal wave had already totally wiped out any sign of civilization near the coast up to about a 5000 foot altitude. It had swept up the west coast of South America and was just reaching Central America, moving north. The farther southern coasts around Chili had received the most impact. The wave was moving both south and north from that point, as well as basically west. The backwash scraped everything down to the hardest of solid rock. Nothing above that was left. To the west, the Philippines, all south sea islands, much of Indonesia, Malaysia, and a massive part of Australia had already disappeared. The wall of water was bearing down on China.

The wall of water crossed all the way over Central America, and many miles into southern Mexico. Anything or anyone within 50 miles of the west coast of Mexico would soon be no more. In a flash there was no Baja, and the wave moved up and filled the Grand Canyon, and most of Utah, Nevada, Arizona, New Mexico, and was stopped only by the continental divide, giving Colorado a west "coastline," and for a while making an island of the Grand Mesa. The Gulf of Mexico instantly increased its depth by a thousand feet, the wall having crossed Panama and moved north through the Mississippi valley to flood the Great Plains, almost to the Canadian border. The vast width of the plains at least served to lessen the depth. Down in South America, the rain forest of the Amazon was left covered with salt water. Cuba and other Caribbean Islands disappeared, as did most of Florida, the Bahamas, and Bermuda.

Anything lower than 3000-4000 feet altitude in the northern Pacific is wiped out by this wall of water. The water that washes over the Arctic Ocean melts massive amounts of polar ice. Japan is left with the top of Mount Fuji still standing above the water. China is terribly devastated. Hong Kong, Singapore, and Shanghai were instantly gone. Taiwan no longer existed. As the impact ring moved its wall of water west around India and Australia, it was still a massive 1000 feet high as it slammed into eastern Africa, flooding the plains of Arabia, Iran, and Iraq.

By the time this has gone around the globe and into the Atlantic, the eastern U.S. and Europe get three floods, not as deep and devastating as the Pacific, but still walls of water hundreds of feet high. They came from the west, and north, and finally from the south and east. People in the skyscrapers of New York would not have expected drowning as a likely death.

As devastating as the wall of water is, it doesn't last long. It is amazing that any sea-going vessels could survive, but some do. Some of the nuclear fallout was washed from the land into the sea where it killed life there. But even the cleansing of the land was short lived. Any nuclear power plants, of which Japan had many, went into meltdown and released new radiation fallout. The nuclear winter continued, added to by new volcanic eruptions caused by the horrible collision.

As a new light tunnel was about to begin, Sheriff Morgan interrupted the viewing for awhile. He needed to separate out some of his officers to start a new cycle of operation. He could leave Willow Springs, and the county, in the hands of his friends only so long. He didn't want the state police to get too curious. He set up a three-day cycle so everyone could work two and be home one. The two work days would cover the town and then the complex. He hoped he could provide security everywhere that way.

There weren't any more reports yet about new Black Forces nosing around. They all hoped it stayed that way. Also, Hank thought that viewing the log was taking so long, he should uncover his secret vault. He asked some of the men to help him. Hank wanted to be able to hide copies of the log instantly if need be. So after the vault was uncovered, he made sure several men knew how to recover it, leaving no trace. He would have to trust them with his last secret.

Doc Payne took a couple of other men and went to the cooler where they had stashed the bodies of the Black Forces men. He needed to know exactly how they died, if possible. When he returned, he had only one explanation for the sudden death of those men—they had obviously seen more than anyone else knew about. Their brains had hemorrhaged and their hearts burst—they died of abject terror. Maybe those angels actually had faces.

After these details were taken care of and another meal shared, it was time to watch again. Two thirds of the sheriff's men had either gone home or were on duty in town. Running 24 hour shifts would be difficult, but it was workable for a short while.

"Everyone ready?" asked Hank. "Okay, here goes."

Everything was happening in such rapid order now, that the light tunnels barely existed. The IDEA still was not landing. It seemed to be traveling at extreme speeds and low levels just to give a detailed overview. Even though the devastation was beyond comprehension, there were signs of rebuilding and stabilizing going on. People were still trying to stand up and survive, no matter what. The IDEA sailed along the Canadian border. There were many Black Forces moving into the U.S. unimpeded. Then, in several large cities, it happened just like before. The Army would get things under control and turn it over to more Black Forces. They were everywhere. Some system of communication was up and running again. The only thing that Hank wished were different on his machine was that the IDEA would only show the time of day and sometimes the month, but unfortunately not the year.

Most survivors who weren't seriously injured but were able to function showed every sign of getting busy and moving ahead, but there was still considerable civil unrest. More than just gangs picking on the populace, there were organized militias staking out territory to govern with their own version of martial law. They would even fight battles with U.S. troops, and especially any Black Forces. Little wars were widely scattered across the continent.

The seas had settled back approximately where they should. There were, however, a few inland seas where none had been known before. They were in notoriously low spots, but landlocked and full of salt water.

The sight of dead fish was quite common. Up in the higher elevation above St. Louis, where the very wealthy used to live, lay a strange sight indeed. Among the high ridges, where there had been mansions and landed estates, were several humpback whales. They must have surfed the wave across the land, up the Mississippi, and hadn't made it back with the backwash.

"I'll bet the dead fish lying around have gotten pretty stinky by now," commented Mike.

No answer was needed.

The IDEA flashed another blip and continued to show similar scenes around the world. Many of the higher elevations, such as Belgium, France, and Switzerland, seemed untouched. The massive wave leftovers had come from directions that had shielded northern France and Belgium somewhat. Also shielded was the Mediterranean. A general rise of sea level was bad enough, but it was nothing like the slamming wall of water that hit everywhere else.

Anything coastal in most of the world was totally desolate. But inland, at higher elevations, one had to contend with the earthquakes, fallout, and the Black Forces. That seemed to be the main thing the IDEA was focusing on. Everyone remarked about where all the black equipment and uniforms could be coming from. With so much of the world destroyed, and the computers down, there was an obvious lack of production of new items. Someone had to have been stocking up for many years. Many of the armaments could come from various countries. All that would be needed for that was a quick paint job. The sinister side of the prospect, though, would mean that the Black Forces would be armed by disarming any possible resistance. What looked so necessary now could become uncontrollable later.

The IDEA then returned to where New York and the UN had been. Neither existed anymore. The nuclear winter was still severe there and worsened from November to May. Then the IDEA moved quickly to Bern, Switzerland, Brussels, Belgium, and Rome. In all of these places they saw extremely heavy contingents of Black Forces—they looked like headquarters. All were equipped with satellite dishes that were aimed approximately straight upward into the sky. IDEA then was back in orbit, showing satellites in tangential orbits, so they would eventually crisscross every continent, and always be in view of one or more of the others in the string. There was always one or two satellites crossing a large window centered over the western coast of France. Most of Europe, northern Africa, and the Mideast would have a direct angle of access to that window.

The group watching the monitor couldn't be certain about what year they were looking at. No more New Year's celebrations had been shown since New York was gone. Everything looked like winter year round.

Chuck Carver mentioned in passing, "We have seen what was supposed to kill a third of living things, destroy a third of the ships at sea, and poison a third part of the waters of the earth, and blot out a third of the sun, moon, and stars. That was basically in Revelation 8. Things should move like a whirlwind from now on."

The IDEA went back to Brussels, Belgium. Something was going on at the NATO facility there. As the IDEA settled in closer, it was apparent that it was now the new Headquarters of the UN. All the flags and the delegates were present. They all seemed secure, and a new order had been accomplished. The facility was so small in comparison to the old UN, not everyone could get inside. The security council had interior seats. Everyone else was seated outside, around a huge wheel of a table. TV screens in the center equipped with cameras were aimed at the table. It was quite an interactive system and looked like it had probably been quickly thrown together.

The man who seemed to be in charge stood to speak. "As Secretary General of this great union, it is my duty to remind some of our dissenting members that the new and now current charter takes priority and precedence over any and all boundaries. Every one of you signed this, and your countries confirmed and ratified it. It is now world law, and without law, there is no order.

"We are now in need of a leader who we will all agree is worth following—one who has the vision and stamina to pull us all together. I believe I know such a man. Most of your heads of state know him as well. He is unique, in that even though he is possibly the wealthiest, he is also the most generous. He has been in the background, often times bailing out whole countries from economic problems. He believes that he has an obligation to do whatever he can to serve our planet. We are in the midst of devastating times. This man can see beyond all that, and a way to restore everything to unsurpassed beauty. Many of you know him by different names, because he thought modesty the best policy. Would you now welcome, and I hope accept and listen to, Mr…"

Beep-beep, the alarm sounded again. The light tunnel was a bit longer this time, and IDEA landed with a thump like the earlier times. Soon Hank was seen checking out the perimeter from the rim. He no longer even acted as if he wanted to leave the ship.

The monitor focused in on the mountains nearby. The IDEA was sitting alone on a high ridge of rock. It all looked quite familiar. It was Ruth who pointed out the general shape of the mountains. It was like a "different colored" photo of a place they had seen before. It was a slightly different angle of the first stop, the one with Noah's ark, but there was no ark visible this time. Eight thousand years and numerous glaciers probably combined to remove any trace from view. But these were the mountains in eastern Turkey and north of Babylon, near Mount Ararat. The headwaters of several rivers would be found in those mountains, two of them being the Tigris and Euphrates. At times, these were mighty rushing rivers. And the swamps of southern Iraq or Babylon were constantly fed by them.

The IDEA shifted its viewers upward. Too close for comfort was a large, falling ball of fire. It was another asteroid. It looked about the same as the bombs in re-entry, but Hank didn't think that any bomb could be this big. It was much, much smaller, though, than the one that hit the south Pacific. It was much too large to just be called a meteor. Its size made it seem closer than it was. As the arc of the trajectory became clearer, one could tell it was going to hit well west-southwest of the IDEA, in eastern Turkey, and northwest of Babylon. It would still be deep into the mountains. It was so close now that if it exploded, the destruction on the ground would be unimaginable.

It did not explode, but collided full force into the south-central part of the range. That put it quite near the general area that formed the headwaters of the Tigris and Euphrates rivers. There was a massive earthquake, just like you would expect in such a collision, sharp as a hammer jolt. And then instead of building in intensity, it proceeded to slowly die away. It was like being an ant sitting near the center of a cymbal or gong. What remained was not aftershock tremors, but fading harmonic vibrations.

Debris blew high into the atmosphere. Most of the rock and dust that made up the debris would be expected to spray a wide ranging pattern laterally, and in a generally circular shape. That didn't happen here. Even though the asteroid came in at an angle due to atmospheric deflection, there was no circular pattern nor skipping. It just seemed to hit and keep going. The debris either went nearly straight up, or a bit of lateral pattern out the south side. All viewers agreed that it was as if it entered a box canyon and buried itself beneath the back wall of the mountain. That canyon must have been formed by the washing away of softer material, and this falling star hit the soft spot right on target.

The heavier debris settled back to earth and only the finer dust hung in the air. Then a heavy cloud of black smoke came pouring out of the impact zone. It was reminiscent of heavy volcanic smoke columns, yet much darker in color, like a large oil fire. Hank watched for some time as the smoke climbed to the upper atmosphere and started spreading westward on the winds.

Then a different kind of cloud began growing. It did not rise in the same boiling fashion as the smoke. It remained at a lower altitude, rather like fog that hugs the treetops. It also seemed to move in separate clusters, very long and wide, but not deep. Ten to 15 feet in thickness, top to bottom, would be an apt description of its dimensions. These clusters flew in all directions. From orbit it would probably look similar to rings in a pool after a rock has been thrown into the water, or the way some artists depict the rays of the sun. The IDEA zoomed in close to one of these clusters.

Schmitty shouted, "Those look like swarms of locusts!"

Beep-beep, the alarm sounded, calling Hank to the target. He was on the move again.

It was good to have Dr. Carver, or Chuck, on hand, because the next scenes might have been too vague except for the thorough scholar. The IDEA just flashed pictures of groups of people. Some wore strange uniform garbs. Others stood in formations, in many different styles of circles, often holding candles or incense. Some filled large auditoriums showing bizarre behavior that was trance-like. Some were obviously meditating in strained positions. Some were walking in desert areas, looking skyward and searching the horizon. Some were small groups in dark foreboding surroundings. Others still were bowing down to the floor, before men. Some were handling various primitive equipment and paraphernalia in bizarre and obscene ways. Others still were wandering around, nearly naked, in forested areas. There were some sitting in circles who were obviously passing around various drugs, some of them being smoked. A few of these groups actually wore robes that would imply some sort of priesthood. There almost seemed to be no end to it, especially when too much of what was shown was in what some would think were Christian churches. Then suddenly it was over. The light tunnel returned for another very short run.

Hank, now confident of the routine, stopped the log again. He spoke as he did this: "Tell me, Chuck, was that the key moment I felt it was, or was it another incidental happening?"

"It certainly was not incidental," answered Chuck. "It is key in at least two ways. The first way is that it is the exact picture shown in Revelation, chapter 9. A second star falls from heaven opening up the pit where the angel of the bottomless pit lives. The black smoke was thought to be allegory, but even if it is, it looks like it could also be oil. The second part that is key is the overwhelming swarm of creatures, which Schmitty thought looked like locusts. That isn't too bad of a description. Revelation describes them as a special kind of creature. They looked like horses, covered with armor for battle, faces like men, long golden hair, teeth like a lion, and a tail like a scorpion. Their king is the angel of the bottomless pit, Abaddon or in Greek, Apollyon.

"I believe the tail like a scorpion is the important feature. They are not allowed to sting those sealed by the Lord. In other words, those who are true believers, not acting, nor following another Gospel will be safe. Just an aside: Only very few present day believers think the current church with true believers will go through any portion of the tribulation, either part or all of it. What we have seen on the log would suggest they're wrong in their interpretation. After all, judgment begins in the house of the Lord, and today's Church has really been asleep, as watchmen at the gate. One thing we are sure of, though, is that any who are appointed to go through it will by God's power be successful in that process. He will keep them by His mighty hand, or remove them before they are tempted beyond their capacity to give in to any pressure. After all, physical death would *not* be a tragedy for a believer, any more than it is now. To be gone from this body is to be with the Lord. Millions are now, and will be, killed for the sake of Christ. Paul says 'Be true unto death and finish the race.'

"All others in the world are fair game for these creatures of torment. The stings will not kill, but will cause pain, which makes the victim seek to die rather than live. Since this will happen to those seeking something different from God's Gospel, it will have the affect of hardening most hearts into an open hatred of God and Christ. It will be a catalyst to stop people's pretense and 'draw the line in the sand.' This torment will last five months and then stop. Revelation also says that through that five months, men will want to die, but they will not be able to. There will probably be even more torment, self-inflicted, caused by such attempts. This should be, if I read it right, one time death takes a holiday of five months, at least where these stings are the problem. I'm not sure about other plagues, starvation, or martyrdom."

As Chuck was sharing some of these horrible things that were going to happen, Ruth instinctively drew Mike closer to her side.

"I mentioned before that the tail of the scorpion has special significance. At least some scholars believe so. It is important as an allegory to the Church. Several places in the Old Testament, scorpions or the tails of scorpions were equated with false prophets and false teachers—those who would enrich themselves by telling people what they like to hear. The people who seek false teachers are described as those with itching ears. It's possible that some who have been following warped and heretical gospels, even if they name the name of Christ, may be damaged and tormented by these other gospels and not even realize it until it is too late.

Paul warned the Galatians in particular of this. The writer of Hebrews did also, as did James. Paul even asked the foolish Galatians 'who has bewitched you?' because they were being counseled to diminish the value of Christ's work of atonement. They were trying to pay their own way to heaven again. These strange teachings usually have some formulary approach that will convince people if they do thus and so, they will get what they want, or increase their own spiritual power. They allude to God occasionally, but misrepresent who and what He is, until the hearers' focus is on themselves. The old original sin of self-righteousness and self-aggrandizement seeps in, weakening the faith God would give them to rely on Him alone. The person's own free will again tries to take control.

"Those who truly belong to Christ will, at least eventually, listen to His voice. They will, through the Holy Spirit, discern the truth and reject the lies. Those who are not truly believing, trusting the Lord, and yielding to His will, continue in the lie until they're stung to death. I believe the significance of the event we just saw, and the follow-up involving people in all sorts of strange actions, shows the the point where they crossover the 'line in the sand' and give themselves over to buying into the lie. From that point on, they are sealed in it, and their growing hatred of Christ will prove it."

CHAPTER 28
The Enemy's Strategy

The IDEA had already landed again when the log restarted. It was in Brussels at the temporary UN headquarters. The scene was like a shadow of the late 1930s through 1945. Black uniformed officers were in control of everything; intimidation and blind obedience was the discipline of the day. The frantic activity combined with many rows of trucks intermingled with tanks suggested a move was on the way.

The viewers zoomed in on an English newsstand and scanned the headlines: "The New Order Completed," "World Leaders Agree," "Peace and Prosperity Promised," and "New Hand on the Helm." One headline after another had to do with the move: "UN to Move to Rome," "Larger Facilities Made Available for World Wide Re-construction," and "UN Seeking Special Security Pact With Vatican."

The light tunnel blipped again and IDEA started a new trip, flashing scenes from around the world. Building was indeed progressing. Attitudes seemed on the upswing for the moment. However, one thing was growing faster than anything else—the Black Forces. They were already rounding up people considered to be an impediment or danger to the New World Order. They saw no national militia anywhere—only Black Forces.

The IDEA showed barbed wire encampments in scattered and remote places. They had all the appearance of the concentration camps of WWII. It was Doc Payne who had the background to recognize the signs. He had been in WWII as a very young man, right out of high school. He was part of the occupation forces at the tail end of the war. He helped dismantle some of these camps and care for the displaced persons found there. What he recognized and then explained as everyone watched was the signs outside the camps. They had numbers as the basic identification of the camp. The types of prisoners were stated by a color code. The signs would be the color of that code, including black, red, blue, green, yellow, and white. These colors basically stated the security level and urgency of neutralization.

Schmitty said he had heard of this, but hadn't seen it personally. It was basically a Nazi system, and he had served in the Pacific. The system hinged on a list of people that was compiled long before the Nazis took power. Whatever was known about anyone was used to assess how likely that person would resist the system and for what reasons. First were those already in positions of power and could not be bribed. Next might be religious people, especially those who were openly so. Then might come teachers who were not corruptible. Another level might be people with money and resources not at the government's disposal. What was alarming was the same color code as the Nazi's had once had in force now seemed to be in use. More and more people were being rounded up. This was happening not just in Europe, but worldwide.

The IDEA then stopped above the Vatican showing a summit. UN personnel were everywhere, making the assembly of Cardinals seem small. There was to be an assurance of peaceful intentions to make Christians and, in particular, the Roman Church feel safe. The strange part was the fact that when it was over, Black Forces controlled security, rather than the Vatican guards. They were reduced to being the Pope's personal bodyguards only.

The IDEA then blipped another light tunnel and was instantly in Jerusalem. The scene was similar to the one in Rome, except at this time the Black Forces didn't stay behind. News headlines, though, read: "Israel Given Guarantees of Security."

The IDEA then began moving about the whole earth again. The swarms of creatures were having a terrible impact on mankind's health and welfare, as well as economic production. Everything seemed to have come to a state of stagnation. But, there were some people who were doing quite well. Those same people could also be found attending Christian services.

"Hey, Dad," called Mike. "Switch that thing off. I have a real question."

Hank quickly stopped the log. "What question is that, son?"

"Isn't Apollyon or Abadon supposed to be an evil spirit?"

"Yes, that's right," answered Steve. "He's Satan."

"Well, then, I don't understand," said Mike. "If he's evil, why would the creatures that he is king over sting evil people? Why isn't it just God's people?"

"That's a fabulous question, Mike," answered Dr. Carver. "That young fellow cuts right through the junk and gets down to the meat. Don't feel confused, Mike. Asking the right question is more than half the problem. I think you'll probably see why,, but I'll try to give you a heads up on it.

"Satan, Apollyon, or whatever we call him, knows that God protects His people. So he must devise a strategy to hide that fact from other people lest they also wake up and turn to God. So, when he turns an evil loose on the world and God's people are protected like Daniel in the lion's den, all that is left to attack are people who have not turned to God. Now they don't feel they've chosen 'evil' as such, but, they just have not sought out God. These people are known in the Bible as the simple-minded, not discerning right from wrong. They then are easily swayed by outrageous claims. If Satan would tell them that all this was caused by God's people, they would believe the lie. Then they'd do their own oppressing of anyone who loved God.

"What Satan just cannot and will not accept and understand is that when God's people are tested under oppression, they get stronger. That fact will eventually prove that Satan is way beyond simple. His horrid pride has made him into the ultimate fool. He believes his own lies.

"The paradox is that this is right in line with God's will. Pretense must stop so that God's judgment cannot be questioned. As His people are strengthened, the same torment thoroughly hardens the hearts of God's enemies. The lines are clearly drawn; and Satan is allowed, by his own trickery, to take away all false excuses. This will guarantee that Satan loses and God wins."

As the log returned to the monitor, they could see some of the people who were tormented by the creatures from the pit. Agony was everywhere. The only difference was the way in which each one handled it. One thing was apparent—the sting had about the same total effect on people's tempers as, for example, too many extremely hot days. As if the physical torment wasn't enough, most people seemed unable to put up with each other, let alone cooperate.

As the months passed by, the exalted leader of the New World Order had to find a way to restore order. With the Black Forces in the same state of torment as most others, He could not rely on their judgment.

The IDEA settled in front of the Vatican just in time to pick up a press conference. A very tall, muscular, and handsome man stepped to the microphones. "I have urgent news that the whole world needs to hear. The wonderful people of earth—all of humanity—have been under torment from an evil that makes great boasts about being good. These creatures are a mutant creation that was the result of a massive conspiracy. This has taken a long time to develop and was unleashed in order to create chaos and disrupt the orderly progress we have been making toward peace. These Christians have used nationalism, imperialism, and hatred toward the common man in an attempt to destroy the hope of peace on earth.

"These Christians are against democratic government, which has been proven to successfully work. I stand here as a result of the democratic process, yet they oppose everything we do. They want everything their way. They don't care what you want. They speak excitedly and boastfully about a king. They even say he is the 'King of kings.' They only want humanity, as proud and noble as it is, to grovel in the dirt before this figment of their imaginations. In democracy, the majority should have their way. We don't need instruction on right versus wrong.

"I tried to make peace with the largest entity in this mess called the Christian church. All the rest are mere sects compared to the church of Rome. Yet I have been unable to deal with any of them. They can't be talked to. I'm sure you noticed how these people who call themselves Christians have not been tormented, nor have a large number of Jews. Even Israel complains about these Messianic Jews that teach Christianity. They are a horrible irritant. They have lost their senses, so they don't even know who or what they are. We have discovered that before they released these awful stinging creatures against us, they made a special tonic they drink. This makes them smell putrid to these creatures so they won't go near a Christian. They smell too bad. They call it communion.

"However, I have organized my own task force. They have created a mild substance that will not hurt humans, but is deadly to these creatures. This horrible torture will be over soon. I will spare no expense to make you safe in your homes again.

"In order to provide continued security, I have ordered the UN forces to declare the treaty with the Vatican void. We will take control and will dedicate the spacious buildings here, built by the blood of its subjects, to a much better use. Rome provided the longest peace the world had known. It will do so again. In order for this to succeed, one other matter must be dealt with. Any Christian activity will, from this time forward, be illegal. Christians who remain Christian are to be considered outlaws, wanted by the society at large, and are to be considered dangerous.

"The UN security forces need your help in rounding them up for trial. They rounded up Jews in the last century. Now they will feel the vengeance of an outraged humanity. Once this is accomplished, we will be free to shed the light of true knowledge out before you. You will find your minds illuminated as never before. This I will do for you, by my own hand. I pledge to you…"

The alarm sounded and Hank returned to the target. There is no recognizable light tunnel, and the IDEA seems to be in about the same location. It was obviously at least days later, and A. Paul Lyons is speaking again. The IDEA's sensors pick it up, but Hank is not seen.

"In order to help Israel solidify her security, I have made a pact with Israel to supply more assistance in slowing the activity of proselytizing Christians. They are creating all manner of disturbance. Also, there are two madmen in particular who are doing amazing magicians tricks, convincing some that their power is from God, whom they claim is Jesus or Yeshua— it all depends on who they talk to. They have been plaguing most of the world for about three years. Our forces, though, are closing in on them. We believe they are the ones who released the stinging creatures. That is one indication that a Christian conspiracy is behind these things. I am about to...huh...what the..."

Suddenly the speaker was attacked in the middle of his rambling speech by a group of men, dressed in Arabian garb. One of them was screaming, "May Allah be praised." Even though most were carrying large swords reminiscent of the Arabian Knights, all of them were cut down by automatic gun fire. When the air cleared and calm returned, it was obvious that A. Paul Lyons was mortally wounded. A huge cut was down the side of his head. It was as if a downward blow of a sword had caught him above the ear and continued into the neck. He was not decapitated, but he was definitely dead, according to those near him. His body was rushed into the Vatican medical building. Then a man dressed in the robes of a cardinal came out to address the crowd. "My little children, a horrible thing has happened here today. We must in our hearts and minds detest and abhor such action. We must pray for this great man, that God may have mercy upon him."

A man hollered from the crowd, "Isn't that illegal now?" and the crowd laughed.

The cardinal answered sternly, "Pray. Amen!"

The alarm sounds beep and blip, and the IDEA is behind the medical building. Visual sensors zoom in tight at an upper window. Conversation inside can also be heard on a laser beam touching the window.

"Would you rather have a general anesthesia, sir?" asked an attending physician.

"Not on your life, Doctor." It was the voice of A. Paul Lyons. "I must be alert at all times. If I am to walk around scarred, I want to know as much about what caused it as possible. We have to pull this off, you know."

"Oh, we will, sir," said the doctor. "This scar will not just look real, sir, it will be real. At least we have your clone to get skin from later, so you will be handsome again."

"Yeah, that poor dope thought he was the real thing. He so wanted to be me. I'm just glad he didn't know what to expect. There is more than one way to rise from the dead."

"Yes, sir. All the world is going to be amazed all right." It was the cardinal's voice. "What a shock it will be when they see prophecy fulfilled right before their eyes, yet later have nothing more come of it."

"You have truly become quite a marvelous cynic. The Pope would have been so-oo...thrilled," Lyons said sarcastically. "Kill him!" He motioned to the guards in the room. Quickly, without blinking, they grabbed the cardinal and slit his throat.

"There is one less security leak," said Lyons. "When does Daniel Nodaba arrive?" he asked his aide.

"In just a few hours, sir."

"Good...that's good. We can't take too long with this procedure. The world must see that I am unable to be harmed. We must awe them into hanging on my every word. But I can't look like nothing happened, just in case someone should happen to wonder about any expendable doubles. Now, hurry it up, Doc, our world is waiting."

Blip, again the IDEA was moving, but not far. This time it settled on one of the buildings at the edge of the Great Plaza in the Vatican. A huge crowd had gathered. Some looked bewildered as if they didn't know for sure why they were there. All of the Black Forces that ringed the perimeter suggested that the people had just simply been told to assemble.

A small group of men, all in formal black dress, came out of the medical center followed by a Black Forces honor guard. Carried on the shoulders of six of these men was a funeral bier draped with black crepe. Laying on white satin was the alleged body of A. Paul Lyons, the Exalted Leader of the New World Order, now fallen. They carried it to a raised platform in the center of the plaza. One man stepped forward to the microphones to speak. He raised his hands to call for calm and attention, and then began.

"Fellow citizens of earth, I come here as a longtime friend of our dear, murdered and martyred leader, A. Paul Lyons. My name is Daniel Nodaba. We who knew Paul best were always amazed at his unmatched abilities. There was nothing he put his hand to that was not mastered almost instantly. That's why, as time passed, we also came to realize the future of the world would be its best possible when A. Paul Lyons was at the helm. He had the ability to see through and navigate safely the most hazardous situations. You might imagine then how deeply pained I am to see the body of this great man lay here, slain by terrible villains. I sincerely hope that...huh...that we...what is this?"

There was quite a stirring among the crowd. Some started yelling at the speaker and pointing. Faking his surprise and joy, Daniel Nodaba looked toward the bier directly behind him. Sitting up and looking for a way to get down was A. Paul Lyons. The scar was quite evident. Lyons rubbed it a little just for the dramatic effect.

As Lyons stirred once more looking for a step, Nodaba called to him to wait and relax. Daniel Nodaba then held his palms out in front of him-

164

self and toward A. Paul Lyons. As he motioned upward, Lyons' body began to float above the bier. He then moved him to the side and gently brought him to a standing position right before the microphones. The crowd went wild. Some were jumping up and down and dancing almost as if a new year were being greeted.

Two very raggedly dressed men pushed to the microphones. They looked strange enough, in contrast to the planned group, that most people just stepped back and let them through. When they reached the microphones, one of them started speaking boldly.

"Don't fall for this charade, please! These men are defrauding you. This man was never dead, and the rest is a magician's trick."

Before they could say any more, someone turned off the mikes. Black Forces Guards grabbed the two men and started taking them to the side of the plaza. Suddenly, the men broke free and started to run. The guards began shooting but missed their targets. The two men turned, facing the guards. As they started to speak a laser-like fire came from their mouths and killed the guards. They turned to leave, and the crowd around them panicked and fled.

Daniel Nodaba raised both hands to the sky and screamed something no one understood. A bolt of pulsing light came out of the blue, and hit the ground several feet behind the two men. They disappeared into the alleyways between the buildings and were gone.

The crowd was so impressed with the fire from the sky they nearly rioted, trying to reach both A. Paul Lyons and Daniel Nodaba. It was evident that everyone believed that Lyons had come back from the dead. And they also believed they had seen overwhelming miracles from Nodaba.

A. Paul Lyons raised his hands for quiet, and the crowd became hushed. He began to speak.

"Our enemies who call themselves Christian have failed again. It is obvious that I cannot be killed by them. It is obvious that they and that thing they call their God are impotent to stop me...to stop us! Even when they pretend to be Arabians!

"I have even better news that I tried to tell you before the brutal attack. My lead bankers in Brussels have been able to launch the last of the satellites they need to make possible a new economic system. This system will make it impossible for anyone to steal your money. They won't be able to rob you because there will be nothing for you to carry. These satellites will connect banking and ID centers in every community around the world. When all is ready, I will have more information for you. In the meantime, let's find those two maniacs."

The IDEA's alarm sounded and blip, it was in orbit again. It went straight up to a satellite. This was a strange looking satellite compared to those shown before. This was a space weapon. It looked to those watching the monitor as though it could be the source of Daniel Nodaba's "fire from the sky." Then the IDEA moved suddenly down to ground level outside of Rome. In a wooded area, in a ditch about to be covered, were bodies. On the bottom lay one that wasn't in view, but it seemed to be dressed in white robes and a golden sash with a large cross. Also there were the body of the cardinal and the guards who had killed him. Mixed in with them were the men who attacked A. Paul Lyons.

"Several more security leaks plugged," said Hank.

He then turned off the log and nodded to Steve and Dr. Carver.

Steve spoke up first and asked, "Did you pick up on that new character's name, Chuck?"

"Yeah, you mean Nodaba!" responded Chuck. "He has to be the false prophet. He obviously has his own scam. The Antichrist is revealed by a phony death and resurrection, as an attempt to duplicate Christ. The false prophet is revealed through a false display of calling down fire from heaven, to copy Elijah. The real prophets or witnesses that come closer to Elijah and Elisha are kept on the run. But, they won't run far; they'll be back."

"What I was getting at, Chuck," said Steve, "was the cute turn of the name. *Nodaba* in a mirror or spelled backwards is Abadon."

"Isn't that revealing!" responded Chuck. "Satan is such an egomaniac, to put it mildly, that he's willing to boast and gloat over his accomplishments. He does that with brain teaser games. He sees to it that his chosen representatives bear his name, and in the languages that matter most— Hebrew and Greek. By using the two languages in which were written the bulk of scripture, it's as though he's sticking his thumb in God's eye. The curious question is whether these men with these names were there by happenstance, or were they acquainted with the old dragon to such a degree that he changed their names? They seemed to come out of the blue, yet we know Lyons was connected with at least one group that dates back several centuries or more. It's possible Nodaba was as well."

Sheriff Morgan spoke up loudly. Everyone could see that he was agitated. "That's all well and good, guys, but what could possibly be going on here. A cardinal?! A cardinal, being so blasphemous as to say the things he just said? I have a hard time believing such a thing. What could make him so cynically evil? And to be following along with this enemy of Christ! I don't think I can take this!"

"Oh, my dear Sheriff," said Dr. Carver, "I didn't stop to think that some of you were not as accustomed to things found in prophetic scripture and would be hit between the eyes by something like this. Of course it is a terrible shock. But imagine the shock the disciples had when Judas betrayed Christ.

"The Scripture is full of warnings about leaders in the church who are really wolves in sheep's clothing. They are interested only in what they see as their status. In a political sense, this is very beguiling. When this man of high rank saw that the Pope had possibly made the wrong choice, in trying to protect his massive flock, his opportunistic tendencies probably took over. He made his own mistake trying to bargain with the devil. Not only was the treaty with the Pope a vicious lie, so were the promises made to him. So he ended up in the same mass grave as the Pope. That's the clear sign that the days of Satan's warfare with the Church are in full bloom. He'll seem to be victorious for a short while.

"Meanwhile, Harold, try to take comfort in the knowledge that there are some bad apples in every barrel. The Lord will justly sort out who they are. Can you do that?"

"I guess I must, and with the Lord's help, I will," Sheriff Morgan said with misty eyes.

Just then the sheriff's relief group arrived for the next watch, and the others headed home. Hank showed the new men how to replay what they had missed. Everyone else said their goodnights and turned in for some rest. It looked like this listening and watching vigil was going to last another day or two at least. They left the monitor for the new shift and went to sleep.

CHAPTER 29
Lies, Madmen, and Chips

The next morning started early. Almost no one had been able to sleep soundly. Their minds were racing with all of the new concepts they were learning. Chuck knew prophecy well enough that he could only anticipate what might be next. How would his visualizing of these events match up with what would be shown on the log? He believed that the IDEA had really taken Dr. Cooper through time, deep into the past and now into what seemed to be the near future. He believed this because of Dr. Cooper's past and background. Having never had a real interest in the particular things shown in the log, he would never have been able to program them into his machine. Also, the log clearly chose to show unique things, mainly scriptural, that even if he had the ability for such programming, he wouldn't have chosen these scenes. Hank simply was not interested in spiritual things at that time.

Steve Lichtman and Doc Payne were having similar thoughts. Hank was just getting more and more curious. He needed to know if the things coming back strongly in his memory now would match the log. Most of the rest were both shocked and exhausted. It was nearly too much to grasp, especially when a few days ago they had no clue as to what was happening near them. So, sound sleep had been almost out of the question for most.

Shortly after they had eaten a small breakfast of Army style rations and were ready to start the log once more, Rick's voice came over the radio, "Calling Animal Control." Sheriff Morgan switched to the secure channel, "I read you, Rick, come back."

"Sheriff, I'm afraid we have another black Lincoln, and the same sort of strange passengers, dark shades and all."

"Where are they, Rick?"

"Well, believe it or not, they're hanging around Farnsworth's truck stop right now. They may be waiting for more back up, like the last bunch."

"Has there been contact with any other people yet?" the sheriff responded.

"Yeah, I talked with them at Dr. Cooper's home, Sheriff."

Ruth let loose an audible gasp and clamped her hand over her mouth. Grandma Schmidt reached over and took her hand to calm her.

"Tell me about that," said the sheriff.

"Bill and I went by the Cooper place to make sure all was secure. Just as we got to their drive, we saw the Lincoln up at the house. Two men were just getting out and going to the front door. We pulled up and they came to their car to meet us. Right off, they asked if we knew where Dr. Cooper might be.

"I told them I didn't think I could help them very much. I said that a sudden emergency had called them away. It seemed to involve either family or dear friends."

"Hey, that's good," piped back the sheriff.

"Yeah, I kind of thought so, too," continued Rick. "But it gets better. I said I knew it involved a long trip, and that I couldn't remember it all. I was sure that part of the trip involved the Seattle area. They seemed to be satisfied by that explanation. When we told them we were watching the premises as security until the Coopers returned, they said goodbye, got in the car, and drove into town."

"Well done, Rick, that was as smooth as vanilla pudding. Just keep us informed, Morgan out."

Hank made sure that everyone was ready. He filled in a few blanks that this particular shift hadn't had time to watch. Then he started the log again.

It seemed that the IDEA was giving an overview of the human condition in the wake of all the disasters and woes. There was agony, illness, biological plagues, radiation fallout, starvation, and extreme cold due to debris in the air from bombs and volcanoes. There was also no shortage of nuclear powerplant meltdowns adding to the radiation. All of this, of course, prolonged the nuclear winter.

One thing seemed strange until the 20 people viewing the monitor could talk it through. What puzzled everyone was the fact that people in more remote and high altitude areas fared much better. After discussing it among themselves, they came to a logical conclusion: First, they were closer to the sun with less atmospheric filtration, so the cold was moderated in the daytime. Second, less population caused biological diseases to move more slowly. Third, water was helpful to wash away radiation fallout, and the water nearer the headwater sources was less contaminated than water downstream. The farther downstream people were, the less they could even use water from rivers. They vividly saw how most of it was poisoned now with radiation, chemical, and biological debris.

From what they saw on the monitor, the lower the elevation, eventually reaching sea level, the less stable and more poisonous became the water and the more dead animals they saw strewn along the banks of the rivers. Large sea coast cities, then, shortly after the tidal wave deluge, were unfit for anyone's return. Even where people congregated, farther up the elevation level, their sheer numbers were making survival almost impossible. They saw the ones who drank the water get radiation poisoning and worse. Others were dehydrating and starving until their tongues swelled up and choked them to death. Either way, these deaths were slow and horrible. Those who had been injured were of course in even worse shape.

Some reconstruction continued anyway, but the IDEA showed them that bitter cursing was a general way of life. Such destitution also brought with it a desperado mentality. People were both fighting and cheering the order that the Black Forces established. As long as it stopped the other guy in his tracks, it was great and worthwhile. Because of lost employment, banks and stores had little meaning for the poorest three fourths of the population. They had no cash to work with.

"Many probably already lost their savings in banks that were totally destroyed," Chuck commented. "And those who saw the possible disasters coming and were successful in surviving them, were probably the only ones who had any cash. In a society like this, bank insurance, backed by the government, is no good at all."

"Hey Mom, look! They're just trading stuff."

"I think you're right, Mike, it looks like the old original system of bartering has reestablished itself. It's all they can do now. The free market is the only true way to establish value. Food and clothing, followed by medicines, are definitely of greater value than cash. I'll bet that precious metals even have lost some of their value because only the few rich people left could even consider such a long-term investment. The most valuable commodity—what do you think it is?"

"That one I know, Mom. It's water. Air is filterable, and food could wait awhile if need be, but water is the lifegiver. Just a few days without water means death—very painful death."

"You're right, Mike," said Hank. "In the past, many parts of the world had experienced these same horrors. There were other places to go, though, or places that could be of assistance. What makes this truly a tribulation with no equal is the fact that it's a worldwide devastation. There's nowhere to hide, and no one to care or assist..."

Not everything was dark, though. The group watched the richer survivors who did have resources, move in to fill many of the needs. They put together new filtration systems that, once purged, were able to filter the contaminated waters and provide potable water.

The IDEA flew over massive tanker ships headed to the poles in order to mine ice from deep inside the polar caps. This was easily transported to various places, again providing potable water. The poorest died, and the comfortable spent everything they had just to maintain life. The few rich piled up the long-term wealth in obscene amounts. They were the ones who joined together to set up the new economic system—a cashless society. The only possible thieves would be those controlling information. In other words, those who owned the system.

Suddenly the IDEA settled again in Rome. Once again Hank was seen checking the perimeter and found he was in the same spot where Daniel Nodaba supposedly called fire down from heaven. Again, a large stage was set up at the edge of the plaza, this time right in front of St. Peter's Basilica. Enough time had passed since the New World Order turned on the church and did away with the Pope that there was now no sign of clergy of any kind. The secular had taken over.

Shortly thereafter, people started arriving by the hundreds and then by the thousands. Hundreds of Black Forces took up positions around the whole plaza. After the area was filled, a procession of limousines arrived and drove to the stage. The second car was flying the UN flag. Soon eight or 10 V.I.P.s were in place and a man walked to the microphones. "As Secretary General of the United Nations, I greet you," he said. "This is one of the most historic days the world has ever seen. I am here to report officially, in the name of the UN, the news that will change all of our lives immeasurably.

"As you know, the new UN charter that was adopted by the nations of the world a few years ago gave us a representative, World Governance, which binds all nations into a Federation for the common good. The implementation of that charter was slowed by a series of disasters, the like of which we have not seen before. But, we have survived, and as before we will thrive. Times such as this, however, call for extraordinary measures in order to prevail. That is why the UN has debated and passed a series of measures that will help us implement and coordinate everything necessary for the ultimate human victory over times of adversity.

"We have recognized, and the whole earth has witnessed, the fact that a very amazing man has the intellect, power, and wisdom to accomplish super-human results in nearly everything he does. He has even defeated death in his own body right before our eyes. For those reasons, the UN has voted and asked him to serve this earth of ours as the single top executive. The UN would be the legislative body. The chief executive or World President would be that branch, and the world court would serve as the Supreme Judiciary branch. This is a lifetime appointment by the UN. His second in command would be of his choice, as would whatever cabinet he deems necessary. I am pleased to report that he has accepted and has chosen his number two person, or chief of staff. I will now ask that man, Mr. Daniel Nodaba, to introduce to you his friend and mentor, and our New World President. Mr. Nodaba...if you please."

From the perimeter of the plaza came a wave of applause and cheering. By the time it reached halfway to the center, it could be heard well enough for those down front to know they should join in. It raised to a mighty crescendo and stayed there till Daniel Nodaba finished basking in the sound and raised his hands to signal quiet so he could speak.

The IDEA's viewers picked up on something that was put on the log for all to see. Everyone in the hangar started commenting about it, because it showed how phony the whole response was. Just as Nodaba stepped forward to the microphones, the Black Forces Guards, who surrounded the perimeter, stepped up behind the people farthest back. They then jammed a weapon of some sort in the backs of several persons. As they did, they leaned forward to say something in their ears. The prompted people immediately started clapping and cheering. The rest just followed the moment. It seemed to be spontaneous enough that the whole crowd figured it was the thing to do. The louder it became, the more they believed it and added to it.

When things finally quieted down, Daniel Nodaba spoke. "Thank you, thank you all. Mr. Secretary, and citizens of the world, I set before you one of the most important days in known history—a day filled with astounding news and opportunity. Many of you already witnessed the great changes and improvements in how we relate to each other. As a single community of humanity, properly concerned about the welfare of our single planet, we can solve the problems together to the benefit of all. But it is not up to me to share with you how this will be done. I am here to introduce to you the man for the moment. Some of you know him, or a least know of him already.

"This man is the true renaissance man—a man for all seasons. Everything he does, he doesn't do just well, he does it superbly. He has organized and run more successful enterprises than most people could name. He has generously used his great wealth to help where disasters have hit. He has single-handedly bailed out whole countries during their financial crises. It may surprise you to know that in different enterprises, and different parts of the world, you may have known him by different names. He felt it was much too pretentious to do so many things under one name. That way most of his charitable effort was unknown by most of the populace. Most people never had the opportunity to put all of the names together and match them up to one person.

"I am proud to introduce to you this man without equal. The name you will know him by from now on is A. Paul Lyons. Let's give him a world class welcome. The man who in this very place came back to life after a terrible attack the day before. I believe you will be astounded at how much he has healed in these few days. I give you your future—A. Paul Lyons!"

The crowd, already fired up by their earlier cheers, went wild. They were really exuberant now. Many of these same people were very likely at the previous mass announcements. They probably saw the attack and believed they saw Lyons killed in the process. Then in a matter of hours, they were the same ones who watched Lyons sit up from his funeral bier. They saw the horrid scar that the surgeon created. Then they saw Daniel Nodaba seemingly levitate Lyons off the bier to the floor.

"I'm sure that they know that he called fire from the sky," said Steve. "We have seen how the UN put great confidence in this one man and his friends. They probably had convinced them that the solution to all their problems was just around the corner. I don't believe that even the Caesars enjoyed such acclamation without first conquering by warfare."

After a considerable time, filling himself up on the cheers and praise, A. Paul Lyons gave a final acknowledgement. He raised his hands to motion for silence. Several minutes later the crowd calmed down enough for him to speak.

"Mr. Secretary, national leaders of the world, my great friends, citizens of earth, thank you for such a wonderful welcome. We all have indeed just crossed the threshold of a marvelous millennium. Mankind has proven that he is capable of surviving anything, and we are more than able to solve our many problems. Don't let anyone tell you that you are going to face insurmountable crisis. All we need to do is work together and show proper adoration and respect for our Mother Earth. For many years we have been moving toward a single language, by which we conduct business at the highest levels. It is somewhat accidental that this language is English. That was natural, because the wealthiest and strongest nations of the last century happened to speak it. All well and good; we all at least have that in common. We can work together more easily because of it. That will do much to obliterate the useless separations that different languages enforce. All languages are fine, but a common one will bring us closer.

"There is a second mighty development that will help draw us even closer. We will become a single entity on earth called humanity. That development is the one I mentioned before—the new economic system that will tie us close enough that we need one another. A system that will give every citizen access to the resources needed for living, and new businesses. The building we have already started, and our future achievements. Let me explain and lay it out for you. I have had a large group of people working many years on the development of this…"

"No! No! Do not believe anything this man tells you! He really is your enemy and slave master, not your friend." The two wild-acting men seemed to come from nowhere.

"Seize them," yelled Lyons. "Those two have caused most of our problems. They and the other Christians." He then vented a long stream of curses on anyone involved with the name of Christ. He found a way to even blame them for the asteroids and all of the earthquakes. It was amazing to hear him take minute mentions of a situation, with microscopic pieces of fact, and turn them into outrageous lies.

The two men were grabbed and brought before Lyons, and in full view of the crowd. When Lyons started to say something, one of the men interrupted him, and shouted for all to hear. "By the power of Yeshua, creator of heaven and earth, the God of Abraham, Isaac, and Jacob, the God of Israel from whom they have turned away, but are now turning back. By His word, there will be no rain in all the earth for six months!"

"Silence," screamed Lyons, "take these men into custody. We will have none of their terrorist threats."

As the guards of the Black Forces started to take hold of them both, the other man spun around facing each of the guards. As he spoke, the laser-like fire from his mouth hit each of the guards, who had started to obey Lyons' order. All four men immediately perished in the heat of the second man's words.

They then turned toward the crowd and motioned that a path be opened for them. No one was willing to challenge them. They just stepped back and gave them room to leave. When they were nearly gone, a repeat of the earlier scene took shape. Daniel Nodaba stood in the center of the stage and screamed words that were unintelligible to those listening, and once again brought fire from the sky. The first pulse beam landed just ahead of the two men. The next was right at their heels. The third one took out the corner of one building as they darted down the narrow streets and disappeared. Wherever Daniel looked, the pulse beam targeted. He and the satellite were nearly one.

After a few moments, A. Paul Lyons resumed his speech. "See the riffraff run? They clearly are in over their heads. I wouldn't worry too much about their threats. They are obviously crazy, and this so-called God of theirs is then a figment of an insane imagination. They are too dense to realize that they are even unable to kill me. You all know now that such a thing is not even possible. I cannot be killed. I proved that before your

174

very eyes. So, don't fear these madmen, and listen to me. I will show you things you haven't even dreamed of."

The crowd once again went wild with cheers and praises for A. Paul Lyons and his associate Daniel Nodaba. After several minutes, Lyons regained control and continued.

"The new system I promised you is now ready to be implemented. After years of preparation, I have established a central computer that has none of the problems that we just went through with the old ones. Many millions of compatible smaller units are being installed worldwide as we speak. The satellites are in place, and in two or three weeks all will be accomplished. Every person will be entered with his or her own account.

"Each of you will be your own living credit card. You will have no need or use for cash money. There will be no unequal exchanges of currency because none is used. Different countries will not have different economies. There will be a single world economy.

"I have even better news for you who are standing here in this plaza—you will be the charter members of a new citizenship. We have things arranged at all exits so that before you leave, you will be given a personal chip implant that will carry all the pertinent information that applies only to you. This will not take long. You state your name and age, your address, and your country's I.D. number for you. The teller will punch this into the computer, and in seconds it will produce a microchip that carries all this information. You can choose to have that implanted above your left eyebrow or on the back of your left hand. It is painless and will not show. However, the computer scanners can read it from a distance.

"When you leave here, you just continue life as you would. But—But—the beauty of it all, when you go to purchase anything, is that you will need no money. Just shop where the proper scanners are in place. Now, isn't that great?"

The crowd cheered again but not so boisterously. They seemed a little bewildered by it all, yet they obediently stood in line to wait their turn to get the mark.

One change was noticed by the IDEA's viewers when it was put on the screen. Each person was asked several questions. Most would raise their hand, and a bit later pass on through. Every once in awhile, there would be someone who did not raise their hand. Usually they would shake their head no vigorously. These people did not go through. Instead they were escorted back to another part of the plaza and were taken into another building.

Suddenly, the IDEA called Hank back to the target, and a new journey began.

Hank knew it was time for Steve and Chuck to tie things together for those in the group who were not involved in the study of Bible prophecy, which was most of them. He, as a matter of course, stopped the log and nodded to Steve and Chuck.

CHAPTER 30
Another Move

Chuck seemed tentative at first, but then spoke. "I suppose that most of us here understand fairly well what we have seen and heard. If not, we're not formal here, speak up if Steve or I don't answer your questions or touch on your personal observations.

"I guess many of us know fairly well what that last part of the log was all about. The misery is growing exponentially until the whole earth's population is totally desperate. It then seems a small thing to throw away freedom and become the vassals of one man who is a successful fraud. Old 666, as you've been calling him, is insidiously in control. The UN armed forces, or the Black Forces, are pledged to him."

"I have a question," said Mike. "Those people we saw led away by the guys in black—were they refusing to take the mark?"

"I think you're right," answered Steve. "They remembered that they should refuse the mark of the beast. When they do that, though, the enemy knows why right away. The only people who would think of that are those who have known the scriptures and the Gospel of Christ. I believe that is the point at which they will be told they must denounce Christ completely if they expect to live. If they refuse, they're killed. Some may be allowed to remain in camps for a while to see if torture will change their minds. Some who previously ignored Christ are probably hoping that being a martyr for the sake of Christ will prove their own true repentance and allow them to be covered by God's grace in the end.

"There may still be room, though, for the salvation of those who understand for the first time, even after the rapture, what the Gospel is all about. Possibly they will hear it from the 144,000, who were sealed to go through the tribulation for the purpose of winning those last few souls. Or from other new converts. We know that much of Israel will be saved, and finally acknowledge and turn to their Messiah. They will believe the lie only a short time, and then their eyes will be opened. Maybe it is just that their political leaders are the main ones that want to make deals with the antichrist. At any rate, many will be saved out of great tribulation. It is just that some scholars don't believe there are second chances for those who, even though they knew the Gospel, just ignored Christ before. They believe those persons would be blinded and bitter towards God, and would be eager to believe the lie instead. Either way, there will be many martyrs then, just as there are already millions martyred around the world today."

"Just a side note," said Hank, "I've been getting some information of one development here in the U.S. that is already being used in some satellite phones. It is also used now to locate cars and planes anywhere in the world. It is called the GPS or 'Iridium' system. Some say they are working on a very tiny chip that could carry DNA information as an ID. Is that the kind of thing we're maybe seeing here, Chuck?"

"I'll bet that would be a good candidate, Hank."

"Have we about covered that now?" asked the sheriff.

"Yes, I believe we have, Sheriff," answered Chuck, and the others nodded.

"Johnny, do you read me? Come back."

"Yeah, Sheriff, what's up?"

"I just need to touch base. Have our dark friends been up to anything more?"

"No, Sheriff. There haven't been any more contacts or sightings. I'm not sure they're even around here anymore. I was just down the highway and by the Cooper's place, and I saw nothing out of the ordinary."

"All right then, Johnny, if anything changes let me know. Okay?"

"You've got it, Johnny out."

It seemed like a good time for a break. Everyone just relaxed for a while and took care of their personal needs. A few minutes later they reassembled, ready for another session watching the log.

They were surprised to see that the IDEA was back outside of Rome. The spot was near where they saw the mass grave of the Pope, the cardinal, and their assassins and guards right after A. Paul Lyons' surgery. There was a new trench now and it was holding many more bodies.

The IDEA then was quickly in a fly-by mode, again—it made short stops in most major areas of the earth. Most of the time, they seemed to be near camps with wire fences and yellow signs showing the camp number. They all were the same in one regard—there were large trench graves just like the one outside Rome containing the bodies of men and women of all ages and also of children. The placing of the mark for economic control had been a very effective roundup of any who were in opposition to the New World Order. Only the Lord would know how many were martyrs for His name's sake. If there were any ways to escape such a purge, they would have to be in very remote areas. They would also need to be extremely self-sufficient.

The group talked about what they were seeing as it passed by, just like a family does watching TV. Doc speculated that if there were some small

178

groups tucked away in odd, remote places, they might also be experiencing some angelic protections similar to their own group's recent encounter. All present thought that it was at least a comforting concept.

The IDEA then returned to its customary perch at the Vatican, just in time for another speech—this time from Daniel Nodaba. "Citizens of earth, I greet you with good news, and news of another change. For the most part, our transition to the new economy is progressing quite well. There are a few people here and there who resist any change. They still think they can do better with a black market or underground economy of their own design. This cannot go on too long without decisive action. It is necessary for a system, such as the one we have adopted, to be complete, or we could continue to have the same confusion and breakdown as we have experienced twice in less than a century.

"What is most disturbing is the fact that the bulk of such resistance comes from those connected, in some strange way, with Christian beliefs. It is as if some people think this 'Christ' of theirs wants nothing more from them but to be troublemakers. Even many groups who were long known as churches have given up on this stupid imagining and have joined in the effort to bring unity to the family of humanity. Helping everyone to love and care for nature and our Mother Earth is where our future belongs. These people only want to claim extremist ideas of human superiority, in the name of Christian superiority. This cannot be allowed; we must stand as one in our own right. The issue of import is not God as our Father, but earth as our Mother! To summarize: If you know of such people who are still carrying out illegal activities, be good citizens and turn them in. We will then help them change.

"Now, the change I mentioned. It seems the controversy over Jerusalem is nearly intractable. Israel is still having major security problems. The Arab states and the Palestinians are very upset over the destruction of the Dome of the Rock during the Russian invasion and coinciding earthquake and storm. All of that resulted in great destruction over much of the city. The Arabs want the Dome rebuilt, but the hard-line Jews say that is where a new temple should be built. Then add to that the Christians and Messianic Jews who are sure there isn't any need for a Temple anymore. There are several different groups besides the nation of Israel that claim Jerusalem as their own capital. So many ancient claims for one piece of land is what wars are made of. At least now we have a world peacemaker in A. Paul Lyons that cannot be successfully challenged anymore.

"In the light of that fact, and the hope the whole world has unanimously recognized this exalted leader who has yet to be given any specific title by the UN, we have deemed it needful for Mr. Lyons and his headquarters to move from Rome to Jerusalem. Since everyone wants this as a capital, he will listen to your wishes and make it so. The decisions about damage repair and rebuilding will be more easily handled from that location. We will keep all informed as the move progresses. Due to the steady hand of A. Paul Lyons, true peace is at hand.

"I will stay here in Rome most of the time as a special envoy to the UN. The UN needs more space, and we can share some of the extra space we will now have here. This will make communications and coordination much easier."

CHAPTER 31
The Tale of Two

The IDEA sounded the alarm again to bring Hank to the target. When it settled with the familiar thump, the hatch opened quickly. Hank stepped out only to see that he was in Jerusalem. The IDEA was perched on the wall of the old city, with the new modern part of Jerusalem on the other side. It was readily apparent by banners and black limousines that the new, nearly finished high-rise was Lyons' new headquarters. It was built quite close to the ancient wall of the old city. Presuming he would use the highest floors for his own quarters, Lyons was in a perfect position to view nearly all of the old city from above. Being at one of the highest points of the total city made it possible to see much of the modern city as well.

"There's an eagle's nest for you," piped up the sheriff.

"Well," quipped Doc, "from what we know of this guy, it may be more like a condor. You know, giant vulture."

"I get the picture, pilgrim," answered the sheriff `a la John Wayne.

While Hank was still checking the perimeter from behind the rim of the IDEA, a disturbance started growing near the center of the old city. There was a crowd of people gathering. It was difficult at first for Hank to see the cause. Finally the crowd moved around a corner and into view. Near the head of the crowd were the two men who had been a continual thorn in the side of A. Paul Lyons—the ones that John's revelation called the two witnesses. They were loudly proclaiming that judgment was about to fall on any who accepted the mark or chip. The crowd was yelling back at them angrily, but most didn't touch them. Whenever anyone did touch them, they were rebuffed in a threatening manner. At widely scattered moments, a very few actually attempted to do physical harm to the two men. When that happened, the words of the two witnesses continued, but when aimed at their attacker, became a laser-like fire that immolated the attacker instantly. They continued to burn in a fashion reminiscent of past stories of spontaneous combustion. After such a show of power, the crowd would fade back for awhile until they were far enough away from the last incident. Then someone else, who hadn't seen what happened previously, would make their own fatal mistake.

Black Forces were sent in, but were continually unable to find the two men. They would just seem to disappear into an alleyway or building. Then soon they would be in another part of the city. This continued throughout the evening and deep into the night. Hank continued to watch, occasionally dozing off. He was awakened suddenly by a long, anguished yell that came from atop the high-rise occupied by Lyons. He could not understand much of what was yelled after that, nor could those watching the monitor. But, everyone was sure they heard the names Apollyon and Abadon a couple of times. It seemed to be an anxious prayer for help.

Shortly before dawn, another disturbance began. It was very close to the Temple mount, which was still cluttered with the ruin debris of the Dome mosque. As the pre-dawn glow was peeking over the mountain tops, a startling sight appeared. It was similar in movement and sometimes in shape to that of the various angels that appeared on the log, as well as outside the lab compound. It was more like a writhing, three dimensional shadow or ominous cloud. It was darting one way and then another, one time high as if flying, and then nearly hugging the ground. There were moments when it seemed to have appendages like arms, legs, or wings. Other times it was just a turning writhing mass of darkness. Finally, Hank could understand the commotion. The occasional flashes of light were the fire bolts from the mouths of the two witnesses. The sudden movements of the shadow were attempts to dodge the missiles of light.

Before long, one could tell that the two men were tired. They were thoroughly exhausted. The dark mass seemed to be taunting them, begging them to expend all their strength. Then, in one sudden move, it totally enveloped them, and seemed for a while to be convulsing. All at once, the two men were flung to the pavement, and the shadow jumped back as if repulsed. The men did not move. They were obviously dead. In almost the same style motion as the angels seen before, the shadowy mass collected itself into a writhing, somewhat spinning column, and flew away ahead of the sun. It seemed to be seeking the cover of night.

The IDEA beeped the alarm that called Hank back. In a mere flicking instant, the pictures returned to the monitor. The IDEA was in a flight and hover mode. It was just above the temple mount area. A crowd of onlookers and mockers had collected there to view the bodies. Some were even checking them to be sure they were dead. One man called out to a friend in the crowd, after he placed his hands on the neck arteries and lifted the eyelids. He said, "What's to be chicken livered about? They're both stone cold and rigor has set in. Their eyes are like in a dead mackerel. They are gone for good, finally."

Several in the crowd shouted obscenities, some of which were so vile

182

that Ruth and Hilga Schmidt looked at Mike. They obviously wished he wasn't there to hear such things. When Ruth and her son's eyes met, Mike just wrinkled his face and shrugged as if to say, "I know, it doesn't matter."

About that time, a black stretch limo drove up close. Lyons and several bodyguards stepped out. Lyons found a high point on which to stand. Then he spoke.

"Fellow citizens, I had hoped to get this cleaned up before you were bothered by it. These two madmen have had quite a run for these three plus years. They were doing so much damage to our city and people last night, I just had to do something about it. I found them here, and we had quite a battle for a short time. Like I have proven before, though, I can not be beaten or killed. They would not believe that until I killed them. It was nasty work, but I have promised safety and security. Now you see, once again, that I deliver. I'll have some crews come bury the bodies in a few moments. That is…No, don't bury them. Let them rot till the birds and the vermin clean them up. If there are any bones left, then bury them."

The whole crowd yelled agreement and started chanting, "Let them rot and swell in the sun." Over and over they chanted this while Lyons entered his limo and was gone.

As the crowd started to party in derision in front of the two bodies, the IDEA began a mode that was different from any previous. It showed a fast forward type of time lapse pictures. Two different crowds were gathering. The one was clearly happy beyond reason that the two witnesses were dead. The other group just stood around as if wondering what it was all about. The biggest difference was that the second group did not seem to respond well to the mockery and derision, and outright vile, blasphemous hatred for any claims concerning God.

This time lapse sequence moved quickly into the night. Then it was daytime again, and quickly nightfall. It was back to daylight, then night changed to morning once more. The pace then slowed a bit until it seemed, again, to be running at normal speed. The IDEA zoomed in on the bodies. Right away Doc noticed something that no one else did.

"Hold it right there, Hank," hollered Doc.

"Now look real close to the people standing around. What do you see?"

Everyone shrugged and looked questioningly at Doc.

Doc continued, "We've just seen a sequence of three days and nights. The people are not wearing heavy clothing. They are dressed for summer. They didn't even get cold at night." He waited for a response but got none.

"Okay, you don't get it yet. Two dead bodies laying three days on an average day, or at room temperature, would send up such a stink, no one would be anywhere near them. The sun has been hot, and the people are sweating enough to wipe their brow, like that guy there. All of this and the bodies have not bloated or changed in any noticeable way," said Doc, quite agitated now.

"I get your meaning," said Chuck.

"Great. Finally!" retorted Doc.

"That is talked about in Revelation 11," said Chuck. "You just keep your eyes open. Let it go, Hank."

The monitor continued for several minutes. Just as soon as some of the revelers thought it was a good time to throw some stones their direction, both men began to stir as if getting up from a long nap. The crowd fell back a long distance, and a few began screaming in panic. Some in the middle were trampled by those trying to flee and the ones moving closer to find out what was going on.

The two witnesses stood and looked around, then their gaze fell on the frightened crowd. The ones closest to them in the first group cowered as if expecting to be hit by the fire. One of the witnesses seemed about to speak but was stopped before he could.

A voice so bold and loud the whole city could hear it came rumbling directly from above the crowd. It said, "Come up here!" The two witnesses looked up with expressions of amazement and wonder. Then immediately gravity had no affect on them. They just raised up above the crowd and kept going until they looked much smaller. Then a cloud came together just beneath them, grew in size, and started rising as well.

In only a moment's time, the two witnesses and the cloud disappeared. The crowd grew ever more fearful, especially when the other people, who seemed only to be bystanders, began praising God. They danced and sang praises to Jehovah or Yahweh. Some Messianic Jews, who had not yet been captured by the Black Forces, began in earnest to convince their countrymen that this was foretold by John. They told them that this was proof that Yeshua was the Messiah or Hamashiach, and that Yeshua and Jehovah are one. They were telling them, "Look up; your redemption is drawing near."

While the excitement was still bubbling, ominous clouds built up over the city and spread for many miles in all directions. As the people began to get worried about the storm, the earth began to tremble. In a matter of minutes, everything broke loose. The earth split open, taking people, cars, and buildings into the chasms. Lightening strikes by the hundreds seemed everywhere at once. The hailstones from the storm were massive and large enough to kill anyone they struck. When the storm dissipated, bodies lay everywhere.

The IDEA picked up and left for another time and/or location. Chuck took the opportunity to explain that even though the monitor did not give a body count, the passage in Revelation says that the count will be 7000 men, besides women and children, in Jerusalem alone.

CHAPTER 32

Here Comes the Groom

When the IDEA opened the sensors this time, the effect was wonderful indeed. It was in a mode that seemed to be everywhere at once. Almost dream-like, interwoven and overlapping images were merged with mixed up moods. Night time was mixed with day. People, events, colors, sounds, all proceeded on their own course, but all at the same time. Ruth told the others that it was like that early morning when the IDEA left and came back at the same moment. It was nearly impossible to separate the ingredients and sensations.

The first thing, though, did seem clear in this sequence. There was a startling yet beautiful blast of sound, like that of a trumpet to end all trumpets. It started on one tone and quickly slurred to a note an octave, and then two octaves higher. It held the high note, then tapered in volume till it was gone. A shrill but sweet singing note that hung in memory, long after it ceased to sound.

Immediately the sun, on the daylight side of the planet, was darkened. Something eclipsed a large portion of the sun, yet without special equipment, one could not tell what it was. It was just a dark silhouette. Also immediate was a universal earthquake. It was as if the earth had the shivers of a great fever like malaria. The IDEA showed scenes on the monitor that jumped all over the world in a matter of seconds. Or was it all at once?

Graves were being ripped open, and live persons were seen standing and looking around. There were people standing on the water of the oceans. The earth continued to shake, and others by the millions appeared. Then, in a flash, all of these, and many more, took on a light-filled glow. They lifted up from the earth to the edges of the atmosphere; and, in a blink of an eye, they were gone. The IDEA changed location to an orbit high above the earth. Everything looked normal there from a distance, but just ahead, looking away from earth, this huge mass of humanity—all gleaming like the stars in the sky—was rapidly heading for the most glorious sight. It was no longer dream-like. There was no need to physically be on multiple sides of the planet. The IDEA could now just observe the beauty of the moment.

"This is just like the prophets foretold. It is God's holy city, the New Jerusalem. It's huge for a city by any standards," said Dr. Carver. "It looks like about one half the continental United States in area." What surprised the people watching the log was the particular shape—it was a giant pyramid. "It's 1500 miles in all dimensions—length, width and height," added Dr. Carver.

The sight seemed almost too glorious for them to discuss. It did, at first, look golden; but, as one looked closer, it was full of beautiful colors. The IDEA was too far away to give many details—it was like viewing earth from a satellite. Differences in depths and size just blurred into a color pattern. Structures of immense size, however, were clearly visible on the horizon. From the top of the city shown a light that enveloped and surrounded everything, so that there was no discernable shadow.

As the great host of people approached the city, everything seemed to shine brighter. The colors emanating from this fabulous mountain seemed to pulsate in a rhythmic response to their approach, giving a feeling of jubilation. The green colors, in particular, seemed to flutter. From what they saw from a distance, with no benefit of sound, it could only be interpreted as "party time." Everything looked joyful and exceedingly bright.

Suddenly, though, the IDEA moved and no longer viewed the heavenly scene. It had returned to the earth. The effects of the earthquake were immediately evident. Huge fissures had developed in every continent. Massive blocks of polar glaciers were loosened and floated out to sea. Three dormant volcanoes exploded back to life. One of these was Mount Lassen in California, one in central Asia, and another in the Malaysian string of islands.

The IDEA seemed to purposely zero in on airplane crashes all over the globe. Freeways of large metropolitan cities were jammed with wrecks. Cars had run off the roads in remote areas. At military bases, there was wreckage of nearly every type of plane, tank, and truck.

In the cities, crowds of people roamed aimlessly, looking in all directions. Ambulances were lined up at hospitals, but no one seemed to be going anywhere very fast. Schools seemed to be in a lock down mode. Jails were, too, and many prisons had alarms sounding.

The IDEA gave a short blip and refocused on a newsstand of a large city. The headlines read: "Into Thin Air"; "Minister Shocked—Third of Parish Missing"; "Quake Opened Graves"; "Morgue Says Some Missing-Most Not"; "Pilots, Drivers, and Surgeons Disappear"; "Husband says, 'Flash of Light and She Was Gone'"; "From Cemetery Administrator, 'Underground Dual Vaults, Body on the Bottom Missing'"; "Ship Captain says, 'They Came Up From the Sea—Stood There and Then Disappeared'"; and "Second Coming Resurrection???"

The IDEA's alarm beeped, the light tunnel returned, and Hank hit the stop button once more. "Well, we've come to the end, huh?" he asked as he turned toward Dr. Carver.

"Oh no, not on your life," answered Chuck. "This is only the beginning of the end. The wildest parts of this story are yet to be. In fact, we may not want to see most of it. I believe most scholars of Scripture would agree that this may start the saddest part of the story when the Holy Spirit is removed from the earth. The only part of God's people remaining will be the 144,000 evangelists who will win Israel back to their Messiah, or to Yeshua Hamashiach. The Jews will finally be able to open their eyes and see that the Hebrew name for Jesus is Yeshua or Salvation. They have continued to sing and dance to scriptural songs that speak of this, yet they could never see the connection. Revelation says in one place that these 144,000 are comprised of 12,000 each from the 12 tribes of Israel. In another verse, it speaks more generically of converts from all nations. Some believe this still speaks only of Jews dispersed all over the world, while some who pay more attention to scriptural numbers see another possibility. They see the number 12 speaking of the 'fullness' of God's total plan. They see 12 tribes of Israel, 12 apostles, etc. Twelve times 12 or 12 squared is 144. The thousands make everything to be multiples of ten, which they read as the 'completeness' of God's plan. Thus the number 144,000 'completely fulfills' the number needed for such a job. These 144,000 and the two witnesses, who show supernatural gifts, are said to be anointed or sealed by the Spirit to go through the tribulation and to complete this final evangel to turn as many hearts to the Lord as possible. The only clear promise in this is that Israel will be saved.

"The sad part is found in the corporate Church. This is where many who have tasted of God's blessing, yet still rejected it by not taking the step of repentance, will be left behind. They will be unable to honestly say, "I never heard or knew." They will probably not have a second chance; at least the Holy Spirit will not strive with them again. A few scholars believe they 'might' receive a second chance by dying a martyr's death for the sake of Christ. Most people, though, are sure that those who rejected the Gospel when it was comparatively easy to do so would be the least likely to go that direction later when it might cost them their lives. Rather, they would be in a category talked about in Hebrews, as well as other places: 'Who's eyes are now blinded.' They are given over to believe a lie. These are likely to become some of Christ's worst enemies."

It was obvious that Dr. Carver was now in his element. He thoroughly enjoyed sharing with the others what had been for him a lifelong study. "As for those caught up to heaven at the trumpet call, or what we have come to call the rapture of the saints, their story is quite a marvelous one," he continued. "This is what is referred to as the marriage feast of the Lamb. The true Church is Christ's bride who will be joined to Him eternally. This is also considered to be the time, while more tribulation is on the earth, when individuals are judged at Christ's Bema Seat. That's the place and time when all a person has done will be judged. That which is not good and righteous, but covered by Christ's sacrifice, will be wiped out. Only the good, done in God's will, will last and remain. On that basis, Christ will assign the rewards, above and beyond His matchless grace. Any selfrighteous acts will be among those things burned away, for our Lord is like a refiner's fire, leaving only the purest gold in the end. Except for His Grace, none could stand.

"After these things are accomplished and all of the horrid tribulation on earth is done, He will close the books. The Lord will return, with His Bride at His side, and by His Word they will overcome and destroy the antichrist and the False Prophet, casting them into the lake of fire. Then and only then will the Lord's Kingdom bring true peace to earth.

"Everything else will bring torment in ever growing intensity until all is accomplished. On earth, those who will rule for a while will…No wait, Hank. Turn it back on. Let's see what the IDEA just saw."

The IDEA continued to show newsstand headlines: "UN Secretary Expresses Relief"; "Government Leaders Glad Troublemakers Are Gone"; "Some Few Still Try to Keep the Faith"; "Israel Seeks New Allies"; and "Hooray, Moralists Away."

"I'm sorry, Hank; please, stop the tape! I slipped up again."

"It's stopped. What's up, Chuck?"

"There's something on the log a few minutes ago that's been bothering me. Because of my preconceived ideas, at first I was surprised at what I saw. I've been thinking it through and feel I may understand it now to some degree. The shocker was seeing the holy city, or heaven, or New Jerusalem, whatever it is called in various contexts as a pyramid with a high wall. Did this bother anyone else?"

"Yes, you bet it did," said Ruth. "Even though Hank thought I was being overly cautious, I have been warning Mike not to get involved in the occult stuff his friends were messing with. I always connected pyramids with occult type worship of anything but God, as well as the tower of Babel, Egyptian gods of the dark spirits, Mayan, Incan, and Aztec worship of the sun, with human sacrifices, and the list goes on. Modern 'new age' occultists put pyramid power and crystal power in about the same league as magic incantations and conjuring up of spirits. You get my drift."

"I certainly do," answered Chuck. "That was exactly my reaction on the initial sight of it on the log. However, I have since come to the conclusion that my reaction shows how much effect this sin-cursed world and its way of thinking has had on my own modes of thought. But, Christ's promise to us is that 'we shall know the truth, and the truth shall make us free.' My reaction basically had been, 'Why would God have anything to do with the symbols used by Satan?' The problem was, I was beginning with a false premise. You see, God doesn't copy anyone. He's the original Creator. Say, Steve, jump right on in here when you feel like it, okay?"

"No need, Chuck," smiled Steve. "You're right on track; just keep going."

"Okay then. God existed before the beginning of the world. He created the angels first, of which Lucifer—whom we call Satan—was one of the greatest and finest. When He and a third of the angels rebelled against God, they were thrown to the earth and away from God's heaven. Ever since, Satan has been the masterful liar who uses little pieces of truth, warping and distorting them into monstrous lies and subtle traps. He uses these to draw simple, gullible men away from God, and into forgeries and fakes that lead to destruction.

"Satan told Eve in the garden, 'You will not die' (a lie); then he said, 'You will know good and evil' (a bit of truth); and he capped it off with 'you will be like God' (a monstrous lie that stirs the self-centered pride that became sin and death). All the other things we see in pagan societies and those who worship idols, and the sun, moon, and stars, all follow the same pattern. Satan cannot create, but he has learned to copy, fake, and conjure just enough to impress mankind with magical manipulation. Add to that twisted phrases that don't really say what they seem to at first, and you have a recipe for getting back at God, doing as much damage as possible."

"Then what are you saying?" asked Hank. "Are you saying you believe Satan knew what heaven looked like, so he set out to convince man that a pyramid was a magic formula shape of sorts?"

"Very close, and…yes. The pharaohs thought that being buried in one somehow put them on the road to immortality. It's just warped enough to fit. The Mayans, Incas, and Aztecs then were much like other orientals. The actual temple was on top of a pyramid.

"I had just gone along with the 'cube shape' that had been passed along to me. I didn't consider further. A 'city foursquare,' as it says in Revelation, would be length and width. If height was considered square as well, would that be called anything different from that?"

Hank just shrugged, but had no disagreement.

"Now consider that the holy city or Zion is also called the mountain of

190

the Lord. The throne on top seems to be the source of the water of life that flows to the whole mountain. The light emanates from the Son—the Lamb. He and His Bride are both talked about as being the Temple. Individuals as part of the Bride or Christ's Body are also called living stones in the house of the Lord.

"The bottom line is that God didn't use Satan's symbols, but Satan plagiarized and warped what he knew was close to God's heart, in an attempt to hurt and, if possible, destroy God. But that ain't possible."

Hilga Schmidt burst with a little yip and started clapping and jumping, all the time saying, "Now that's the truth, that's the whole truth, and nothin' but the truth."

Everyone turned and looked at her. She had taken them all by surprise. When she saw them watching her, she got a funny grin on her face and blushed a bit. Then she said, "Oh I'm sorry, but it *is* the truth!"

Everyone laughed and joined her in her joy at the knowledge of it all. After a short breathing spell and personal break time, the log was resumed.

CHAPTER 33
Collusion

In the next sequence on the monitor, the IDEA was still in Jerusalem, near the temple mount again. A. Paul Lyons was beginning to speak.

"Citizens of earth and especially citizens of Jerusalem, this is a momentous day. I have just completed a special treaty with Israel. It is a singular nation that seemingly all others wish to blame for everything they find troublesome, even problems of their own making. I have guaranteed the safety and security of Israel. All earth knows that I cannot be killed, so I expect your support and cooperation in this matter. We will have peace!

"As proof of my intentions and sincerity, I have promised also that I will rebuild the temple that belongs on this mount. We will do our best to duplicate the temple as built by King Solomon 3000 years ago. I will begin construction with my own funds. This should settle the question on Jerusalem. Judaism will flourish as before.

"As you all know, we finally got rid of the two madmen that have plagued the world for over three years." He began to get agitated as he went along. "Just as it was for the Russians, it was a mistake to plague Israel and and it was an even bigger mistake to plague me. We have dealt with that problem by disposing of great masses of these foul Christians in one massive sweep. We are close to finalizing any leftover business in regard to the total liquidation of the Christian hazard." His voice began to get louder and louder. "They will soon know that this Christ of theirs has no claim here. Humanity has no need for His hand in our matters. We will not be bound by figments of the imagination of madmen." By now he was so wound up he was screaming every word. He made Hitler look like a tired professor.

As he continued in the same vein, the more agitated he became, the more his words became vile and obscene until he suddenly seemed to realize that he was not going over so well with his audience. He immediately toned his speech down and ended with a few calm and charming remarks, full of positive hope for the future, and it was over.

As Lyons rode back to his high-rise complex, the IDEA hovered above the limo. The monitor showed a small laser pattern, from the IDEA, touching the roof of the car. Lyons could be heard speaking on his satellite phone. "Daniel, has the doctor made any headway on our project?"

"Yes, Paul, he's making good use of the tissue from your clone. It's looking quite promising."

"I know that much; you've said so several times before. Can he really pull off a believable copy?"

"Yes, I believe he will."

"But will I have to worry about it really being alive, is the question. It won't be in the cards, this time, to need to kill it. It is only to be an image that seems alive when we want it to be. We don't dare let it have a mind of its own."

"Yes, Paul, please relax. We know all of that. The skeletal part and exterior flesh will be all that is used from your clone. He'll look like you, the voice will sound like you, but all else is computer technology very securely programmed to only follow your lead and input."

"All right then, Dan, you have about six months—nine at the most—to have it ready. Give my best to the Secretary, goodbye."

"Wow!" Mike exclaimed as he watched the tape. "He won't stand for any foul-ups, that's for sure. It'd be dangerous to work for that guy!"

The IDEA pulled away from the limo, and the light tunnel returned. It began to hover again, but now before the UN headquarters in Brussels. There were crowds of Asian people holding signs and yelling slogans. Some of the signs were written in Chinese characters, others in various European languages. They were voicing complaints that the countries of the Far East, especially China, were being shut out of the New World Order. Some were saying that they were being ignored when it came to their need for food and power, oil in particular. The long drought, just such a short time after other disasters, had left their people starving. One sign a young teenager carried simply said, "No house—no food—no heat—no medicine!"

As the IDEA hovered over the crowds, they could hear the people blaming Lyons for the trouble because he was too overly concerned with taking care of Israel and hating the Christians. Some said that he had left the Far East to carry the brunt of the curses that they believed were placed on the earth by the two madmen.

The IDEA moved again and found the Vatican area, where Daniel Nodaba was stationed, under the same siege of protest. By now, though, the Black Forces were breaking up the crowds and making many arrests. The Vatican Plaza was reminiscent of the happenings in Tieneman Square a few decade before.

There was a moment of dark screen, and the IDEA began looking at the main cities in China. There was not much left at all but rock and some gouged out foundations where the populous cities of Hong Kong, Singapore, and Shanghai had been. The tidal wave from the asteroid had wiped the land almost completely clean.

In the higher elevations and inland cities, the sight was different. There was obviously massive damage from the repeated earthquakes. The rubble of the cities looked more like an area that had been bombed in the mid-twentieth century. With the myriad of fresh graves they saw and the bony, sick looking people shuffling down the streets, it was obvious that starvation and disease were killing men, women, and children by the millions.

Military installations, though, were functioning as if no problem existed. China was obviously diverting everything to the needs of her military machine.

Chuck commented, "It doesn't take much to realize that China and probably a few allies were preparing for a showdown. Looks like the Pale Horse was still riding hard and the Red Horse is being remounted."

The IDEA picked up and soared over the southern hemisphere. It looked as though nothing were functioning in Australia, New Zealand, and the many islands. Death and starvation were everywhere. The resources of these countries had been totally destroyed by the wave, subsequent earthquakes, many volcanic eruptions, nuclear plant meltdowns, and finally drought.

Then the IDEA moved east and showed that South America was also a continual scene of death. Any of the people who looked like they had some strength seemed to be surviving by violence. It was as if civilized society was a thing of the past. All the ones who had put their faith in God had been a control valve helping to maintain some form of moral order. Since they had been taken away in the rapture, only chaos and death reigned.

The IDEA moved on to Africa only to show similar conditions. However, death was much stronger there. Disease and starvation had nearly annihilated humans and animals. No one searched for the bountiful riches of gold and jewels anymore. They only scratched for food.

As for the land itself, both South America and Africa showed the strain placed on the continental plates. Both had several great fissures that had developed. Hank speculated that the asteroid impact and the sideways tidal forces caused by it, probably were responsible for most of these faults.

As the IDEA began to come into a light tunnel again, Hank turned off the log.

Chuck Carver spoke briefly. "You know, we had become so interested in the shenanigans of A. Paul Lyons that, at least for my part, I had nearly forgotten the horrors that were still befalling most of the planet. Just because the highly developed Europe and the Middle East were pulling things together, it really had not much to do with the total reality of life on this planet. Did it have that effect on you, too?"

Everyone nodded agreement, but no one could speak. They were all becoming emotionally fatigued by the devastation and horror on the tapes. They wanted to continue to watch the log, but they were unsure how much more they could absorb at this time. Especially stunned by it all were the few there who had not been involved with the Church or the study of the Scriptures. They were frightened and overwhelmed by sudden exposure to what the real world was like. They became aware of what wonderfully sheltered lives they really had and reminded of how dear life itself is.

Beep - beep, "Sheriff Morgan, this is Bo. Do you read me?"

"Sure do, Bo, how are you doing?"

"Oh fine, Boss, just a little sore in spots, but I'm fine."

"What can I do for you, Bo? Are you ready for work?"

"Yeah, I'm ready, but I'm bustin' a gut with curiosity, I guess. It sounds like my getting beat to a pulp had something to do with that complex out there. Trouble is, no one will tell me a thing. Herb said it was best I call you."

"Well, thank Herb for me. He's right. This isn't one of those grapevine things. It only makes sense if you get to the root of it, if you get my drift."

"Not really, Sheriff. Sure would like to, though."

Sheriff Morgan looked at Dr. Cooper with a questioning gaze. Hank nodded assent. It was only right. After all, Bo was the only player in this whole thing, except possibly Hank, who actually suffered physical injury. He had played it correctly, but had put himself on the line. He had earned his stripes.

"Okay, Bo, bring yourself a bag with some stuff to stay awhile and we'll catch you up to speed. But, say, we heard earlier there were some more of those guys in another black Lincoln. Have you seen anything of them?"

"More guys? Do you mean these aren't the same ones?"

"No, Bo, they can't be the same ones. I'll explain that later. So, what about them?"

"They just cruise around between the airport and the truck stop. That's all I know."

"Okay, Bo, get yourself out of town when they're not looking. I'll meet you at the front entrance off the highway. Don't call again unless something changes. Morgan out."

"Well," said the sheriff to the others, "I guess we'll need another cot."

Hank spoke up. "Let's wait on the log until we get Bo settled. I think we could all stand a change of pace and scenery. Stretch your legs, wander around, and if you see some debris that really bugs you, feel free to do something constructive with it. But, above all, try and relax."

Hank motioned to the sheriff to come with him. When they got to the corner of the hangar, Hank lifted another security panel to reveal a space containing a small file box. He took a thin pocket-sized pouch from the metal box and slipped a folded paper out of the plastic envelope.

"We have come so far in this thing," said Hank. "I believe I must entrust you with this additional bit of information, Harold. We didn't know each other much before these last few days. However, I've come to count you as a friend as well as a necessary confidant. I don't know why, but I have a feeling something very serious will happen to this whole complex—you know, those anxious premonitions that tell you that just around the next corner is a surprise for which you better be ready. Sheriff, you do remember, don't you, about the secret vault that's under the lab, and how to open it and seal it?"

"Sure do, Hank. What now?" responded Harold.

"Well, what if there is ever a real violent confrontation that completely destroys the complex? Or, what if it becomes necessary just to keep the complex out of the wrong hands, to wipe it out so it can't be found?"

"Boy, Hank, you're getting jumpy, aren't you?" asked Harold.

"No, Sheriff, I thought about these things years ago and built them into this place," said Hank. "I just didn't know half of why it was needed. I know the Lord can and probably will take care of anything important. I just believe in doing all I know to do as well. Now here's the deal. We'll close this up soon. I'll take copies of the log with me, but just in case, I've got the the complex rigged to self-destruct if need be. Another copy of the tapes will be hidden in the vault.

"Now this layout shows how to find the vault from outside the complex. I did that just in case I would lose control of the complex or if it was destroyed in some way. Now the only reason this talk is necessary is in case something happens to me. Not only will the log be there, all of my records, calculations, plans, and journals of my progress are inside. If that fell into the wrong hands, they could duplicate the IDEA. Then if they studied the log, it could help teach them how to navigate. Now, Harold, that must not ever happen! I need your promise that even if the log is saved, all the rest must be destroyed."

"You've got it," responded Sheriff Morgan. "And we'll just have to trust the Lord to see to it that one of us, at least, stays around to accomplish the task. What if we just opened the vault now and did it?"

"We don't have time for it now, and I don't want to disturb too many people. Until we see more of what is on the log, we won't know if there is something we need to know before we destroy it. I suppose inside I feel some resistance to wiping out my life's work, but I really don't think it's the proper time yet. Who knows, but it might be taken care of for us. This might seem weird, but if I need to get rid of the IDEA, I can always put in a rabbit, or something like that, on the target, punch in a number for infinity, set the power sequence and send it nowhere forever. Maybe you should go meet Bo, and we'll get him all set up with the log."

"Yeah…okay, Hank, I'm out of here. Be back soon."

CHAPTER 34

Dastardly Deeds

After Bo arrived, he was given what was now being called, "the bug-eyed tour" of the IDEA. He received an even shorter orientation from the early scenes on the log. He took to it fairly well. He said he'd been a faithful believer since childhood, so what he saw on the screen was really just a confirmation of what he'd already learned in Sunday School classes but often wondered about. What he couldn't imagine was why anyone would let themselves be zapped into particles just to prove a theory.

Hank assured Bo that he now agreed with that point of view. Then he said something else that was heavy on his mind. "I know Ruth and Doc in particular, and probably the rest, are concerned for how much older I'm now looking. I've seen the same things in the mirror. I'm guessing that this trip has taken a good 20-30 years off my bodily life span. I feel much older as well. Since I obviously traveled 6-10,000 years in the past, and who knows how many years into the future, I'm amazed I'm not feeling 50-100 years older. Now directly to your point, Bo. Once I was trapped unexpectedly, I had no choice but to finish the ride if I ever hoped to return. We don't really know all the physical damage I experienced by all that zapping. All I know now is that it shouldn't have been possible for me to do that yet. And there was no way that I could have programmed this ride. Of course, I had faith the total machine could work, but the fact that I survived the ride in the smaller circuitry had to be only the grace of God and His protection. I have a feeling that the purpose behind all of this is to reach men of a totally different mind-set, with a story of fact they had been refusing to read or hear."

With that, Hank resumed the playback of the log.

The IDEA settled again in Jerusalem. The temple had been finished, and the smoke of sacrifices was rising into the air. Except for the obvious modern setting of the newer city outside the ancient walls with its cars, buses, and all sorts of tourists with video cameras, one would almost feel he had arrived at the time of Solomon. Everything on the temple mount was immaculate and beautiful again.

Something special was stirring, though. Crowds were filling the grounds outside the walls surrounding the temple. The outer courtyard was full, and the separate niches that were part of the wall surrounding the courtyard were filled with what seemed to be entire families or elite parties of some sort. They had places to sit and tables for their use.

The altar of the outer court had a constant parade of priests in white linen coming to the altar with whatever sacrifices had been given. Animals or birds were killed there and the proper portions, according to the law, were added to the fire. Once the rest of the unused portions were properly roasted, they were taken to feed the priests and their families. Everything seemed for a while to be normal, except for the overpowering presence of the Black Forces. Dr. Carver was disturbed by what he was watching. He said, "Watch close, I'm sure some kind of trouble is about to happen."

There was, almost immediately, a disturbance at the gate of the temple. There were 12 men in typical Jewish garb—yarmulkes and prayer shawls—pushing their way through the crowds. They insisted they must go inside for a special purpose. The crowds gradually relented and let them through. Some of the waiting families speculated, "Maybe they are part of the special program?"

Just as they got near the altar, the great doors to the sanctuary, where only Jewish men could enter, slowly opened. There was a great flight of stairs leading up to the doors and a sizable portico top. The massive doors, 30 feet tall, dwarfed the men standing in the opening. They were not dressed in any special robes or ephods, and they were escorted by men in black. The crowd in the courtyard looked confused as to what this could mean. One man lifted his hands as if to pray and all grew quiet. Just before he spoke, Mikey whispered, "That's Daniel Nodaba!"

Instead of praying, Daniel spoke boldly, "Hear the words of the lord of heaven and earth, the one promised to you and your fathers for millennia. The promised 'Hamashiach' has finally come to you. He has rebuilt this temple on the place where it once stood so that you might come into his presence and receive his blessing. See, now, he comes at this moment through the king's gate, for there is no other king but he. You have known him for a while as A. Paul Lyons. From this time forth, he is to be known as the lord, the one who has brought you peace."

The men who had pushed their way to the altar area began to object to what they were hearing. They were drowned out by the roar of the crowd, shouting, 'Hamashiach, Hamashiach,' over and over. It was noticed right away by those watching that the chant had started at the outer edges and swelled to the front and center. It was the exact same pattern as that produced at the Vatican many months before. The Black Forces, surrounding the crowd, forced the people just in front of them to start it, yet it seemed to come from all directions at once.

With a real show business flourish, A. Paul Lyons appeared with a massive guard contingent around him. He was dressed in a very sharp white silk suit. "At least he got the colors right this time," quipped Doc Payne. "I guess one lie is as good as another," he added. Doc was obviously considerably irritated.

Lyons lifted his hands for silence and then spoke. "I am the god of your fathers. The god of Abraham, Isaac, and Jacob. I am here as I promised I would be. I could not reveal myself to you until the temple was finished. That time is here. Peace will now reign forever.

"Since I have now taken bodily human form, I will be limited in where I can be. So I have arranged a way to be both here in my house that I have built in your midst and also elsewhere at the same time. I have placed a portion of my spirit in a perfect image of myself. Whatever the image says, I have said. Whatever he blesses, I have blessed. Whatever he does, I have done. He will forever be in the temple. I will sometimes be here and sometimes elsewhere. But, through my image, I will always be here. The connection between us will not be broken. Now I would like for you to meet the image of your lord. Mr. Nodaba, if you please!"

At that, Daniel Nodaba gestured with his hands, and the huge curtain or veil at the front of what should be the Holy of Holies pulled up and out at the center. Seated on one of two gold thrones was what looked like A. Paul Lyons. He was dressed identically to Lyons. All the image did at this time was wave a gentle acknowledgement to the assemblage. Then he spoke. It was the voice of Lyons. He said, "Hear the words of my servant, Daniel. He will instruct you in all you must do." Then he motioned to Daniel Nodaba, as if to say, "Carry on."

Before Nodaba could speak, the group of men, who were still protesting, rushed partway up the steps and began yelling, "This is an abomination. The glory of Jehovah filled the temple when He was here. No one could look upon Him and live. There should be the Ark of the Covenant inside, not two thrones. This is a fraud. Blasphemy!"

"Silence!" cried Nodaba and the image in unison. Then they continued in unison, "The cloud of glory is not needed and neither is the Ark because, your god now lives among you."

The leader of the men spoke up and said, "The Lord walked among us 2000 years ago, and we rejected Him. Yet He was, and is, the true Messiah or Hamashiach. His name was, and is, Yeshua, Jesus, or Gesu, or if you will, Jehovah! He is Lord then, now, and forever! This that you do is an abomination!"

"I will show you who is god," screamed Nodaba. Again he raised his hand to the sky and yelled a jumble of words no one understood. Then he flung his hands down and pointed at the 12 men on the steps. A laser type bolt struck two sides of the group, and a third laser came from the eyes of the image and converged in the center of the group. In a flash it was over. Twelve bodies lay sprawled and smoldering on the steps.

The crowd went into a confused state of shock. They had heard how Nodaba called down fire from heaven, but they had not witnessed it until now. While they were still not sure if they should stay or run, Nodaba spoke again.

"Now hear the word of the lord. You will worship and seek the blessing of him and his image only. If you do not, you will die as these who lay before you. Now instruments play, singers sing, and all others kneel before your lord!"

The music started, and nearly all of the crowd fell to their knees. Many seemed to truly believe in Lyons, the image, and Nodaba. Yet there were a few who did not kneel or who tried to hurriedly leave. Three or four were struck down by the eyes of the image. The others were shot by the Black Forces. The temple had been dedicated.

The IDEA sounded the alarm, and Hank obeyed. There was really no light tunnel, and the IDEA just did a fly-over without landing. China was the subject once again. It was obvious that they did not believe anyone was listening to their demands because the pictures showed a massive military buildup. Ships of any size at all were being outfitted to carry missiles. Already piling up on China's western borders were tanks, mobile artillery, troop carriers of various sizes, and hundreds of thousands of trucks, about a third of which were tankers. Some of the tankers were for fuel, the others for water.

The infantry divisions seemed endless and communication companies were everywhere. The one unique addition was a very sizable horse cavalry seemingly attached to each division. Supplies, equipment, and troops were gathered all along the western boundaries. It even looked as if the southwest coast would load men and supplies on large ferries and other barges to cross over to the east coast of Vietnam. China was definitely preparing to move across Asia in a big way. From the coast or borders, this scene stretched back into China for many miles.

Dr. Carver spoke about what they were watching. "Revelation states that this army would number 200,000,000 men. China, for 20 or more years, has boasted they had this same number of troops ready to fight. Their plan is to overwhelm their enemy like a swarm of locusts. Anything in their way will just be trampled underfoot. Men and bullets are all the same to them.

"Please forgive the break in the flow here, but I feel I must digress once more. Everything is moving so fast now. I'm sure you all understand that when Lyons set his image in the temple, that was an abomination. But for those of you who may be new to the Gospel, one other thing must be made clear. The very act of rebuilding the temple, for the purpose of renewing the sacrifices, was in itself an abomination to God. It was an abomination because new sacrifices were a rejection of the Perfect Sacrifice that was provided 2000 years before. That's why the Messianic Jews rejected the renewal of sacrifices. Salvation 'God's way' is already accomplished. There is nothing more for man to do. Nothing more man can do. Only Christ is sufficient.

"Now back to the rest of the story concerning China," Chuck continued. "Revelation says that in this onslaught, a third of the population of the earth will be killed. Due to the six months without rain in all the earth, most people standing in the way of China's hordes will not have the strength or ability to greatly resist. What is amazing to those who do not know God personally, through His Son, is the fact that God knew exactly where the greatest mass of humanity would be at this time. Revelation clearly states that this great army would march out of the east. China is as far east as it gets. It has such an army, and nearly half of the world's population is either there or between there and Israel."

The IDEA left China and was immediately back at UN headquarters in Brussels. A. Paul Lyons and Daniel Nodaba were together before the microphones outside the assembly hall. Lyons spoke.

"Members of the press and citizens of the world: We had thought peace was secured, but there are still power hungry warlords in the East. Especially in China are those who seem to be nostalgic for the days of Genghis Khan. They seem determined to dream up excuses for destroying our steps toward peace. They will not accept the fact that peace is under *our* control.

"We, the United Nations of the world, have been trying in vain to bring China to negotiations, where we might reason together. They keep refusing our attempts at a peaceful settlement. The General Assembly, at the request of the western countries, has voted a condemnation of China for its obvious threat of military assault. China has responded thus far with belligerence and defiance.

"Speaking for the UN, I am now suggesting that all nations mobilize their forces and have them in position to counter China's action. If China does not relent and still goes through with its threats, we must be ready to put an end to this aggression."

The IDEA closed the sensors and was off again. In just a moment's time, it had landed in a mountainous area in North America. Sheriff Morgan said it reminded him of the Tetons or the northern Rockies, but said there were a few places in Canada that he thought were similar as well.

The IDEA was on a slight ridge overlooking a small rustic little community. There seemed to be 40 or 50 people there, counting men, women, and children. All told, there were 10-15 households. There were large, low built storage buildings that were set into the sides of the hills. It looked to Hank as if anything dug back into the mountain was dug just beneath very thick rock ledges. The rest of the buildings were blended into the forest by being strategically placed under the trees and covered by their canopy so that they would not be seen from overhead.

Also hidden in that similar fashion were many tanks holding fuel or water. A few lines coming out of the ground implied there were more tanks that were buried. The only indications of civilization that could be noticed were a few garden plots scattered through the woods in various clearings. Even though they tried not to use obvious row planting in order to avoid detection from the air, these still didn't look entirely natural.

Children were involved in various activities commensurate with their ages. For the most part, everything just seemed calm and peaceful. Life was definitely laid-back, and the people enjoyed a settled routine.

There was one road, barely passable, leading to the village and beyond. It was really only a firebreak running along a ridge. Suddenly two large explosions shattered the calm. Children started screaming in fright, and the adults rushed outside, each one looking for their own children.

The blasts tore two gaping chasms into the roadway—one on either side of the camp. The firebreak would no longer serve as a road or means of escape. The rest of the terrain was so rugged, any attempt to flee was useless. The roar of choppers could be heard below the ridge and also at the backside of the camp. The two at the ridgeline came quickly into view and set down in the middle of the village. The Black Forces were here in strength. Ten troops with automatic weapons piled out of each chopper, while the pilots stayed in the plane with engines running.

As the troops from the chopper behind the camp emerged from the woods, the commander of this cadre spoke in a loud voice.

"Everyone, show yourselves immediately. I want the one in charge in front of me, without delay. Is that understood?"

"Yes, sir," answered a tall slender man in his 50s. "We understand quite well. We are all here except for …"

Just then, two young men in their 20s emerged from one of the storage buildings. One was holding a rifle.

"Correction, sir," continued the speaker, "we're all here now."

"Drop that weapon, now!" shouted the Black Forces commander.

The young man, obviously shaken, looked in all directions quickly. He just let go of the rifle, and it fell at his feet.

"Now, get over here with the rest," barked the commander. He turned and addressed the first man. "What's going on here? Why are any of you at this place? And why does this fellow carry a rifle?"

"My name is Frank Harkness," he answered. "This is my property, and I live here. I have for years. I own about 500 acres of timberland. The rest are my friends whom I asked to join me. After all the disasters, they needed a place to live, and I had plenty of room. As for the rifle, these young men were going hunting. I thought they were already gone."

"So you admit to trespassing and poaching then?" asked the commander.

"Not on your life," responded Frank Harkness. "This is my land and my game. I stocked these woods with turkeys and a small lake with bass and trout. My place is full of deer, elk, rabbits, and the like. I take care of their habitat, and they provide me with the food we need."

"I'm sure you're aware," said the commander, "that there is a new worldwide system and order. The UN is the official owner of everything. Something is yours to use only if the UN formally says so. Until then, you are trespassers and poachers. Now if you have the proper papers authorizing your presence here, show them to me."

"What do you mean? I don't have..."

"Come on, Frank, give it up. You know very well what's happened, and you're great at trying to get around it." It was Frank's friend and supplier, George Syngh.

"George, what are you doing in that Black Forces outfit?" asked Frank. "I thought you were my friend."

"That was just an undercover scam, Frank. I've been a member of the Black Forces for over 15 years. How else are we going to round up you well prepared hold-outs? Personally, survivalists give me fits."

"Well, we're not what you would normally call real survivalists, and we're not paramilitary. We're just peaceful people of conscience," said Frank.

"People of what?" roared the commander. "Step up here and show me your mark, or if you prefer, your ID implant."

"We don't have any marks or implants here."

"So you are black market as well, then," said the commander. "We'll change that right now." He turned to George, "Lieutenant, have your men bring the kit. These folks can be put in the system right here. Then they won't have to hunt so much."

George motioned for the men to carry out the order. Frank spoke again. "I believe you'll find that unneeded, sir. The last I checked, everyone here was in agreement that no such mark would be accepted."

"On what grounds?" roared the commander.

"On the grounds of knowledge, conscience, and a greater long term hope," answered Frank.

"I don't follow you."

"On knowledge—that this whole system is in place because of who we call the antichrist, meaning A. Paul Lyons and his false prophet Daniel Nodaba."

The commander was furious and tried to stop him from speaking, but Frank continued. "You wanted an answer, then hear it," he demanded.

"All right. You have five minutes to make an explanation," sneered the commander.

"We here knew trouble was coming back before the computer problems. We were not, though, paying any attention to Christ or His Church, or the Gospel. When the devout Christians were suddenly taken off the earth in what we call the rapture, we were left behind like other non-believers.

"We all lost someone from family or friends in that sudden event. We knew enough to seek out what happened. Then we learned from the Bible to watch out for the very things that are going on now. We believe that to accept the mark or implant is sure damnation. Since we were left behind, we may not get much help at this time. If we *choose* to follow Jesus the Christ, who is truly God and Messiah, possibly we can prove our faith in Him."

The commander started to roar, "What blasphemy! Si..." and was cut off by Frank's curt, "Cut it, commander. Five minutes, remember?"

When the commander reluctantly fell silent, Frank continued, "We resist on the grounds of conscience because we know Christ and who He is, we not only dare not, we *cannot* relent. We depend on a greater long term hope because we know this devil who is pretending to be god is doomed, but for us to be forever with the Lord is a wonderful prospect."

"We'll see about that," growled the commander. He pointed to a young family and motioned for them to step forward. Then he demanded of the father, "Step up here and hold out your hand."

The man refused to do so. Then the commander grabbed his son and pulled him to the table. He then demanded, "Hold out your hand."

The lad jammed his hands in his pockets and shouted, "No, I won't!"

"Okay, Dad," yelled the commander, "Tell him to do it right now."

The boy's father answered, "I will never tell him that."

"Have it your way, mister," said the commander who nodded to one of the troops. The soldier stepped up behind the boy and shot him at the base of the skull. The boy fell forward dead. His mother let out a small scream and sagged to her knees sobbing.

The commander asked her if she was ready to accept the implant. "Never," she sobbed. At that point the same soldier shot her as well. The commander looked at the young husband and father and asked, "Now?"

The young man said, "If we accept it, we will surely die. So you see, we have nothing to lose. By joining Christ in His death, we shall join Him in His resurrection and future glory." With that he set his jaw, looked the commander in the eye and shook his head no. The commander shot him in one knee.

"Now?" the commander asked.

The young father writhed in pain but again shook his head no. The commander screamed, "Why?" and shot him between the eyes.

This scene continued in a similar pattern, family by family, until the only one left standing was Frank Harkness. He had just watched all his friends and his wife be executed, staying true to their commitment. He asked George, "How can you do this after pretending to be such a friend?"

"That's easy," answered George with a mocking tone. "I just kept selling you everything I could 'til I figured we had about all your cashable assets. When we finish here, we'll take back all this stuff you won't need now and sell it to the next camp leader. That's why you got such good deals. We've done this many times over. All you 'Goody-Goodies' are easy touches." He then started laughing and jeering.

"Before you kill me then," Frank began to prophesy, "I have some information for you. 'Be not deceived, God is not mocked.' Only one third of you will leave here alive. The other two thirds of your forces will perish within the hour. The rest will be spared so they can spread the word. Your doom is assured."

With that, George flew into a rage. He nearly cut Frank in two with automatic fire and even hit one of his own men with stray ammo. But he got even with Frank, or so he thought.

The Black Forces left three men to guard the compound until transports could arrive to load up the supplies. The rest then boarded their choppers and lifted off. The two choppers at the front of the compound flew out over a small valley in formation to await the third chopper.

Just as the third chopper came around the point, the action started. Mikey jumped up and hollered, "Look, there they are again!"

"You're right, boy," chimed in Doc Payne. "Hang on to your hats!"

Coming up out of the trees were two spinning columns of light; one to the left of the commander's chopper, and one to the right of the chopper carrying George. They moved in fast and shoved the two choppers against each other, and they became one giant fireball in mid air.

The two columns then moved together toward the third chopper. It turned and peeled off, and tore out of the area at top speed. The two columns chased them a couple of miles, then disappeared.

The IDEA sounded the alarm and began the next journey through the light tunnel.

CHAPTER 35
The Earth Fries

Mike was upset. "Now that whole thing is unfair! Why didn't those angels help those people before they were killed? And...and ... ," he was choking up. "That George guy said they'd been doing a lot of the same thing. They're just butchers!"

Ruth and Hilga rushed to him and wrapped their arms around the lad. "This isn't something that a 12 year old should have to see, especially when it's not just a piece of fiction," said Hilga.

"Yes, I agree...to a point," said Steve. "On the other hand, we know that the end result is that the people who're martyred for their faith are with the Lord, and that is a wonderful prospect. Of course, it would have been better for them if they had turned to Christ for salvation before all these terrible things began, before the rapture."

"There's even more to it than that," said Chuck. "Those angels *could not* help those people without destroying them. All they could do was avenge the evil and let some escape so it would be known what happened. It could also be that this was purposely put on the log to help us all gain some understanding. Let me try to explain.

"Before the rapture, the Holy Spirit of God was at work in the world. He dwelt in the true Church, within honest believers. So the Body of believers and followers of the Lord now comprised His earthly Body. His Body, therefore, was able to fill the whole earth. His Body was the force that held all that was evil at bay and made it possible for more to be saved, and thus increase itself. It also kept humanity from destroying itself and the earth with it. When the fullness of time was completed, changes took place. Parts of the church, that were not truly part of Him, began to rebel. Thus judgment began in the house of the Lord.

"As time progressed, when the apostasy within and evil enemies without were joining forces, God said, 'Enough!' and called His Church away in the rapture. With that happening, the Holy Spirit was removed. Until then, the Spirit had stirred men's hearts to awaken and turn them to the Lord. But once the Spirit left, men *only have* their free will to choose, to give them any power to face the extortion of their soul's worst enemy.

They have only one way now to prove their choice. That way is to defy Satan and to accept nothing given or demanded by him and his agents. Most of the time that means resisting unto death. To deny them that proof of devotion might deprive them of new life.

"Look at the alternative. If they chose to die rather than live in slavery, what have they lost but a short time of slavery? Is that much of an alternative? Their only hope was to trust that the Lord would raise them up. After all, many martyrs have been killed. Sometimes the Lord intervened; sometimes He didn't. But, you can be sure He turned it all to good in the long run. If we are this close to the culmination of all evil, He just spared them from going through all that. Mikey, God is just.

"There's one exception to what I just said, Mikey," continued Chuck. "That is this. Remember the two witnesses and the 144,000 evangelists who were sealed by the Holy Spirit because they were needed to go through the whole tribulation? Their function is to tell the world what happened, and that Jesus Christ is God. It's their job to win as many as possible to the Lord during all of this. Because of their work, most of the nation of Israel will become followers of Jesus, or Yeshua in Hebrew, and thus claim their Messiah. You can be sure the mass of the 144,000 will be protected so nothing can harm them. But you see, they were already followers of Christ. He just covered them so they could survive the horrors to come. Any others who were left behind at the rapture were unbelievers, non-hearers, or false pretenders at that time. It is up to God's justice, tempered by His grace, that gives any of these a later chance. He is true and just.

"One last thing may further help your understanding. These verses— John 3:16,17—capsulize the Gospel:

For God so loved the world, that He gave His only begotten Son, that whosoever believeth in Him should not perish, but have everlasting life. For God sent not His Son into the world to condemn the world; but that the world through Him might be saved.

"This means that God does not *send* anyone to hell and damnation because they are all headed there under their own steam, with no escape. What God did was to provide a way for His holiness and justice to be satisfied and to freely give any men, who would accept it, a way of escape and a chance to live in unimaginable fulfillment. If anyone is lost, it is because he believed the lies of Satan's world and chose to reject God and His gift. So you see, God provided a payment for His justice, because He loved us so much. Then when men still despise Him and reject Him, His love also allows them to make that choice. The damnation that results is only the natural extension and result of an unloving way of life. This is otherwise called selfish pride. Its end result is total destruction, because its whole principle of existence is destructive in essence. Let's face it, if a man rejects God after having been given God's gift of life on earth, he would not be happy in a loving and selfless heaven anyway. The proof is found in Satan who, as Lucifer, had everything but was too selfishly proud to appreciate it. So he rebelled. God's love won't let that happen again.

"I only ask any of you who have not yet accepted God's gift to do so before it's too late for you. Think about it, folks."

Wanting to give the people time to digest what he said, Chuck concluded, "I think that should cover it, Hank, let's get to the end of this story."

Dr. Cooper nodded and hit the button, and immediately the pictures reappeared. The IDEA was staying in a flight mode this time. The position was high above the south China Sea. The assault was just beginning.

China had learned much from watching the tactics of the U.S. in Iraq and 1991's Desert Storm campaign. Ships and barges carrying medium range missiles had skirted south of Vietnam and Thailand. They fired most of their missiles at known military installations in Thailand, Cambodia, Laos, and larger ones in South Vietnam. The land-based, truck launched missiles left the southwest coast of China, and flying low, concentrated on Saigon and Hanoi in Vietnam. The heavy air and supply bases in the south and the mass of Vietnam's army, poised at the border in the north, were the major targets. Small nuclear warheads were used in the south. In the north, heavy explosives were interspersed with chemical weapons.

This barrage lasted for 36 hours and then was followed by China's typically massive wave upon wave of soldiers. Everyone was dressed for chemical contamination. Tanks led the way, followed closely by long range artillery, and then truckloads of soldiers as far as the eye could see. Regiments took turns leapfrogging each other. One would be on the ground in "search and destroy" mode, while the others rode and rested. After several hours, another regiment would take over on foot while the old crew rested in the trucks. If ever they met heavy resistance, their reinforcements were right at hand. Cavalry was used to run down any fleeing opposition. No prisoners were being taken. In a matter of four days, they had covered the total Indonesian peninsula.

They regrouped and filled their empty trucks with supplies and fuel they seized from their victim countries. A large part of the expense of this war was covered by looting each country they conquered. As the last of the army left an area, all of the usable water was taken as well. Then biological poisons and diseases were planted in all water sources left. Once this was done, they left and moved west.

At this point, the IDEA pulled away and came to rest again in Jerusalem. A. Paul Lyons was broadcasting his latest tirade. This time he sounded as though he were on the edge of panic. He demanded that the nations he had urged to mobilize begin now to counterattack the Chinese. "If they do go ahead and attack India, it is certain they mean to cover the earth. They must be stopped *now*! Bring your ships and your planes and stop them where they are. Your future depends on it."

The IDEA moved again and hovered almost directly above what looked like it could have been Mount Everest. It zoomed in on the areas to the east and west of the mountain. A huge rift had opened up sometime during all of the massive disasters. It was as if the sub-continent of India had already begun to move away from Asia. The fault line was massive and clearly seen. A large part of the mountain had fallen into the chasm acting as a giant wedge, pushing the sides farther apart. It seemed apparent that this was causing continuous tremors in the region. All the small countries of the Himalayas showed total devastation. Also hard hit were India, Bangladesh, and Pakistan.

Flying over these countries, the IDEA confirmed their suspicions and showed them that some of the earthquakes had been heavy enough that a large part of the infrastructure of these countries was destroyed, leaving them unable to accomplish much repair. It looked as though the only thing that would slow up the Chinese would be the need to rebuild the torn up roads and bridges as they progressed.

Chuck commented, "From his speech, you can tell that A. Paul Lyons' hope is that all of earth's armies and navies would arrive in time to engage the Chinese right where they were and prevent them from moving forward."

Sheriff Morgan replied, "If Lyons was serious, this would be the perfect time to nuke the whole Chinese army, but I don't see anything like that happening yet."

Suddenly two plumes rose from outside one of India's military bases. They soared in a trajectory going straight for the front line Chinese troops, one toward north Thailand and the other toward Bangkok. Within moments, the fireball and resultant mushroom cloud proved that the missiles were nuclear, and Bangkok had been hit. There were only two problems: Very few of the heavily armed armies were near Bangkok, and, for some reason, warhead number two did not detonate. They saw a few casualties and some radiation leakage where the second warhead had hit the ground in some heavily forested terrain. Chinese troops thinned out near that point until heavy choppers found the crater. They carried in dozens of heavy tanks of concrete and covered the crater with cement. They hastily built forms 20 feet wider than the crater in all directions and 10 feet high. By the time they were finished, this warhead was covered by a large concrete mass—enough to protect the oncoming troops.

The IDEA focused its cameras to record the first missile barrages in India. High population centers and military installations were again the first targets of the Chinese all along the east to southeast side of the sub-continent of India. They used the same tactics they had used from Vietnam to Thailand. They were utterly without mercy; it was pure slaughter. The only thing they did not bother with was any attempt to move northward to the mountain kingdoms.

It took the Chinese a couple of weeks on the log's clock to transverse Bangladesh and India. When they reached Pakistan, Afghanistan, and Iran, it was apparent that the Islamic countries considered this a real Jihad, or holy war.

"Do you see what's happening here?" Dr. Carver asked. When most of them slowly shook their heads, he said, "The biggest problem most of the Moslems have is the fact that they carry the mark or implant. They had no problem easily rejecting Christ. Only later did they find out that Lyons expected to be worshiped, along with his image, as the god of Israel. Now they stand between the Chinese—whom they had considered as devils—and the true devil. How can they win this Jihad? Yet facing annihilation, you know they're going to try. It's rather ironic, but the Chinese hordes will soon face the missiles they had originally made and sold to these same countries during the previous decade or two."

The IDEA moved quickly to three separate air bases where the scenes were identical. In each case, a shadowy skulking personage would emerge from an official looking building with an attaché case in hand. They wore flowing cloaks, large brimmed hats, and dark, large sunglasses. They boarded luxurious business jets and flew off with an escort of two fighters. One left the Vatican and went west. One from Jerusalem went south. The third one left from an outpost by the large open pit and flew to the north.

The IDEA took up a new position near the opening of the pit, which had been caused by an asteroid hitting the earth. The watchers saw the utter desolation that had once been Iraq. Much of western Afghanistan and Iran were in somewhat similar condition, as was southeastern Turkey. The mountains of Ararat to the north and east, however, were naturally so rocky and desolate that it was hard to tell much difference.

Signs of world resistance to the Chinese were showing up now. Naval forces were the first ones on the scene, coming from the Indian ocean, the

Arabian Sea, the Persian Gulf, and the Mediterranean Sea. It looked like whatever was left of naval power from every country on earth had gathered in one place. Most of the ships carried troops and heavy armament, tanks, artillery, and many trucks with missiles of all sorts. There were launchers for surface to air missiles as well.

When the battles began, it seemed to be a standoff for some time. The three Islamic countries on one hand and China, their enemy, on the other, had almost identical weapons. The power of numbers, though, was on the side of China. Once the Islamic allies were overcome, the next barriers to cross on their westward trek were the Tigris and Euphrates Rivers.

There was one major surprise, though, and it was just beginning. The sun looked as though it were growing or exploding. Looking closer, they saw that it was a massive solar flare, much larger than any in recorded history. Many of the worst solar storms of the last century had played havoc with radio transmissions. When satellites became a major link in communications, they had all manner of protective apparatus and backup systems installed, hoping to survive solar power surges. But those surges were nothing to compare with this one. When the IDEA trained its sensors on one flare, it seemed it would reach all the way to the moon and consume it. The sky was covered in flames as the light began to filter through all the debris in the air.

Even with the heavy overcast of dust and radiation fallout that still remained in the atmosphere, nuclear winter now dissipated into a sauna-like searing heat. After many days, the massive flare was drawn back toward the sun to rejoin the rest of the storms, but not before most of the satellites were fried. Some had even exploded. The IDEA picked up transmission of some shortwave bands from a few sources that survived. It was apparent that the earth was now an evil, bitter place where the only reference to God was to curse Him. A few confused souls even remembered Lyons claim to be deity and blamed him as well.

The IDEA refocused on the headwater areas of the Tigris and Euphrates Rivers and located at their mouth near the asteroid pit. The battle now being waged contained several nuclear exchanges. One or more of China's warheads had mistargeted and landed near the pit. A massive earthquake resulted in the collapse of a large portion of the mountains on either side of the canyon. Any water from this area was dammed up and could not move south. If it would ever build up to one half the height of the barrier, it would spill into the bottomless pit first. The solar flare made short work of drying up not only the rivers but also the low lying swamplands of southern Iraq as well. Nothing stood between Jerusalem and the eastern hordes now but the armies of the world. Those armies moved in from all directions and set up massive defenses over the one major valley that would amount to drawing a line in the sand in the valley of Jehoshaphat known as Armageddon. This valley and its surrounding ridges were just to the north and east of Jerusalem. Syria, Jordan, and Saudi Arabia were now in the crossfire, unless air defenses could slow China.

CHAPTER 36
When Frogs Did Fly for Armageddon

Again it was time to stop for awhile. Everyone was spent emotionally. Hank needed some time to copy more of the log. He felt it was urgent to get as much hidden in the vault as possible since he expected that more uninvited visitors would soon show up. Hank knew now that the Lord would protect everything, but it also made sense to him to use his head and follow common sense procedures as well.

"Let's all rest and freshen up a bit," he said. "When we get back together, maybe Chuck can tell us what those three guys in comic book get-ups were all about."

About an hour and a half later, everyone had gathered back in front of the monitor. Meanwhile, the sheriff had checked in with his men on duty in and around Willow Springs and found that everything was still quiet.

Hank turned the discussion over to Dr. Carver. "I think we probably know what's coming very soon now on the log. I was somewhat taken aback by that solar flare, because it was one of those details I tended to pass over. The context of that event and the three strange characters are consistent with John's Revelation. Also the damming up of the rivers is dealt with there as well. Before the final Armageddon itself, these events all take place. The stopping of the rivers was a task given to four angels, according to John. We saw mistargeted missiles on the log. I'll just surmise that they were pushed off course for that purpose. Then men would think that they did it themselves.

"As for the cartoon styled characters, as Hank put it, they're mentioned, too. Revelation 16:13,14 says three evil spirits came from the mouths of the Dragon, that is Satan, and the antichrist, who is Lyons, and the False Prophet, or Nodaba. John described them as being like frogs. I believe this to be an allegory for something despicable. That might account for their secretive clothing and actions, especially if they really are somewhat ugly in form. It also says they were sent to all the nations to stir them to evil action. I believe they insisted that all the militaries were to come as bidden by A. Paul Lyons. Verse 14b says 'to gather them to the battle of that Great Day of God Almighty.' It is my guess that battle is what we'll see next, or very soon. And this won't be Hollywood. This will be real.

"May I bore you," continued Chuck, "with one last musing that has been going through my mind? I've mentioned before how some scholars pay much attention to numbers, although I have been leery of anything that looks like code. To these men, the number *five* carries much weight. *Ten* is considered to be the completion of a matter. When it is divided by *two* the number of God's people—Israel and the Church—it gives us *five,* the number for the Gospel or God's grace. Remembering the last century and how we believe the Four Horsemen have already ridden and continue to do so, we see *five* great wars. These are more terrible than anything before. They make Alexander, the Romans, Genghis Kahn, etc., seem to be babes in pre-school. There was W.W.I, then W.W.II, and W.W.III, which we thought was quite devastating even though we called it the Cold War. During that war, the worst of modern day weapons was developed. Then when Russia tried for Israel and set off the nuclear holocaust, number *four* was experienced. This move by China that will end at Armageddon is number *five.* Isn't it a little interesting that this is the one that Revelation says will be ended by Christ, when He brings redemption to earth with finality? The Pentateuch was five books. These same people claim to show the Bible as being a string of Pentateuchs, repeating over and over the Gospel message. It just made me wonder about the pattern here.

"Scholars have also shown a possible way that there were only *three* great wars in the last 100 years. W.W.III would be the Cold War and include all of the smaller wars during that time. Also included would be Russia's attack on the U.S. and Israel, as well as Armageddon. All of these could be but escalating battles in one continuous war at the end. Men kept crying, 'Peace, peace,' when there was no peace. They were only regrouping for the next battle. Now with this grouping, we find the number *three* where God in His perfection wins. We do know God to be orderly in everything. Whatever the truth is in this regard, we do know with certainty that the real message is: 'Look up, for your redemption draweth nigh.' Hallelujah!"

It was all Hilga could do to hold her peace. She lifted up her hands as a praise offering at the same time Hank reached over to restart the log.

The Chinese troops were still pounding away. Pakistan was under control, or nearly so. Many of those forces had retreated into Afghanistan and Iran, making those armies a bit tougher. In the meantime, China had taken on the few naval forces in the Persian and Arabian Gulfs. They used their troops as though each man was totally expendable. The waters along those coasts turned red with the blood of men. They effectively neutralized those naval forces with commando action.

As the front kept moving westward across Afghanistan and Iran, Saudi Arabia seemed to pull back to let them pass by.

"I think I know why that just happened," remarked Steve. "They knew the real target was Jerusalem. They had mixed loyalties and feelings themselves. Israel had been their enemy for millennia, yet the man they pledged to follow was now saying Israel was his protectorate. Why then shouldn't they let China pass by without an overt challenge? Also, Arabia could then be in a flanking position if they had to support Lyons."

Huge masses of coordinated Allies poured from the Mediterranean Sea and through Turkey. They moved across Syria, Lebanon, Jordan, and Israel. The stage was set for them all to "meet China at the pass."

"Look at the Allies covering the foothill ridges surrounding this huge valley," Steve explained. "I'll bet their hope is to lure China's hordes into the valley, and in essence, set up their own turkey shoot. They know China has chemical, biological, and nuclear capabilities, but several of the Allies have one or more of the same. Now look, the U.S. is unmasking its pulse laser or death ray, similar to the one on the satellite used by Nodaba."

The IDEA flew close enough to the English troops to hear their leaders talking. "Men, we have to hand it to France. They've finally perfected their infra-sound ray that uses extremely low frequency sound waves. These are too low to be detected by the human ear, but so tightly focused they can turn the insides of a mammal to mush in just a moment's time. Five to 10 seconds in the path of that beam would be fatal. The body would literally shake itself into a puree. As with microwaves, an extended period of time and the flesh would cook from the friction. Let's hope that's all we'll need to win this lousy battle and get home."

Even though many in the Chinese army had died already, there were as many more standing ready to do them battle. So about two hundred million men would be fighting in the valley called Armageddon.

The IDEA was picking up and recording audio messages. It was apparent that many of the communication and ground control satellites were again functioning. Those listening could hear the battle plans being made and the position of various units documented. Air strikes were being attempted against the Chinese positions. The Chinese had far better defenses than anyone would have guessed. The SAM missiles they employed destroyed many planes. The pilots were forced to change their tactics to flying around and behind the Chinese, doing as much damage to the supply units as possible. This had the effect of driving the Chinese forward, toward their own desired goal, Jerusalem.

Chuck spoke up during this scene. "Look at their faces. They are so full of themselves. They have rolled across nations and the largest of continents and still have most of their massive forces. They think they're really about to conquer the world. They don't know they're being guided into the corral of the slaughterhouse and they will be mere grapes in the wine press."

The only response was the nodding of 20-some heads, and Hilga quietly humming the first phrase or two of the "Battle Hymn of the Republic."

Only moments later, the monitor showed the Chinese front lines and point contingents beginning to move into the Valley of Jehoshaphat, or Har Magedon. Chuck shared from Joel 3:14, "Multitudes, multitudes in the valley of decision," and from Revelation 14:15, "Put in your sickle for the harvest of the earth is ripe." Then he began to weep profusely, 'til most of the rest were joining him. Those who were people after God's own heart could not help but feel the God's pain over so many that would not be saved. Such tragedy was beyond expression, except for their wordless moans and groans. Chuck continued, "The remnant is safe, but swift and just wrath must now fall. Not only on this mass of evil armies, but on the whole earth."

Most of China's army had now found its way into the valley. It was a perfect place to group for a siege. Jerusalem was just over the mountains to the southwest. They quickly set up security units to hold the roads leading through the passes to the southwest. Next were tanks seemingly without number. Lighter artillery was pulled up the inner side of the ridges. They seemed to have no awareness of the armies surrounding them on the outer sides of the same ridges. Infantry and cavalry followed close to the tanks. Rockets were near, but back a short distance from the southwest ridges. It looked as though everything was ready for one final push to Jerusalem.

Suddenly all sorts of missiles, artillery, and mortar shells were landing along that same ridge, coming from behind the Chinese. The sources were just over the ridges north and east of the valley. Aircraft were flying from the north and west, cutting off any supply troops still outside the valley. Confusion reigned for several minutes while the problem was assessed. China's commanders were convinced the enemy was behind them, so they began to turn their heavy armaments in that direction, while the infantry and cavalry simply tried to find any possible cover. Death was in the air.

As soon as the turn was completed, the same sort of attack came from the south and west, and Israeli aircraft started bombing and strafing runs down through the middle of a very confused Chinese army. Tanks and artillery were hit with heat-seeking missiles. Chaos ruled and then darkness covered the battlefield. At first everyone thought it was the smoke from the battle that had turned things so dark.

Mike said, "Something's blocking the sun. I can't believe they wouldn't know a solar eclipse was coming. It's got to be something else."

At first the fighting just stopped. All eyes were on the strange sight. Satellite reports showed this object casting a shadow over the entire earth. In moments, everyone on the daylight side of earth was watching. They became afraid that another planet was about to collide with the earth, and panic began.

As the earth turned on its axis and this object moved with it, a corona could be seen along the edge of the object. It was not a planet. It was a giant pyramid with an astounding golden glow about it. A light brighter than the sun now shone from atop this golden mountain.

"It is so awesome to once again see the 'Mountain of the Lord,' the 'Holy City,' 'The New Jerusalem,'" said Steve. "Heaven is standing ready to reclaim earth. Only the redeemed saw it the first time in the rapture. Now everyone in the world can see it."

The earth was now brighter again, not so much from the sun, but from the light atop this wonderful mountain. All of the armies stood and watched. It was as if a moment of silence had captured the universe. It lasted a good half hour.

Mike blurted out "Why is nothing happening? They just stand there."

"It'll happen soon enough, Mike," said Chuck Carver. "I think the Lord is waiting to let men prove how evil they are. They do know who He is, or they're afraid they know."

About this time, the IDEA picked up a sound that sounded like many voices at once. It was a simulcast on every radio and TV channel in the world. It was the voice of A. Paul Lyons screaming his remarks to the world. "How many times have I told you? We are not each other's enemies. There is the enemy. That enemy is not of this earth—it is alien. I am your god and your guide to a life of peace. You have worried for years about alien beings attacking earth. Well, there they are. You have your weapons with you. That much is good. Now fight for your lives, and the survival of earth. Join each other and win this father of all battles. This *&%@#!…" at this point he cut loose with all the vulgar blasphemies he could muster. He was arrogantly daring the Lord to act.

Suddenly, it was as if he were cut off the air. Another voice proclaimed: "People of Israel, hear me now. A. Paul Lyons has told you only one thing that is true. What you see is not of this world. Now hear the truth! This world is one belonging to your God Yahweh, Jehovah; it is Yeshua Hamashiach! Lyons is false. Yeshua is your redemption. Do not fight Him! Run to Him at your earliest opportunity. THE GREAT DAY OF THE LORD IS COME. Hallelujah!"

Lyons' voice was back and he screamed, "Kill that squealing pig. Let the battle begin." There was a burst of gunfire and then a moment of silence.

Then with only one word on his lips, Lyons' voice was heard again. "FIGHT! FIGHT! Fiiiight!"

By this time, the golden hued mountain was near enough that several of the armies believed it to be in range of their weapons. They fired their longest ranged missiles as a first barrage. All the armies in the valley now joined to help each other, all except Israel. Instead, Israel fired several nuclear warheads right into the valley. Yet even those fireballs seemed dim next to the blinding light moving toward them from above.

All of the long range missiles shot at the holy city only got about a third of the way, and then, as if hitting a barrier, they exploded in space. The light moved from the top of the mountain at very rapid but deliberate speed and headed straight for Jerusalem. The sight was not unlike that of a comet. Following after the light was a stream of shining, shimmering particles that came out of the golden pyramid like a comet's tail or a never-ending train. As they got closer, it was obvious that these particles were actually people—human beings, so gleaming white it was difficult to see them clearly. All around them were more dazzling beings that were not quite so bright, but fearsome in form. Some had wings like eagles, but most were like those seen on the monitor before—spinning columns of light capable of throwing lightening bolts. Occasionally they seemed to have hands and feet, but mostly they were just spinning light. Their very presence threatened the armies of the world.

As this band of heavenly hosts entered the atmosphere, the beings who were obviously angels fanned out across the skies and surrounded the entire earth. Everywhere they went, huge storm clouds grew to the stratosphere. Over the valley of Armageddon, the most massive storm imaginable formed. Again it was as if the angels were guiding the storm right over the valley and many miles beyond. About the only place not covered by the clouds was Jerusalem.

As Christ, "the Light," the Bright and Morning Star, entered the atmosphere, everything moved before Him. His form was not only too bright to behold, it was also gigantic at first. All channels, transmitted from satellites, told the story so that all the earth was able to see the Son of Man descend from the skies with clouds beneath His feet. The pictures on the log showed scenes of panic from everywhere on earth. Either the IDEA was acting nearly omnipresent with its time and space capability, or God Himself was putting the images on the log for their benefit. At any rate, everyone who saw Him was either terrified or eagerly worshiping their Savior.

As to His size when they first saw Him, the titans of Greek mythology would be as tiny gum machine toys. He stayed for a while in the air above the surrounding mountains. He could look directly at the valley full of armies below him. The soldiers who looked straight into His eyes did not survive. When their eyes met His, they would melt in their sockets, and then the rest of the man would melt as well. Soon the call went out—"Don't look at Him." That was hard to do and still aim a weapon. Men were dropping and melting where they had been standing. They were like moths drawn to the flame only to be burned.

Missiles and artillery were all used to no avail. Either they just blew up prematurely or were knocked down or caught by the Lord's hands. When He spoke, it was as if lightening were a controlled and accurate weapon. The storms grew to monstrous proportions and lightening strikes were close enough together to be as beads on a pair of moccasins. Then hail as big as 100 pound blocks of ice hit the earth and its people all around the globe.

The Lord then set a foot on the Mount of Olives. At that instant, massive earthquakes worldwide began to rumble. Continental plates shifted and moved away from each other. Mountains that had been pushed to extreme altitudes by continental collisions and pressure now were allowed to drop into the chasms left behind.

The first rift or chasm to open was directly under the Lord's foot. The Mount of Olives split in two, and the rift ran westward to the sea. When the people of Jerusalem saw a major part of the city was collapsing, they ran directly into the rift and under the foot of the Lord. There they found safety, and none were lost. That place remained stable, and no bombs or other weapons could touch them.

The pulse lasers and sound beam lasers began firing at this giant being and the gleaming chorus of the redeemed around Him, but to no avail. The songs of praise rising from them were so powerful as to deflect everything. They just could not be touched. Any such beams directed at the Lord were reflected back by His hands. The returning rays melted those using them. Blood from men and horses flowed like a river from the ridges to the lower parts of the valley. There it pooled as deep as a man's shoulders. All of the armies of the world had been totally destroyed in a moment's time. The storm lifted and the melting hailstones continued to wash down the ridges. This cleaned much of the debris of the battle from the high points and washed it into the pool below.

"You have just seen humanity follow its natural depraved nature to its logical conclusion," said Steve. "But praises to the Lord arise because He had saved Himself a remnant to whom He could give the joys of life as they were meant to be. These were born again to a new life and a new nature. They had chosen to partake of the cleansing power that was found in the blood of the Lamb of God. He gave himself as sacrifice for them. They then gave themselves to Him. God the Father adopted them and now has made them the children of God."

"That's right, Steve," said Dr. Carver. "In just one day, the proof of God's might, justice, and unbounded love was shown to all."

Now the King of Kings and Lord of Lords stepped back from the field of battle. He directed his younger children and brothers to come away to the city and out of the shelter they had found under His feet. These were those out of Israel who had claimed their Messiah and were alive and present for that terrible day. He preceded them into the city. His size was now that of the average man. His glory was again cloaked for the time being.

Whole bands of angels were now returning from around the entire earth. They were bringing with them the balance of those saved during such great tribulation and who were yet alive. As this was happening, the Lord raised His voice and cried out, "Come, now, to me, and enter into your rest, My beloved." Immediately another great earthquake shook the world, and the bodies of those killed for the name of Christ—those who refused the mark of the beast—rose to new life. They were changed like their brothers and sisters in the Lord into new bodies incorruptible. The earth and the heavens rang with the shouts and songs of praise and triumph as all came quickly to stand before the Lord they loved.

There was no sign of life left in all the armies and navies who made war with the Lamb. Yet one bit of business remained.

"Bring the pretenders before the Lord." The call rang out, and immediately four angels went to retrieve A. Paul Lyons and Daniel Nodaba. The angels' present appearance was similar to the spinning columns of light, except the colors were dark and foreboding. Shades of black and deep blue mingled with the same spinning and churning motion. They moved in pairs, looking like hunters that would bring back their man.

Very shortly, they returned with their quarry. Two of them had Lyons suspended between them. Likewise the other two brought in Nodaba. The glory streamed from the Lord to such a degree that the two men fell backwards before Him and whimpered for mercy.

One angel spoke, "You who created nothing but lies now beg for your lives from the Creator of all things. He created you in His own image, but you defiled that image and sold yourselves to the old dragon Satan for power to kill God's other creations. Do, Lord, what your justice demands."

"Leave me, workers of every evil. This will now be your home, away from my face forever." This the Lord said as He pointed toward the sea.

Immediately the heavens and atmosphere above that point writhed as a dimensional shift took place. There in the vortex a massive lake appeared that looked like magma, spitting and sputtering as it literally boiled away. The angels grabbed Lyons, the antichrist, and Nodaba, his false prophet, and soared into the air with them. As they came close to the opening of the vortex, they cast the two men into the lake. The two screamed in fear and agony as they went ever deeper into the vortex. Then as quickly as it appeared, it was gone. It was sealed shut in another dimension.

The IDEA immediately shut down its audio and video and moved again into the light tunnel. Hank thought this a good opportunity, so he hit the off button once more.

"Wow," he said, "I'm not sure how much more I can take. The memories are pouring in now. It almost killed me the first time through. I'm certainly glad it's just pictures right now. I don't know if I want Mikey to see some of the rest."

"Hey, no, Dad, please," responded Mike. "We know why we're seeing it. That's nothing like the guys who will be there for real. Anyway, I have a question. Why does Jesus look 10 times bigger than any of Hollywood's monsters? And, and…that mountain splitting all the way to the sea, just because He stepped on it. And then He…He was the size of every other man. Does that have a meaning?"

"It sure does," answered Chuck. "The way we knew for sure that Jesus was who He said He was, depended on prophecy. He fulfilled every prophecy in the Old Testament that applied to the suffering servant part of Messiah. We trusted by faith, but 100% fulfillment was absolute assurance. For that reason, then, we know He will return. All the log has done is to let us see it from the viewpoint of someone still on earth when it happens.

"As for the size, and earth splitting quakes, this was also foretold more than 400 years before Christ's birth. I believe it's found in Zechariah 14:14. It tells how the believers would run into the chasm beneath His feet and there be sheltered. As again to size, even Greek mythology considered size as some evidence of deity. That was mainly because they saw everything in human terms. Size meant power. In a way, the Lord used some of that same psychology, if you will, to bring fear and panic to those fighting Him. It's another way of saying, 'Your god is too small.' If, though, He had shown His complete fullness and glory, they would have been destroyed instantly. They would have no concept at all of His true majesty, because they wouldn't know what hit them. He wanted them to know and gave them only what they could manage to understand. After all, Mikey, His greatness surpasses the universe.

CHAPTER 37
All Things New

"Sheriff Morgan, this is Johnny, come back. Sheriff, do you read me?"

"Affirmative, Johnny, I read you clear. What's so urgent?"

"That's just it, Sheriff, I don't know if it's all that urgent. I thought it was better to tell you now instead of waiting until tomorrow when I cycle out there."

"Okay, fine, let me have it," said the sheriff.

"There seems to be a gradual build up of these guys in black vehicles and sunglasses. They try to act like they belong here, but I don't think they realize how conspicuous they really are. What bothers me is that the more the people of Willow Springs see of them, the less the Black Forces seem out of place. They're getting more people to strike up conversations with them. I think they're pumping people for information."

"How do you mean, Johnny?"

"I think it best," answered Johnny, "if I save that 'til I'm out there with you. Any ideas in the meantime?"

"Johnny," said the sheriff, "you're the guy with the info. I'll presume for now all the men on your shift know what you're thinking. But, if not, see to it they do. We all need to be working on the same page right now. Follow me?"

"Yeah, I sure do, Sheriff. I'll get back to you, or see you when I get there. Johnny out."

Hank spoke up. "Harold, you know how Johnny thinks. Do you think we're on the edge of another set-to with these guys?"

"I'm sure we are, Hank. That's what Johnny's thinking, too. The question will be more like when and in what form. You obviously know, don't you, that the man behind these goons is the worst you could ask for?"

"That's all right," chimed in Steve. "We know something he doesn't—we're not alone here."

"Well and good, Pastor," said Hank. "We have enough supplies here to hold out for several weeks if need be. But I think I better get these last copies of the log into the vault. We can continue watching after that. It can't run much longer. You folks just relax and care for your needs. I'll be back shortly."

About a half hour later, Hank returned to the viewing room. As soon as everyone got settled, he started the log once more. The light tunnel continued for a couple of minutes this time, which implied a considerable time had elapsed.

As it circled the globe over and over, the IDEA showed pictures of the land moving violently. Mountains were literally being swallowed up by great fissures in the earth. Volcanic action was everywhere. It seemed the earth was almost turning inside out. Graves were opening and the dead were being raised to their feet. Many were even coming up out of the oceans, rivers, and lakes, surprised that they were walking on the water. Some were fearful that they would sink once again. After awhile, when they saw that that didn't happen, they began to walk gingerly toward land. Some reached it quickly, but the land was convulsing so much that it was small comfort. Those far out to sea didn't know which way to go. Their panic continued.

This was eerily different from the resurrection that was part of the rapture. These walking dead had bodies, but there was no change in appearance and nothing was shining or bright. Whatever their age or condition had been at death, that was exactly their condition now. Wounds were not fully healed, and youth was not restored. Some were mostly naked, and with the others, even fine clothes were as dirty as the grave from which they came. There was no light of joy nor recognition in their eyes, only a blank, dull stare. Bodies that had been totally dismembered were restored only to the point of knitting the body together so it might function, however poorly. But they were all there, millions upon millions of those who sought their own lusts rather than their Creator's will. From the dawn of time till the end, those who rejected whatever they knew that was of God came forth. From cave dwellers to 21st century sophisticates, everyone was in the same state. There were all ages from very young adults to the most aged. The only exception seemed to be infants and most very young children. The older the people were, the more there were of them. Even here was some evidence of God's grace. A just God knew when innocence was lost.

Suddenly the earth was covered by the same sort of dark looking angels that had captured Lyons and Nodaba. They moved in teams. Hell, death, and the grave had given up all those beings held for this moment.

Dr. Carver shared, "It's written, 'It is appointed to men, once to die, and then the judgment.'"

As all were collected into one place, they saw before them a great white throne. Seated on that throne was the One who had created them and now would be their judge. His appearance alone was painful to them. They fell on their faces and cried out with fear and agony. It was as if time stood still and each one was checked to see if his or her name was found in the Book of Life. Yet, at the same time, it was as if it all happened at the same moment, as if aeons had been pressed into a few minutes.

Everyone watching the monitor agreed that the effect of time compression had the same dizzying affect on them as when they had watched the IDEA come and go at the same time. Doc thought that everything was simultaneous—that each person knew and confessed his own history, and that each one in essence could not argue, at least at length, because they were aware of their own guilt. It just couldn't all go on this log.

In the background was a wild commotion. It became almost unbelievably loud and violent, with vulgar and blasphemous words beyond imagination. Then they saw him. A considerable cadre of powerful angels had trapped between them the cause of all evil and torment that had plagued the world. They had Satan himself in chains and surrounded.

As they approached the throne with him, the Light turned away. Satan tried to reclaim Lucifer's form once more. He wanted to prove how beautiful he was, in hopes of impressing God. But each time he would try, he would slip back to his hateful evil self. Each time the end result was more hideous than before until his appearance was nearly reptilian. His metaphoric name 'the old dragon' was becoming a reality.

The Light would look nowhere near him. A voice thundered from the throne, "Away with him. The lake of fire that was made for him and his angels is ready."

The skies opened up, and the same magma-like environment was just beyond the portal. In anticipation of the agony he saw before him, Satan writhed and screamed until he was flung like a rag doll into the seething portal. Then from out of the pit suddenly came a swarm of most hideous creatures that had been entrapped there. It was as if Satan's "train" were following their beloved. But they were not going willingly. They were already screaming their anguish as a mighty angel drove them into the lake of fire to join the one they had followed for so long. A steady stream poured into the lake, much like the clouds of stinging creatures they had seen during the tribulation. Then suddenly, silence returned.

The IDEA suddenly moved as if to run alongside the dimension to the lake of fire. Its cameras found a veil through which to peer. The picture zoomed in deep within the caverns of what was much like a volcano. There was room to move about. Deep in the lowest parts was a writhing, slithering, mass that was reminiscent of worms or maggots in a rotting carcass. A closer look showed it rather to be demons clawing at each other and shoving for position. The ultimate irony was beginning to play out. Satan was no ruler here. In this place, he is the most tormented. In the same way that Pharaoh had named his own curse, so had Satan, in the blasphemous mind games he had used for millenia. The fighting was for the opportunity to pull off some of the seeming "flesh" from Satan for food and nourishment.

If ever a creature would desire to die, Satan was now such a one. But he would never die. They watched as every piece of flesh that was pulled from him would continually be replaced. He who had wished to depose God and control everything and everyone for his own pleasure now sustained all of those who had chosen his way and believed his lies. Those most like himself and closest to him now continually devoured him. These were the ones who had known God's heaven, yet believed and followed Lucifer. God, in his judgment and grace, now allowed their desires to be fulfilled forever. Their "communion," so to speak, was now forever real.

Immediately after viewing this horrid scene, the IDEA moved back before the throne and above all the mass of lost people from ages past to present. All had now been judged and stood as convicts awaiting sentence. They now acknowledged what they used to deny. Jesus, or Yeshua, or Gesu—however their language pronounced His name—He is Lord, the Christ, the Ancient of Days, Almighty God!

Steve commented, "It was He who created them, and He who did all necessary to save them. But they had denied, ignored or even hated Him and anything having to do with His holiness and purity. Now He must be their judge."

Suddenly a voice thundered from the throne. "Depart from me, you workers of iniquity. I do not know you. You have no place with me. Go to the one you desire."

Instantly the radiance of glory became so overwhelming that all to whom He spoke were in immediate agony from the blaze of it. The dark angels of death who had rounded them up now began to push them toward the portal of the lake. When they were close, the vortex suddenly widened, and they poured into it as if drops of water in a massive waterfall. The portal, still open enough to be seen, began to move away.

The IDEA quickly pulled along side for another look through the thin veil. The cameras zoomed in once more to scan a massive area both wide and deep. At whatever level life could be seen, there seemed to be one constant pattern. The gravity of each sinful life found its own level. The greater depravity, as a constant way of life, seemed to settle deeper and nearer the core. Those who were obviously open enemies of God, those of absolute rebellion, were found closer to the one they adored and openly served. There the fire was the hottest and the insanity the greatest. Yet, those who knew of God's goodness but put off or ignored a relationship with Him and those who just merrily went their "don't really care" way were at the outer edges. It was still hot, still dark, still miserable enough to induce total aloneness. It was agony enough that time and attention for anything but one's self was impossible. They were forever alone without the possibility of God and His presence anymore. They lived a personal burning, dark, solitary existence with only their own screams for company.

Another very dark portal opened and the lake of fire poured into it, trapped in this greater vortex. Whatever this new dimension was, there would be no escape, for even the light of the fire disappeared. Satan, hell, death, the grave, and all they owned were now swallowed by this voracious black hole. All was still. And victory over all that had tormented humanity was now complete and fulfilled.

The IDEA pulled away quickly, in order to avoid any proximity to that final vortex. As it did, its sensors looked in the opposite direction. The great throne and all the heavenly hosts that had stood behind it all moved rapidly to the magnificent mountain of the Lord. All light was coming from the throne, wrapping around and permeating the entire city.

Once everyone was safe in the Lord's fortress, the holy city moved up and away from the immediate area above the galaxy. The IDEA promptly followed. It seemed that the whole edge of the galaxy, in the general locale of earth's solar system, was involved in a sudden gravitational shift. The source of the pull, though, was not visible. The center was approximately between the earth and the sun. The large outer planets broke from their orbits and moved quickly toward that point. The earth was at first moving away on its normal orbital path, but it, too, turned and began moving to the center.

The sun had nearly reached the central point when a monstrous vortex opened and became visible because of the light reflected from all the space debris. As it moved in the ever tightening pattern of a funnel, it showed the size and shape of its doomsday trap. It was like watching water go down a drain in an otherwise still basin. It began to affect that entire corner of the Milky Way galaxy. The earth was drawn through the asteroid belt, colliding with wave upon wave of them. Since it was now so much closer to the sun, the earth began to burn until it split open with a mighty blast. That blast was nothing compared to the next one they saw. As the sun and the other planets drew nearer to each other and the vortex, the sun exploded like a super nova, causing the large planets to also explode. The vortex, like a celestial vacuum cleaner, swallowed the debris of about a three-billion mile diameter area of the cosmos. Then it suddenly closed up as if it had never been there.

Dr. Cooper hit the off button. He could hardly hold back his excitement. "Einstein was right," he said. "I believe we just saw the result of the fabric of the space-time continuum being ruptured. Very likely it was one of those farthest galaxies we were watching. But, in the billions of years it took for the light to reach us, it has gone on that much farther. During those billions of years, I surmise, a black hole has developed that not only ate much of that galaxy, but was able to pull away a chunk of this galaxy where we live. From the viewpoint of earth, the whole sky fell in upon it, and all was destroyed."

"You got all of that out of what we saw?" quipped Doc Payne. "Whatever happened to the idea that God is in control?"

"That doesn't affect God's part at all," answered Hank. "He set it up so it would happen that way. He then told us what to expect. Now He's shown us how."

Dr. Carver broke in. "Hank, can we finish the log now? There has to be at least one more scene."

"Right you are, Chuck." Hank turned the log back on.

It didn't take long for the next scene to develop. The holy city began to move right back to the same area where earth's solar system had been. As the city and the IDEA moved that direction, a new dimensional shift began. Rather than a vortex that destroyed, a writhing mixture of color formed. Light patterns were mixing as if a veil was being pulled back. The cosmos was giving birth again.

In what seemed but a moment, the light show ceased, and in its place appeared a new system of planets and smaller satellites. In this system was a new earth. Lush vegetation and many colored fields were in full bloom. One great difference was immediately evident. Unlike the old earth, there was no sea—no great masses of water to separate vast continents. Everything was comparatively level with no mountains of extreme altitude and no extreme crevasses of similar depth. There were just enough high and low places to give spectacular beauty and room for streams to flow. The atmosphere was rich with moisture needed by plant life. Because there was no extremely hot sun, it would not be uncomfortable.

The holy city hovered for a while over this planet. A large, somewhat barren area came into view. The New Jerusalem settled on that spot. It was a perfect fit. The capital of earth was now in place. The throne of the King of Kings was established. A beautiful light as the green of an emerald came from the top of the mountain of the Lord, permeating the atmosphere and surrounding the whole earth.

"It's as if the upper atmosphere is made up of photo-active gases that were catalyzed by the light of the Lamb," Steve commented. "He was not only the Light of the City of God—He was the Light of the World. In the old earth, He was the spiritual light and all else was darkness. In the new earth, He's *all* the Light. 'And in Him there is no darkness at all.'"

The IDEA moved in close to the city. Its walls were about 700 feet high and 600 feet thick and made of precious stones too beautiful to describe. It was larger than all the habitable land that had been on earth.

Music was everywhere. Music of praise and thanksgiving. Music of worship. Music of peacefulness. Music of grandeur. And all of it was music of joy. Gone were the harsh sounds of depravity. People by the millions were moving in all directions to fill the new earth. It was obvious that everything was organized by a supreme Power.

The IDEA again lifted and moved away. As it left this new earth, the clearest change was evident. Earth no longer reflected light from a sun—it was now a *source* of light. God was now dwelling with His children. Earth was now the home of the "Israel of God."

Suddenly the pictures and sound ceased. The light tunnel returned. When it continued for several minutes, the group in the lab realized this was probably the trip home.

CHAPTER 38
Prepare for Battle

There was an extra jolt or thump of some kind when the IDEA landed this time. The first pictures were even broken up. When they settled, all that could be seen was Hank almost clawing his way to the rim. The ladder dropped and Hank started down, but lost his footing. He bounced pretty hard on the concrete. Looking up he saw all manner of debris about to fall on him—heavy girders, sheet metal, insulation, you name it. He was about to be buried under it all. He dove under a large heavy steel table and covered his head.

Everything had come full circle, and they were back where it had all begun just a few days ago. It took Hank a while to gather his senses again. Then he began to laugh. It was so contagious, the others joined him. After a bit, Hank said, "You'd think the guy who built that thing would know where the steps were. But seriously, if that's possible now, I really don't know, at this point, how long I was gone. The things we saw happen in the cosmos should take thousands of years to be accomplished, even at the speed of nuclear explosion. The distances were just too great for those happenings, and for the IDEA to survive and maintain power.

"On the other hand, we have seen in just a few days all the thousands of years we can account for, plus all this future we could not possibly know."

Steve broke in. "Hank, the Lord never did intend for all timing to be known. Either He used His power to move things, no matter how far or fast, as His will demanded, or He has graciously run the film in fast forward or time lapse fashion, so we would have time to view it. Either way, He lets us know what we need to know. The rest is discerned by faith, which we know is His will. That is because He wants us to trust Him and His faithfulness."

"Yes, that's true, Pastor," said Hank. "There were many places when we knew things had been overlapping in their timing. The IDEA was following themes and purposeful story lines rather than strictly chronological sequences, for the most part. I've said it before, but I was only a passenger. God was obviously the pilot. Also, He was only interested in telling His story."

"Well, Hank," said Dr. Carver. "The only reason for that is so you can pass the story on. I suggest you make any last copies and get the log hidden. You will likely need that security. Mr. Lyons is not going to let you alone. In fact, we may all need to think of alternative places to go if he finds out who we all are. His people obviously know where you live. They aren't in Willow Springs for their health. There's a possibility they know most of your personal friends live there. Only time will tell."

"What if..." queried Hank, "What if I managed to get rid of the IDEA? What if there was nothing left for him to use?"

"Oh, Hon," cried Ruth, "that's your life's work."

"I know that, believe me, but this can never be allowed to fall into enemy hands. It can't go to anyone like Lyons. I was a fool to take funding so blindly. Anyway, I learned what I wanted to learn. Actually, in a strange way, I learned far more than I thought I wanted to. The paradox is I'm not sure I learned anything about time travel because I didn't really make the IDEA work. It would have taken me 100 years to learn to program that much, no matter what the topic was. I went 6000-10,000 years into the past and worked my way back, and who knows how many years, possibly thousands, into the future. And I still came back to the exact same moment when I began. I have no concept of how fast or far the IDEA took me. Either it worked and God made use of it, or He just honored the effort and gave me the experience. I tend to believe the first option when I look into the mirror and when I notice how my body feels. But, on the other hand, the seeming lost years of my longevity may not matter. This leaves me sure that some of the future we have seen is ready to happen very soon now. We may not need long life to be a part of it."

Hank had been running the fast dub copies all during the conversation and noticed it was finished. "Come on, you guys," he said to the men to whom he had given the vault's secrets. "Let's put this baby to bed."

They were gone about 30 minutes. Hank recapped how to seal and unseal the vault. During that time, Ruth and Hilga put together a good lunch so everyone could relax and think about what they had witnessed.

Lunch was just about finished when a loud squawk sounded on the sheriff's radio. "Calling Animal Control!" It was Bo's voice. The sheriff quickly switched to the secure channel.

"Go ahead, Bo, I read you."

"Sheriff, it looks like these Black Force dudes are going to try another assault. Tess at the truck stop cafe says she overheard them accusing Dr. Cooper of killing some of their people. One guy was saying he saw two of their Lincolns burned up. She was real upset to think Dr. Cooper could do such a thing. So she was asking me if it were true."

"Uh-huh. What did you tell her?"

"I just said, 'Don't be too quick to believe characters who are so strange. You never know what they're trying to stir up.' Was that all right?"

"I guess it will have to be, Bo. I don't know what else you could have said. What makes you think they plan something new?"

"Sheriff, all of us have been watching their numbers grow steadily. They now have three Lincolns, two Suburbans, and six cycles. The only thing we haven't seen is another chopper. I sent Alex over to the Schmidt's farm to see if they're hiding out there again."

"Well done, Bo. Well done! Now, do you have your men spread about the way we did before?"

"No, I've got a third of our force there. I could call the ones off duty back and have two thirds out here."

"Do it, Bo, but remember what happened last time. You probably don't need too many men in any one place. Spread them in similar fashion, just a bit thinner. Also, you might bring one or two up behind anyone using this road, so as to block any retreat. We will prepare here to be lively bait. God's speed, Bo. Morgan out."

"Hank," said the sheriff, "How many of those automatic weapons and how much ammo do you have here?"

"More than I ever thought I would need, Sheriff. There are also quite a few standard weapons, and also some bows and crossbows, throwing knives, a few grenades, and of course flares."

"Do tell. You don't happen to have a mine field, too, do you?"

"Nope, sure don't, Pilgrim."

"Hey, wait," cried the sheriff. "John Wayne is s'posed to be my gig."

"Yeah, are we serious yet?" asked Doc Payne.

"Sure are, Doc," said the sheriff. "Hank, take my guys and bring that arsenal to the room next door here. Let's see if we can get organized."

Within the hour, everything had been distributed, and the sheriff had planned where he would put each man around the rim of the crater. The plan was for Hank and the sheriff to act as if they were the total force, just like before. But they planned to stop any cars closer to the bottom, rather than let them come near the top this time. They weren't sure that talking with them would work this time. The Lyons organization, or NICE, had lost a number of men the last time. This time they probably expected to make a surprise assault upon the complex.

But Hank was glad they could anticipate what lay ahead in their next encounter with the Black Forces. The people in the complex spent a few minutes in prayer together and then went to their own stations to wait for the upcoming skirmish. Doc, Pastor Steve, Dr. Carver, Ruth, Mike, and the Schmidts stayed in the hangar, just as before.

Dr. Carver opened the channel and gave a quick reminder to Bo's posse, as well as all in the complex. "We have made ourselves as ready as we can be. We know those who will assault us are definite enemies, enemies of all we hold dear—liberty, righteousness, and even God. The Lord has proven He has an interest in this situation. All we must do is stand firm and trust Him to see to it His will is accomplished. We may fight some of the battle, or we may just get to watch again. Two words I have for you—stand and trust. Victory is assured. Carver out."

"Sheriff, this is Bo. Do you read?"

"Yes, Bo, go ahead."

"We may be about down to the last minutes of this countdown. It's strange, but they seem to be setting up the identical approach they had before. They just have more troops this time. The two Suburbans went out south Maple Street. The bikes all went west and south. The three Lincolns just left the truck stop and are about at the edge of town heading south on the highway. I've already sent two bike teams. They should be hunkered down just north of you. Sheriff, heads up. The Lincolns just started out. Nine of us will lay up behind them."

"Roger that, Bo. Hold your course, you're doin' fine. Give a yell, anyone, if you see any choppers. Morgan out."

Sheriff Morgan and Hank slipped into their vests, and slung the guns and ammo over their shoulder. They took a shortcut down the side of the berm so they could be as low as possible on the roadway. They hoped to stop the Lincolns early. They were almost to the bottom when they spotted the cars on the access road. They stashed their ammo uphill a bit and then stood there blocking the roadway.

Johnny was in command of the other third of the sheriff's troops inside the complex. He had them spaced evenly around the rim, but just low enough on the inside that they could not be seen by the Black Forces.

Once again the cars stopped, and four men in suits and dark sunglasses stepped out. They all looked for a moment at the line of brush to their right. They made sure that Hank and the sheriff knew that they could see the burned hulks of the first Lincolns. Then they walked up just in front of the two men.

"Do you feel you can destroy foundation property just because you feel like it?" asked the head man.

"Oh I never just feel like it," answered Hank. "The sign you passed warned you about what happens to trespassers."

"You obviously knew we were coming. I'm impressed. But, trespassers we are not. Neither were those men. What have you done to them?"

"We did nothing to them," said Sheriff Morgan. "They did things to themselves. We did push the cars off to the side later."

"I don't believe you. We were sent to investigate you and your work. The people who funded this project want to know the details of what is going on. They want what they've paid for. I'm here to fill their wishes."

"Sorry," said Hank, "I don't believe you. You haven't even shown us any proper identification. You're just phonies. Now, turn around and get lost. I know how to report important details without your help."

"Then let me introduce myself, Dr. Cooper. I am Alex, Alex Thorson. You are an educated man acquainted with the classics of history and mythology, no?"

"Yes, I am. Your point being?" asked Hank.

"My point, ah yes, my point is that I live up to my name in all regards. My thunder is in my hands. I can order whatever is necessary to fulfill my mission. I have no time to waste on you two, so step aside. Better yet, be a good host and show me around. We have many questions that need answers."

"Not likely. I don't really care about your name. You've shown no credentials or any such proof of your connection with NICE. You also have not shown any government clearance. As for your thunder, it is only the empty echo of lightening. Now, pack up your hyenas and leave. Don't come back. It's not safe for you here. You are in over your heads, and I'll bet you can't swim."

CHAPTER 39

Away Barbarians!

Alex Thorson raised his arms and waved a big high sign. Rifle fire from 16 troops rang out. These were the men from the Suburbans. Alex and his men raced toward their car while Hank and the sheriff took cover and tried to see who was firing. The men in the Lincolns looked back and saw three squad cars now blocking their way and nine men in swat team styled garb covering their every move. In a moment, the 16 Black Forces troops were caught from three sides by the sheriff's deputies. Some were behind them and the two bike units were on either side. The far off sound of the Black Bikers was getting louder.

"Sheriff, this is Virgil, come back."

"Yes, Virgil, I read you clear."

"Can you hear the chopper?"

"Not yet. Go on."

"Well, they weren't parked at Schmidt's this time, but they'll come from about that same direction. If they come straight in, you should see them soon. Virgil out."

"Stay alert, Hank," said the sheriff. "Let's not do any shooting here until we have to. If they try to move those cars, go for the tires and radiators."

Hank and Sheriff Morgan could see Alex's hand pointing out of the window. The three Lincolns started backing down the road in unison. It looked like they intended to ram the squad cars and push them off the road. The deputies at that end were prepared and quickly shot out the Lincolns' tires. They got all of them and then aimed at their gas tanks. The cars' wheels thumped to a halt.

Hank and the sheriff noticed that everyone was looking over their heads. They looked up, too, and gasped. Above them were four spinning columns of light that just floated in mid-air. It was as if time had stopped because no one moved. The men in black were frozen with fright.

Hank started climbing up the berm right toward them. He motioned to Harold to follow, so he did, somewhat reluctantly. When they reached the top, they saw eight more just like the first ones. The whole complex was surrounded by a heavenly host.

The sheriff's men were all standing, no longer hidden. No one who had witnessed the log was frightened. It was as if everyone knew that they needed to let the fiery angels fight the battle. The six people in the hangar came out to see as well. About that time, four of the angels moved down by the hangar. A thunder like rumble could be heard up on the rim, but no one understood anything.

There was a moment of conversation among the six. Then they all went into the hangar rooms where everyone had been bunking, came out with their arms full of personal belongings, and threw them into the Suburban that had been confiscated from the first assault. After three or four trips, the men all climbed into the Suburban, and Ruth and Mike climbed into the Cooper's car. Doc Payne used the radio and pointed to four of the deputies he could see. He instructed them to come get the other vehicles parked by the hangar and take them to the rim. Then they all drove to the top where Hank and the sheriff were.

Sheriff Morgan got on the radio and told the men outside: "Don't let anyone move."

Then he turned to Doc Payne and Chuck Carver. "What was all that roar? Did they actually say something you understood?"

"Sure did," answered Chuck. "They said: 'The battle is the Lord's. Take your belongings and all people out of this place. It will soon be gone. After seven days you may return to your secret place. After that time, you will tell this story. Perhaps a few more will open their eyes and turn to the Lord before it is too late. The soul harvest is ripe. Look up, your redemption is very near.'"

Doc pointed back down to the hangar and all eyes followed his lead. The four angels, still in the form of light columns, began moving back the camouflage and the heavy timbers that had hidden the IDEA. There it sat shimmering as it reflected their light. They then placed themselves under the rim as if they were four props or legs. Gently and slowly they lifted the IDEA from the ground and raised it a bit above the hangar.

At this point the sheriff called all the other men off of the rim. "Bring what you can, but climb to the outside and keep coming downhill. We can use you here now anyway."

During the time that took, the form of the angels began to change. The cloak of whirling light subdued to reveal winged creatures of wondrous beauty. They still had a fiery appearance, but with more substance. Highly polished brass or bronze would be close to describing their appearance. And yet, they were rather translucent like glass. Even so, one knew they were definitely living creatures and not machines. They and the IDEA were a perfect complementary set.

Each had four wings and four faces—the face of a man back to back with the face of an eagle. On the left side was the face of an ox, and on the right, the face of a lion. As they hovered there in mid-air, it was like watching a beautiful precision ballet. They had human appearance in general form except for the feet. The feet were straight down and seemed to be hoofed. The body and arms were humanoid. Only the feet, wings, and four faces were different.

One set of wings swept upward as if holding the IDEA. The wingspan was so great that the wing tip of one reached and connected with that of the next angel. Each one then reached one fourth of the way around the IDEA. It was as if the IDEA was nestled like a bowl into a rack.

The other two wings wrapped gracefully, almost demurely, around its body. The sound of their flying was like a large waterfall. When they spoke, it was as if a hundred were speaking in unison. From their hands came either instructive gestures or lightening bolts.

The multiple voice spoke, "Show now the power of the Lord."

Immediately they soared high above the rim of the complex and out over the men in the cars. Then they flew over the Black Forces troops who had been standing paralyzed since the angels had first appeared. The IDEA was not spinning. It was just along for the ride. The angels did not turn or spin. Instead they just moved together in unison, right, left, forward, or back, always facing the same direction as when they first gained altitude. They went high and low, fast and slow.

Chuck Carver started quoting Psalm 2:4,

He that sitteth in the heavens shall laugh: the Lord shall have them in derision.

Then he said, "Now I know the Lord has a sense of humor and irony. He is teasing them with this dance."

All this while the other angels, still dressed in their columns of light, stayed as they were. It was as though they were at attention until needed. For now they, too, enjoyed the dance.

Suddenly, coming up from behind the other side of the hill were two black choppers. One went immediately on the offensive. It fired a missile at the IDEA and its angel escort. The angel facing the chopper raised one hand and the missile changed course and missed wide. It blew up harmlessly a quarter-mile on the other side of IDEA. Three black cycles roared up the backside of the complex and started around the top of the rim. Then they saw the eight angels hovering there. They skidded to a stop, and then saw the IDEA riding on the backs of four angels. The cycle troops panicked and began firing. Three columns of light each picked their own target. Three lightening or laser pulses went to their marks. The bikes remained, but the troops and their weapons just vanished. Down below, the other three bikers came up the road behind the deputies. Three other angels, three new flashes, and three more men had vanished. Their bikes crashed into the ditches just short of the squad cars.

The angels carrying the IDEA continued for several minutes with their dance. They were teasing the men in the choppers. Nothing the aircraft shot at them could hit its mark. Several times the angels seemed ready to ram the choppers head-on, then they would suddenly shoot straight up to an extreme altitude. Just as Alex and his forces were at a peak of frustration, they slowly lowered to just above the troops in the brush. Sixteen men cowered as if they expected to be killed.

Then a low hum began. It was so low in pitch, it was felt more than heard. The pitch began to rise and the IDEA began to rotate. It began to rise above the angels. As it moved higher, they followed without changing the direction they were facing. The IDEA had been started and was ready to launch on one final journey. It widened considerably before starting to fold in upon itself. It was moving rapidly now, and the sound was shrill and piercing. The ground and the atmosphere for a mile around seemed to be writhing. The IDEA shot nearly straight up, all the while changing shape. Then poof—the IDEA and the angels were gone. The immediate surroundings settled quickly as if nothing had happened.

All of Alex Thorson's men who were on the ground were standing in the open, their weapons dropped and their mouths agape. All the people who had watched the log and kept vigils for these few days were cheering and jumping. The choppers were circling in confusion.

Four of the eight angels, still hovering above the complex, moved suddenly toward the choppers. In a repeat of the first encounter, they grabbed the choppers as if they were toys. On each chopper, one angel grabbed the main rotor, and one the tail rotor. They then did their own little dance. One time it almost looked like a square dance do-si-do. When the occupants were completely terrorized, they shot straight up and suddenly disappeared.

When they saw this happening, Alex and his men picked up their guns and began firing at the remaining four angels. Two columns moved over the cars, and two over the 16 men in the brush. As they came close and above their quarry, there were screams of fear and agony from the men. Then all went silent. All the Black Forces were either dead or had disappeared.

The four columns of light then approached the 20 people who were left. They came down to ground level, and their size became more like that of large men. The posse in the brush was already running up to the roadway to see what was going to happen next.

One of the angels spoke. "Henry Cooper, you must find another place to live for now. These evil men know who you are. But, do not fear, they will be blinded so they cannot find you or your family. Your new friend Charles Carver already knows where you can move. He will help you. The rest of you are basically unknown. You may return to your homes. You will be safe.

"All of you have found favor because you have trusted the Lord. He has given you the power of faith, and you have used it. After seven days, this story must be told. Many will think you are out of your minds. But a few will believe and trust the Lord before it is too late. Look up, He comes quickly, and He brings glory for all who love His coming.

"Now take these vehicles and your belongings and leave this place. It's usefulness is over. It will be no more."

Within 15 minutes, everything was gathered up, and they started down the road to the highway. About a half-mile away they stopped and looked back. Four huge pillars of fire hovered above the complex. Suddenly the crater of the complex was like a furnace. Flames shot high into the air. This only lasted for 10 or 15 minutes. Then it was as if each column of light were a galactic-sized earthmover. They started pushing the rim of the berm into the crater. When they stopped this land fill operation, there remained only a sizable hill. It was identical to the one Hank started changing so many years before.

Stunned, but extremely happy, the people who witnessed the unimaginable waved to each other. They climbed into their vehicles and headed for home. They would meet again in a week or two to decide how they would get the word out.

They also would have reason by then to wonder about:
• What happened to the bodies?
• How did the hill grow trees in a week?
• And, what happened to the road leading to the complex, as well as the warning sign that didn't exist anymore?
• Why did others in town not remember some of these things?
• Was the Lord using time to protect them?
• When could they meet to baptize many new believers?

Whatever the answer—it's time to rejoice, for our redemption is drawing very near. LOOK UP !

CHAPTER 40
EPILOGUE
Consider and Discern

This last few words are especially for you, dear reader. If you have read this far, I trust that you found the story interesting. The story, though, must be viewed with a careful eye, and grasped by a knowledgeable mind. If that then is the end result, you are holding a healing medicine for the heart and soul. But, it must be taken as directed. So consider carefully what I tell you now.

In this day when most of our society has lost sight of truth, we find them blinded by relativism. They are rapidly becoming like the simple minded person described in the Bible's Book of Proverbs: "People with no concept of truth and wisdom." People have come to believe that nothing is absolute as a fact. A few might even be willing to argue that 2+2 could equal 5, if you really want it to.

Many in our society are enamored with science as the answer to all of our needs. They would ignore the need for wisdom and moral judgement in order to handle and use science properly. Some ignore the actual fact that scientific study and research, as we understand it, was first introduced to us by devout believing Christians. It is true that some scientists suffered at the hands of ignorant Christians. But, science itself was born out of a deep belief in God and a desire to understand the creation of His hand. When some scientists ignored this fact, they began to twist their knowledge to accommodate their desire to do away with any belief in God's existence. The greatest attempts to assuage this desire are to be found within only the last 200 years. These people bow down to a new god they call science.

This story came to you labeled "Science Fiction," and that is what it is. If it had been told by Jesus of Nazareth, we would call it a parable. Just as Christ used many parables of an agricultural nature in His day, I hope to use science now.

The story of a time machine is not new, except possibly in how this one operates. It is useful, though, to span the time necessary to tell the story within. The modern day people involved with the ship IDEA and its revealing log are part of the fiction. Even their contemporary enemies from NICE are fiction as well, as are any battles between them and the existence of such a complex. Any angels involved in the present day battles just discussed are fiction as well. But they are patterned after similar reported occurrences, reported both historically and in Scripture.

My hope in writing this is to give some basis for those who might worship "science," to realize that what they read in scriptural prophecy is not all that outlandish. God's enemies have contended that all supernatural sounding occurrences are not to be believed, and the images reported by various prophets are beyond the realm of reality. They ignore the fact that many of these visions were explained by those prophets as allegory and metaphoric images. They also ignore the fact of consistency, over hundreds and thousands of years, in how these allegories and metaphors were used. Over a great time span, and communicated through many different human writers, the evidence still points to a single Author. One of the reasons believers can give for believing that author to be God is the perfect record of consistency mentioned above.

Statistical probability would limit the accuracy of chance foretelling of actual events in the single digits percentage wise. Yet it was necessary for a prophet of Israel to be 100 percent accurate in every detail, if he dared say "Thus says the Lord." If he was wrong, he was put to death as a false prophet. It is true that many true prophets were also killed just because those in power didn't like the message. But, over millennia we have a very good picture of which ones spoke the true words of the Lord—they are found in the Old and New Testaments of the Bible. It would take volumes to try to convey how these men have been 100 percent accurate even in minute details. Over 300 of the prophetic details concerning the coming Messiah were fulfilled in one man. That man, who is also God, is Jesus of Nazareth. It was proven by His resurrection from the dead. The existing proofs of that single fact fills volumes.

Suffice it to say that this book, *The Earth Between*, suspends the reader between fiction and fact. The vehicle of the story is fiction. What is found on the log of the IDEA depicts facts to a degree. The things shown or described are word pictures of history at particular chosen spots we all recognize. As it moves past the present and into the future, it includes scenes of how the events of future history could possibly unfold.

The events pictured are prophecy already put forth in actual and allegorical form. I have done my best not to change anything in this retelling. My goal is to show it is possible, in this day and age, to understand how these occurrences are possible and even probable. This statement is made from an understanding of present technology that is meager at best. Even so, just 60 years ago, it was beyond even the imagination of science's most brilliant minds. At that time, many brilliant minds were so brash about what they thought they knew that they didn't realize how little that was. Now, a novice such as I, can even see it coming rapidly upon us.

In an attempt to show the things, spoken of in Isaiah, Ezekiel, Joel, Daniel, Zechariah, Matthew, Revelation, and a few other books of the Bible, I have told the story in a purposeful way. Revelation is one book where the same story is told several times from different viewpoints. Many of the happenings seem to overlap in time, which causes some of the arguments various scholars get into. I have purposely let the IDEA backtrack in time and space in order to be as careful as I believe God was, in order to be true to Christ's statement in Matthew, "It is not for us to know the exact day or hour of his coming." This holds true for the rapture as well as the end of things at Armageddon. But we do know the signs of the times and the season. Do not consider the order on the log of the IDEA to be exact. It is purposely mixed yet tries to remain generally consistent with supposed order.

Now reader, if you are among those who have been kneeling before the altar of science, rather than bowing humbly before your Creator, please re-think the matter in clear meticulous form. God has said in His Word, "Come let us reason together." And again "Come, prove me here if my word is true." He lays the evidence before us, if we are not too proud to read and hear it. Don't just regurgitate what some professor may have told you without investigating for yourself. A true scientist does not live by prejudice and rumor. He searches out the truth wherever it may lead, even if he may find that truth really is God, the One who has always known the beginning to the end.

Or, reader, if you have mentally acknowledged that there is a Creator, the lover of your soul, but have been choosing to give Him no real heed, look around you. You can see what is going on, and you know the time is short. Come to the Saviour now before it is too late. There is nothing He can't forgive. There is nothing He won't forgive, except the rejection of His Son. Repent of your self-absorbed sin and ask Him to make you into a new creature, and take control of your life and future.

Or, reader, if you are one who has at some time come to Christ, and you know what a relationship with Him is, but have fallen away: Wake up. Be alert. Turn back to Him and be one who looks forward to His coming. Renew your vows to Him. Do what is right. Stop sinning that He may protect you or lift you away as the case may be. Also, remember that we must always willingly forgive anyone who has wronged us. This lets the Lord be the judge, not we ourselves. Then He can forgive us our trespasses.

Give up any root of bitterness, for that in its essence is a lack of trust and true faith.

Or, reader, if you are enjoying a walk with the Lord and feel personally secure in Him, do more. You know the time and the season. Do not be complacent and uncaring for those around you. Remember that the Lord does not desire that any would perish, but that everyone should have life eternal with Him. Reach out with the urgency of a rescue worker trying to save a fallen mountain climber. The life of their souls could be in your hands. The harvest time is upon us, and all hands are needed in the field. Get busy, you are needed. Also remember to forgive willingly, because the Lord has forgiven you. Love those who have despitefully used you. The root of bitterness causes many ills, and destroys our walk with the Lord. It also injures our witness because it belies the faith we profess.

Or, reader, if you are by birth a son or daughter of Israel, a Hebrew according to fleshly lineage: You also need the great salvation of your Messiah. He is Salvation or, in the Hebrew, *Yeshua. Yeshua Hamashiach,* Son of God, Emmanuel, meaning God with us. As was repeated many times in the history of your forefathers, they drifted away, over and over, from their God. Sometimes just being stubborn, a stiff-necked people. Sometimes even turning to the idols of their neighbors. But, for 2000 years now they have fulfilled the words of the prophets Jeremiah, and Ezekiel in that they have been unable and possibly unwilling to understand God's word on this matter. They have had the "eyes to see, and see not, they have (had) the ears to hear, and hear not:" All of this is common the world over, Israel being the world's teacher in the eyes of God.

This Gospel or "Good News" of Salvation was to the Jew first, and then to the Gentiles. For through Abraham, via Israel, are all the nations to be blessed. That is why much of the early church were composed of the priests and Levites who had been serving in the Temple. Now, the eyes are beginning to see, and the ears are opening to hear. The Lord has said "My sheep hear my voice and follow me." Is it not time you hear His voice as well? The time of His return is near, according to the signs. Though the exact time is not told us, we know it is at least 2000 years closer now than it was for the early church. Therefore, open eyes and ears can show you the truth, and the truth will make you free. That truth is Yeshua. He brings us freedom from the curse of sin that troubles and enslaves all of us. That is the true "Shalom," the peace of God. Pray for the peace of Jerusalem, for it is the "Prince of Peace" who will accomplish it.

Finally, keep straight what is fiction and what is prophecy. I have attempted to show prophecy as unfolding in a form that is understandable. Therefore, some of what is shown interspersed are the type of things that could possibly "trigger" the prophesied affect.

The machine, the IDEA and its log, are but tools to be able to see it happen. The timing follows a general overlapping picture, similar to the story told by prophecy. This, then, is not an exact pattern of what is to come. It only shows the possibility that these things *can happen* within a short period of time, such as a seven-year tribulation. It could be slower, but it is far more probable to move much, much faster.

Get into God's Word. Ready your heart. Prepare yourself and your loved ones to be ready to withstand persecution if need be. Always remembering that no matter what happens to the Lord's people on this earth, we are in the Win - Win position.

So, with hope in your heart, the hope provided by a risen Saviour, stand. Stand firm, and look up, your redemption is near.

"Even so, come, Lord Jesus."

AFTERWORD

What Is Your Decision ?

In the book of Isaiah we find two distinct pictures of the coming Messiah, or in the Hebrew, *Hamashiach*. The first was of a "suffering Saviour" who would bear the sins of His people. The second was of an "Almighty Conquering King."

When He arrived as the suffering Saviour, He found a populace and religious community wanting *only* the mighty King. This is what helped God's plan to succeed. It made possible the "God-purposed Sacrifice" needed to pay the price for man's sin, a price no man but Yeshua could successfully pay. The "Lamb of God" had to be "perfect" before God. He paid the final sacrifice that no mere man could pay. This was to fulfill Abraham's words to Isaac, that "God would provide for Himself a sacrifice." Yeshua died as the Passover Lamb the day of that feast, and arose as the First Fruit on the day of that feast.

This book has ended showing Him as the second picture of Messiah, returning as the conquering King of Kings and Lord of Lords. That seems like a fearsome picture. Yet, His first coming as a baby was the act of love that removed the fear of the second coming. He waited, so long, to give you and me time to come to Him. He is powerful, yet meek, waiting for you.

In Matthew 11: 28-30, He calls to us:

Come unto me, all you who labor and are heavy laden, and I will give you rest. Take my yoke upon you, and learn of me, for I am meek and lowly in heart, and you shall find rest unto your souls. For my yoke is easy, and my burden is light.

He has paid for our sins and offers to forgive all of it. Receiving Christ and His forgiveness is as simple as A B C:

Admit that you have sinned:
As it is written, there is none righteous, no, not one (Rom. 3:10)
...for all have sinned and fall short of the glory of God (Rom. 3:23).

247

Believe - that Jesus Christ died for you:
Yet to all who received Him, to those who believed in his name, He gave the right to become the children of God (John 1:12).

Confess that Jesus Christ is Lord of your life:
That if you confess with your mouth, "Jesus is LORD," and believe in your heart that God raised Him from the dead, you will be saved. For it is with your heart that you believe and are justified, and it is with your mouth that you confess and are saved (Rom. 10:9-10).

If receiving Jesus Christ is your decision, then take time right now to tell Him so. This is called a sinner's prayer of repentance. Pray something such as this:

"Dear Lord Jesus, I know that I am a sinner. I believe that You died for my sins and arose from the grave in triumphant power. I now turn away from my sins and invite You to come into my heart and life. I receive You as my personal Saviour and purpose to follow You as my Lord. Thank you, Lord, for Your wonderful grace toward me. Amen.

If you have taken this step and meant it with all of your heart, you can be assured that you have been heard and have been saved to new life.

And this is the testimony, God has given us eternal life, and this life is in His Son. He who has the Son has life, he who does not have the Son of God, does not have life (I John 5:11-12).

If you have made such a decision, please let us know. We can be helpful with your move into your new life in the Lord. We also can hold you up in prayer and blessing.

Find a good church in which to grow, one that is not ashamed of the Gospel of Christ. May the Lord build you up into a strong tower for His glory and the blessing of all around you.